CONFRONTING ANTI-SEMITISM:
SEEKING AN END TO HATEFUL RHETORIC

CONFRONTING ANTI-SEMITISM: SEEKING AN END TO HATEFUL RHETORIC

Amos Kiewe

t

Troubador Publishing Ltd
9 Priory Business Park
Kibworth, Leicester LE8 0RX, UK
Tel: (+44) 116 2792299
Email: books@troubador.co.uk
Web: www.troubador.co.uk

ISBN 9781848767034

Typeset in 11pt Stempel Garamond by Troubador Publishing Ltd, Leicester, UK

Contents

Preface

As a rhetoric scholar I have known for a long time that one day I would write about anti-Semitism from a rhetorical perspective, but activating my plan took many years until one event was too disturbing for me to keep postponing this project – the 2001 United Nations World Conference Against Racism in Durban, South Africa. The Durban conference would highlight how anti-Semitism is alive and well and that it is being used throughout the Arab world as the preferred rhetorical stance and a means to attack the State of Israel. The anti-Semitism this conference spewed was ostensibly anti-Jewish while the focus of criticism was Israel and its policies toward the Palestinians. The Durban Conference was antithetical to the 1965 Vatican II statement on the relationship between the Catholic Church and the Jewish people, but since the perpetrators were primarily of the Muslim world, I had to figure out what was happening and why. Thus, the years of thinking, reading and speaking on the larger issue of anti-Semitism were over; I had now to put my thoughts into writing.

I must admit that writing about anti-Semitism was not easy given the centuries of pain associated with it and the multiple explanations for its roots and historical developments. As an unjustified and hurtful discourse, any writing on anti-Semitism is sure to be accusatory of perpetrators, and justifiably so. Studies on anti-Semitism are plenty and this subject keeps yielding new scholarship, yet scholarship on anti-Semitism from a rhetorical perspective is almost none existent. The objective I set for this project is not that of charging others with centuries of hateful rhetoric and action but in pointing to the unwarranted charges in order to have them cease from continuing for centuries to come. The views offered here are that of a critical nature and, in following the classification of Barbara Warnick (1992, p. 232), my work here fits that of the advocate-critic who views text as power and whose critical study seeks to unravel assumptions of power in order to give voice to those who have been marginalized or worse. The advocate-critic does bring the critic's values into criticism in dealing with the selected texts (p. 232) and thus engages in criticism that is personal or that the critic has a stake in its prospects. This, in short, is my take on, and my stake with, the issue of social justice in communication studies when considering the scrooge of anti-Semitism. I hope to have been productive in exposing this hateful rhetoric for its rhetorical function and objectives and ultimately bringing this hateful rhetoric to an end.

In pursuing this project I wish to thank several individuals whose support and encouragement were critical to the project: David Frank, Professor and Dean of the Honors College at the University of Oregon, and Fritz Rohrlich of Syracuse, Professor Emeritus of Physics at Syracuse University. Their insightful and critical comments are most appreciated. I have presented my thoughts on the subject of anti-Semitism over a spread of some twenty years in smaller gatherings of a Jewish group in Syracuse called the *Khug* (Club in Hebrew) and I thank the members of this group for letting me try these early presentations for the sake of generating feedback. I am grateful to an anonymous reviewer of an earlier essay that is part of this project for the added comments on the notion of temporality and the Catholic Church. Special gratitude goes to Omar Swartz of the University of Colorado Denver and editor of Troubador's series on communication and social justice for recognizing the value of this project and supporting it throughout the publication process, and for his conscientious suggestions during the editing phase. Finally, I wish to thank Syracuse University for granting me a research leave, allowing me the time to read, research, and write this book.

1

Introduction
Anti-Semitism: A Rhetorical Perspective

In 1965, the Catholic Church Synod known as Vatican II issued a document that included a profound statement on the origin, length, and reason for anti-Semitism. It identified the accusation of Jews as "Christ Killers" some two thousand earlier as the key reason for anti-Semitism and asked that the accusation of deicide and the eternal guilt of Jews thereof come to an end. This millennia-old accusation, argued the Synod, was in error and should not have been used to charge Jews eternally for a crime committed centuries earlier. This document touched on the theological center of Christianity — Jesus' death on the cross — and, yet, despite a series of disputes within the Council over this tectonic shift, a significant portion of the theology of eternal guilt came to an end. The sought effect of this statement was clear — to bring not only a theological end to centuries of Christian anti-Semitism but a practical one as well.

That the theology had to change first is significant, pointing to anti-Semitism as a construct, a rhetorical creation that despite its entrenched hold over many centuries was now challenged and refuted. The Church made it clear that an earlier theology was erroneous and no longer acceptable and that its harm was now realized as horrifying, especially after the Holocaust. A new page in the Christian-Jewish relationship was written and, with it, the hope for an end to Catholic-based anti-Semitism. Various Protestant groups have similarly rejected "replacement theology," the one that claims that Christianity has replaced Judaism, arguing instead for respect and even close relationship with Judaism (Brog, 2006, pp. 3-5).

Unlike Christianity, the Islamic-Jewish relationship for centuries has not been as horrifying as the Christian-Jewish relationship and the hatred of Jews was, by and large, less harsh. Only in the past century, especially with the rise of Zionism, an Islamist strain of anti-Semitism has developed; a strain not fully shared nor exercised by all Muslims. Yet, similar to Christianity, a theological cover — a rhetorical construct — has grounded this rather recent hatred.

In both religions, then, theological resources constructed anti-Semitism, and in the case of Christianity, theological resources also sought to bring it to an end. *Anti-Semitism, I argue here, is a rhetorical construct prompted by theological precepts in order to create a mass persuasion. Anti-Semitism is a means whose ultimate end is often obscured but its victims are always the Jews.* Ostensibly, anti-Semitism can cease to exist by tackling its constructed theological grounding. In short, I argue here that anti-Semitism was constructed for rhetorical purposes to suit a theological set of arguments and its end lies as well in rhetorical means. This book delves into the rhetorical construction of anti-Semitism, its theological motivation and its horrid consequences in the hope that it could cease to exist.

The "eternal guilt" accusation inherent in anti-Semitism, whereby Jews are forever charged with deicide — that of killing Christ, is a most entrenched yet puzzling if not a disturbing conception. It is with this profound puzzlement that one enters the complex and by-no-means easy discussion about anti-Semitism. The puzzlement can be summed up in few simple questions: How did the charge of eternal guilt come to life? Why has it survived for centuries? The persistency of the charge of deicide — killing Christ — and eternal guilt thereof has been sustained for centuries due to successful mass persuasion in the form of liturgy, myth, and narrative. Anti-Semitism is thus the persistent hatred of Jews as a collective and as individuals; a hatred that is grounded on suspect, if not altogether, false and malicious reasoning that through the ages has brought much misery, persecution, expulsion, torture and death to millions of Jews for no other reason than that of being Jewish.

From antiquity to the Middle-Ages, and to the modern age, anti-Semitism has reared its ugly head despite changing circumstances, times and locations. Anti-Semitism has often been promoted during political turmoil or economic hardship ostensibly to obviate dwelling on real causes. Given the changing grounds, reasons and justification for practicing anti-Semitism, the topic becomes one of great bewilderment when contemplating its origin, causes and perpetuation. As Robert S. Wistrich (2010) has observed, "anti-Semitism is probably the most adaptable of all group hatreds, exuding a protean quality that seems to guarantee longevity" (p. 600). This is the task undertaken by numerous scholars over a long period of time and from various disciplines and perspectives, seeking to understand the origin and motives of anti-Semitism. I enter this task by following with trepidation the tracks of many other scholars who sought the same through the ages. I hope to shed light on the matter in some unique and original way and I do so by taking a perspective rarely contemplated — a rhetorical one.

Among the few exceptions to the neglect of rhetorical studies of anti-Semitism is a study by Omar Swartz (1996) who relies on rhetoric scholar Kenneth Burke to explain that anti-Semitism lies in the nature of language that allows unity by division via the scapegoat mechanism (pp. 183-185). Swartz posits that "Perspectives are our reality," and that symbols and perspectives bring "people to use and misuse language in their attempt to create meaning for their lives and for their society" (p. 186). My critical approach is similar though my starting point is slightly different. I begin with the Burke's notion of guilt to understand anti-Semitism.

A unique persuasive reasoning, I argue, has established this "eternal guilt," and this unique feature is what I set to explore. Guilt, according to Burke, is foundational to the rhetorical process as it motivates a fairly predictable frame of attitudes and actions. Put differently, since guilt appears inherent to anti-Semitism, the rhetorical process ought to reveal insights into this form of racism. This is the view taken here — that of considering anti-Semitism a rhetorical artifact or a trope — a persuasive process and a prop that has allowed it a longevity that would not be accorded to other historical charges. Though guilt would be foundational to Christian anti-Semitism, a cursory look into Islamist anti-Semitism reveals striking similarities in seeking to establish an eternal guilt of the Jew, charging him/her with the carrying acts against the Prophet Muhammad. This similarity ought to indicate that in anti-Semitism a significant rhetorical force is at play and that a consistent pattern of guilt projection appears to run across these two religions, as well across time and place.

Anti-Semitism is a commonly used term but an erroneous one, if not altogether misleading. Though the term has been cast for more than a century as hatred of all Semites, it was very narrowly conceived as the hatred of Jews only. The more accurate descriptive term is anti-Judaism or anti-Jewish sentiments. Indeed, for some seventeen centuries the prevailing terms in use were "anti-Judaism," "Jew-hatred," or worse, "Christ Killers." Only late in the nineteenth century, when the term anti-Jewish or Jew-hatred was no longer fashionable, the less innocuous term and the more scientific sounding, "anti-Semitism," was coined and as such, set roots as the common reference. Yet, the very consideration of anti-Semitism as "hatred of Jews is itself erroneous as it stands for the anti-Semites' definition of anti-Semitism."[1] However, since anti-Semitism is the more frequently used term, its usage here is done with the clear understanding that it means anti-Judaic sentiments or hatred of Jews and actions thereof, and that the term itself is inadequate for defining the hatred of Jews.

The United States Department of States official definition of anti-Semitism (2005) acknowledges that the "definition of anti-Semitism has been the focus of innumerable discussions and studies. While there is no universally accepted definition, there is a generally clear understanding of what the term encompasses." In a report issued by the United States Department of State (2005), anti-Semitism is defined as

> hatred toward Jews — individually and as a group — that can be attributed to the Jewish religion and/or ethnicity. An important issue is the distinction between legitimate criticism of policies and practices of the State of Israel, and commentary that assumes an anti-Semitic character. The demonization of Israel, or vilification of Israeli leaders, sometimes through comparisons with Nazi leaders, and through the use of Nazi symbols to caricature them, indicates an anti-Semitic bias rather than a valid criticism of policy concerning a controversial issue (Report on Global Anti-Semitism).[2]

This definition is rather comprehensive and seeks also to distinguish between anti-Semitism and anti-Israel sentiments, clarifying the dividing lines between hateful rhetoric uttered against Jews and Judaism that are considered unacceptable and those uttered against Israel, which are. This distinction seeks to clarify that valid criticism of Israel or Israeli policies are acceptable but not attacks that are anti-Semitic — those that attack the Jewish character of Jews be they citizens of Israel or of other countries.

A Rhetorical Perspective

Most studies of anti-Semitism take a historical, religious, sociological or psychological perspective in seeking to explain this disturbing phenomenon. The perspective that has not been fully explored is the rhetorical approach, and given the observation that anti-Semitism is inherently a highly persuasive phenomenon, this stipulation requires an explanation. After all, anti-Semitism would not have set roots had it not succeeded in persuading individuals, groups, communities, institutions, and nations to become hostile to Jews. A perusal of studies on anti-Semitism in the discipline of rhetoric and communication reveals a surprising silence on this issue. A special issue of the *Journal of Communication and Religion* under guest editor David A. Frank, as well as his co-authored book with Robert C. Rowland, *Shared Land Conflicting Identity* (2002), and Omar Swartz's essay entitled "Symbols and Perspectives in Burkean Rhetorical Theory: Implications for Understanding Anti-Semitism" (1996), are among the few studies in the communication and rhetoric discipline.

Rhetoric, or its more simplistic synonym, speech, is inherent to the history and practice of anti-Semitism. In referencing Jean Paul Sartre's famous study of anti-Semitism, Cary McWilliams argues that anti-Semites "like to play with speech because by putting forth ridiculous reasons, they discredit the seriousness of their interlocutor; they are enchanted with their unfairness because for them it is not a question of persuading by good arguments but of intimidating or disorienting" (McWilliams, 1948, p. 264). The persuasive, hence the rhetorical, is central to the millennia of anti-Semitism. Here, perhaps, lies the opening to examining anti-Semitism rhetorically. Had anti-Semitism been considered unreasonable and illogical, it stands to reason that it could have been countered and perhaps even ceased to exist after a while. But precisely because anti-Semitism has been carried by appeals to logic and reason, distasteful and manipulative though they are, it has been taken by adherents as rationalized, reasonable, and, therefore, assumed to be justified.

Though the hatred of Jews is base, often emotionally charged, highly generalized and prejudicial, it has been accepted as well as perpetuated because persuaders succeeded in their endeavor. This we must acknowledge if we are to understand why this hatred has persisted. As a purposeful and indeed strategic form of persuasion, anti-Semitism has been the design of early Church leaders, especially in the fourth century who saw in hateful rhetoric the best means for a complete separation of Christianity from its mother religion, Judaism. This hatred, then, as a top-down strategic persuasion, was designed for a harsh separation that could not be revoked or be modified later. The longevity of this hatred ought to indicate that something of a profoundly grand scale was and is practiced here, and rather successfully. The logical questions that must follow any questioning of anti-Semitism are these: Why has anti-Semitism succeed in different places and at different time? What rhetorical strategies made anti-Semitism last for some seventeen centuries? What is in anti-Semitism that has appealed and continues to appeal to so many people? In short, what has sustained anti-Semitism despite changing circumstances, locality, time, language and political settings?

By setting a rhetorical perspective in studying anti-Semitism, I seek to explore the persuasive process that influences or "instructs" people to accept certain precepts, notions and attitudes, reinforcing "desired" feelings, and suggests specific acts. I do not use the term "rhetoric" in its limited scope to mean lies and manipulation but, rather, as the study of persuasion including its design, process and reception, as well as its verbal and visual manifestations. The study of rhetoric has both an illustrious and infamous history. As an art of persuasion, rhetoric is a neutral process, covering the means by which individual are able to persuade others by considering situational variables, audience predilections, reasoning processes and conventions. The art of rhetoric is guided by ethical norms yet, from antiquity onward, the art has been recognized as easily falling into the hands of charlatans and manipulators, able to twist premises and manipulate logic and reasoning in the service of suspect objectives and false hopes. Unethical and unwarranted reasoning goes often undetected precisely because the practices of lies and manipulations are often no different from ethical ones.

The rhetorical act functions symbolically and metaphorically, allowing for persuasion via symbols and signs. Such has been the nature of anti-Semitism whereby hatred has functioned symbolically and metaphorically. By the symbolic nature of anti-Semitism I mean that the Jew is much more than a word with denotative and definitional reference to individuals of a Jewish faith and origin. The word "Jew" is loaded with complex meaning, often carrying negative connotations, stereotypes, and prejudicial attributions. Thus, the word "Jew" often functions as a metaphor, a representation that includes verbal narrative and visual depictions that their very triggering easily fall synecdocichally within "acceptable" frames of prejudice. Put differently, the Jew as a word and as an individual symbolically fits well within various constellations of prejudice, casting the individual both as metaphoric and literal devil, prone to evil and detestable behavior. The symbolic meaning that historically has conjured up the Jew as evil and diabolic has made anti-Semitism a rhetorical entity that was and still is available as a trope.

To suggest that anti-Semitism is beyond logic, or that it is illogical, may not be a productive way of understanding this phenomenon. I subscribe to the position of rhetoric scholar Roderick Hart who writes that "in persuasion, everything is rational to the behaver at the time of behaving" (Hart, 1997, p.. 84). The rhetorical perspective means that a certain logical process is in play and that a certain sensibility, however abhorrent, has grounded this hatred. This is so because anti-Semitism is about forming and sustaining opinion, and suggesting action. Though unethical and unwarranted, anti-Semitism cannot be termed illogical persuasion. The longevity of this hatred means that a fitting reasoning has been forwarded to convince communities in different times and at different locals to accept this hatred as reasonable, or as fulfilling certain communal, social or religious needs. Stated more succinctly, where there is persuasion, a rhetorical process is underway and where one can find anti-Semitism, one is sure to find a persuasive process grounded by specific reasoning and objectives.

The attitude and actions called by anti-Semitic tracts, speeches, liturgy, iconography, myth and innuendoes have constructed, among others, narratives that accuse Jews, first by Christians as "Christ-killers" and much later in Islam, as infidels in the eyes of the Prophet Mohammed. Original or *ur*-narratives of the so-called enmity *of* the Jews toward others had become entrenched and timeless Christian and Islamic theology, allowing for the compounding of additional charges no matter how false, capricious, outrageous, or contradictory. These "narratives of origin" have functioned rhetorically by casting the Jew in negative light through libels, accusations, hateful speeches and vile statements. As a narrative addressed to one generation after another, anti-Semitism has become a rhetorical and, therefore, a cultural trope, available whenever "needed," and often immune to changing circumstances, context and location. In its foundation, anti-Semitism is theological. As John T. Pawlikowski (1986) argues:

> No other Christian accusation with a seeming New Testament basis against the Jewish people has been responsible for more Jewish suffering throughout history than the charge of deicide . . . This claim laid the groundwork for a highly developed theology within Christianity claiming that Jews, for the reminder of human history, were to be subjected to continual suffering and to live in a state of perpetual wandering without a homeland as a punishment for this monumental crime (In Curtis, 1986, p. 107).

This theology of eternal anti-Semitism would be recognized for its folly in 1965 when the *Vatican II* Council sought to end its culpability for the history of anti-Semitism and that such a significant move was possible only if the temporal variable — eternal guilt — was to be taken out of the Catholic Church's argumentative and theological stance. This much, the Catholic Church has done.

Anti-Semitism, like most prejudices, has succeeded where a society has already accepted certain perceptions and stereotypes of Jews. It has also existed longer than other forms of hatred and prejudice. Anti-Semitism is indeed a unique phenomenon. Blind and base, used as a means, sometimes calculated, and other times spontaneous, yet always focused on blaming Jews for sins or crimes that they did not commit. A distinct cause-and-effect logic can be identified in many anti-Semitic acts throughout history, often by the perpetrators themselves, and used as justification for attitudes and actions. The justification for hatred of Jews included the ancient and original accusation of being deciders — killers of Christ — whereas later accusations mingled religious causes with financial, social, and economic ones, pointing to Jewish wealth and economic control, as well as sociological and racial causes that blame Jews for their separation from mainstream communities. These accusations share naive, almost childish narratives that are structured in God-Devil terms, pointing to a simplistic plot of *Good* and *Bad*, no matter the specific story line. These narratives, like most stories, are attractive for their naïve and linear logic, clear cause and effect reasoning, and the reaffirming plot line that reinforces one's community. Subsequently, such narratives unite a community by distancing itself from a hated group and by pointing to its moral and ethical superiority by comparison with Jewish immoral and unethical conduct. These are the base ingredients of anti-Semitism. These are also the ingredients of many foundational narratives hence the key to understanding their attractive function is to consider their rhetorical functions.

In undertaking this writing, I do not suggest that the questions posed here have not already been dealt with or that the persuasive elements in anti-Semitism have not already been discussed. I do suggest, however, that a systematic rhetorical approach to anti-Semitism is yet to be explored. This is the task I set for this study. The working formula that guides this book is that once religious anti-Semitism was institutionalized and formalized as an inherent policy of the early Church, a rhetorical context of hatred and racism became well established and purposefully practiced. Once this hatred became institutionalized, it became possible to "download" additional reasons for hatred, usually covering social and economic charges and later also racial, cultural, and political accusations. By "rhetorical context" I mean a setting that is already rife with suspicion and ill-feeling toward Jews, such that any additional charge is easily anchored on existing negative feelings. The rhetorical device operating here is the enthymeme (a rhetorical syllogism) whereby existing beliefs and premises are used to ground new allegations, no matter how fallacious they are. In a syllogism, a general premise taken often as a cultural truism serves as the reservoir for specific charges that are "consistent" with the general premise. The rhetorical syllogism stands at the root of hatred and prejudice in general, and anti-Semitism is not immune to this logic inherent in this rhetorical device. If anything, the enthymeme has been kept as a powerful rhetorical device that explains how quickly anti-Semitism rises to the surface either intentionally or spontaneously.

Identifying different sources and causes of anti-Semitism, as can be found throughout history, may suggest that the so-called "causes" are no causes at all but just symptoms of a basic motive — the religious one. In other words, the religious tension, I argue, has remained the primary cause of anti-Semitism and the tendency to discuss different kinds of anti-Semitism such as "modern anti-Semitism" as distinct from earlier forms of anti-Semitism is erroneous; or that the distinctions made between different types of anti-Semitism (economic or racial) are artificial and misleading.

Pursuing the investigation of anti-Semitism from a rhetorical perspective points to the possibility that the evidence for its persistence may lie in more ingrained individual and social needs — the desire to believe that one's life framework is better than another or others. Such an implied or assumed hierarchy allow humans to construct their lives as worthy and ideal but that such values are possible only when contrasting them with the undesirable; therefore, negative attributes and that when such attitudes are attached to a distinct and disliked group, one's hierarchy becomes that much more potent. The premise that undergirds this perspective is that humans are inherently hierarchical being, seeing the world around them in hierarchies that function as guides for thought and action. The use of hierarchical thinking implies that someone is at the top and someone else is at the bottom of the hierarchy. The Jew, cast historically and generically as the identifiable "other," becomes the available entity for hierarchical reasoning. How and why the Jew became the construct of the "other" is the task of this volume.

Rhetorically and ideologically, anti-Semitism offers ready-made *topoi* or common places — resources for the invention of arguments, reasoning, and rationalizations that are often used to advance tried-and-true explanations. Ideologies work by identifying an "enemy," or the "other," as the antagonistic agent against whom a group supposedly struggles and whose demise will ensure the success of the group. This is often the rhetorical screen through which a group is instructed to perceive its situation and the way out of difficult predicaments. A group's objective, be it freedom, equality, or independence, is rhetorically made attractive by casting its belief system in antagonistic relationship to another entity, often depicted in simplistic and attractive *good-bad* or *God-Devil* terms. Put differently, an ideology is but a rhetorical screen or veil through which individuals and groups are taught to view a given phenomenon. Anti-Semitism offers ideologies such as German Nazism, Italian fascism or Iranian Islamism the ideal narrative for such antagonistic relationship. This is so because the Jew has been cast historically as the outsider, the "other," the stranger, and the ready-made devil, and thus easily blamed and hated for things he has not done.

Practically, such narratives become useful in seeking to solve, or at least, to rationalize society's ills. Thus, if a society suffers from poverty then Jews are guilty because they are wealthy and they acquired their wealth on the back of innocent people; if many died of the plague, then Jews brought the disease; and if others became sick, this is so because Jews have poisoned the wells; if a society confronts corruption then Jews are to be blamed because they are all corrupt; if a society turns radical, the Jews are at fault because they are inherently radical; if the landed nobility taxes the farmers harshly, Jews are behind the plan because they are agents of the rich; and, if an undesirable war began, Jews are at fault for seeking to start it in the first place; and if a war has been lost, Jews are to be blamed for stabbing the country in the back. This short survey of historical arguments made against Jews is factual and covers well some several centuries of anti-Semitism. These so-called justifications share one variable in common — they all seek to blame Jews for undesirable events that befell a community and its need to avoid self blame and painful reflection. The Jew as the scapegoat is an entrenched and thus generic resource of reasoning. When this postulation is put in the context of the sinful nature of human beings that is foundational to Christianity, anti-Semitism ought to have been rejected and prohibited, at least on theological grounds. But it has not, and thus in seeking to find the answer to this quandary, a rhetorical possibility is offered as a plausible explanation.

The rhetorical perspective of examining anti-Semitism is justified at several levels. The gap between the miniscule number of Jews worldwide and the enormous space devoted to Jews throughout history is simply incongruent. The small number of Jews, estimated today at about 13 million (Julius, Rifkind, Weill, & Gaer, 2001, p. 2), and a persistent small number of Jews over the past two thousand years, ought to indicate that something else must explain the enormous focus on Jews as their sheer number alone (i.e., generally, no more than .0002 percent of the world's population) could not have been threatening to others. Yet, anti-Semitism has been found even in places where very few Jews live as well as in places where Jews no longer reside. The absurdity and intensity of many charges, and the many contradictions thereof must point to other motives for anti-Semitism. Since material substance such as the small number of Jews or the tiny geographical region that is the State of Israel can hardly explain the hatred of Jews, other reasons must explain this prejudice. Such an explanation, I believe, can be found in non-material substances, thus rhetorical entities such as memories, habits, tradition, and customs as well as motives, myth and expediency.

The varied and inconsistent charges made against Jews are equally suggestive of a rhetorical process. As Michael Curtis (1986) writes,

> no other group of people in the world has been charged simultaneously with alienation from society and with cosmopolitanism, with being capitalist exploiters, and agents of international finance and also revolutionary agitators, with having a materialist mentality and with being people of the Book, with acting as militant aggressors and with being cowardly pacifists . . . with being a chosen people and also having an inferior human nature, with both arrogance and timidity, with being guilty of the crucifixion of Christ and at the same time held to account for the invention of Christianity (p. 4).

Likewise, historian Walter Laqueur (2006) suggests that notwithstanding the multiple contradictions of Jews being blamed for being radicals, socialists, capitalists, usurers and parasite, Jews as the cause and the motive for multiple beliefs and ideologies is at the root of perpetual anti-Semitism as a convenient agent in world history (pp. 128-129). Anti-Semitism as practiced for some two thousand years was and remains possible due to a simple yet devastating rhetorical formula – a much practiced and therefore, ready-made negative agent cast throughout history as evil, the devil or the Anti-Christ. In short, the Jew-as-devil is in often use because it is easy and convenient, regardless of the truth.

Emil Fakenheim points to the fact that in anti-Semitism, Jews are hated for their vices as well as for their virtues and since the vices are not so much vices but "bear the stamp of uniqueness," we are dealing therefore with "a collective psychology" that cannot be "altered by a little more enlightenment." Fakenheim does not even consider anti-Semitism a genuine prejudice since "unlike a genuine prejudice, anti-Semitism does not seem to disappear when knowledge comes on the scene" (In Curtis, pp. 22-24). Similarly, Jean-Paul Sartre considered anti-Semitism "not a legitimate opinion, not a prejudice, but, rather, a criminal passion and that it is criminal because its ultimate goal is the death of the Jew" (cited in Fackenheim, p. 24). If anti-Semitism is not a prejudice or a legitimate opinion, then what is it? I suggest that it is a purposeful, though not always fully realized, process of managing a community's complex and often frustrating set of challenges and constraints through simplicity of objectifying one convenient culprit or agent on whose shoulders all of the community's impediments are saddled.

Fakenheim also writes that "the missionaries of Christianity had said in effect 'you have no right to live among us as Jews'. The secular rulers who followed had proclaimed: 'You have no right to live among us.' The German Nazis at last decreed; 'You have no right to live'" (Fakenheim, pp. 24-25). Consequently, no matter what Jews do and do not do, they are always to be persecuted. They are to be punished by God for not following the Old Testament and they are to be punished by Christians for following the Old Testament. St. Chrysostom suggested as much when, in his vitriolic sermons, discussed in detail in Chapter 4, he stated that Jews are worse off for keeping the law of God and Moses than when they were disobeying them.

In concluding his seminal study on *The Devil and the Jews*, Joshua Trachtenberg (1943) explains

> how the magic of words has transmuted a pernicious medieval superstition into an even more debasing and corrosive modern superstition. Antisemitism today is "scientific"; it would disdain to include in the contemporaneous lexicon of Jewish crime such outmoded items as Satanism and sorcery . . . To the modern

antisemites . . . the Jew has become the international communist or the international banker, or better, both. But his aim is still to destroy Christendom, to conquer the world and enslave it to his own . . . devilish ends. Still the "demonic" Jew. (pp. 219-229)

Words, and hurtful words at that, have constructed and sustained anti-Semitism, and though the circumstances have changed, sometimes drastically, the basic theological accusation has remained. But words are entrenched in people's psyche and extricating them is no easy task as their very act is to construct our reality and our understanding of the world around us. Yet, new realities can be constructed and unfortunately, it took the Holocaust to bring people to realize how far centuries of anti-Semitism had gone.

The fourth century "invention" of anti-Semitism as a way to elevate Christianity at the expense of Judaism is now repeated in the Islamic world. Jews are now blamed for a host of acts against Islam which supposedly occurred at the beginning of the seventh century CE. Various interpretations are forwarded with Quranic "proof" in order to ground hatred. Though the context of this anti-Semitism is often Zionism and the State of Israel, the rhetorical process is rather similar to the one early Christianity promoted. Islamist anti-Semitism is inherently theological as it draws its arguments from religious tracts to prove their credibility and secure its mass persuasiveness, turning a relatively benign century-old relationship between Muslims and Jews into a hatred that did not exist until about a century ago, a relatively new phenomenon.

This development is significant as it would replicate the Christian "need" to hate Judaism as a strategy for separating itself from Judaism. Islam would intensify its anti-Semitism, not so much for theological reason but use its theology a political means to combat the Zionist movement and later the State of Israel. The reliance on a theological justification for opposing Zionism and Israel, I suggest here, was made with the recognition that it would yield successful mass persuasion. Seeing in the Zionist project a religious motivation that would "compete" with Islam over religious narrative and holy sites, Islam opted for anti-Semitism as a the strategy of opposition that could successfully be grounded in Quranic text and thus be powerful and persuasive.

Finally, the rhetorical process in anti-Semitism also worked in reverse. Anti-Semitism which brought untold death, destruction, expulsion and social hatred, also forced Jewish people to identify ways to unite and maintain its community survival through a continuous process of constructing memory, aspiration and hope. An external rhetorical process of hatred ushered in an internal rhetorical process of self preservation that strengthened identity and heritage, but subsequently further exacerbated hatred of the Jew. Anti-Semitism has also brought Jews unintended consequences, that of turning inward to find ways to preserve their heritage and devise means for continuation despite the odds. This inward look and severe professional restrictions would also be featured prominently in anti-Semitism, often in the form of accusation of Jews of their separateness and social exclusion.

Only in the late nineteenth century, with the rise of nationalism would Jews develop their own national movement — Zionism — in aspiring to construct their own nation-state. The intensification of anti-Semitism would add urgency to this project which eventually culminated in the Zionist Congress calling for a Jewish homeland. In 1917, following Great Britain's win over the Ottoman Empire in the Near East, the British Government would issue the Balfour Declaration which called for the creation of a Jewish homeland in Palestine, a development that would eventually lead the creation of the State of Israel in 1948, closing a circle of some two thousand years of expulsion of Jews from Judea and their dream since for their return. Zionism was developed as a nationalistic movement to gather Jews from around the world to a place that would allow safety and self expression, often in short supply in various parts of the world, especially at the end of the nineteenth century and the beginning of the twentieth century (discussed later in this volume). Yet, anti-Semitism would not subside in the Middle East but would intensify as Islamic opposition to Zionism and later to the State of Israel would consider both in religious-theological terms, infringing on Islam and its own religious and national aspirations.

The larger objective of this volume is to confront anti-Semitism; the means for this end is to expose anti-Semitism for its discursive scrooge used in this rhetoric of hatred. Confronting anti-Semitism is as necessary as confronting all forms of racism, prejudices and stereotypes. In a report submitted to *The United Nations World Conference Against Racism, Racial Discrimination, Xenophobia and Related Intolerance* (Durban, South Africa, August-September 2001), the American Jewish Congress spelled out the reasons for fighting anti-Semitism. It states that "anti-Semitism ultimately is harmful to societies that tolerate it. It denies Jews the opportunity to contribute to their societies and denies the societies the benefit of those contributions. It also represents an irrational avoidance of real problems . . . . Antisemitism also pollutes political discourse, driving out reasoned discourse with wholly irrational, but nonetheless potent myths" (cited in Julius et al.., p. 4).

Though I do not fully subscribe to the irrationality of anti-Semitism, I do concur with the notion that when anti-Semitism goes unchallenged it becomes detrimental not only to Jews but also to the welfare of any given community. Given the premise that in anti-Semitism Jews are accused for things that they have not done and that this hatred functions primarily for obviating society's ills, I suggest that when anti-Semitism erupts, it becomes reflective of a dysfunctional community. Anti-Semitism, then, is symptomatic of other problems not signified, and can thus be a barometer of the health of a given society. The rhetorical efforts that are invested in promoting anti-Semitism can be used as predictive of serious rupture in a society or a community, not willing or able to face its difficulties and challenges, preferring instead the easy way out by resorting to the tried-and-true scapegoat mechanism.

Anti-Semitism has lead to the death of millions of Jews throughout history and, despite the horrors of the Holocaust, it has not dissipated. Incidents of anti Semitism have increased in recent years, often in relation to Israeli actions, causing great concern to Jews and non-Jews alike. And though incidents of anti-Semitism are not as acute today as they were prior to World War II, the United States Department of State, in a special report (2005) states that "The increasing frequency and severity of anti-Semitic incidents since the start of the 21st century, particularly in Europe, has compelled the international community to focus on anti-Semitism with renewed vigor."

Yet, confronting anti-Semitism is primarily a rhetorical process since countering it is primarily an act of persuasion or, more succinctly, an act of counter-persuasion. Such a task is quite daunting, as its effects are frustratingly limited for several reasons: The variables of anti-Semitism are historical and religious in nature, some of which are entrenched in stereotypes and prejudices, and others are foundational to specific theologies, developed over centuries and embedded in the suasiveness of sacred narrative, myth and ritual. Yet, for successful critique of anti-Semitism, it is important first to understand the rhetoric of hatred with its motives, nuances, and devices.

A note of caution is warranted here. This book does not seek a theological debate or a discussion about the nuances of theological disputes between Judaism and other religions. I am not a theologian, nor a historian or a religious studies educator. I am a rhetorician and my interest lies in understanding the role and function of persuasion in the formation and sustainability of anti-Semitism. Anti-Semitism is viewed here, disturbingly so, as primarily a successful form of mass persuasion. This statement is based on the perspective that anti-Semitism was borne of rhetorical reasons and that it functions primarily through rhetorical means, using the symbolic means of verbal and visual texts. The task undertaken here seeks to show how precepts that grounded religious convictions have also promoted anti-Semitism. The objective of this writing is to confront anti-Semitism and, in so doing, to point to centuries of set dogma and convictions with the clear understanding that any attempt to challenge strongly-held beliefs is often ripe with criticism and defensiveness. Vatican II's statements regarding anti-Semitism were a significant step in this direction and an exemplar of the possibility of bringing an end to this hateful rhetoric.

The study of anti-Semitism commences by first setting the rhetorical perspective that guides this inquiry. I then develop several case studies and instances that illustrate different experiences that prompted or reflected upon intense anti-Semitism. The case studies covered here allow for observing emerging themes of anti-Semitism and the drawing of conclusions about anti-Semitism as a unique case of racist and hateful rhetoric. Thereafter I move to discussing foundational issues that stand at the root of anti-Semitism, issues that could potentially be considered in seeking to bring an end to anti-Semitism.

Notes

1. The term anti-Semitism was coined in the late 19th century when racial explanation became popular, arguing that it was natural to dislike those of different culture and races. See, McWilliams (1948, pp. 88-91).
2. *Department of State to the Committee on Foreign Relations and the Committee on International Relations*, The Bureau of Democracy, Human Rights, and Labor, http://www.state.gov/g/drl.rls/40258.htm).

2

From Guilt to Scapegoating:
The Rhetorical Grounding of Anti-Semitism

In seeking to theorize about the causes or reasons for the noxious continuation and perpetuation of anti-Semitism, the perspective that is often invoked is that of *scapegoating*. Accordingly, anti-Semitism is initiated and promoted by individuals and groups who, in the face of difficulties and setbacks, need to find someone else to blame, instead of the warranted self-blame or responsibility of the in-group. Given the fact that Jews have been the traditional evil-agent for centuries, referred to as the "devil" and assigned many diabolical characteristics, they have thus become a convenient scapegoat on whose shoulders the guilt of others is carried.

The scapegoat mechanism, however, is only the manifestation of another motive, without which the causes or reasons for anti-Semitism cannot be fully understood. If scapegoating is the end of the act of hatred; its beginning, or its motivational starting point, is *guilt*. Put differently, scapegoating is not only the projection of guilt in an otherwise *un*-guilty entity; it is the result of guilt experienced by the one who practices scapegoating. The rhetorical process, then, does not begin with scapegoating but with guilt as a basic motive inherent to human beings who can never fulfill all societal expectations, prohibitions, sanctions, and requirements. Guilt needs to be understood as a generic term that encompasses a host of experiences such as inadequacy, incompleteness, insecurity, and deficiencies, and the attempt to overcome them by following a process that rhetoric scholar Kenneth Burke refers to as *dramatis,* whereby such feelings are overcome by the projection of counterforce such as scapegoating, victimage, and sacrifice of another or others in order to achieve redemption and ultimately purification (for simplicity sake, the terms "sacrifice" and "victimage" can be considered synonyms for scapegoating as they are the operative terms for hurting others unjustifiably). The scapegoat, then, is a substitution whereby "one character may be redeemed through the act or agency of another" (1961, p. 176). It is also crucial to understand that while guilt is a feeling not often expressed or experienced in a material way, the scapegoating mechanism is experienced materially and is often quite visible and pronounced. This distinction explains why the focus on scapegoating materially often ignores its triggering motive.

The means-to-end reasoning process in the scapegoat mechanism is far from being justified or ethical. On the contrary, the dramatistic process that moves one from guilt to sacrifice, scapegoating, victimage, redemption and purification is replete with the hurting of others, just as in ancient times communities absolved their sins by sacrificing animals and even other human beings. As a general rule, people prefer not to sacrifice themselves for their iniquities; such an act would be literally too painful, and worse, terminal. It is easier and relatively painless for anyone to sacrifice another or others. This is the essence of the scapegoat theory named for the goat that in ancient Jewish tradition was allowed to escape from a deep slope in Jerusalem carrying symbolically with it all the sins of those who set the goat free. Yet, one should not take lightly this literal ritual as it has grounded the act of scapegoating for centuries to come, and with increasingly devastating consequences, sending people, instead of goats, to their death and on mass scales.

For the scapegoat theory to work in identifying its role in anti-Semitism, it must also be present at the roots of anti-Semitism. Since the roots of anti-Semitism are inherently religious, the question that guides this query is whether scapegoating can be found in the initial struggle between Christianity and Judaism. As discussed later, the roots of anti-Semitism can be found in Christianity's frustrations and anger over Judaism's rejection of Jesus, the popularity of Judaism in Rome during the first three centuries CE, and the guilt associated with its ultimate cooption of Judaism and the need to reject Judaism altogether. The formation of Christianity does point to the scapegoat mechanism. Once the scapegoat mechanism was employed with some success, it became over the centuries a tried-and-true device, ready and available for use as needed.

In his seminal essay on Hitler's *Mein Kampf*, a reading that did much to solidify Burke's notion of guilt as foundational to Nazi anti-Semitism (and his rhetorical perspective in general), he argues that the scapegoat mechanism allowed Hitler to offer a "'curative' process that comes with the ability to hand over one's ills to a scapegoat, thereby getting purification by dissociation" (1941, p. 749). That anti-Semitism could function curatively, was likely derived from the Catholic Christian Social Party Hitler knew in Vienna, whereby unification through division was the preferred scapegoating formula. But, as Burke, cautions us, the "curative" device is based on "a fictitious devil-function," and that "people, in their human frailty, require an enemy as well as a goal" (1941, p. 753). Not to be overlooked is Burke's point that Hitler's anti-Semitism was appealing because it relied "upon a bastardization of fundamentally religious patterns of thought" (1941, p. 756).

For the scapegoat mechanism to work, writes Swartz (1996), the Jews must be transformed into a monstrosity and animality that distinctly characterizes Nazi anti-Semitism as a necessary "precondition to ground Nazi extermination policies" (p. 186). Rhetorically, "people are encouraged to hate each other based upon crude symbolic differentiations rather than to investigate critically the system that is causing them to have such negative feelings" (Swartz, p. 186). Subsequently, the rhetoric of hate is premised on people's misunderstanding of language "as both source and mystifier of strife" (Swartz, p. 187), whereby the mortified (the one suffering negative feelings) is, according to Burke, "saying no to another aspect of himself — hence the urgent incentive to be 'purified' by 'projecting' his conflict upon a scapegoat by 'passing the buck,' by seeking a sacrificial vessel upon which he can vent, as from without, a turmoil that is actually within" (cited in Swartz, p. 187). In "naming the Jews as the *Other*, anti-semites gain agency over their own weaknesses," allowing individuals to assert control over the source of their guilt. Thus, Nazi propaganda transformed the Jew into a monster, stating that they were not human and in so doing, made persecution and genocide possible, all done by a "symbolic transformation of the victim into monstrosity" (Swartz, p. 187).

The ultimate objective of the scapegoat mechanism is the need of individuals or groups of a redemptive outlet and that in executing the redemptive process humans engage in a form of substitution in which "as a character can redeem another by suffering in his stead, so one character can impute guilt to another by sinning in his stead," and that accordingly, "Adam's disobedience represents a guiltiness in Everyone with regard to Covenants ("In Adam's fall, We sinned all"), and thereby 'a second Adam' can serve as sacrificial substitute for mankind when the categorical guiltiness is being 'paid for'" (Burke, 1961, p. 176). The "fall" of mankind and its redemption are accepted as one version of an Order that can also work in reverse whereby "the terms in which we conceive of redemption can help shape the terms in which we conceive of the guilt that is to be redeemed" (Burke, 1961, p. 218). In short, Burke suggests that the Bible, viewed either logologically or theologically, takes victimage (which is redemption by vicarious atonement) as intrinsic to the idea of guilt (1961, p. 219).[1]

Guilt, then, is the place to begin contemplating the origin of anti-Semitism and as an encompassing term, it means any feeling of short-coming, inadequacy, but primarily it means sin. "Theologically, there are two kinds of 'sin', 'original' and 'actual.' 'Actual' sins are those committed by an individual sinner, in his own right. But 'original' sin is that of the 'old Adam' in us. It is sin 'in principle.' Hence it is the kind of guiltiness that, as translated into terms of temporal sequence, we 'inherit' form our 'first' ancestor" (Burke, 1961, p. 223). We sin, states Burke, because no one can fully comply with all of world's temptations and the Order that they require us to follow. Humans are "forever guilty," and therefore "forever demanding 'redemption,' thus forever inciting anew to the search for a curative victim" (1961, p. 223).

The Nazi projection of the Jew as the ultimate enemy allowed for cleansing "by ideology" that identified the Jew as "the 'perfect' victim in the guise of a total enemy." The "perfect" enemy was made possible by biblical teaching of the correct Order whereby a progression from crime to guilt serves as justification for action as well as the reverse whereby guilt leads to crime. This is so because guilt is "intrinsic to the social order" and that "the offender would feel guilty first, and afterwards commit the crime that justifies the guilt (or, more often, the crime that defies the guilt)" (Burke, 1961, p. 224).

The scapegoat theory is grounded in the explanation that suggests that "anti-Semitism is the result of neurotic resolution of conflict, meaning that problems which actually originate elsewhere are compulsively transformed into anti-Semitism" (Bergmann, 1988, p. 9). Bergmann, in an introduction to a two-edited volumes on anti-Semitism, accepts the scapegoat theory, stating that the "Jews, as a foreign and powerless group, are often the victims of affective release." That Judaism is the "'paternal religion' may be an added reason for anti-Semitism. Furthermore, Bergmann states that "by making the others 'victims', the anti-Semite wins back some of the lost omnipotence and . . . gains recognition in his own group" (Bergmann, pp. 12-15).

Psychologists explain the essence of anti-Semitism as a prejudice, the result of "ego defense mechanism," and that anti-Semitism follows a bi-polar stereotype whereby the Jew is "both communist and capitalist, cosmopolite and Zionist, rich and impoverished, brilliant and stupid, lazy and industrious" (Bergmann, 1988, p. 12). For the rhetorician, these bi-polar stereotypes are but short-hand terms for convenient accusations used as needed (i.e., *topoi* are common places that can serve as resources for arguments) and whose primary function is effective persuasion. This, in principle, is how the scapegoat mechanism operates. With such an array of sentiments, most conventional characteristics can trigger basic human emotions such as fear, inferiority, hate, and envy. These emotions often bring stereotypes and prejudices and this has been the lot of the Jew throughout history (Bergmann, 1988, p. 16). The key process, I highlight here, is that a rhetorical construct allows for the prompting of a mass psychology in the form of hatred of the "other."

Psychologists also add that the function of the stereotype affords the anti-Semite the opportunity "to destroy in the Jew that which he hates in himself." The psychological perspective describes the process of transfer which is the essence of what the theory scapegoating is all about — transferring one's guilt onto another. Herbert A. Sallen argues that the scapegoat theory of ethnocentrism is not an abnormal phenomenon but rather part of conformity expectation (cited in Bergmann, 1988, p. 23). Flory contends that the scapegoat mechanism is a human invention to overcome internal fear and the need to overcome it by inventing an external source for its replacement. Scapegoating does mean lying to self and that this lying brings also guilt (cited in Curtis, 1986, p. 242). When individuals are in such a state, an outsider can "guide" them in a given direction, which is what Hitler's rhetoric offered, moving the German people a rather short distance "from fear to hatred" (Flory in Curtis, 1986, p. 245). Anti-Semitism, Flory adds, is a prejudice and prejudice does not begin "with hatred but with the selfish impulse to reinforce our sense of our own worth at the expenses of others. A sense of inadequacy aggravated by fear is likely to lead to hatred of a scapegoat, but the hatred fulfills the specific function of rationalizing the bigot's sense of guilt" (in Curtis, 1986, p. 247).

Flory contends that prejudice is a fundamental human impulse and one manifestation of the most "instinctive of all human drives — selfishness — and its persistence is the result of another human characteristic that is equally predictable — the pride that makes us ready to go almost any length to avoid admitting to ourselves that we were in the wrong." As a prejudice, and similar to racism in general, anti-Semitism is explained as an "attempt to inflate one's sense of self-worth, and often to compensate for one's feelings of inadequacy, by choosing to treat differences as though it were a moral falling" (Flory in Curtis, 1986, p. 241). The real motive, then, is to deny "others the fundamental human right to be judged as individuals" (Flory in Curtis, 1986, pp. 240-241).

One frequent anti-Semitic charge that can be found in prevailing myths and conspiratorial theories is that Jews display great solidarity among themselves (very much the essence of the forged *Protocols of the Wise Elders of Zion*, discussed later in this book). In short, Jews follow an Order that is not shared by the larger community. Yet anti-Semitism in the form of scapegoating has often been triggered precisely to unify a community or society, hence a desired Order against an identifiable "enemy" and its so-called Order. The scapegoat theory explains much about this often used charge by anti-Semites. Indeed, anti-Semitism has often been used precisely to unify a nation (to project Order) when strife threatened its stability, blaming the Jews instead of dealing with difficulties that could not be easily solved, whether in Czarist Russia or Nazi Germany. Swartz writes that "the appeal of Adolf Hitler in Germany

. . . can be found in his ability to offer explanations for the problems facing people and in being able to resolve those problems. Such 'resolution' often involves taking a 'hard line' (a euphemism for heartless cruelty), but such excesses are legitimized by the authorizing force and the 'ends' that such policies bring (usually 'order' at the expense of diversity)" (Swartz, 1998, p. 90).

The scapegoat theory has not received universal agreement and some prominent thinkers have rejected it as an explanation for anti-Semitism. As stated earlier, Emil L. Fackenheim rejects the scapegoat theory "because those accepting it fail to explain why the scapegoat is almost always the Jew." In rejecting the scapegoat theory, Fakenheim also rejects the notion that anti-Semitism is a prejudice. This is so because a prejudice can be modified "when knowledge comes on the scene" which is not the case with anti-Semitism (Fackenheim in Curtis, pp. 22-24). Fakenheim subscribes instead to Reinhold Niebuhr's view that when a minority is hated "for its virtues as well as its vices, and when its vices are hated, not so much because they are vices, but because they bear the stamp of uniqueness, we are obviously dealing with a collective psychology," and that mass psychology cannot be altered with "a little more enlightenment" (Fakenheim, in Curtis, p. 22). Rhetorically, I contend, a mass psychology is a form of collective persuasion operating on a community, influencing it in one way or another, accepting and believing in set premises that condition groups to behave in a certain way without much reflection and introspection regarding actions taken.

But how was a given community influenced in the first place, and by whom? The sources of persuasion bring us back to those agents who ushered in a new religion — Christianity — not just by persuading others of its new ideas and merits but also by contrasting it with a group that they sought to outcast — Judaism. This, unfortunately, is often the way persuasion works. Instead of persuading others of an idea and letting the auditors weigh its merits, the group is persuaded to accept an idea by contrasting it with an undesirable one, thus adding negative attributes that carry people's opinions and attitudes. A Manichean worldview becomes the vehicle that carries the persuasive process and, along the way, a group that represents the opposing view is criticized, demonized, and scapegoated. This scapegoating suggests that the undesirable group carries "false" ideas that must be rejected and, by implication, the proposed idea of the in-group is superior and ought to be adopted. This persuasive process appears crude but historically it has worked repeatedly. Robert Hariman (1986) offers a similar observation regarding the strategy Socrates and his followers used to denigrate rhetoric in ancient Greece in order to endorse philosophy as the "superior" mode of inquiry. They attacked the sophists and ridiculed their practices and, in so doing, they sought to diminish the rhetorical practices that the sophists advocated (pp. 38-54).

A variation on the scapegoat perspective lies in considering Jews as "generic" agents or "generic middlemen" whose role and function one can find in different cultural settings. The Jew as the "generic middleman" originates in different communities and in different locations, yet its characteristics is similar. This view is supported by evidence that minority groups, such as Chinese or Lebanese, have been referred to as "Jews" even though they are not but appear only to emulate so-called "Jewish" characteristics. The generic middlemen function as intermediaries who mitigate social and economic functions among different social groups, and given their unique ethnic origin, they receive the brunt of criticism and frustration of others who represent the majority in a given community. These "generic middlemen" are often suspect of their achievements and skills at acquiring wealth and status which bring resentment, and instead of being rewarded for hard work they receive the scorn of others who cannot accept a logical explanation for their success. Instead of being praised for "their value, their discipline, and their culture," they are often labeled "clannish," and are accused of being deceptive, unscrupulous and unreliable (Sowell, 2006, p. 73). Consequently, "the tragic history of middlemen minorities around the world shows that often there are many substitutes for Jews in the role of scapegoats, as well as in their economic functions" (p. 109). The question is whether this explanation is warranted in the first place.

As I attempt to show in this study, there is some merit to this explanation but that the force of this perspective goes only so far. What needs to be recognized is not just the function of such a middleman group but that, in the selection of the reference to them as Jews, the "generic middleman" perpetuates a long-standing acceptance of the stereotype of the Jew as the middleman. The identity of the Jew as carrying these negative characteristics is the foundation of the generic stipulation. The practice of scapegoating was instituted at the inception of institutionalized Christianity when dogma and anti-Semitism went hand-in-hand. Since this practice of scapegoating falls well within the function of human psyche to blame others, the repeated use of the scapegoat theory has became a common place or a familiar line of reasoning to be used repeatedly.

Like Fakenheim, Hannah Arendt (1951), too, rejects the scapegoat theory as foundational to explaining anti-Semitism. She claims that "the theory that the Jews are always the scapegoat implies that the scapegoat might have been anyone else as well. It upholds the perfect innocence of the victim . . . and that no evil was done." However, those adhering to the scapegoat theory usually explain that "a specific scapegoat was so well suited to his role," that once they engage in such an explanation they left the theory of scapegoating and entered the more common historical research looking to explain why one group was more suited than others for the role of the scapegoat. At that moment, the scapegoated group "ceases to be the innocent victim whom the world blames for all its sins and through whom it wishes to escape punishment" (p. 7). In other words, if Jews became the scapegoat for the Nazis, it did not happen arbitrarily.

Arendt blames those seeking to rationalize anti-Semitism by using the scapegoat explanation for escaping "the seriousness of anti-Semitism and the significance of the fact that the Jews were driven into the storm center of events" (Arendt, 1951, p. 7). With Arendt's rejection of the scapegoat theory, one is left with a very narrow room for an alternative explanation for anti-Semitism. Arendt's thesis remains relatively constant as she puts the weight for bringing or causing anti-Semitism on Jews themselves. Given her thesis, the rejection of the scapegoat theory makes sense when one seeks to find internal causes for anti-Semitism such as Jewish behavior and practices as the weighty causes.[2]

Yet, Arendt's rejection of the scapegoat theory is not altogether tight, and despite her initial rejection, Arendt does allow for the possibility of the scapegoat theory, stating that "if there is any psychological truth in the scapegoat theory, it is as the effect of this social attitude toward Jews;

for when anti-Semitic legislation forced society to oust the Jews, these 'philosemites' felt as though they had to purge themselves of secret viciousness, to cleanse themselves of a stigma which they had mysteriously and wickedly loved" (1951, p. 86). So, Arendt allows for those who shed their anti-Semitism and became supporters or defenders of Jews to do so not out of genuine motives but out of guilt of previous unwarranted scapegoating. The key term in her sentence is "purge" as akin to sacrifice, victimage and, subsequently, a redemptive act. Yet, if some individuals became philo-Semites because of a certain scapegoating mentality, as Arendt suggests, does not this stand to reason that their initial sentiments toward Jews were also of the same mentality? Put differently, why assign the scapegoat theory only to the act of philo-Semites but not to anti-Semites? Despite conceding a bit on the scapegoat theory, Arendt narrows the possibilities of explanation.

Hitler's Scapegoat Theory and the Rhetoric of the Kill

During the twilight of World War II, Hitler began talking about sending German airplanes into Manhattan's skyscrapers so that this metropolis of the Jews would be destroyed (Kuntzell, 2007, pp. xix-xx). The concentration camps were not sufficient for Hitler's plan to exterminate Jews. His plan to kills Jews had to be complete and, in his hatred of them, he saw the United States and, especially, New York City as "the center of world Jewry" that must be destroyed as well. German scholar, Matthias Kuntzell (2007), has wondered if the perpetrators of September 11, 2001 were inspired by Hitler to blow up the twin towers in New York City (pp. xix-xx). More revealing of Hitler's motives was his claims that "in resisting the Jew, I am doing the work of the Lord" (Kuntzell, 2007, p. 95). The so-called "secular" Nazi had turned religious when contemplating his hatred of Jews, substantiating again the premise that anti-Semitism is inherently religious at its core. As Swartz, following Burke, notes, though Nazi Germany suffered from a severe economic depression, it psychologically identified with the ultimate "hero" that traditionally had been Jesus, "the man the Jewish people allegedly betrayed. Because Christians associate Jesus with 'presence' in the world, Jews, in their alleged betrayal of that presence, vicariously betrayed the World. Thus, attacking the tormentors of this 'hero', the Christ-figure, anti-semites lash out at the new-found tangibility of their symbolic tormentors" (1996, p. 188). To this I would add that Hitler constructed himself in similar fashion, the hero-leader — the *Fuehrer* — as a God-like leader whose authorizing figure carried the ultimate credibility and whose statements and call to actions had to be obeyed.

Upon reading Hitler's *Mein Kampf,* Kenneth Burke wrote his seminal essay "The Rhetoric of Hitler's *Battle ''*." In it, Burke observed the plan Hitler concocted to unify the German people and the "medicine" he would implement in solving the plight of Germany. The rhetorical analysis of Hitler's text, written before Germany's invasion of Poland and prior to the knowledge of what was happening in Nazi concentration camps, centers on selecting the Jews as the scapegoat for Germany's ills, identifying the international Jew as the common enemy. Burke was quick to realize that in focusing his attention on Jews, Hitler practiced the "materialization of religion" as a most effective "weapon of propaganda" (1941, pp. 744-745). Indeed, one cannot separate Nazi anti-Semitism from Christian anti-Semitism as the former is clearly drawn from the latter.

As a propaganda tool, Burke observed that "once Hitler has thus essentialized his enemy, all 'proof' henceforth is automatic. If you point out the enormous amount of evidence to show that the Jewish worker is at odds with 'international Jew stock exchange capitalist,' Hitler replies with one hundred per cent regularity: That is one more indication of the cunning with which the 'Jewish plot' is being engineered. Or would you point to 'Aryans' who do the same as his conspiratorial Jews? Very well; that is proof that the 'Aryan' has been 'seduced' by the Jew" (Burke, 1941, p. 745). All argumentative bases are covered and the Jew is consistently the culprit, no matter how shallow the evidence. The Jew is selected precisely because he had been recognized as the devil unifier. The Jew, then, functions as the ultimate projection device whereby "the 'curative' process that comes with the ability to hand over one's ills to a scapegoat, thereby getting purification by dissociation" (Burke, 1941, p. 749). The sentiments that in killing Jews, society is cured, is not a recent advocacy. Though Hitler would spell out in 1939 his plan for "the annihilation [*Vernichtung*] of the Jewish race in Europe," the intent to harm Jews goes back to Martin Luther's diatribe "against the Jews and their lies" (Hilberg, 2003, pp. 409-410), which I will discuss in detail in Chapter 10.

Kenneth Burke (1969) writes that the scapegoat "is profoundly consubstantial with those who, looking upon it as a chosen vessel, would ritualistically cleanse themselves by loading the burden of their own iniquities upon it. Thus the scapegoat represents the principle of division in that its persecutors would alienate from themselves to it their own uncleanlinesses" (p. 406). The mode of operation then is that of transference whereby the guilt or uncleanliness of self is transferred to another who is "selected" for the task regardless of his innocence. However, Burke points to the fact that scapegoating does not cure, and that despite the obviation and transference of one's iniquities onto others, scapegoating does not relieve oneself of the guilt that prompted the scapegoating in the first place. The strategy, however, allows one to feel purified temporarily by the act of scapegoating but not eternally. This, perhaps, is the design inherent in anti-Semitism whereby the hatred of the Jew is turned perpetual, continuous, and eternal precisely because the scapegoating accomplishes only a temporary task but does not eliminate the inherent reasons for guilt in the first place. The scapegoated Jew, then, is available for the next scapegoating. The impossibility of identifying another group for perpetual scapegoating is in itself a revealing notion.

In Hitler's cult of anti-Semitism, Burke (1969) finds the scapegoat as the "'essence' of evil, the principle discord felt by those who are to be purified by the sacrifice," and whose ultimate motive in scapegaoting is the "*rebirth* of the self." Thus, "the Hitlerite Anti-Semitism as scapegoat principle clearly reveals a related process of dialectic: unification by a foe shared in common" (pp. 406-407). Nazi anti-Semitism and the Holocaust as a detailed killing-machine was the ultimate scapegoat mechanism of building a new Germany on the principles of purity and redemption from sins assigned to the Jews. This was the ideology espoused by Hitler and put into practice via a powerful propaganda system.

The origin of anti-Semitism, as argued here, commenced with a Christian theology that centered on the accusation of *deicide* — that of killing Christ. The root cause — death on a cross — would become the ultimate punishment of Jews and the justification for their hatred. This was the Nazi's ultimate objective and the justification that was well imbedded in this Christian theology. It is noteworthy that Islamist anti-Semitism, grounded significantly on Nazi propaganda (developed further in Chapter 7), also speaks the language of killing Jews in, and outside, Israel. Basing Islamist hatred of Jews in Quranic and related religious writing, a fairly recent development, proves the objective of justifying killing. Such actions are possible when they are accorded religious justification because in the religious context, all statements are true because they are sanctioned by God.

Anti-Semitism as *Topos*

A variation on the scapegoat perspective can be found in the "rhetoric of cause" whereby anti-Semitism is a simplified post-hoc cause-finding justification for hatred. I situate anti-Semitism as a historical *topos* (a topic or common place) that has functioned conveniently as a resource for argumentation whereby a cause is drawn from the tried-and-true list of possible causes. The longevity of anti-Semitism and the purposeful attempts to perpetuate anti-Semitism at many historical junctures, keeping it from fading for some seventeen centuries, must have been sustained by a unique logic. As stated earlier, anti-Semitism has been explained throughout history citing numerous causes, ranging from religious to social, ethnic, cultural, linguistic, economic, racial and political causes. None of these completely explains anti-Semitism. If anything, these so-called causes are but convenient rationalizations that address temporal contexts but they do not explain this form of hatred for the sheer fact that the causes cannot change and always yield the same effect. The changeable nature of the explanation for anti-Semitism must point to a more profound cause. I point here to the possibility that once anti-Jewish hatred became entrenched in the religious narrative of Christianity, and to a lesser degree later during the founding of Islam, a habit of sort was established; a habit situated in the foundation of historical narrative.

History as a survey of facts that describe a purposeful eventuality is but a narrative of causes. This is so since facts and events cannot be sustained unless causes are attributed to specific agents and an overall coherent narrative coupled with measured sense of fidelity is forwarded. But history is far from being objective or truthful. On the contrary, history is a selective account of events, and its narrations are meant to rationalize that which is acceptable to a community. Idioms such as "history is written by the winner" or "history, like beauty is in the eye of the beholder" are illustrative of the less-than-objective nature of history. As Hayden White (1987) explains, "in the historical narrative, experiences distilled into fiction as typifications are subjected the test of their capacity to endow 'real' events with meaning," and that "the historical narrative does not, as narrative, dispel false beliefs about the past, human life, the nature of the community, and so on; what it does is test the capacity of a culture's fictions to endow real events with the kinds of meaning that literature displays to consciousness through its fashioning of patterns of 'imaginary' events" (p. 45). In short, history is formulated narratively and carries rhetorical qualities. Perhaps, more pointedly, White contends that "one can produce an imaginary discourse about real events that may not be less 'true' for being imaginary" (p. 57).

With a conceptualization of history that considers it to be as good as its narrative coherency and fidelity, I argue that anti-Semitism in history is but a rhetorical trope: a figure of speech or a linguistic device that is used as topic of invention. History, then, is written for, and out of, persuasive reasons whose aim is to forward an attractive (therefore, persuasive) tale of origin and significance. However, no narrative is completely truthful or comprehensive, as it often glosses over the less appealing or undesirable tales. Likewise, anti-Semitism is an entrenched source of argumentative possibilities, the kind that can obscure and obviate more truthful but undesirable accounts of events. Ostensibly, anti-Semitism is a ready-made cause (*topos*) to be used as needed and it has been used as a replacement for less than favorable tales.

Since history's rationalization requires a cause, and given history's more subjective nature, the "tried-and-true" act of blaming the Jews for all sorts of events has become such an entrenched notion, and has been repeated so many times over so many centuries, that many of its assertions have become accepted as "self-evident" facts. Blaming the Jews, then, has become a *habit* and, in so doing, it has become a conventional source of scapegoating. Yet, this scapegoating often does not appear as a devious practice when obviating other more truthful or honest causes because Jews have been identified as the cause or culprit so often. History, then, is replete with so many examples of Jewish "faults" and conspiracies that these many assertions have become acceptable, and often, *unquestioned* resources for argumentation and reasoning. The notion of guilt as motivating hatred can be illustrated in the insightful observation of Germany's guilt over the Holocaust by Israeli psychiatrist Zvi Rex, stating that "the Germans will never forgive the Jews for Auschwitz" (cited in Wistrich, 2010, p. 253). The perpetrators of one of the worst crimes against humanity resent the victims' charge of committing the crime; hence the hatred continues, and now because the victims dare to speak up. A cause is conjured up out of a familiar narrative but it is presented in a twisted way whereby the Jew-victim of Nazi Germany is now the Jew-victimizer of Germany's Nazi past.

Take, for example, a recent accusation by Iranian President Mahmood Ahmadinejad, stating on , that "these heinous acts are committed by a group of Zionists and occupiers that have failed. They have failed in the face of Islam's logic and justice . . . They invade the shrine and bomb there because they oppose God and justice … But be sure, you will not be saved from the wrath of power of the justice-seeking nations by resorting to such acts." Ahmadinejad made this statement in reference to "the bombing of a major Shiite shrine in Iraq by Sunni insurgents" ("Iran's President Mahmoud Ahmadinejad in his Own Words," *Anti-Defamation League*, 2006). The internal strife between Sunni and Shiite factions of Islam is obviated in this example with the more "conventional" and "acceptable" culprit who has nothing to do with the conflict or with the specific bombing of an Islamic holy shrine — the Jew. Given the larger context of repeated diatribes against Jews by the Iranian president Ahmadinejad, why should this accusation not fit the already accepted narrative of hate? In short, the Jew as the agency of evil is a convenient cause and therefore in preferred use.

Conclusion

The scapegoat perspective, as illustrated by Kenneth Burke, is based on the notion that people "in their human frailty, require as enemy as well as a goal." Hitler provided such a scapegoat mechanism by identifying the Jew who was "made to look like a world menace by rhetorical blandishments" (1941, p. 756). Indeed, the most extreme form of anti-Semitism took place in Nazi Germany where Hitler and his henchmen validated anti-Semitism by allowing individuals to be free from the feeling of guilt. Once the Germans were free of guilt the cruel phase of torture and extermination began precisely because there was no longer a reason to hate (Flory, p. 247). The freedom from guilt was possible by the use of the scapegoat mechanism whereby a simple transference of guilt to others was sufficient for people to feel absolved of their sin. In the scapegoat mechanism lies the objective of anti-Semitism, that of "gratification rather than enlightenment" (McWilliams, pp. 185-186). It is this particular point that explains why anti-Semitism is not illogical or unreasonable. Rather, it appears reasonable or rational to the person who is offered a "convenient" or "comfortable" explanation out of a complex or unwanted strife. This is so because enlightenment or knowledge is not the objective here but the need to alleviate an internal state of some inadequacy and this can be achieved only by the process of gratification. In short, in anti-Semitism the anti-Semite seeks to heal oneself; a rather reasonable process but one based on misdirection and misuse of language. The resultant social injustice is not seen as such once the process of objectifying Jews appears reasonable.

Finally, it is worth noting that the scapegoat theory has also carried an unintended but an important consequence in Jewish history — that of solidarity and survival. Historically, anti-Semitism has functioned in two distinctive ways: It allowed varied communities in different places and at different times to find a scapegoat for their local ills, setbacks, and misfortunes as a diversion from having to deal with difficult and perhaps insoluble issues. In that sense, anti-Semitism is but a strategy of obviation whereby the Jew is taken as the historical cause of things gone badly. Anti-Semitism has also functioned to unite Jewish communities and maintain a continuous existence through millennia. Yet, this very need for community and unification also added to the list of charges against Jews — that of preferring to be separate and different. Anti-Semitism, I argue here, is the act of searching and justifying causes of hatred. But why hate the Jew in the first place? This I shall explore here in the forthcoming chapters.

Notes

1. Logology means words about words, or as Swartz explains, they are relationships between words and actions (1996, p. 187).
2. Hannah Arendt does not subscribe to historical anti-Semitism that pivots scapegoating as the primary explanation. She forwards instead a perspective that ties the hatred of Jews to the rise of the modern nation-state. While the scapegoat theory implies that the victim is not guilty of its victimization, she faults Jews for not understanding how their association with political elites would give justification for their hatred.

3

The Messianic Conception in Judaism:
The Foundation of a Fatal Misunderstanding

In accusing Jews of *decide* — the killing of Christ, or the Messiah — the Messianic idea would become the most prevalent and continued source of tension between Christianity and Judaism. The Messianic idea would remain foundational to the Christian theology and its rhetoric of hate until the Vatican II synod (1962-65). For comprehending the tension between the two religions regarding the Messianic conception, the discussion must center on the Judaic conception of the Messianic idea, the specific conception from which Christianity developed its own Messiaship, the one it was quick to claim that Jews have missed and thus entered into God's disfavor. Understanding the origin and development of the Messianic idea in Judaism is necessary for setting both the context and substance of the eventual tension and anti-Semitism.

The noun "Messiah" is derived from the Hebrew verb "to pour," and it describes the act of pouring oil on the head of the individual inducted to be king or high priest. Saul was anointed the first King of Israel by the prophet Samuel, and as such he was given the title "Messiah of God" (I Sam. 24:7). When David was anointed as the second King, also by Samuel, he, too, became known as the Messiah, and decedents of King David were referred to as "Messiah son of David" (Maccoby, 1973, p. 99). Anointment, then, was the symbolic act of the royalty and deity, investing an individual with a title of great honor and importance. Christianity would adopt the same noun in Greek, *Christos*, to designate its Messiah, or God's anointed.

The Messianic idea in Judaism develops shortly after the reigns of the father and son kings, David and Solomon, on whose reigns was founded the doctrine that God had designated the House of David and his descendants to rule over Israel until the end of time (II Samuel 7:23; 1-3, 5, in *Encyclopedia Judaica Jerusalem*, pp. 1407-1417; Greenstone, 1972, pp. 25-27). The Messianic idea would continue to evolve and function as a "sign of the times," reflecting specific historical developments and the yearning of the people of Israel for a restoration of a glorious past. Thus, following the subsequent division of the kingdom of Israel into two parts (the northern kingdom that would retain the name Israel and the southern kingdom that would be known as Judea), the Messianic idea expressed the doctrine of hope, yearning for the House of David to be restored to its old glory and reign again over a unified kingdom. This is the Messianic idea in Amos 9:11-12, where rebuilding the City of David and the return to the former glory is prophesied. Isaiah (7:14; 11: 1-9) introduces the notion of the Messiah as a future-savior and he names him Immanuel which in Hebrew means "God is with us."[1]

Another common practice in the Hebrew Bible is the attribution of the title Messiah to different individuals. As discussed earlier, Samuel assigned the title to the first two kings. The prophet Isaiah called Cyrus (Koresh), King of Persia, the Messiah, for returning the Jewish exiles to Jerusalem (Isaiah 45:1). Haggai referred to Zerubbabel, governor of Judea, as the Messiah (a signet; Hag. 2:23). Malachi, the last biblical prophet, declared that another prophet like Elijah would announce the arrival of the great day of the Lord (Mal. 3:22-24). The book of Daniel provides a richer conception of the Messiah that includes the eternity of the nation of Israel and its glorious future, and the conversion of the heathen to the Hebrew faith (Greenstone, 1972, pp. 67-68).

These several instances, covering a lengthy history of ancient Israel, describe an evolving Messianic conception that responded to, and corresponded with, the growing internal strife as well as external pressure by different regional powers. With the passage of time, the Messianic idea began to gradually incorporate the doctrine of hope and with an ever-despairing present. Subsequently, the Messianic idea developed more along the lines of hope and aspirations for an ideal king who would redeem Israel and whose reign would be founded on the notion of justice (Isa. 9: 1-6; 16: 4-5). Yet, despite the evolving nature of the Messiah in Judaism gradually being transformed from a king or prophet into a deliverer and a redeemer, even in late Judaism (from the last prophet Malachi around 400 to Jesus' time) the Messiah remains a human being and never a superhuman figure (Maccoby, 1973, p. 99; Becker, 1977, p. 87). Indeed, the reference to different individuals in the Bible who were bestowed the title Messiah illustrates its primary function as an honorary or titular, thus symbolic function, and as noted, the title was not exclusively assigned to those of the Hebraic faith. Finally, and most crucially, it did not refer to a deity.

David Hartman (1976) argues that the exodus from Egypt provided the theological model for the Messiah by allowing God to break history so that divine presence in people's lives becomes a reality. The Hebrew Messiah then is conceived as a mediator between the people and God whose task is to ensure that people follow God's teaching. The Messiah is not the performer of miracles. Despite variations on the Messianic conception, the Hebrew Messiah remains a human being who assumes only human functions and appears alternatively as a king, high priest, warrior, and defender. No reference in the Hebrew Bible is made to the Messiah being God, the son of God, or being made in the image of God. The injunction against the creation of an image of God, not to speak of assigning familial relation to God, is rather explicit in Judaism. Here, then, lies one major gap between Christianity and Judaism over the Messiah and a source for much misunderstanding and tension.

One reasonable explanation for the Christian conception of the Messiah as God and Son of God is perhaps the latter's limited knowledge of Hebrew and mistranslation thereof. The honorary "God, my father," which is metaphorical and poetic in Hebrew, has been taken literally by early Christians, who perhaps were no longer in possession of the knowledge of Hebrew, or who relied on translations that lost their metaphorical and symbolic meaning. Noting the Christian conception of the Messiah as based on a blood relation to God that does not exist in Judaism, Rabbi Abahu stated in the fourth century CE the following: "Let us compare this to the case of the human monarch. He rules but he has a father, or a brother, or a son. But the Holy One, blessed be He, said: I am not so. I am the first and have no father, and I am last, having no son" (Chernick, 1980, p. 403). This principle is crucial for understanding the

Jewish rejection of Jesus as the Messiah and the Christian misunderstanding of the Jewish injunction against a too close proximity to God, not to speak of any blood relation to Him.

Gershom Scholem (1971) argues that the notion of redemption which stands at the foundation of the Messianic idea in Judaism is of *this* world, experienced publicly, and that accordingly, the eschatology of the prophets such as Amos, Hosea, and Isaiah are by-and-large *nationalistic* as they seek the return of the House of David, Israel's return to God and the establishment of an everlasting peace. Scholem traces the changes in the Messianic conception from initially a material to the more spiritual Messiah in later books of the Bible such as the book of Daniel, and post-biblical books of Enoch and Baruch. Similarly, Joseph Klausner (1955) suggests that the Messiah as a savior and redeemer does not appear in the Hebrew Bible and that it is found first in the book of Enoch written during the time of Herod's reign and that it was not connected to the notion of anointing (p. 8).

Judaism provides no hint as for who would be considered the Messiah and thus the flexibility of its conceptualization as well as the variation in its application. In Isaiah and Micah, a more comprehensive Messiah is presented relative to the more limited and even vague conception found in Amos and Hosea, where the Messiah is a "a light to the Gentiles," and "the servant of the Lord," who "bears the sin of many" (Klausner, pp. 238-241). Klausner also points to the fact that initially God alone is the redeemer (keeping the honorary title "anointed" to the king or the high priest). In Amos and Ezekiel there is no individual Messiah but a collective entity that revolves around a Messianic period that would restore the House of David. As Klausner notes, in Judaism spirituality is not taken to an extreme and faith is not separate from the social life, leaving the Messiah as an earthly concept (p. 10).

In the post-Biblical period (second century BCE) the Messianic idea undergoes further developments that include notions such as life-after-death and the world-to-come, sometimes confused with the "Days of the Messiah." There are also "signs" attributed to the Messiah that include his arrival, the birth pangs of the Messiah, the war with Gog and Magog, the days of judgment, and the resurrection of the dead (Klausner, pp. 241-250; 384-385). The richness of signs of the Messiah's coming are situated in the continued turmoil in the life of the Jewish people during the second century BCE and continuing to Jesus' times. Clearly, during this period of turmoil, the suffering of the Jewish people became the source of a more imaginative Messiah but also a modified conception of the Messianic idea that included repentance as a prerequisite to redemption. The despair of many and the yearning for an end to suffering gave rise to Messianic aspirations but also to numerous individuals claiming the title.

Though Jesus declared himself a Messiah and his followers were hoping that he was who he said, he was not considered as such by many since any hope in Him ended with his death (Cott, 1979, p. 499). Jesus was not the only one at his time who claimed to be the Messiah and in countering this trend of multiple individuals claiming to be the Messiah arose also the notion of a *false Messiah* (Klausner, pp. 408-411). The designation of the Messiah, in biblical as well as in post-biblical periods, was very much a matter of hindsight reasoning and based on the dream of restoring the kingdom of Israel and the reign of the House of David (Cott, pp. 496-498). Any failure to accomplish this task would negate the Messianic designation. When Jesus declared that "The Kingdom of God is not coming with signs to be observed; nor will they say, 'Lo, here it is!' or 'There!' for behold, the is in the midst of you" (LK. 17: 20-21), he did not follow the Messianic idea that his contemporaries could recognized and thus, the likely reason why he was rejected (cited in Cott, p. 500).

The Messiah that Christianity advanced was no longer a mortal being as the concept expanded beyond the limitations of mortality. Christ's task was no longer to redeem Israel from political oppression but to redeem the world from spiritual evil, and since He was no mere mortal he would come again (Klausner, p. 526). These notions, however, were anathema to Judaism of Jesus' time as they bore no biblical reference Jews could recognize. Yet, Christians would blame Jews for being blind to Jesus and thus unable to realize he was the Messiah. While the Messianic idea in Judaism combines the political with the ethical expectations of redemption and moral perfection, it is in Christianity that the political and nationalistic notions are removed and replaced with the ethical and spiritual ideas. In Christianity, claims Klausner, through error of interpretation, various biblical references are used as evidence of the Messiah (pp. 9-10, 26). As further elaborated by Martin Goodman:

Despite the eventual emergence of Christianity from late Second Temple Judaism, the figure of the Messiah is either missing or unimportant in many Jewish religious texts of this period. Christian interest in messianism may explain why much more is to be found about the figure of the Messiah at the end of days in the early Jewish literature preserved by Christians than in the Jewish literature of the second and third centuries CE preserved by the rabbis. (p. 190)[2]

The Hellenistic base of Christianity also explains the inner conflict and doubt Christianity carries regarding its Jewish origin.[3] While Christianity is much more Hellenistic than Judaic, it needed Judaism for foundational reasons. When Marcion suggested the complete rejection of Christianity's Jewish roots, a strong attack was mounted against him and his doctrine because "it was unthinkable to reject the Old Testament, precisely because it was said to contain the prophetic passages whose fulfillment in Christ they had preached from the first generation." The primary reason for the "usurpation of Israel's identity by Christians," argues Goodman, was the need of the Old Testament for "Christian thought and worship" (2007, pp. 503-505).

Early Christianity, then, was significantly influenced by Hellenism yet claimed its roots in Judaism as a necessary proof of its foundation. This is the source of the initial tension between Judaism and Christianity, since such an admission was not easy nor desirable from the Christian point of view. Put differently, the formula of the "Old Testament = Judaism warrants the New Testament = Christianity" makes Judaism subservient, but essential to Christianity. Judaism, then, was needed but only to warrant Christianity since Judaism's remaining role was/is to support Christianity's theological claims and in that role Jews had to suffer.

But since such an admission would weaken Christianity, it was easier to usurp Judaism and to claim that it no longer counted in God's eyes. But this was not all. Jews were accused by the Church of rejecting Christ and for not understanding His message. The alternative option, that of Christianity not understanding the Judaic conception of the

Messiah has not been considered. Yet, Christianity accepted the essence of the Messianic idea in Judaism — hope. In short, all rhetorical resources were mounted to prove Christianity's Messianic conception and all that stood in Judaism for the same, was sought to be squashed. So strong was the belief in the Middle-Ages that Jews did know that Jesus was the Messiah that we find numerous tales and plays that would argue that Jews rejected Him because of their evil nature (Trachtenberg, p.153).

The Messianic Idea as the Rhetoric of Hope

Though Jesus was hailed as the Messiah (and rejecting the Jewish denial that Christ was God's anointed), with His resurrection, the Church accepted the Messianic conception in Judaism that it initially rejected. Following the resurrection, Christianity implemented the Judaic Messianic notion of apocalyptic deliverance, the very idea that was initially rejected with Jesus' arrival (Cott, p. 508). The Judaic Messianic idea that in essence stands for the rhetoric of hope was claimed by Christians to have materialized not once Jesus the Messiah (or Christ) has arrived on the scene, but after he left it. Shortly after his crucifixion, a new Messianic idea emerged in Christianity — the second coming— that is still operative, and that in essence is identical to the existing Messianic idea in Judaism.

The hope for better days, for overcoming setbacks, for the resumption of old glories based on cherished memories, are all rather universal qualities and necessary in motivating individuals and groups to sustain themselves against unexpected odds. Hope, then, is an essential ingredient in the tool box of human psyche whose purpose is to manage life's often difficult and unexpected turns. The importance of hope to human existence manifests itself in various rhetorical forms such as national dreams, myth, fantasies and iconic depictions. For the sake of clarity, my focus here is on *hope* and not on *faith*. I consider hope a positive and motivating force that is based on "concrete plans, or strategies," while faith is "alienating and anti-human," as it relies on "the unwarranted belief that things will work out according to some larger plan or directive" (Swartz, 1999, p. 83). With hope, writes Swartz, a person is not asked to "give up his or her critical facilities; on the contrary, hope encourages people to maximize their critical talents," and that hope depends on "the richness of the human imagination," while "faith panders to the poverty of our spiritual and moral imaginations" (p. 83). More succinctly, hope, argues Swartz, is pragmatic while faith is dogmatic (p. 83).

Hope, then, is central to theology. This very conception of hope, I contend, stands at the foundation of the Messianic idea, vested with religious metaphors and symbolism to formalize its importance and enshrine it with doctrinal power. Hope is well captured in the idea of redemption as the highest form of motivation. Since hope gives people the motivation to continue despite setbacks and difficulties, in redemption one finds the ultimate attainment of sustainability. No wonder, religious rhetoric, clearly the case in Judaism and Christianity, have endorsed this conception of hope and developed it around the Messianic idea.

In a larger sense and perhaps from a more philosophical perspective, life is meaningful when it is guided by hope and hope, in turn, gives individual the aspiration, motivation and strength to do that which is not always easy. Taking this concept a step further, the three religions that are tied together — Judaism, Christianity and Islam — have all developed their respective theology of hope as a necessary concept. Hope, then, in one conception or another, is essential for any religious system. Stated differently, hope can be considered the primary reason for religion in the first place and as such hope is the rhetorical trajectory of religion. In more simplistic terms, a given religion may incorporate the rhetoric of hope in the direction of its theology. Religion gives hope a formal, metaphorical and symbolic importance such that its narrative or iconic manifestations are sanctioned with great authority such as the deity. In Judaism, the rhetoric of hope allowed for continuous aspiration for better days and the motivation to continue to believe, especially during difficult and challenging times.

Hope, as discussed thus far, is essential for human continuity; but in aspiration and hope also lie an inner and not an insignificant contradiction. For hope to continue its motivating influence on humans, it cannot be realized, at least not in a religious sense. Hope cannot come to an end since its very fulfillment would be the end of hope. Hope can survive only if it continuous and not be fully consummated or materialized. Thus, if the Messiah has already arrived, hope would end. In that sense, Judaism made the conception of the Messianic idea important, continuous and evolving, but not central or conditional to its existence. In Judaism, then, people continue to believe in the arrival of the Messiah, who, at least rhetorically, cannot arrive since his arrival will negate hope. Perhaps intuitively, in Judaism the greater importance is given to the rhetoric of hope than to its materialization. Hope, and its transcending rhetoric and not its consummatory quality in the form of the Messiah's arrival, is the essence of the theology at hand.

Now, what is a religion to do when the aspired hope has already been realized? Which brings us to the Christianity's inherent dilemma: When Jesus was declared Messiah, hope has been realized and thus the messianic idea in its fulfillment came to an end.[4] In short; what now? And, how could the new religion sustain itself without the notion of hope? For hope to continue, the Messianic idea had to appear *again* and the mechanism for continued hope centered on the theology of the resurrection. The conception of hope in Christianity lies in the narrative of Christ's second coming whereby Jesus rose from the dead, and since His resurrection Christians await His coming, *again*. Hence, the rhetoric of hope of Judaism was re-introduced in early Christianity so that believers would continue to hope and believe. That Christianity had to "borrow" from Judaism's messianic conception the second time was not a comfortable thing to do and would thus bring later accusations of Jews ignoring their own Biblical teaching and not respecting their prophets.

From the perspective of the rhetoric of hope, Judaism and Christianity have a similar, though not an identical conception of hope; Jews still await the Messiah and Christians await his second coming — the frustration of which fuels anti-Semitism. Theologically at least, Christianity understood the Judaic Messianic idea only after Jesus' arrival. Thus, in the conception of Christ's return Christianity brought back the Judaic conception of the Messiah that it initially rejected. Conceptually, the Jewish Messianic conception and the Christian expectation for Christ's second coming are rather similar as both aspire for ultimate days of peace, and justice.

Yet, despite the conceptual similarity, there is also a wide gap in the rhetoric of hope of the two religions and therein lies the source of Christian uncertainty, doubt, and even guilt about theological claims related to the Messiah. Ultimately, these gaps commenced hatred of Jews. Several reasons stand in the way of a secure Christian conception of the Messianic idea. While Judaism can and has survived without the Messiah's arrival as the aspirations for such a future event are sufficient to sustain its continuity, symbolically and metonymily, Christianity is wholly based and dependent on the Messiah, both in concept and in the literal body of Christ. Without the Messiah, Christianity cannot exist while Judaism can continue as it has for millennia. The uncertainty and doubt about Jesus as the Messiah springs from the very Judaic conception of the Messiah that bears no resemblance to the Christian Messiah.

As discussed earlier, no affiliation to God is allowed in Judaism, no central importance is assigned to the Messiah as God continues to be the central figure in Judaism. The biblical references to the Messiah and the evolving nature of its conception cannot sustain a single notion of the Messiah. The attribution of the title "Messiah" to several individuals in the Hebrew Bible is indicative of the rather honorary value but innocuous practice of its use. In short, Judaism had a rich volume of references to the Messiah, yet none of which would have supported accepting Christ as the Messiah who also claimed to be God. Finally, biblical references to Jesus' foretelling, a practice of looking backward and tracking those references that are interpreted as "proving" Jesus were not known to his contemporaries. Yet, later and repeated references to these biblical sources as "proof" of Christ's foretelling without acknowledging the difficulties of Jesus' contemporaries of contextualizing them vis-à-vis a Christian conception, is the source of much tension and misunderstanding between the two religions. Judaism's rejection of Christ, at his time must be put in the context of the knowledge Jews had about the Messiah of the Hebrew Bible and not of the Christian Bible.

Yet, for some two thousand years Christian anti-Semitism has maliciously blamed Jews for committing numerous crimes — none as foundational as the accusation of killing Christ. Surprisingly, throughout these two millennia, no effort has been made to consider the opposite — that Jews have remained faithful to their Mosaic and Messianic conceptions and that had they accepted Christ as their Messiah they would commit an act that was incongruent with their biblical teaching. What complicates the matter for Christians, and thus constitutes a possible source of doubt thereof, is the alternative argument that Christians rejected the Jewish notion of the Messiah. Put differently, is it possible that Judaism did get it right with its conception of the Messiah? However, with the theology of the second coming, Christianity has accepted Judaism's notion of the Messiah yet kept blaming Jews for rejecting Jesus as the Messiah. Such inconsistency and confusion is the fault of Christianity; not of Judaism. Yet, for centuries Jews have been presented with the Messiah formula — that of "proving" Christ by referencing verses in the Hebrew Bible. Yet, for Jews, the Messiah formula in Christianity, based on tenuous interpretation, ignores biblical verses that do not support this Christian doctrine.

Conclusion

The messianic conception on whose foundation Christianity rests is argued on Old Testament grounds, but its materialization in Jesus as Christ is not consistent with Jewish teaching or in Old Testament verses. Only after Jesus was pronounced to be the Messiah — Christ — and died on the cross, I argue, has Christianity embraced the essence of the messianic idea in Judaism. The Christian's conception of Christ's second coming follows rather closely the Judaic conception of Messianism in which the rhetoric of hope is its essence. Rejecting Jesus as the Messiah that Jews yearned for is the initial and foundational charge Christianity leveled against Jews, a charge that would be repeated again and again over many centuries. It would serve as the justification for anti-Semitism, for hating and punishing those who, supposedly, should have known better.

The 1965 Vatican II statement rejecting Catholic anti-Semitism (discussed later in this volume) has attempted to address some of these concerns but only indirectly. It is unlikely that the gap in the Messianic conception between Christianity and Judaism would ever be narrowed, primarily because any deviation from the dogmatic Christian conception of Christ as the Messiah would negate Christianity. Judaism, though in the possession of a more flexible Messiah, is also bound by specific principles that guide prohibition regarding the visualization of God and the holiness of His being such that no human being can claim blood relationship to him. The rejection of Christ became the primary and purposeful source of a hostile break from Judaism and specific Church leaders led the way using the persuasiveness of sermons as the best means of constructing an image of Judaism that was negative and diabolic. The setting for virulent anti-Semitism was now underway.

Notes

1. Christians often refer to this verse as proof of foretelling Jesus though no connection exists between the names Immanuel and Jesus, or Yeshua in Hebrew.
2. The sects whose writings were found in Qumran, may be the exception than the rule.
3. As Christianity spread through the Hellenic and Roman worlds, it fused Greek philosophy with Judaism, integrating philosophies such as Stoicism and Platonism with Judaism. The influence of Hellenism must have been significant given Paul's warning against such practices (1st Corinthians 1:18-31), whereby Paul argues that Jews require signs in order to know God, while Greeks rely in wisdom, or in Colossians 2:8 where Paul considers Greek philosophy hollow and as of this world rather than that of Christ's world.
4. I fully acknowledge that Christianity as we know it today was developed centuries after Jesus' death and that the theology thereof was developed after events surrounding Jesus' teaching and death have long been part of history and memory. The issue at hand, though, is the theology of hope.

4

Saint John Chrysostom: Rhetorical Invectives and the Foundation of Anti-Semitism

The disengagement and separation of Christianity from Judaism would usher in anti-Semitism as an institutional Church dogma. The anti-Semitism that the Church espoused would set the course of history for some seventeen centuries of hatred as a strategic and purposeful rhetorical act that was seen as necessary for the survival of Christianity and guarantee its separation from Judaism. Inherent in the need for a clear separation between the two religions, I argue, was also the lingering doubt and uncertainty about claims Christians have made about its own theology and subsequently, about Judaism. Anti-Semitism, then, was constructed as a necessary step in "proving" Christianity's theological claims and usurpation of Judaism. Hostility towards Jews and Judaism was the preferred mode of operation over the more reasonable debate about competing beliefs, especially those about the messianic conception, a debate that perhaps early Christians did not wish to pursue.

Though several Church leaders would speak with great hostility toward Jews and Judaism, none would be as viciously anti-Semitic as St. John Chrysostom (ca. 347-407 CE). James Parkes (1974) argues that in the eight sermons, known collectively as *Adversus Judeaus*, St. Chrysostom delivered in Antioch, in 387 CE, he spoke with "bitterness and lack of restraint unusual even in that place and century" (pp. 163-166). Christianity, claims Parkes, was no longer in danger and St. Chrysostom suffered no challenges from Jews. This was the century in which the

Church "won," and there was no reason for such severe attacks on Jews. Yet, claims Parkes, "in these discourses there is no sneer too mean, no gibe too bitter for him to fling at the Jewish people. No text is too remote to be able to be twisted to their confusion, no argument is too casuistical, no blasphemy too startling for him to employ" (p. 163). Had these homilies been just taken as contemporary lashing out of a local preacher, then not much credence would be assigned to them. But such is not the case with the sermons of St. Chrysostom. As a Church father, he set the tone and reinforced a dogma that subsequently made anti-Semitism a Church policy for centuries to come. As David Brog (2006) put it, St. Chrysostom upped the ante a notch higher advocating a "link between replacement and elimination," arguing not only that Christianity replaced Judaism but that Judaism should no longer exist (p. 25).

The situational context of St. Chrysostom's homilies reveals much about anti-Semitism as intentional hatred. Antioch was rather placid where the local Jewish community, prosperous and well-integrated, was quite acceptable by the Christians of the city. Yet, this friendly relationship between Christians and Jews is precisely what triggered St. Chrysostom's wrath (Parkes, pp. 163-166). His eight *Adversus Judeaus*, homilies depict a Jewish community that appears attractive to many Christians who have joined them during Jewish holidays and festivities, visited their synagogues and maintained good relationship with them. A separation and a complete break with Judaism is St. Chrysostom's aim. Indeed, Parkes suggests that the vicious rhetorical attacks on Jews were borne out of the "close fellowship between Jews and Christians in Antioch" (p. 164). St. Chrysostom's attacks on the Jews must be seen as part of a larger effort to confront many who doubted and resisted Christianity (St. Chrysostom, 1985, pp. 18-19). St. Chrysostom would battle pagans and various Christian sects such as the Anomoeans, and though his addresses are similar to the homilies *Adversus Judeaus* in their rhetorical development, proof, structure and appeals, they lack the anti-Semitic or hateful bent preserved for his attacks on Judiazing Christians (St. Chrysostom, 1985, pp. 165-166; St. Chrysostom, 1984, p. 72).

More recent studies of St. Chrysostom's treatment of Jews aims at claiming that his anti-Semitism has been misunderstood and that he actually attacked those Judaizing Christians and that he did not attack

Jews per se (Wilken, 1983). It is indeed the case, that most of St. Chrysostom's appeals are directed at those Christians who enjoyed the fellowship with Jews. But what he has to say about Jews is the reason for finding him unnecessarily hateful. Had he limited his concern to those Judaizing Christians, no serious charges of anti-Semitism would be uttered against St. Chrysostom. But his many statements about Jews and Judaism are not only biased but hateful to the extreme. His own words will make the case here.

It is important to note that St. Chrysostom was also a rhetorician — a teacher and a successful practitioner of rhetoric, versed in the cannon of classical rhetorical theory. His saintly name means "golden mouthed," and his homilies are developed with a solid knowledge of how to construct persuasive messages and the various persuasive strategies available to the speaker (St. Chrysostom, 1985, pp. 45-46). In particular, he understood the power of rhetorical questions, analogies, and metaphors, and how to incorporate them in his rhetorical appeals.

One distinct feature of St. Chrysostom's homilies against the Jews is the use of logos — appeal to reason — often constructed in the homilies as rhetorical questions whose answers he forwards and whose acceptance often appears as the most logical conclusion and the ones the audience should draw. The use of logos is also limited to the traditional *topoi* (common places) from which he draws his arguments — namely the Hebrew and Christian Bibles. He specifically seeks to prove Christ's foretelling by using verses from the Hebrew Bible as proof of Christianity's superiority to Judaism. Yet, his evidence is weak, indirect and not all together convincing, at least not to those who still leaned on the Judaic side of the religious divide. Given this rhetorical limitation, St. Chrysostom also resorts to reasoning from hierarchy, whereby Judaism is mocked and ridiculed while Christianity is presented as the superior religion. Anti-Semitism, then, is constructed as a rhetorical tool to depress Judaism and convince suspecting Christians that they should cease all association with Judaism.

St. Chrysostom's homilies carry a consistent message: that of convincing people to avoid all things Jewish. He does so by repeatedly demonizing Jews and using their demonic depiction as proof of their ungodly ways. He is rather fond of using verses uttered by Moses or other Hebrew prophets, primarily for the purpose of putting Christ among these illustrious individuals and subsequently for their cumulative rhetorical weight. Since in Christianity, Christ is considered a prophet, St. Chrysostom builds his arguments such that he can question why Jews opted to listen to some prophets and not to others; why did they listen to Moses or Jeremiah but not to Jesus? This inconsistency, argues St. Chrysostom, is proof of the error in Jewish practices and God's punishment. Rejection of Jesus, then, is the primary sin incurred by Jews and this act justifies hating them and disengaging from them.

With this basic rhetorical formula of Jews being inconsistent in their practices, I identify two related themes that run through St. Chrysostom's homilies in *Adversus Judeaus*: *The Sinful Synagogue* and *the Sin of Rejecting Christ*. His purpose is to drive a wedge between the two religions such that a separation between them would be complete. St. Chrysostom's primary objective is his thesis that the Jews committed the sin of deicide and given this sin he advises Christians that they should cease all fellowship with them. Subsequently, the synagogue, the metaphor for all things Jewish, ought to be disparaged and be avoided for it is an evil place.

Rejecting Christ: The central message of St. Chrysostom's homilies in *Adversus Judeaus* is that Jews have rejected Christ and that they are responsible for his death. The sequence of these two events is important to St. Chrysostom as he argues time and again that Christ's arrival was foretold in the Hebrew Bible. Thus, Jews have committed not only the sin of killing Christ but also of rejecting prophecies of him as foretold in their own Bible. The so-called proofs that he provides though — references to Biblical sayings — are vague, unspecified and suggestive, but the language is intense and replete with invectives against Jews. The hateful statements against Jews are important to this study not because of the unique experience of the tension between Jews and Christians in Antioch in the fourth century, but because they set the tone and the depth of anti-Semitism. In short, with St. Chrysostom, the rhetoric of anti-Semitism is shaped for centuries to come.

Jews, St. Chrysostom tells his audience in the first homily, "are enemies of the truth," and never cease in "blaspheming our Benefactor" (Homily one: I: 4). The Jews, then, are evil because they attacked Christ.

St. Chrysostom's immediate objective is to prevent Christians from joining Jewish festivities and associating with them. "I wish to drive this perverse custom from the Church right now . . . now that the Jewish festivals are close by and at the very door, if I should fail to cure those who are sick with the Judaizing disease. I am afraid that, because of their ill-suited association and deep ignorance, some Christians may partake in the Jews' transgressions" (One: I: 5). Judaism, then, is a disease, and Jews seek to infect unsuspecting Christians with their false religion.

What exactly bothers St. Chrysostom? He is concerned with the charge Jews make against Christ: "that He called God his own Father and so made Himself equal to God" (One: I: 6). He is bothered by the charge Jews have made that Christ called himself son of God and thus equal to him and that such a presumption does not accord with Judaism. Rejection of Christ, then, is the major Jewish offense. Says St. Chrysostom: "The morning Sun of Justice arose for them, but they thrust aside its rays and still sit in darkness," and that "they crucified him who the prophets had foretold" (One: II: 1). Jews have erred in not accepting that which was done for them. The stark metaphors of sun and darkness are meant to project a great divide between the two religions such that Jews are seen as ungrateful and miserable, and thus deserving of his scorns.

In rejecting Christ, Jews, says St. Chrysostom, "fell into kinship with dogs; we who were dogs received the strength through God's grace" (One: II: 1). Opposing hierarchies are presented as metaphors for the superiority of Christianity over Judaism. He confronts Jews for attacking their "own salvation," mocking them for resisting to observe God's Law and, now that the Law is no longer binding them, "they obstinately strive to observe it." Jews provoked God twice, early on by resisting his Law by rejecting Christ, and now by following God's Law that, with Christ's arrival, is no longer binding (One: II: 3). Clearly, for St Chrysostom, Judaism is irrelevant and should cease to exist.

Christ's foretelling in the Hebrew Bible is established prima facie as when St. Chrysostom asks: "When they say that Moses and the prophets knew not Christ and said nothing about his coming, what greater outrage could they do to those holy men than to accuse them of failing to recognize their Master . . .?" St. Chrysostom does not deal with the theology that stands at the heart of the issue, that of Moses foretelling

Christ, which he did not. He resorts instead to rhetorical questions whose very utterances signify self-evident answers that are suggestive and, therefore, appear reasonable, but are nonetheless, factually wrong. The Christian premise is inherent in the question which implies that there is no room for the Jewish perspective. This is so because St. Chrysostom leaves Christians with only one option: "And so it is that we must hate both them and their synagogue all the more because of their offensive treatment of those holy men [Moses and the prophets]" (One: V: 4). Jews are to be hated for not heeding Moses and other prophets who foretold Christ, which these prophets, as far as Judaism goes, made no such prophecies.

St. Chrysostom warns his audience to "be overly careful in searching to see if anyone favoring an alien faith has mingled among you" (One: IV: 9). Complete separation between Judaism and Christianity is the call again as Christians are advised not to associate "with those who shouted: 'Crucify him, Crucify him'" (One: V: 1). Continuously, St. Chrysostom seeks to draw comparisons between Judaism and Christianity such that Christianity is always presented as the superior religion. States St. Chrysostom: "for the man who strives to gain salvation from the works of the Laws has nothing in common with grace," and that "if justice be by the Law, then Christ died in vain" (Two: II: 1). This argument is akin to the often heard truism that those who died in battle, however controversial, did not die in vein. A post-hoc justification is the appeal of the last resort.

Crucially, Judaism is presented as a religion of *Law* while Christianity is presented as the religion of *grace*. The gap could not be wider and starker. And here lies St. Chrysostom's concern — that some Christians are still following the law and that the law is Jewish. Under such circumstances, Judaism could not become the ostracized religion St. Chrysostom sought it to be. The intent, therefore, is clear — to cast Judaism in the worse light and turn it into a hated religion so that Christianity would survive, not by the substance of its teaching or the merit of its theology but by the dogma of its edicts. The irony of this reasoning is revealing; Judaism is frowned upon as the religion of law and not of grace, yet Christians are told to obey specific laws if they are sanctioned by Christ. Yet, the equation of Judaism with law would prevail for centuries and function as a resource of anti-Semitism whereby Judaism would be reduced to a set of laws and Jews would be mocked as their blind following. Christianity as the religion, not of law but of grace, would by implication be held as a superior religion. The Talmud, in particular, as a codex of law and the study of legal disputations, would be featured prominently as a source of evil and deceit, and be used time and again in many cases of anti-Semitism (Laqueur, p. 48).

St. Chrysostom spares no invectives against Jews and his metaphors are revealing of his deep hatred. And though some contemporary views of this Church Father have sought to temper his negative and outrageous views, putting his sermons in a context such that he is not considered the anti-Semite that others consider him to be, St. Chrysostom's own words betray such a tempered assessment. The Jews, he says, are "the most miserable and wretched of all men" and "today, the Jews, who are more dangerous than any wolves, are bent on surrounding my sheep" (Four: I: 1-2). The intense animalistic metaphors function to not only separate Christians from Jews, but also to cast fear and suspicion of Jews, knowing quite well that if reason cannot bring the sought change, fear and hatred could.

At the foundation of the tension between the two religions is Christ's death which St. Chrysostom puts squarely at the hands of the Jews:

> The difference between the Jews and us is not a small one, is it? Is the dispute between us over ordinary, everyday matters, so that you think the two religions are really one and the same? Why are you mixing what cannot be mixed? They crucified the Christ whom you adore as God. Do you see how great the difference is? How is it, then, that you keep running to those who slew Christ when you say that you worship him whom they crucified? You do not think, do you, that I am the one who brings up the law on which these charges are based, nor that I make up the form which the accusation takes? Does not the Scripture treat the Jews in this way? (Four: III: 6)

One can read St. Chrysostom's frustrations over the fact that the grave sin of killing Christ is not an issue for some Christians who willingly mix with Jews. The context of these attacks illustrates a rather productive relationship between Christians and Jews, such that only extreme rhetoric of hate could alter. Since the association with Jews continues, St. Chrysostom retches up his attack on Jews. He also elevates the severity of the matter by putting his credibility on the line by asking his audience whether they question his statement. Clearly, he felt the need, time and again, to prove his assertion about Jews being evil:

> Let me say what Elijah said against the Jews. He saw the unholy life the Jews were living: at one time they paid heed to God, at another they worshipped idols. So he spoke some such words as these: "How long will you limp on both legs? If the Lord our God is with you, come, follow Him; but if Baal, then follow him." Let me, too, now say this against these Judaizing Christians. If you judge that Judaism is the true religion, why are you causing trouble to the Church? But if Christianity is the true faith, as it really is, stay in it and follow it. Tell me this. Do you share with us in the mysteries, do you worship Christ as a Christian, do you ask him for blessings, and do you then celebrate the festival with his foes? With what purpose, then, do you come to the church? (Four: IV: 1)

In using biblical references, though selective and misleading, as proof to support his claims about Jewish sins and transgressions, St. Chrysostom illustrates his rhetorical skills. From all available means of persuasion, the Hebrew Bible is indeed a most credible source for making derogatory statements about Jews as the Bible includes many examples of the Israelites who at one point or another strayed away from God's teaching. References to worshiping idols are numerous, and most prophets have spoken against these practices and warned the people of their punishments. But St. Chrysostom takes these references out of context and applies them to his current struggle. He also seeks to create distance between Jews and their biblical icons, such as the prophet Elijah. For instance, the deliberate phrasing of "Elijah" and "the Jews" implies two estranged entities, which they were not.

In another homily St. Chrysostom brings forth a random list of biblical events such that they cohere with his preferred commentaries:

> What about this? After the waters of the sea were divided, after the rocks were broken asunder, after so many miracles were worked in the desert, did you not worship the calf? Did you not try many times to kill Moses, now by stoning him, now by driving him into exile, and in ten thousand other ways? Did you ever stop hurling blasphemies at God? Were you not initiated in the rites of Baal of Peor? Did you not sacrifice your sons and daughters to demons? Did you not make a display of every form of ungodliness and sin? (Six: II: 6)

Casting negative references about Jews is not a difficult task when consulting the Hebrew Bible. However, St. Chrysostom is short on the context for the various saying and he stretches their implication and falsifies biblical narratives (Moses went into exile not because of the Israelites but because the Egyptians were after him. See, Exodus 2:11-15). The link St. Chrysostom makes between these iniquities and Christ, however, cannot be found in the Hebrew Bible.

Overall, the homilies against the Jews are replete with "proof" of the Bible foretelling Christ's as well as of God's abandonment and punishment of the Jewish people for their iniquities. The proofs are presented as arguments for ceasing all fellowship with Jews because of their evil ways. A deeper analysis also reveals that the homilies imply doubt and uncertainty about the theological claims St. Chrysostom makes. The heavy dose of "proof" that he forwards throughout his homilies are suspect for the sheer amount of space he devotes to proving Christ's saying, surveying Jewish history, and especially for attacking Jews and Judaism.

St. Chrysostom is aware that what he practices is heavy persuasion and that he relies on propaganda technique of forwarding a shred of truth as necessary proof for larger unsubstantiated and suspect claims.[1] He states, for example, that "the demons wish to open the door to their deceits and to create confidence in their lies. And so they give some admixture of truth, in the same way that those who mix lethal drugs smear the lip of the cup with honey to make the harmful potion easy to drink" (Six: VI: 10). Further:

This is why Paul was very much grieved and why he hurried to stop up the demons' mouths when they took to themselves a dignity which ill became them. This is why I hate the Jews. Although they possess the Law, they put it to outrageous use. For it is by means of the Law that they try to entice and catch the more simpleminded sort of men. If they refused to believe in Christ because they did not believe in the prophets, the charge against them would not be so severe. As it is, they have deprived themselves of every excuse because they say that they do believe in the prophets but they have heaped outrage on him whom the prophets foretold. (Six: VI: 11)

The demons (the Jews), then, spoke with some dignity, such that Paul was quite bothered by the practice and sought to stop them from talking. And for this, St. Chrysostom makes it clear that he hates Jews. So, when Jews spoke, presumably the truth, they were to be hated, because they did so for evil purposes. Though he blames Jews for mixing falsehood with a grain of truth to confuse adherents, this is the very rhetorical formula St. Chrysostom uses against the Jews.

But St. Chrysostom's hatred of Jews is also due to a related cause, and here, as before, his reasoning is rather misleading: if Jews rejected Christ because they did not believe in the prophets that would have been acceptable. But the greatest sin, for him, is that Jews state that they believe in their prophets yet rejected one of them. Jews, then, are charged by St. Chrysostom with inconsistency and this charge grounds the primary thesis he has developed against the Jews — the rejection of Christ as inconsistent with Jewish teaching. The inconsistency in accepting some but not all prophets, means, according to St. Chrysostom, that Jews have erred and given this error, Christian fellowship with Jews is in error too. The notion of grouping all prophets is a rather sweeping of a long historical development. Including Christ among the Old Testament prophets, though he is not mentioned in the Hebrew Bible, except for a highly interpretive Christian theology, simply does not accord with Hebrew teaching. St. Chrysostom also mixes Messiah and prophets whereas the Hebrew Bible makes no such connection. Indeed, the continuous references to Jesus as Messiah and prophet, a concept not to be found in the Hebrew Bible, shows that the objective here is argumentative and polemic.

The need to prove that the Hebrew Bible foretold Christ's arrival is of course central to Christian teaching; thus, the constant references to such foretelling. St. Chrysostom clearly wishes to disconnect Christians from Jews; however, in so many places in his homilies he makes it clear that Christianity *needs* Judaism as proof of its — Christianity's existence. This ambivalence toward a group that is needed theologically but is also rejected and scorned socially cannot but result in an uncomfortable philosophizing. Hence, an inherent uncertainty and guilt thereof that stands as the twin motives for the rhetoric of hatred. Anti-Semitism, then, had become the outlet for Christian tension and uncertainty over its history and theology whereby hating Jews and Judaism was the counter statement to the heavy reliance on Judaism for the establishment and sustainability of Christianity.

The Synagogue: The Synagogue, the Jewish house of worship and learning which has replaced the Temple upon its destruction is, for St. Chrysostom, a metonym of all things Jewish, and a negative one at that. The synagogue is the immediate and tangible manifestation of Judaism, and no wonder that given his views of Jews and Judaism, his wrath against the synagogue is particularly harsh.

When Jews fast, he says, "they go in for excesses and the ultimate licentiousness, dancing with bare feet in the marketplace," and "they act like men who are drunk." "These Jews are gathering choruses of effeminates and a great rubbish heap of harlots; they drag into the synagogue the whole theater, actors and all. For there is no difference between the theater and the synagogues" (One: II: 5-7). For St. Chrysostom the "synagogue [is] not only a brothel and a theater; it also is a den of robbers and a lodging for wild beasts." The source for this description is a verse St. Chrysostom takes from Jeremiah who, when seeking to dissuade people from their iniquities, said: "Your house has become for me the den of a hyena." St. Chrysostom takes the verse out of context as well as changes the metaphor, yet uses the credibility of the source as proof of his assertion about the synagogue (One: III: 1). Needless to state, there were no synagogues in Jeremiah's time.

St. Chrysostom mocks Jews for claiming that they love God as much as Christians do. He calls Christ his witness and his very words that knowing Him would mean also knowing his Father, as proof of the opposite (One: III: 2). Putting the matter in the form of a rhetorical question, St. Chrysostom states that

> if, then, the Jews fail to know the Father, if they crucified the Son, if they thrust off the help of the spirit, who should not make bold to declare plainly that the synagogue is a dwelling of demons? God is not worshiped there. Heaven forbid! From now on it remains a place of idolatry. But still some people pay it honor as a holy place. (One: III: 3)

Of course St. Chrysostom glosses over the alternative possibility that Jews love *their* God and not the Christian God. Clearly, St. Chrysostom is bothered by the continuous operation of the synagogue and its rather positive impact on the larger community. Is it possible that some Christians did not fully accept Christ and the Christian theology, and continue to give credence to the Jewish God or Jewish practices?

St. Chrysostom's frustration over the respect Jews have been able to uphold among Christians is well displayed when he sought to dissuade one individual from visiting the synagogue. When he asked the individual to explain his action, "he answered that many people had told him that oaths sworn there [at the synagogue] were more to be feared." This answer infuriates St. Chrysostom, but he claims that he quickly realized that what was happening was the work of the devil who "had the power to seduce men; I grew angry when I considered how careless were those who were deceived" (One: III: 5). His aim, then, is to stop the Judaizing disease that appears to have plagued his community affecting those he calls "half-Christians." His homilies are directed not at those visiting the synagogue as much as at those who could save those Judaizing Christians "from the devil's snare and to free him from fellowship with those who slew Christ" (One: IV: 5).

Not being able to dissuade Christians with reason, he resorts to fear whereby the Jew is presented as the devil. St. Chrysostom uses not only evidence to drive his arguments, but he resorts to strong metaphors and puts them into hypothetical questions. He asks whether anyone who had power over others would save a man on his way to his execution. He, then, intensifies the rhetorical dilemma, but this time he asks whether anyone who had the power would save a man from the hands of the devil. The conclusion St. Chrysostom set for his audience to accept is that just as he would risk his life so should anyone else "rather than let him enter the doors of the synagogue," calling on others to prevent Christians from having any fellowship with Jews (One: IV: 6).

St. Chrysostom acknowledges that the arguments Jews make about rejecting Christ appear to resonate with some Christians and could be the reason for the fellowship and good relationship Christians have with Jews. He is bothered by the fact that Christians find the Jewish festivals attractive as well as by the fact that some Christians find the synagogue holy because of the holy books therein. St. Chrysostom asks that Christians stop attending the synagogue because of what Jews did to the Holy one — Christ. Killing Christ then is his formulaic and foundational reasoning for rejecting Jews, and this is the ultimate objective of his homilies.

His rhetorical dilemma is how to stop Jewish theology that has continued to resonate with the Christian community. He does so primarily in two ways. The first one is to use biblical verses that prove the foretelling of Christ's arrival. For this strategy, he resorts to biblical statements that appear to support his thesis. However, the passages he selects are not specific to the case at hand, and are not altogether clear how they support his overall claim. For the second strategy, he resorts to rhetorical questions whose answers he presents as self-evident. Both strategies are complemented with invectives and harsh statements about Jews that stand often in place of reasoned rhetoric.

Asks St. Chrysostom: "What deed of theirs should strike us with greater astonishment? Their ungodliness or their cruelty or their inhumanity? That they sacrificed their children or that they sacrificed them to demons?" For proof, he forwards the following: "Hear what the prophet says of their excesses. 'They are become as amorous stallions. Every one neighed after his neighbor's wife'" (One: VI: 8). A similar approach is taken when arguing against Christians who join Jewish festivals. St. Chrysostom states that God has said: "Take away from me the sound of your songs and I will not hear the canticle of your harps" (One: : 2). None of these so-called proofs support the assertions.

His arguments against the synagogue are harsh, primarily because they also weak, even in St. Chrysostom's views. In an attempt to strengthen his argument against the Jewish house of worship he compares it to a pagan temple. The comparison allows him to present a clearer and a more tangible point. Accordingly, the synagogue is worse than a pagan temple because its inhabitants are demons. And while, "in the pagan temple the impiety is naked and obvious," and thus it is easy for prudent people to understand what is going on there, in the synagogue "there are men who say they worship God and abhor idols, men who say they have prophets and pay them honor. But by their words they make ready an abundance of bait to catch in their nets the simpler souls who are so foolish as to be caught off guard" (One: VI: 3). The comparison between the pagan temple and the synagogue is not only weak but continues a biased and hateful line of reasoning whereby nothing good can be found in the Jewish house of worship. It is also interesting that no proof is forwarded for the claims St. Chrysostom makes about the synagogue. He simply puts evil words in the mouth of Jews and asks his audience to consider them as factual.

St. Chrysostom has nothing to pin against Jewish theology except that Christians ought to reject it. Had he left the discussion there, that would be fine, but in the absence of good reasoning, he resorts to word choice, specifically the invectives and hateful statements. His so-called proofs are but empty statements that he asks his audience to accept as truthful. Such as, "in their synagogue stands an invisible altar of deceit on which they sacrifice not sheep and calves but the souls of men" (One: VI: 4). This is how he solves his thesis about rejecting the synagogue. First, he compared it to a pagan temple and then he distinguishes between the visible rituals of pagans with the invisible, therefore, insidious rituals of Jews. Yet, this rhetoric of suggestion and manipulation would become prominent in the history of anti-Semitism practiced often as false assertions to be taken as facts.

Another rhetorical staple St. Chrysostom resorts to is to damn Jews and Judaism by false dichotomies. He says to his audience that "if the Jewish ceremonies are venerable and great, our[s] are lies. But if our[s] are true, as they are true, theirs are filled with deceit" (Sermon One: VI: 5). The formula is straightforward: "us" or "them," "theirs" or "ours." Either they, the Jews, are right or we Christians are right, but we cannot both be right. This rhetorical strategy speaks to the urgency of "saving" Judaizing Christians from Jewish influence. Time and again St. Chrysostom appeals to his audience to avoid associating with Jews and more importantly, he instructs Christians to find Judaizers and bring them back to the Church: "Like a pack of hunting dogs let us circle about and surround our quarry; let us drive them together from every side and bring them into subjection to the laws of the Church" (Two: I: 4).

In bringing Judaizing Christians back to mother Church, St. Chrysostom sought to prevent these "half Christians" from following Jewish practices such as circumcision, fasting, and festivals. His rhetorical approach is by now familiar. He puts the matter in a question form and provides the answer his audience must accept. In so doing, he seeks to inoculate his audience against the arguments Jews have supposedly made: "But someone might say: 'Is there so much harm in circumcision that it makes Christ's whole plan of redemption useless'? Yes, the harm of circumcision is as great as that, not because of its own but because of your obstinacy" (Two: I: 6). In other words, no substantive reason is given for opposing circumcision and no rationale is forwarded to explain the reasons for its rejection except that in practicing these rituals Christians are suspect of preferring Jewish practices. Yet, this dogmatic theology is central to St. Chrysostom's theology. He says as much when he reminds his audience that all "who run to Christ are saved by his grace and profit from his gift. But those who wish to find justification from the Law will also fall from grace. They will not be able to enjoy the King's loving-kindness because they are striving to gain salvation by their own efforts" (Two: II: 1). Being Christian, then, means not only the acceptance of all of Christianity's practices, it also means rejecting all things Jewish. This is St. Chrysostom's primary thesis.

In another homily, the approaching Jewish festivals such as Passover pose a major concern to St. Chrysostom and the reason for another address specifically aimed to inoculate those who might find these festivals attractive. St. Chrysostom states that "nothing is worse than contentiousness and fighting, than tearing the Church asunder and rending into many parts the robe the robbers did not dare to rip" (Three: I: 6). The unity of the Church, then, is the primary reason for rejecting Jewish festivals and holidays. The metaphors of robe and robbers are powerful as they allow St. Chrysostom to depict the tension Jews and

Judaizing Christians, whereby the latter are worse than Jews for hurting the Church-robe, whereas even Jews did not dare to touch his robe. The strategy here is to position Judaizers as more despicable than Jews, hoping that such a designation would be powerful enough to stop such individuals from their fellowship with Jews.

His aim is consistent throughout his homilies — to separate Christianity from Judaism and to create clear lines of demarcation: "What belongs to the Jews: what belongs to us?" (Three: II: 5). Citing Paul, St. Chrysostom urges his audience "to renounce circumcision, to scorn the Sabbath, the feast days, and all the other observances of the Law" (Three: III: 1). All symbolic acts that can remind Christians of their Jewish roots are to be eliminated. And though the Council of Nicea of 325 CE made the separation between the two religions official, it is clear that many Christians did not completely separate themselves from the mother religion.

Another inventive strategy St. Chrysostom uses to drive a wedge between Christianity and Judaism is to negate the viability of Judaism since most Jews no longer reside in their ancestral land: "How can you do that when the Jews have been driven from their ancestral commonwealth and way of life and have no sacred festival to celebrate?" (Three: : 6). In other words, Jewish practices are meaningless given the fact that none of their practices make sense outside their ancestral land and that absent a direct connection to the old Temple with its rituals, Jewish life outside the holy land is worthless. In a related strategy St. Chrysostom questions contemporary Jews for why they follow God's message, now that they no longer reside in His land or worship at His temple. In short, what is the point of being a good Jew now when it no longer counts? Says St. Chrysostom:

> Tell me this. In those days you were guilty of ungodliness, you worshipped idols, you slew your children, you stoned the prophets, and you did ten thousand dreadful deeds. Why, then, did you enjoy such great kindness and good will from Him? Why did He offer you such protection at that time? Now you do not worship idols, you do not slay your children, you do not stone the prophets. Why are you now spending your lives in endless captivity? (Six: II: 8)

The message St. Chrysostom wishes his audience to accept is that outside the holy land Judaism is meaningless and so are all its practices. His objective here is rather limited — to dissuade Christians from joining Jewish festivals by arguing that these practices no longer count in the eyes of God. Perhaps inadvertently, the larger implication here is important as well; Jews are forever identified by themselves and by others as a people associated with their ancestry land: the land that God gave them.

Much of St. Chrysostom's hateful rhetoric against Jews is developed by using a back-track or post-hoc logic, whereby acceptance of Christ as God and the son of God is proven by going back to the Hebrew Bible in search for evidence thereof, also referred to as "prophecy historicized" (Carroll, 2002, p. 129). Not surprising, then, that Jews are presented as in the wrong and, therefore, sinful since biblical teachings and references are skewed to support the Christian claim and giving no credence to the Jewish conception of the Messiah. But St. Chrysostom's rhetoric is also misleading because his proof is suspect, and he was likely aware of this. And since the proof is questionable, what is left, then, is to intensify the language, hence the hateful and hurtful words. In short, St. Chrysostom's attacks are harsh precisely because they are at best weak and at worse, erroneous and manipulative. Says St. Chrysostom:

> The cherubim and the ark were still there, the grace of the Spirit still abounded in the temple when Christ said: "You have made it a den of thieves" and "a house of business." And He said this because of the transgressions and blood-guilt of the Jews. Now, after the grace of the Spirit has abandoned them, after all those august solemnities have been taken away, they are still stubborn with God and carry on their irreligious rites. What worthy name can we find to call their synagogues? The temple was already a den of thieves when the Jewish commonwealth and way of life still prevailed. Now you give it a name more worthy than it deserves if you call it a brothel, a stronghold of sin, a lodging-place for demons, a fortress of the devil, the destruction of the soul, the precipice and pit of all perdition, or whatever other name you give it. (Six: VII: 5-6)

The synagogue was clearly a source of great concern to St. Chrysostom as he spends many efforts to denigrate and humiliate this house of worship. By sheer delineation, the synagogue must have been a well-functioning and much respected center of religious as well as communal activities for both Jews and those who favored some Jewish practices. The context for virulent anti-Semitism could not have been more undeserving.

Conclusion

Rhetorical questions, assertions, false dichotomies, and metaphoric as well as literal God-Devil terms, comprise the primary rhetorical staples of St. Chrysostom's homilies. His main proof on which he constructs his attacks on Jews and on other heretics and doubters is "fulfilled prophecy," whereby signs of foretelling Christ are referenced as "empiric fulfillment" that proves Christ's divinity (St. Chrysostom, 1985, p. 25). Put differently, the "fulfilled prediction" is used as the strongest proof that Christianity has used in claiming that the Hebrew Bible foretold Christ. The argument relies on the rhetorical device whereby if the evidence about Christ comes from his enemies — the Jews — all the more the reason to consider the source, the Hebrew Bible, credible. If the argument is believable, then those questioning or doubting it should act accordingly, meaning embrace Christ (Parks, pp. 168-169).

While the rhetorical structure St. Chrysostom selects assisted him in constructing the proof he wishes his audience to accept, the word choice reveals his motives. Though the thesis of a fulfilled prophecy is inclined to work with pagans and other non-believers, especially when accompanied by non-offensive language, the thesis cannot move Jews. The humiliation and the continuous references to Jewish errors in understanding their scripture, as well as the harsh invectives, cannot be taken as designed for persuading Jews. After all, a skilled rhetorician who implements well rhetorical stipulations would have also consulted rhetorical theory in seeking to appeal to his audience and as such antagonizing an audience cannot secure persuasion. But then, the *Adversus Judeaus* was not meant to address Jews but those Christians still influenced by Jewish tradition. The harsh language is necessary for St. Chrysostom to describe Jews and Judaism in bad light in order to dissuade those leaning Jewish to cease such inclinations. Hence, attempts to put St. Chrysostom's homilies as not altogether hostile to Jews are not credible. The anti-Semitism in these eight homilies, whether strategic or personal, is straightforwardly hateful. It is not altogether clear if St. Chrysostom was successful at his time as his arguments were consistently weak. His reasoning illustrates an overall theology that was uncertain and in search of firmer grounding vis-à-vis doubting population. But the seeds of extreme hatred were sewn by him and his theological reasoning would gain traction, primarily by framing them as rhetorically attractive and thus ready for adherents to accept and follow.

St. Chrysostom must have known that Jews would not accept his thesis about fulfilled prophecy and this was not his objective. From a Jewish perspective, the so-called biblical references he uses as evidence are but sham evidence, suggestive and manipulative, and his theology does not accord with Jewish teaching. Thus, the either "this or that" reasoning must be understood as the strategic foundation for the hatred of Jews necessary in the eyes of the Church as means for its survival. And though the proximity of the two religions was obvious to many early Christians, Christianity's survival was also seen, especially to Church Fathers, as conditioned by the rejection of Judaism. It was not enough to have the separation between the two religions be accomplished by prohibiting specific practices, it was also necessary to institutionalize hatred of Judaism in order to secure Christianity. Judaism, then, had to suffer and be humiliated so that Christianity could survive, hence the invention of hatred. St. Chrysostom's homilies against the Jews reveal as much as he consistently seeks to demonize and disparage Jews and Judaism. Thus, anti-Semitism was a strategic decision designed to advocate and practice hatred that once established was perpetuated for centuries and sewed into the social and religious fabric of the Christian world.

Note

1.   For an insightful discussion on this propaganda device see, Jacques Ellul, *Propaganda: The Formation of Men's Attitudes* (New York: Alfred A. Knopf, 1965), pp. 56-61.

5

The Protocols of the Wise Elders of Zion: Beyond the Lie

In 1920, Winston Churchill published a newspaper article blaming Jews for their significant role in the Bolshevik movement and for their conspiratorial inclinations to spread revolutions (Gilbert, 2007, p. 44). As a friend and supporter of the Jewish people, and as the individual directly credited with advancing the cause of a Jewish homeland in Palestine, his accusations were shocking, especially to many Jews. What was not known at the time was that Churchill wrote his newspaper article shortly after receiving a copy of the *Protocols of the Wise Elders of Zion,* and before it was revealed to be a forgery. That Churchill, a historian, and a rising politician would fall for such a forgery is indicative of the significant persuasive force of the *Protocols*. Despite the wide acknowledgment that the *Protocols* are a forgery, they must be acknowledged as being among the most successful anti-Semitic tracts of the past century, as they have influenced both friends and foes, and continue to function in this capacity in spreading anti-Semitism.

The *Protocols* have not only survived numerous challenges and proofs of being forged, but they have been so widely spread that a century after their first publication, they are extensively read and often believed. This is especially the case in the Islamic world where numerous Arab and Muslim leaders cite its thesis of a Jewish plan of world domination as self-evident. The *Protocols* have been instrumental in serving Czarist Russia, especially those opposing the Bolsheviks during the early years of the twentieth century; they have been foundational to Nazi anti-Semitism and especially to Hitler's propaganda; and, they have found adherents in the United States during the 1920's by individuals such as Henry Ford. Ford would go about a well publicized campaign against Jews that was based on the Protocols.[1] Further, the *Protocols* today are part and parcel of Arab and Islamist anti-Semitic and anti-Israeli propaganda and have given modern anti-Semitism a new life after more historical anti-Semitic accusations such as deicide were no longer fashionable or acceptable.

That the pamphlet *The Protocols of the Wise Elders of Zion* is a lie and an infamous forgery is a well known fact. But what is in it is revealing of those wishing to perpetuate the lie as well as for those inclined to believe it to be true. Two trials, one in South Africa in 1934 and one in Bern, Switzerland in 1934-35, were brought by Jews, challenging the *Protocols* and its claims. In South African in 1934, the trial was the result of a charge by a local anti-Semitic group that they had in their possession a document taken from the local Synagogue and that in it was evidence that Jews seek "the persecution of the gentiles by organized Jewry throughout the world" (Ben-Itto, 2005, pp. 232-233). The trial concluded with a clear repudiation of the plot committed by the perpetrators and their anti-Semitic intents. The trial in Berne, in 1935, was more complicated but also revealing as the research required by the defense exposed the details of the forgery and the identity of the individuals involved in its instigation. The trial proceedings clearly show that the *Protocols* were conceived purposefully to incite Russians against Jews and identify them as the cause of the upheaval the Russian people were suffering during the last years of the Tsar's rule. Indeed, the *Protocols* were directly responsible for various pogroms during the early years of the 20th century (Ben-Itto, 280).

What is known about the forgery is that Sergei A. Nilus of the Russian Synod published the document in 1901 under the title *The Great in the Little and the Anti Christ as a Proximate Political Possibility*. The purpose of this document was to promote the Holy Russian Empire and the Czar's absolute power against opposition forces described strategically as belonging to the anti-Christ. The specific objective was to have Jews become the scapegoat to divert attention from the growing strife in Russia (Ben-Itto, p. 25). In 1905, the document was re-issued but for the first time it included the *Protocols* which are minutes of supposedly secret gatherings of Jewish leaders whose aim was to outline the plan for world domination.

In 1921, Phillip Graves, the Constantinople reporter for the London *Times,* came across the *Protocols* and noticed similarities between it and another book written by a Frenchman, Maurice Joly. Upon further scrutiny, the *Protocols* were found to be largely a word by word copy of the entire text by Joly titled "Dialogue in Hell between Machiavelli and Montesquieu," a satire directed against Emperor Napoleon III, published in 1864, and that had nothing to do with Jews. This tract became the foundation for the *Protocols* whereby every reference to France and the Emperor in Joly's book was changed to Jews in the *Protocols*. The London *Times* devoted three issues to this forgery, on August 16, 17 and 18, 1921, putting the *Dialogue in Hell* and the *Protocols* side by side to show how the forgery was developed (Ben-Itto, pp. 94-102). Graves concluded that the *Protocols* "were designed to foster the belief among Russian conservatives, and especially in Court circles, that the prime cause of discontent among the politically minded elements in Russia was not the repressive policy of the bureaucracy but a worldwide Jewish conspiracy," and that the "Protocols were paraphrased very hastily and carelessly" from an earlier fictional book titled the *Geneva Dialogue* (another name for Joly's book about the dialogue between Machiavelli and Montesquieu). In Graves' view, about two-thirds of the *Protocols* were copied verbatim from Joly's book (Ben-Itto, pp. 100-101, 124).

The events leading from Joly's book to the *Protocols* are insidious, convoluted, and disturbing as they point to specific individuals who sought to spread anti-Semitism and use it as a weapon for political reason. The hands of several individuals involved in the forgery is revealing of a unique conspiracy which began in France where anti-Semitism in the second half of the nineteen century was wide-spread and became the answer to various societal and economic ills. During the trial in Bern, Switzerland, one key witness speculated that no other but Edouard Drumnot was behind the forgery. Drumont was a known French anti-Semite whose writings on Jewish conspiracy were widespread. His book *La juive* (1886) became a best seller and, in it, Drumont accused Jews of seeking world domination through economic means. A suspicion also exists about the possible connection between the forgery of Joly's book for anti-Semitic purposes and the Dreyfus Affair.[2] The close proximity of the events is striking as well as the fact that both events were based on forged documents whose ultimate objective was to spread anti-Semitism (Ben-Itto, pp. 195-196).

The most immediate background for the forgery is the likely opposition of several key figures in France who opposed the Franco-Russian alliance. The alliance was the plan of Sergei Iulievich Witte, the Czar's finance minister during the final years of the 19th century, who sought bank loans from France to finance major economic reforms in Russia. Those opposing the alliance sought to squash it by accusing Witte of being sympathetic to Jews and that of having a Jewish wife. None of this was true but the charge was a convenient political weapon. The Jews, the accusation goes, were collaborating with Witte because they wished to dominate that country (Ben-Itto, pp. 197-199).

Witte was quite convinced that the *Protocols* were a forgery used for political reasons. Concerned with Russian's deteriorating reputation regarding its appalling treatment of Jews and the widespread coverage of recent pogroms, Witte tried to stop the *Protocols*' publication. He reasoned that no one would believe that Jews wish world domination when several millions of them lived in Russia "in appalling conditions, prey to discrimination both by law and in practice, [and] in daily danger of pogroms and massacres" (Ben-Itto, p. 28). Even the Czar, once he realized the *Protocols* were a forgery, ordered their publication be stopped (Ben-Itto, p. 34).[3] The publication, however, continued. The *Protocols* found fertile ground in many political circles in Russia where anti-Semitism was rampant and political instability and growing revolutionary sentiments needed to be confronted. The Jews, by the perpetrators' own design, were the convenient scapegoat against whom other frustrations could be directed.

The publication of the *Protocols* from 1905 onward was timed perfectly as the political upheaval of the next twelve years needed an agency on whose shoulders all misfortunes could be put, including Russia's loss to Japan in 1905, the rise of revolutionary groups, attempts by the old regime to hold on to the power, fear of Bolsheviks, and then the revolution of 1917 (Ben-Itto, p. 45). The same agency would be needed at the end of World War I, especially in Germany where a culprit had to be found and whose shoulders the loss of the war could be pinned. The Jews were the perfect agency to rationalize the causes of these events. Subsequently, Jews were accused of sponsoring a German-Bolshevik alliance against England as well as causing Germany's defeat in 1918 (Ben-Itto, p. 140; Elon, 2002, p. 353). In short, a conspiracy of Jews against European powers became the most frequent accusation, often based on the mere fact that some Jews could be found to be members in revolutionary or radical movements. The fact that Jews could be found in literally every other segment of society or political movement was irrelevant to the various conspiracies. A mere sign stood for erroneous conclusions, and with devastating effects.

One witness during the trial in Berne, Rabbi Ehrenpreis, the chief rabbi of Stockholm, made an apt comment, stating that "this trial is not about the forgery of the Protocols of the Elders of Zion . . . or about the Zionists. This is about the forgery of Judaism" (Ben-Itto, p. 311). The judge who issued the verdict, stated the following: "I hope that a time will come when nobody will understand how in the year 1935 almost a dozen sane and reasonable men could for 14 days torment their brains before a Berne court over the authenticity of these so-called *Protocols*, these *Protocols* which, despite the harm they have caused and may yet cause, are nothing more than ridiculous nonsense" (Ben-Itto, pp. 346-347). The judge's foretelling would prove in matters of only few years how correct he was.

Indeed, the *Protocols* are ridiculous and nonsensical but devastatingly dangerous. Clearly, Judaism was and continues to be on trial every time the *Protocols* are invoked. Yet the charges are so sweeping that the resources of logic are not always sufficient for countering them, especially when the charges carry a heavy dose of emotional appeal such as fear and conspiracy. The formula of emotional appeal in the context of losing a war, revolution, political upheaval and great uncertainty makes for a dangerous context. The success of the *Protocols* is based on the function of its unique narrative that carries some semblance of a reasonable explanation to any contemporary upheaval and is thus conveniently considered acceptable. Ostensibly, the fact that the *Protocols* are a forgery is set aside as another case of a Jewish conspiracy.

The Semiotic of Hate: Hannah Arendt (1951) found the *Protocols* to be the base for the "most efficient fiction of Nazi propaganda," which presents "the theory of a Jewish world conspiracy." She states that

> Lies about a Jewish world conspiracy had been current since the
> Dreyfus Affair and based themselves on the existing international
> interrelationship and interdependence of a Jewish people
> dispersed all over the world. Exaggerated notions of Jewish world
> power are even older and can be traced back to the end of the
> eighteenth century, when the intimate connection between Jewish
> business and the nation-states had become visible. The
> representation of the Jew as the incarnation of evil is based on
> remnants and superstitious memories form the Middle Ages. (p.
> 344)

The grounds for the claims made in the *Protocols* as well as for those using
this forgery, I contend, are inherently a matter of purposefully confusing
signs with causes — of taking existing signs that are available to many,
and assigning them fictional motives. The *Protocols* are but a classical case
of the rhetoric of hate based on the semiotic of collecting disparate and
unrelated signs that are put together to argue a premise or an assertion
of fact — that of a wide-spread Jewish conspiracy to control the world.
The *Protocols'* success lie in taking basic facts about Jews and their
tradition and manipulating them to construct conspiratorial accusations
developed as a treatise.

The essential ingredients of the *Protocols'* success are based on the
conspiratorial interpretation of key facts in Jewish experience: the
preservation of historical language, liturgy, and kinship. At the heart of
the conspiracy stands the argument that Jews have developed a secret
world government that controls world affairs including world capital and
industries. The *Protocols* are presented as the minutes of twenty-four
secret sessions conducted by a selective and secretive group of Jewish
elders who are responsible for the plot. The overall implication of this
conspiracy is that various countries and nations unknowingly engage in
doing their bidding and are therefore slaves of this secret Jewish group.

The primary sign of the so-called conspiracy is language. No matter
where Jews reside, the claim goes, they have a secret language that only
they understand, namely, Hebrew (or Yiddish which is a mixture of

German and Hebrew, using the Hebrew Alpha-Bet). The language of the Bible and the language of Jewish education through the ages have thus been turned into a secret language and a code that allows conspirators to argue that Jews possess a communication network known only to them.

Another sign that "proves" the conspiratorial plot is the dispersion of Jews in many countries and in most continents. While such was, and still is the case of a host of people of many origins, Jews residing in various countries have often been a source of suspicion that lent themselves easily into conspiracies about ill-intent as well as loyalty to another entity than the one in which they reside. For the anti-Semites, the dispersion of Jews amount to a plot against gentiles, often seen in economic terms.

A related sign of the plot is Jewish wealth. While the vast majority of Jews were throughout the Middle-Ages and even in modern times rather poor, especially in Eastern Europe, the few Jews who became wealthy stood in the eyes of non-Jews as metonymic for all Jews. Put differently, few wealthy Jews meant all Jews were wealthy and if the country in question was suffering economically, the Jews were to be blamed for bringing poverty to the people. No other sign was so "obvious" to anti-Semites, and a likely background for the accusation in the *Protocols* about world domination, than the case of the Rothschild family.[4] The fact that the founding Rothschild patriarch stationed each of his five sons in one key European capitol, heading the local branch of the family banks, was taken as evidence of a Jewish plot. The Rothschild's enormous wealth, their successful banking enterprise and the reliance of European nations and leaders on their wealth to develop various economic enterprises brought much jealousy and hatred.

The signs used by anti-Semites to substantiate their accusations are complete anathema to Jewish tradition, yet defending Judaism against such vile charges are rather difficult. Indeed, the posture of defense carries the presumption of guilt and exonerating one of baseless charges often leaves a taint of guilt no matter how unjustified the charges are. The signs of conspiracy, then, are no signs at all as any sinister interpretation of such signs runs counter to Jewish history and tradition. The *Protocols* have allowed a persistent formula of hatred to become a persuasive tract, putting Judaism itself on trial whereby any challenge to the *Protocols* means defending Judaism itself.

The Minutes of the Protocols: Selective themes and arguments in the *Protocols* illustrate the objective of this document. The first sentence of the *Protocols* reveals an insidious plot by highly immoral peoples: "Right lies in Might" (Protocol no. 1, p. 11).[5] The so-called Jewish plot is immediately set as a contest about power and control of non-Jews by Jews. The control is to be achieved by replacing liberal rulers with "the power of Gold" such that "the despotism of Capital" would be in Jewish hands (Protocol no. 1, p. 11). Thus, from the outset, a premise is set forth whereby Jews, their God and their money are but the means to power and control. The objectives are clear and what is left for the plotters to do is to find the best means for exerting control and accomplishing the plot.

Indeed, the first *Protocol* includes several references to mass psychology and mass persuasion as necessary for the plot's success. The *Protocol* asserts that "men in masses and the men of the masses, being guided solely by petty passions, paltry beliefs, customs, traditions and sentimental theorism, fall a prey to party dissension," and that "every resolution of a crowd depends upon a chance or packed majority, which, in its ignorance of political secrets, put forth some ridiculous resolution that lays in the administration a seed of anarchy" (No. 1, p. 12). The mass or the mob, then, is to be used as a means to an end, arguing for example that "the might of the mob is blind, senseless and unreasoning force ever at the mercy of a suggestion from any side" (no. 1, p. 12). These passages could profitably be read as a propaganda tract and no wonder Hitler found the *Protocols* useful as his own propaganda campaign relied heavily on manipulating the psychology of the masses.

Another propaganda technique that would become the staple of Nazi propaganda has also a corollary in the *Protocols*: that of using passions in appealing to the masses as well as the use of deliberate misinformation to bring "a state of bewilderment by giving expression from all sides to so many contradictory opinions and for such a length of time as will suffice to make the *GOYIM* [A Jewish reference to non-Jews] lose their heads. . . and to see that the best thing is to have no opinion of any kind in matters political" (no. 5, p. 22). And thus by multiplying "to such an extent national failings, habits, passions, conditions of civil life, that it will be impossible for anyone to know where he is in the resulting chaos, so that the people in consequence will fail to understand one another." In short, the purpose is "to sow discord in all parties," and use the divide-and-rule mechanism for the ultimate control of the people (no. 5, p. 22).

The first *Protocol* spells out the immoral intention of the plotters. It states that "the political has nothing in common with the moral. The ruler who is governed by the moral is not a skilled politician, and is therefore unstable on his throne" (no. 1, p. 12). Jews, then, are not interested in moral principles and the implication is clear; Jews are immoral and no wonder they would favor an immoral rule over a moral one. The guiding principle of this *Protocol* is that "great national qualities, like frankness and honesty, are vices in politics" (no. 1, p. 12). The power Jews would gather will remain hidden and invisible "until the moment when it has gained such strength that no cunning can any longer undermine it" (no. 1, p. 12). The objective of the plot is "to direct our attention not so much to what is good and moral as to what is necessary and useful." In short, all means are justified in pursuing the objective of complete control of the political machinery "brought to naught by liberalism" (no. 1, p. 12). The reference to liberalism is revealing as the forgery stands in clear opposition to any deviation from autocratic regimes, like the one held by the Czar. Indeed, the *Protocols* are replete with references to Jewish opposition to liberalism as in the statement that "we shall root our liberalism from all the important strategic posts of our government" (no. 15, p. 42). The inconsistency between the tendency of Jews to gravitate toward the liberal end of the political continuum and the claims in the *Protocols* to the opposite is striking. Jews are said to believe only in an autocratic rule thereby all means justify the ends.

The supposedly Jewish disdain for the ideals of liberty and freedom is cited in the opposition to the ideals of the French Revolution. The reference to the French Revolution also points to the carelessness of those behind the forgery of Joly's book. The first *Protocol* states that from "far back in ancient time we [Jews] were the first to cry among the masses of the people the words 'Liberty, Equality, Fraternity'," and that "in all corners of the earth the words 'Liberty, Equality, Fraternity' brought to our ranks, thanks to our blind agents, whole legions who bore our banners with enthusiasm" (no. 1, p. 14). The motto that would indeed fit a fictional dialogue between Machiavelli and Montesquieu would clearly not be the slogan for Jews from time immemorial. Neither would such ideals be uttered in ancient times as such political concepts were none existent in ancient Jewish tradition or any other tradition at that time. The careless and hurried forgery makes the context of the *Protocols* evidently suspect. But the message, nonetheless, is unmistakable; Jews oppose liberty and equality, but would use it to as a means to mislead people in order to gain world domination.

Time and again the *Protocols* advocate despotic rule as the only workable political system and thus it "is inevitable that a satisfactory form of government for any country is one that concentrates in the hands of one responsible person. Without an absolute despotism there can be no existence for civilization" (No. 1, p. 13). A Hobbesian logic pervades the *Protocols* whereby the anarchy of the masses can be controlled and order restored only by a despotic rule.[6] Put in the context of Russia and the political upheaval, especially during the years of 1905 to 1917, this advocacy, from the Czarist perspective, makes sense. However, from a Jewish perspective, there is nothing here that remotely emanates from experience, practice, or vision. The despotic rule takes on a monstrous depth with the statement that "we are obliged without hesitation to sacrifice individuals, who commit a breach of established order, for in the exemplary punishment of evil lies a great educational problem" (no. 15, p. 43). The notion that Jews would favor a despot, especially given their extreme poverty and persecution in Russia, is completely inconsistent with Jewish history and experience. And though one is tempted to call such a vile line of reasoning illogical, it is not when put in the context of fear and uncertainty.

The tract carries a clear penchant for the persuasive and for propaganda techniques. In one key statement, the *Protocols* argue that Jews believe only in "Force and Make-Believe," that "cunning and make-believe [are] the rule for governments," and that "this evil is the one and only means to attain the end, the good" (no. 1, p. 13). The means-to-end logic is the only one that makes sense to this secret Jewish cabal, the argument goes. That such a statement would be made by a Machiavelli, whose theories of political statecraft were based on means justifying ends, makes sense. That Jews would make such a statement, when they held no position of power, does not. However, and here lies the key to the persuasiveness of the *Protocols*, if some facts are true then the entire concoction is believed to be true. Jacques Ellul (1965) refers to the "use of accurate facts by propaganda," and that "based on them, the mechanism of suggestion can work best" (p. 57). Accordingly, those presented with propaganda would accept its bold claims if some of its assertions are true or can easily be verified as such. And the few signs available, such that of the Rothschild's family bank or of Benjamin Disraeli, a converted Jew serving as the Prime Minister of Great Britain, were considered sufficient proof that all Jews are in the position of power and influence, then the entire Jewish plot might be true as well. The *Protocols*, then, are persuasive as long as suggestive assertions therein can be matched by signs recognized in the larger societal context. The syllogistic reasoning is the mechanism at work here.

The objective of the Jewish plot is to create an international body that will "wipe out national rights" (no. 2, p. 15). A symbolic snake is used to depict the plot whereby "we [Jews] appear on the scene as alleged saviours of the worker from this oppression when we propose to him to enter the ranks of our fighting forces — Socialists, Anarchists, Communists — to whom we always give support in accordance with an alleged brotherly rule . . . of our social masonry" (*Protocol* no. 3, p. 17). And how will power be exerted? Very simply, "our power is in the chronic shortness of food and physical weakness of the worker because by all that this implies he is made the slave of our will" (no. 3, p. 17). Power will be further enhanced "by all the secret subterranean methods open to us and with the aid of gold, shall throw upon the streets whole mobs of workers simultaneously in all the countries of . These mobs will rush delightedly to shed the blood of those whom, in the simplicity of their ignorance they will then be able to loot." But, of course, Jewish property would suffer no consequences; "'Ours' they will not touch, because the moment of attack will be known to us and we shall take measures to protect our own" (no. 3, p. 18). The sinister and the selfish are the twin values that Jews are alleged to possess and that would guide them in the plot to control the world.

In the fifth *Protocol*, the Jewish plot seeks to manipulate the relationship between kings and their people:

> In the time when the peoples looked upon kings on their thrones as on a pure manifestation of the will of God, they submitted without a murmur to the despotic power of kings: but form the day when we insinuated into their minds the conception of their rights they began to regard the occupants of thrones as mere ordinary mortals. The holy unaction of the Lord's Anointed has fallen from the heads of kings in the eye of the people, and when we also robbed them of their faith in God the might of power was flung upon the streets into the place of public proprietorship and was seized by us. (no. 3, p. 21)

The convoluted plot had Jews insert liberal ideas in the heads of the people which subsequently diminished the power of kings. In liberalism, which they supposedly do not believe, Jews found the means to divert people from their faith, all manipulated with exactitude to the benefits of the plotters.

Also, in the fifth *Protocol*, Jews have managed to instill discord as a strategy for mass confusion: "We [Jews] are secured by the discord existing among them [non-Jews] whose roots are so deeply seated that they can never now be plucked up. We have set one against another the personal and national reckonings of the *goyim*, religious and race hatreds, which we have fostered into a huge growth in the course of the past twenty centuries." As a warning to anyone contemplating resisting this so-called Jewish power, the *Protocol* warns that "we are too strong — there is no evading our power" (no. 5, p. 21). No outrageous lie is too big in this tract. Jews are said to have fostered religious and race hatreds as a means to control nations and that they have done so successfully for some two thousand years. Thus, centuries of suffering and persecutions was now presented as a period of great Jewish power and manipulation. Anti-Semites sought now, with the aid of the *Protocols*, to erase their responsibility for instilling anti-Semitism. This is still the objective of those who continue to use it.

Another strategy of the supposedly Jewish plot can be found in controlling various enterprises of the non-Jews: "We have got our hands into the administration of the law, in the conduct of elections, into the press, into liberty of the person but principally into education and training as being the cornerstones of a free existence" (no. 9, p. 27). Jews then are alleged to have penetrated primary professions such as law and education for the sole purpose of controlling them. This rhetorical device of pointing to Jewish membership in multiple professions seals the possibility of Jews claiming that the accusations in the *Protocols* are blatant lies. Stated differently, if anyone can find a Jew in any of these professions, law, politics, press or education, then the presence of these Jews proves the assertion to be correct. Indeed, following the French Revolution Jews began to enjoy various liberties not accorded to them previously, and subsequently, Jews began to enter various professions, including those cited in the *Protocols*. The propaganda device is by now a familiar one: the presence of a Jew in a given group asserted to be part of the plot proves the plot to be truthful. Indeed, signs for accepting the assertion were plenty to allow people to see the so-called "fit" between reality and the conspiratorial assertion. Guilt, not so much by association, but by signs, is the primary rhetorical strategy of the *Protocols*, and no matter how fictional or outrageous the assertions, the mere presence of a sign stood for accepting the whole forgery as truthful.

Throughout the *Protocols*, the language used denigrates non-Jews, describing them as foolish, stupid, and easily manipulated by clever Jews. For example, "The *goyim* are a flock of sheep, and we are their wolves. And you know what happens when the wolves get hold of the flock?" (no. 11, p. 32). Such a line, representative of a children's tale, is used here precisely to trigger immediate rage and thereafter hatred of Jews for their evil intent. Non-Jews are depicted as stupid and whose mind is "underdeveloped in comparison with our mind" and that the very ability of Jews to bring non-Jews "to such a pitch of stupid blindness is . . . an amazingly clear proof" of their stupidity, which in the end "guarantees our success" (no. 15, p. 40).

It is also worth noting that Jews are referred to in the *Protocols* as "we," or "us," in order to designate clearly the demarcation between "us" and "them." Added to this dichotomy are the self attributes of "us"-smart and "they"-stupid and the recipe for hatred is readily available. Repeatedly, the *Protocols* describe Jews as the "chosen people," a variation on the positive-negative attributes that are assigned to Jews and non-Jews respectively. Thus, the *Protocols* claim that "God has granted to us, His Chosen People, the gift of the dispersion, and in this which appears in all eyes to be our weakness, has come forth all our strength, which has now brought us to the threshold of sovereignty over all the world" (no. 11, p. 32). The simple fact that Jews are dispersed throughout the world, not the result of their doing, is rationalized in the *Protocols* as proof of dispersion by design, intent on world domination.

The phrase "chosen people" has done much to intensify anti-Semitism for the simple fact that the phrase stands for elitism and arrogance. To be chosen over others yields jealousy; to be chosen by God over others breeds hatred. Not surprising, the *Protocols* repeats the phrase, as in *Protocol* no. 14, when contemplating the final victory: "when we come into our kingdom it will be undesirable for us that there should exist any other religion than ours of the One God with whom our destiny is bound up by our position as the Chosen People" (no. 13, p. 37). The ultimate goal of the Jewish plot is "to discredit the priesthood of the *goyim*" and "the complete wrecking of that Christian religion" (no. 17, p. 45).

The religious foundation of anti-Semitism has been resurrected again and with the powerful device of highlighting the Jewish claim to superiority. And what is a better way to spew hatred of the superior than to argue from both sides of the continuum? If a Jew is powerful and superior, he should be hated for his vanity. If a Jew is weak and poor, do not believe that this is so, as this is just the manipulation of the strong and mighty. Thus, the weaknesses of the Jew are but a camouflage for the game the strong Jew play on non-suspecting non-Jews. The strategy of reasoning by opposite signs is well displayed in the statement that "until we come into our kingdom, we shall act in the contrary way" (no. 15, p. 39). Put differently, any sign to the contrary is a sign that affirms the plot. The Jew cannot escape any suspicion or accusation since his weakness or poverty are signs of the opposites and any sign of his wealth stands for the wealth of all Jews. The Jew is guilty all the time, and all proof to the contrary is presented as part of the plot in the first place.

When the plot is completed, the *Protocols* claim that "our authority will be glorious because it will be all powerful, [we] will rule and guide, and not muddle along after leaders and orators shrieking themselves hoarse with senseless words which they call great principles and which are nothing else . . . but utopian" (no. 22, p. 55). Disdain for the oratorical and the parliamentary babble, then, is spread throughout the *Protocols*, depicted as foolish and useless. Hitler would repeat this claim in rationalizing how he developed hate and disdain of Jews for their "parliamentary babble," the kind he saw in Vienna. Indeed, the *Protocols* must be read as highly un-democratic as the plotters consistently vie for a despotic political system as the only viable and warranted political system.

The *Protocols* continue to be widely published and are often cited, especially in the Islamic world, as proof of a Jewish plot to control the world (for example, Wistrich, 2010, pp. 926 and 936). During the 2003 meeting of the Organization of the Islamic Conference in Malaysia, Malaysian Prime Minister Mahathir Mohamad repeated this very charge, stating that "today Jews rule this world by proxy. They get others to fight and die for them." This statement generated much criticism and condemnation from several world leaders. In the face of such an outcry, Prime Minister Mohamad's reaction to the criticism added fuel to the fire but was also quite revealing. He stated that "the reaction of the world [to his initial statement] shows that they control the world . . . . Israel is a small country. There are not so many Jews in the world. But they are so arrogant, they defy the whole world" (*After the Promise: Keeping OSCE Commitments to Combat Antisemitism*, 2004, pp. 26-27). Both statements show why the *Protocols* are so attractive to those inclined to hate Jews. The two statements display the principle arguments in anti-Semitism: Jews are few in number yet they make too much noise; therefore, they should suffer for their arrogance. Since Jews, as far as the charges go, are able to control the more powerful nations by proxy, this is proof of their true power. Jews, then, are manipulators of world affairs and hating them should be warranted and not be a source of criticism.

The rhetoric of hate as displayed in the *Protocols*, functions through the devices of sign reversals and outrageous exaggerations. These techniques are exemplified by using simple propaganda techniques of turning things around whereby the weak is actually strong, the poor is actually wealthy, the powerless and dependable are among the most powerful and, subsequently, the despised minority is controlling the world and its economic machinery. Once this basic premise is taken for granted, additional attributes are easily accepted as well. Thus, Jews are described not only as wealthy but that their greed is insatiable as they now seek world domination. The enormity and complexity of the plot to dominate the world is unfathomable. It is so grandiose that the plot has secured all political, social, and economic aspects to ensure the execution of the plan. The enormity and complexity of such a convoluted plot is designed to refute any argument to the contrary. The ultimate objective of the *Protocols* is to have everyone believe the plot such that they will quickly turn to hate the plotters. Indeed, hating Jews is rather predictable and the expected effect. It is, in short, a tract based on the device of the "Big Lie" which would become the foundation of Nazi propaganda. I submit that it is not beyond speculation that the former informed the latter.

Hitler's own words would illustrate this point. He writes in his autobiography *Mein Kampf* (1971 translation): "Was there any form of filth or profligacy, particularly in cultural life, without at least one Jew involved in it? If you cut even cautiously in such an abscess, you found, like a maggot in a rotting body, often dazzled by the sudden light — a kike!" (p. 57). Or, "the relation of the Jews to prostitution and, even more, to the white-slave traffic, could be studied in Vienna as perhaps in no other city of Western Europe" (p. 59). And perhaps more aptly, in discussing the so-called Jewish charge that General Ludendorff caused the collapse of Germany during World War I, Hitler writes that the Jews "proceeded on the sound principle that . . . the great masses . . . more easily fall a victim to a big lie than to a little one" (p. 231), and that "the foremost connoisseurs of this truth regarding the possibilities in the use of falsehood and slander have always been the Jews; for after all, their whole existence is based on one single great lie, to wit, that they are a religious community while actually they are a race — and what a race!" (p. 232).

The plot to control the world is extreme in all aspects of the plan and its continued objective is to have no one ever find out about the plan and those behind it. But critical questions must be contemplated as well. Indeed, one is tempted throughout the reading of the *Protocols* to ask the simple questions: Are Jews, or any other group for that matter, capable of such a devious plot? Why would anyone plotting to control the world put in writing such a vile plan, knowing very well that its exposure is extremely risky? And, finally, what in Jewish history can stand even remotely as an explanation for a plot to take over the world? Questions about the viability of such a plot as well as the wisdom of those supposedly behind it should by itself prove this document to be a forgery. Yet, despite the ample proof that the *Protocols* are a forgery as well as an anathema to Jewish history, character and experience, and despite a century of condemnation, the tract is wide-spread and its acceptance and use, past and present, continue to be a cause for alarm. It served the Nazis to design the most extreme method of annihilation of an entire people and it is used today in the Arab and Islamic world to motivate similar sentiments of extreme hatred.

Conclusion

The overall rhetoric one finds in the *Protocols* is designed to spew hatred by anyone accepting the premise that Jews have designed a plot of the most grandiose proportions. The *Protocols*, like other forms of anti-Semitism, can be read as one overwhelming rhetorical syllogism whereby the consumers of the *Protocols* are positioned to hate Jews as a "normal" reaction to such a vile plot. The lies of the forgery are not questioned because hateful sentiments against Jews are already present and need only be triggered or reinforced. This would be Henry Ford's logic, stating in 1921 that "the only statement I care to make about the Protocols is that they fit in with what is going on. They are sixteen years old and they fitted the world situation up to this time. They fit now" (the *New York World*, February 17, 1921, p. 5). The plot as a syllogism, to use Henry Ford's own words in accepting and spreading the *Protocols*, "fit" existing events. Portions of the *Protocols* can likely fit numerous realities and thus be used as proof of its complete authenticity. This is how propaganda works and this is how easy it is for the rhetoric of hate to find adherents where mere conspiracies are taken as facts. This is the key to understanding why the *Protocols* have and continue to be widespread; as long as people can find factual and innocent signs around them that "fit" a concocted plot or any portion thereof, then the *Protocols* as a whole are taken to be true. Ultimately, the obvious question should not be "why would anyone believe such outrageous charges?" but rather "what motivates someone to believe in such outrageous charges?"

Those espousing the *Protocols* know that the guilty-Jew is not guilty of the conspiracies attributed to them, but they do not wish to correct the lengthy history of this contrived but favored accusation, hence the guilt of perpetuating the lie and the way to overcome it is to keep perpetuating it.

Notes

1. In an interview with the New York World (February 17, 1921), Ford sought to warn Americans against the "Jewish financier" who is controlling European countries. "He [the Jew] is not on top here because there has always been a strong group of gentiles in this country awake to the situation. But the gentiles of America must be kept informed of what the international Jews here are trying to do. They would control America, as they control the Old World countries, if they could" (p. 5). Six years later and after much criticism, in a letter to Louis Marshall of the American Jewish Committee, Henry Ford would issue an apology to Jews for perpetuating a hateful tract.

2. Captain Alfred Dreyfus was a Jewish officer in the French military. He was wrongly charged with espionage in 1894. He was publicly humiliated and sentenced to prison in the infamous Devil's Island. The fight for his acquittal as well as for finding the real culprit would bring upon France one of the worst cases of anti-Semitism. The relentless efforts of Dreyfus' family, as well as prominent individuals such as Emil Zola would finally bring justice to Captain Dreyfus but the anti-Semitism it produced remain a stain on France's image for quite some time.

3. The person who bares the primary responsibility for the forgery of the Protocols is Piotor Ivanovich Rachkovskii. For an excellent description of the person and the events surrounding the forgery, see, Ben-Itto, *The lie that wouldn't die*, pp. 212ff, especially, 227.

4. One of the most famous financial dynasties in Europe, began by Amschel Rothschild in the late 18th century, a German Jew and his five sons whom he stationed in key European cities. The family created a very successful bank

that was kept in the family and became instrumental in lending money to European governments throughout the 19th century to pay debt, to finance war and construct various projects such as the Suez Canal. The enormous wealth of the Rothschilds would become a source of envy and anti-Semitism.

5. I am using Victor E. Marsden's translation of Sergyei A. Nilus, The Protocols of the Wise Elders of Zion www.flholocaustmuseum.org/history_wing/antisemitism/primarysources/The_Protocols. Hereafter, references to the Protocols are cited in the text.

6. In the chaotic and brutish context of England in the first half of the seventeenth century, Thomas Hobbes advocated that "the sovereign should be absolute," considered "the final arbiter in all matters of law, morals and religion" (Hobbes, 1962, p. 11).

6

The Pariah Jew: Guilt or Guilty?

In a book on anti-Semitism, its history, and causes published in 1894, Bernard Lazare covers Jewish history through the ages and its relation to various communities in which Jews resided, from antiquity to modern times. His specific purpose was to locate the roots of anti-Semitism and his central thesis would become foundational to the thinking of many anti-Semites — that Jews brought anti-Semitism on themselves by choosing to be different from others and in so doing have behaved historically like a pariah. Lazare's conception would become influential on Hannah Arendt who would further develop this thesis several decades later. Lazare's thesis is that anti-Semitism has "always resided in Israel [in Judaism] itself and not in those who antagonize it" (Lazare, 1967, p. 8). Both Lazare's and Arendt's conception of anti-Semitism is revealing as it sheds light on the relationship between old and modern anti-Semitism, as well as on the controversies surrounding the location of causes and erroneous assumptions therein. That both Lazare and Arendt are Jews who would identify Jews as primarily responsible for anti-Semitism did not go unnoticed by anti-Semites who could point to these writings as proof that Jews are indeed responsible for their hatred.

Bernard Lazare and the Conception of the Jew Pariah

Lazare finds anti-Semitism to exist as early as the Roman times when it was attributed to Jewish feelings of exclusiveness. He admits that these sentiments of exclusiveness were sanctioned by God and His dictation that Jews worship no idols, believe in one God, subscribe to rules of hygiene, ethics and morality, and live in a designated land. These qualities were summed up in the phrase that itself would bring much anti-Semitism – "The Chosen People" (Lazare, p. 9). Lazare is sympathetic to the reason for exclusiveness which mandated strict adherence to God's dictation, yet he blames Jews for the behavior that constructed their relationship with God in the first place. Anti-Semitism then, at least for some, was the result of constructing a special relationship between Jews and their God, not realizing the subsequent and negative implications of such a unique bond with the deity. Practically, the resultant envy and jealousy of being God's "chosen" should have been realized, argues Lazare, as resulting in unwarranted consequences.

The sentiments of exclusiveness, claims Lazare, have been displayed throughout history at different times and places in separation of Jews from the community in which they lived. In cloths, habits, and customs, Jews brought nothing but mystery and suspicion by others (Lazare, p. 21). Yet, claims Lazare, many of the accusations leveled against Jews in ancient Alexandria and later Rome were aimed not at Jews but at early Christians who could not be distinguished among Jews. Only when Christianity broke completely from Judaism in the fourth century, did Christian anti-Semitism take on a new face (this point is not altogether accurate as Romans had no difficulties distinguishing between Jews and Christians).[1] Until this juncture, claims Lazare, Christain anti-Judaism was apologetic but it ceased to be so when Jews were no longer considered potential Christians but a hostile entity. At that moment, Jews became known as killers of Christ (Lazare, pp. 40-42, 84).

This thesis I argue has been proven to be only partially true as evidence has shown that Judaism was rather popular in Rome (more on this in a later chapter), and that despite Jewish revolts in Judea, the Jewish influence and respect for Judaism, especially during the first century CE was high. Yet, Lazare's view, written at the end of the nineteenth century, is important as it reflects a prevailing thesis accepted for centuries, constructed by early Christians to deflect blame for resorting to anti-Semitism sentiments and sustaining it through the ages.

With the sermons of Chrysostom in the fourth century, Lazare views anti-Semitism as taking a distinct religious and vicious tone that lasted until the 16th century when most legal and legislative anti-Semitism dissipated (some of which would be reenacted by Nazi Germany). Lazare argues that by the 4th century CE the Church became secure and no longer feared its believers would remain adherents of Judaism or that they would practice some semblance of Judaism (Lazare, p. 79). In other words, there was no reason for promoting anti-Semitism in the 4th century; yet, it is this century that anti-Semitism is intensified and institutionalized. The reason for this intensification of anti-Semitism, argues Lazare, was borne out of the act of being uprooted from Judaism and the insecurity inherent in the claims the Church made in its early pronouncements as it sought to establish a new religion. It took some twelve centuries, according to Lazare, for the Church to believe that its independence from Judaism was no longer suspect. This point is significant as it illustrates the degree to which the early Church's doubt, uncertainty, and hence guilt over its theological foundations affected its attitudes toward Judaism. Lazare argues that the Church's insecurity over its theology lasted all the way into the end of the Middle Ages.

During the millennia, hostility towards Judaism came with vicious and even gruesome anti-Semitism, depicting Jews as monsters, deformed, and criminal. Later causes of anti-Semitism are identified by Lazare as envy over economic success and the acquisition of wealth. He admits that philo-Semites have argued that Jews were initially forced to engage in the professions of credit and usury as a form of humiliation and that over time Jews became experts in all matters financial. Anti-Semites, on the other hand, claims Lazare, believe that Jews have always displayed inclination toward things financial. Regardless of which sentiment is the more accurate, by the fourteen century Jews became "the bankers of the world" and that distinction brought much envy and jealousy (Lazare, pp. 59-60).

From a rhetorical perspective, Lazare's view reveals a tension between two primary explanations of anti-Semitism: a *scene-act* and an *agent-act* as the rhetorical framing of a given situation and the motives for actions therein.[2] More specifically, at issue here is what motivation one finds for an act or what conditioned the act: in the case of anti-Semitism, are the questions of causes to be found in the circumstances of the Jew (scene) or in his character (agent)? For the most part, Lazare subscribes to the scene-act ratio whereby situational conditions and circumstances are argued as forcing Jews into becoming a stranger, a pariah. In a more specific explanation, constrained by professional restrictions, Jews became involved with financial matters as one of the few professional venues left open to them. A related aspect of financial matters that would play a role in anti-Semitism is the Jewish expertise in currency and gold. Here again, Lazare would add a sympathetic note that explains the long historical scene of the tenuous hold Jews had in their community of residence, forcing them always to keep an eye on the need for quick exit, a hurried escape, and the need for keeping one's assets liquid and handy for such an eventuality. Gold and currency would become valued assets in such dire time and not surprisingly, a source of envy and hatred.

At other times Lazare also subscribes to the *agent-act* ratio whereby the Jew is responsible for his or her own pariah status. The metaphor of the pariah speaks to the agent as being responsible for his own lot. This shift in the ratio explanation, between *scene-act* and *agent-act* illustrates the dilemma of accounting for anti-Semitism; is anti-Semitism the result of various conditions, be they social, economic, religious and political that have affected Jews, or is anti-Semitism the sole responsibility of the Jew? For Lazare, the Pariah conception of anti-Semitism is his guiding thesis, yet, his explanation, time and again, is leaning situational, hence, a *scene-act* framing. The rhetorical analysis of Lazare's account of anti-Semitism reveals that though he is inclined to side with the Pariah argument, his explanations point to the greater conviction that the Pariah conception was imposed on Jews, and that it was not of their own making.

A new wave of anti-Semitism, explains Lazare, rose during the late 18th and throughout the 19th century, the result of a backlash against the liberties brought by the Napoleonic wave of freedoms. Western European Jewry began to enjoy greater freedom and full standing as free citizens in their respective societies; yet, once Napoleon was defeated, the freedoms granted to Jews at his urging in various countries were not only reversed, but Jews were now blamed for Napoleon's war and the destruction it brought. Indeed, new restrictive legislations against Jews were meant to curtail some of the freedoms they just won. Several decades later, the rebellions of 1848 in various European capitals brought renewed anti-Semitism but the kind that was left at the level of opinion and, for the first time, without hostile legislation (Lazare, p. 101). This anti-Semitism, argues Lazare, was brought by economic, hence competitive reasons, given the Jews' tendency to compete well in commerce and industry. Lazare's argument is that Jews, once legal, economic, and social the barriers fell, rushed in to conquer the area of economics which they understood best, and that subsequently, their successes bread jealousy and henceforth, hatred (Lazare, p. 108).

There is also an inherent cause-and-effect fallacy that Lazare often resorts to in rationalizing anti-Semitism. Accordingly, "on the eve of the French Revolution, they [non-Jews] saw him [the Jew] humble, timid, an object of general contempt, exposed to insult and injury. They found him after the tempest, free, liberated from every constraint, and from a slave, become a master. Such a rapid exaltation was offensive" (p. 108). Given their rapid social and economic gains, Jews were accused not only of enjoying the fruits of the French Revolution, but, in slippery slope logic, of causing it in the first place. It is the wealth of the Jew that offended people the most and, in their attempt at rationalizing this phenomenon, they concluded that the Jewish wealth must have been gained at the expense of the Christian.

Writing his book primarily as a reaction to the wave of anti-Semitism in France displayed during the trial of Captain Alfred Dreyfus, Lazare claims that those "who maintain that the Jews are the sole cause of the present state of things succeed only in establishing their own absurdly marvelous ignorance" (p. 166). Yet, he also identifies modern anti-Semitism in the Jews' refusal to assimilate and that they "did not cease to be a people" in the midst of other nations (Lazare, p. 138). He also points to the secret of their success in their ability to "stand united as one" (p. 169). But Lazare does not delve into this unity of Jews to explain in rather simple terms the reasons for this affinity of Jews borne out of the need to survive amidst continued challenges and profound insecurity.

The pariah accusation surfaces again when Lazare blames Jewish community leaders of opposing Jews from pursuing professions and occupations such as non-Jews. Some Jews, he states, became philosophers but against the wishes of Jewish leaders who preferred to focus on Jewish law. Even attempts by Maimonides to reconcile faith with science ran afoul with those advocating the "the purity of Israel" (p. 63). The charge of pariah is harsh given the reality that in the face of historical threats and persecution Jews sought ways to preserve Judaism for posterity. This principle does not excuse the punishment Jews have inflicted on other Jews, like Baruch Spinoza, who sought other occupations not traditionally Jewish.[3] Yet, against constant threats of persecution and annihilation, Jews found in their tradition a source of continuity and thus looked inward for perseverance.

In his survey of anti-Semitism, Lazare repeatedly points to a transformation of a religious-based anti-Semitism into an economic based hatred of Jews. What Lazare ignores is that no cause should have resulted in anti-Semitism, yet once a cause is identified it turns into a justification for the course of action. His own account of the constraints put on Jews and the limited professional outlets available to them made any charge against them a circular argument. Lazare's explanation, though framed in line with his pariah charge, is largely sympathetic.

Lazare admits that anti-Semitism was an easy practice for non-Jews because the Jews have already been blamed for all the evil in the world: Christ killers, collectors of taxes, usurers, and bankers. Coupled with a long-standing tradition of being a hated group, any accusation was easy to accept and perpetuate. Lazare singles out the church in particular for fighting Jews dogmatically, and for prohibiting them from reading their scholarly tomes such as the Mishna and the Talmud, forbidding Jews from appearing in public on certain days, imposing on them special taxes, subjecting them to being boxed on the ear, not to speak of the more brutal acts that included killing in various European cities, such as burning them in York and Strasbourg, hanging them in Spain, or ripping them with pitchforks and scythes.[4]

Against these terrible suffering a sense of brotherhood developed, bent on survival by connecting their present suffering with the long-standing aspiration of returning to Zion (Lazare, p. 71). Lazare admits that anti-Semitism has had the unintended consequence of forcing Jews to look inward for survival since all external forces were usually against them. Lazare betrays his Pariah argument when in middle of his discussion about modern anti-Semitism (of the late 19th century) he writes the following:

To tell the story of Israel is to tell the story of France, or Germany, or Spain. This is what the Christian antisemites see, and their anti-Semitism is purely theological, it is the anti-Semitism of the Fathers, that of Chrysostom, Saint Augustine, Saint Jerome. Before the birth of Jesus, the Jewish people was the chosen people, the beloved son of God; since the time it had disavowed the Saviour, since it had become a deicide, it had become the fallen people par excellence, and having before brought the world's salvation, it now causes its ruin. (p. 112)

Here, Lazare contradicts his earlier assertions about Jews being responsible for their own plight, or giving temporal and even circumstantial explanation for various forms of anti-Semitism. One root cause — a theological one — lies at the base of anti-Semitism. In the language of rhetoric, anti-Semitism was easy because it functioned as a *metonymy* — the single representation of the whole, whereby the Jew as a metonymy for evil is a device that is already known to yield the sought result which is hatred.

Even more profoundly and originally, Lazare rejects racial theories used to explain anti-Semitism. His view here is rather advanced given the fact that he wrote his tract when racial theories were relatively a new phenomenon. He considers racism a fiction, claiming that "there is no such thing as a race" and he acknowledges that racial theories have brought to life pseudo-historical and pseudo-anthropological arguments. In rejecting racial theories, Lazare contends that the theological conflict is foundational and the real cause of anti-Semitism. When one takes Lazare's view to its critical end, he points to the inconsistency in having Jews who brought the Savior Jesus to the world and then being accused of killing him, are to suffer thereof, and for eternity. As pure narrative, Jews are cast as killers, the convenient "other," the villain, and the ultimate evil. All other narratives follow this basic rhetorical plot line and regardless of the variations on this plot line — the Jew as the killer who must be killed therefore — has remained constant throughout history and with dire consequences. Indeed, the identification of "the kill," I argue, is crucial in seeking to understand anti-Semitism as a thread that has continued from antiquity to modern times.

In contemplating philosophical anti-Semitism, Lazare points to an attack on the Semitic (Hebraic) conception of the divine and of ethics. He addresses, in particular, Eugen Dühring's claim that Christianity "is the last manifestation of the Semitic spirit," and that nations will "not be done with Semitic spirit until they have expelled from their spirit this present second aspect of Hebraism" (p. 117). Here is the rhetorical formula fully exposed — Jews must be eliminated because the perfect spirit of Semitic values and ethics has already been perfected by others. The need to eliminate Jews is mandated by their uselessness. The Jews who originated Hebraic conception of morals and ethics have been replaced and are now relegated, at best, to second place, and at worst, should be eliminated altogether.

But why would Dühring suggest that Jews must be done with their Semitic spirit? Taking Lazare's description critically, the Jews' continued existence is a bothersome reminder of being the first to conceive the morals and ethics others usurped and have claimed as their own; an inconvenient act of usurpation that is best handled by ridding society of those usurped from; those who can make the charge of usurpation. The rhetorical process explains this phenomenon well: redemption and purification are possible by sacrifice and victimage whereby a community cannot exist without ridding itself of the one who stands in the way of the need for perfection. But, again, why the "kill"? Why the ultimate form of elimination? Because there is no other way to stand as a usurper whose act of usurpation is that of co-opting another's entity (in this case, a religious foundation), not until the usurped is no longer present and guilt is no longer experienced. The presence of the Jews is a reminder of the usurpation and it keeps the guilt on and this is an uncomfortable feeling one must rid oneself off.

In the end, Lazare concedes that no accusation against Jews can make sense as no fact can support anti-Semitism. Whether racial charges, religious charges, political or economic, "none of these grievances of anti-Semitism are well founded. Some, like the ethnic grievance arise from a false conception of race; others like the religious and political charges are due to a narrow and incomplete interpretation of historical evolution; and last of all, the economic count, has its justification in the necessity of concealing the strife going on within the capitalist class" (p. 175). So what is left is to cast the Jew as the pariah and then hate him for being one. While earlier in his book Lazare would use both *scene-act* and *agent-act* framing to explain anti-Semitism, ultimately he would conclude that anti-Semitism was a projection of one's evil onto others, whereby the guilt of one's doing (casting the Jew as evil) is projected onto the victim who is now blamed for his action (for producing the evil) in the first place.

So, while Lazare's treatment of anti-Semitism presents his discussion as generally accusatory of Jews, the rhetorical analysis reveals a sympathetic view of the circumstances Jews were put under and that out of these conditions stands the probable cause for the Jew as a pariah. In subsequent years, especially following the *Dreyfus Affair,* Lazare would modify his initial views on anti-Semitism as he realized that emancipation and integration of Jews in their respective society, the solution to the pariah criticism he advocated, did not end anti-Semitism (Laqueur, p. 29). If anything, emancipation exacerbated anti-Semitism.

Hannah Arendt's Conception of the Pariah

Arendt would take Lazare's argument about the Jew as pariah (*parvenue*) and expand its conception further. While Lazare would begin with the pariah but ultimately blame Christians for anti-Semitism that caused the Jew to become a pariah, Hannah Arendt's thesis lies in her conception of Jewish history as consciously seeking to be treated as unique and separate. Subscribing consistently to the *agent-act* ratio, she argues that Jews purposefully avoided all political action during two thousand years of history in Diaspora and, in so doing they have unknowingly become dependent on the historical forces of others. Her conclusion is that the Holocaust and its "catastrophic end to the history of the Jews in Europe was neither accidental nor inevitable" (Introduction, 1978, p. 22). Jews, Arendt argues, were "politically blind" to the conditions they helped create, which resulted in growing hatred and subsequently, the Holocaust (p. 22). In seeking to understand Arendt's thesis — her indictment of Jews for failing to be active in political causes which subsequently brought anti-Semitism on them — it is important to note Arendt's thesis — that of expecting Jews throughout history to become advocates of their cause and plight. Jews had to realize, Arendt opined, the need to persuade others of their religion and circumstances instead of becoming, throughout their history "dependent upon unforeseen, accidental factors than the history of other nations, so that the Jews stumbled from one role to the other and accepted responsibility for none" (Arendt, 1978, p. 22). Her primary claim is that "survival has been the single aim of Jewish political thought and action since the Babylonian exile," and this single issue brought the dissociation and separatism from the larger communities within which they resided (1978, p. 22).

In subscribing to the *agent-act* ratio, Arendt's thesis is premised on the philosophy that looks at individuals and groups as being directly responsible for their action. For Arendt, action is a most central feature of her philosophy. She clearly rejects situational circumstances as conditioning events. As Stephen H. Brown notes, for Arendt, action "denotes that which actualizes our shared capacity for living freely in a world inhabited by others," and that pride includes "pride of place" (in Phillips, 2004, pp. 53-56). Yet, such pride of place when put in the context of public memory may not relate just to the here and now but, as has been the case for Jews, to a distant and ancient past and embodied in a land that has remained alive in peoples' memories. Therein is Arendt's inconsistent reasoning — of blaming Jews for constructing barriers around them and discounting the possibility that centuries of anti-Semitism brought an inward outlook and that the separation from the larger community was done not by choice but by force. More crucially, Arendt discounts the possibility that what kept Judaism alive was in no insignificant sense, their "pride of place."

Action for Jews, the kind Arendt advocates, albeit, theoretically, if plausible at all, was related only to questions of improving their conditions, and in idealistic terms it meant only one thing — that which is recited continuously — a return to the ancestry land. After all, it was not Jews who put themselves in ghettos (physical enclaves with walls and a gate) of Venice or Frankfurt, preventing them from stepping outside at certain times and days. It was not the Jewish community that prohibited Jews from entering many professions and designating restricted professions open to them, such as lending money, purposefully to further humiliate them. With such hostility over many centuries, one should not wonder that suspicion of the larger community would become pervasive and entrenched in a people's psyche. Indeed, entrenched habits, professions and mindset, forced on people for a long time, affected their psyche over centuries, and easily shaped the Jewish character. The distance between a people's character and stereotypes is rather short as it is often based on visual signs and external depiction. Indeed, the hatred of the Jew was easily triggered for many centuries when signs such as dress, customs, and even smell, were used deterministically as judgments about evil character and immorality. Arendt conveniently ignores the obvious — that anti-Semitic accusation turned so vicious and ridiculous that Jews, erroneously or otherwise, were not inclined to argue with those possessing such sentiments, or worse, that they saw no chance of succeeding in swaying people who held such noxious notions. In facing outrageous charges and lacking the power to counter them, Jews turned inward, "despising those who denigrated them" (Cohn-Sherbok, 2006, p. 39).

Arendt's account of Jews avoiding political action from antiquity onward is not altogether fair or accurate. The severe limitations put on Jews in terms of residence and occupation made political action throughout the Middle-Ages rather limited, if not impossible. When restrictions became more flexible Jews have also acquired some political clout. In the Middle-Ages, few Jews served as bankers to nobility, and when possible, were able to influence the plight of their brethren, at least to some degree. It is true that their association with landed aristocracy brought the hatred of many who were heavily taxed by them. However, with more freedom, Jews did exactly what Arendt advocated. Following Emancipation, and especially during the mid-19th century, Jews become active members of assemblies in several Western European nations as well as revolutionaries of several causes, and even leaders of various freedom movements (Elon, 2002, pp. 152-153, 171ff). Arendt's thesis does not hold when numerous leaders of the 1848 revolts and later of the Russian revolution were of Jewish origin. The involvement of Jews in various radical movements is one important reason for the success of *The Protocols of the Wise Elders of Zion,* as those claiming that Jews were intent on world domination could point out in the late nineteenth century, that Jews posses radical tendencies.

Arendt is also critical of the Jewish occupation with the "politics of memory," arguing that this focus was detrimental to their historical plight (1978, pp. 22-23). Indeed, public memory has been crucial to Judaism as the means to a strong link to the past and as a force for a continued future and identity. Since the Roman exile, Judaism would develop its liturgy, worship, and religious symbolism around the loss of Judea. The objective of these symbolic acts was meant to secure a public memory that would be transmitted from one generation to another. What seems to concern Arendt on this particular point is her view that Jewish engagement in public memory was exclusive and extensive to the detriment of other more needed occupations and interests. Yet, when put in the context of multiple professional and social constraints, including physical threats, it stands to reason that the mechanism of self-preservation would take prominence. The pivotal point, though, is the connection between Judaism and Judea (the land of Israel), and this connection was one Arendt considered not very important. Jews, she advocated, had to find the formula of living among others despite century-old victimization.

In Arendt's view, responsibility for the human world is shared by the victim as well as by the victimizer (1978, p. 33). While the morality of individuals being responsible for their action is laudable, the shared responsibility of victimizer and victim is naïve, as one would assume that, at a minimum, the victimizer ought to be more responsible than the victim for the victimizer's actions. But this is not Arendt's view. She expects the victimized to shore up the necessary strength and fight his victimization. This is fine, at least in theory; however, is it possible that the victimized by the very act of victimization is unable and or limited in his or her ability to resist or fight? Is the implication here that Arendt is critical of the Jews for never challenging anti-Semites or even worse, that those trapped in concentration camps did not fight their Nazi oppressors?

Arendt assumes that in all situations, the victims still have a venue of political activity available to them. And though this may be true in some cases, one is hard pressed to generalize this notion. The Jewish revolt at the Warsaw Ghetto, though crushed, was a heroic act that illustrates the great difficulties Jews had of resisting the Nazi killing machine in other locations. [5] For most Jews trapped in Nazi concentration camps, the oppression was too difficult to mount successful resistance. It is true that prior to World War II, the growing attacks on Jews, especially in Germany, were alarming enough for some to flee Germany while others stayed, hoping for the mad phase to dissipate. Arendt's thesis holds if Jews had protested and opposed their treatment. Yet, such a move was increasingly difficult, if not improbable to implement. While Jews were prominent in politics during the Weimar Republic, which proves their active role in the state, the assassinations of Kurt Eisner, the Prime Minister of the Republic of Bavaria (1919) and Foreign Minister, Walther Rathenau (1922), to use two examples, did not bode well for Jewish politicians. It is thus possible that attacks on Jews in general, and on Jewish politicians in particular, sealed the fate of practical opposition to Nazi Germany and its anti-Semitism, not to speak of fear of the Gestapo and the violence they spread.

Arendt is critical of finance as a Jewish inclination that did nothing but bring additional anti-Semitism. Just as in Lazare's view, scenic and situational constraints that brought Jews to financial professions in the first place are discounted in her analysis as the effect of anti-Semitism and instead are identified as its cause. Only Zionism, according the Arendt, the political answer Jews developed in fighting anti-Semitism, was the political activity she could identify in Jewish history (Arendt, 1978, p. 28). This is a significant point yet, it, too, is not without its complications. For one, if her thesis holds, then why not account for earlier and similar attempts to gather the Jews of Diaspora and bring them to their ancient land? For example, Shabbtai Zevi's movement of the seventeenth century would surely be considered such a political move, though it ended rather disappointedly.[6]

Arendt's view is not separate from her pariah accusation. Indeed, unlike Lazare, the pariah accusation runs consistent throughout Arendt's philosophy. She considers the *Yishuv*, the initial pre-state political entity that would later become the State of Israel, to be an artificial creation, implying that it should not have been created in the first place (1978, p. 35). In the introduction to her volume *The Jew as Pariah* (1978), Ron H. Feldman writes that Arendt saw in the *Yishuv*, and later the State of Israel, an artificial creation brought on by "unrealistic political demands of the Zionist movement" (p. 36). This state established in the midst of millions of Arabs would require it to request the protection of a great power (p. 37), such as the United States, which is what happened. She also was critical of the Arabs for seeking to "expel the Jewish 'invaders' from Palestine without consideration for Jewish achievements there" (p. 197). Subsequently, she argues, "the Jewish and Arab claims were perfectly incompatible and mutually irrefutable, for both were the result of nationalistic policies reached within 'the closed framework of one's own people and history'" (pp. 200-201).

Arendt believed that with the establishment of the State of Israel, the Jewish people as a pariah would become a pariah state (1978, pp. 38-39). This view, I contend, is not without merit, and indeed, anti-Israel or anti-Zionism has replaced anti-Semitism, at least in some circles. With hindsight, Arendt's prediction regarding Israel's vulnerability proved correct though likely for different reasoning. Arendt saw the pariah syndrome as the motivator for a history of anti-Semitism and now these sentiments, she believed, would be used against the State of Israel primarily for its inability to defend itself, bringing upon itself a "second catastrophe so soon after Hitler" (p. 38). But Israel's military weakness Arendt feared did not materialize.

Arendt's interest in a Jewish political movement is limited, and if such a movement were to be established, it had to be worked out within the nation in which Jews resided in and be part of its political discourse, be it France, Germany, or any other country. Arendt did not accept an independent Jewish state and saw in Zionism only a political movement — she did not accept the link Jews have kept with their ancestral land. This as much is obvious in Arendt's philosophy. As Feldman offers, Arendt's Zionism is in the mold of Lazare, that of becoming a pariah for refusing to be a dissident, for refusing to be "a revolutionary among his own people, not among others" (p. 33). It is Zionism without Zion, a limited movement of self assertion, a rebellious movement whereby Jews would take responsibility for their plight and act upon it. This was Arendt's answer to anti-Semitism. The Zionism that ended up in creating a state Jews could call home was a perpetuation of the old pariah and she opposed it.

Yet, if she considered Israel an artificial creation, she ignores similar state creations as no more artificial than the State of Israel. What would she say about most Arab countries established immediately following the end of World War I, such as Iraq, Kuwait, Jordan, Syria and Saudi Arabia? All these Middle Eastern states, just like the Jewish Homeland of the Balfour Declaration, did not exist prior to World War I. Once the Ottoman Empire ceased to exist, the League of Nations, with the active participation of England and France, carved new states in the Middle East, often using a ruler for straight lines to designate specific geographies. Such artificiality was not limited to the Jewish Homeland but to the entire Middle East following World War I.

Arendt admits that "so small (and, in world politics, so unimportant) a phenomenon as the Jewish question and antisemitism could become the catalytic agent for first, the Nazi movement, then a world war, and finally the establishment of death factories" (Arendt, 1951, p. viii). She also states that, there is hardly an aspect of contemporary history more irritating and mystifying than the fact that of all the great unsolved political questions of our century, it should have been this seemingly small and unimportant Jewish problem that had the dubious honor of setting the whole infernal machine in motion. Such discrepancies between cause and effect outrage our common sense. (1951, p. 3)

One is quite taken by Arendt's accurate description of events leading to the Holocaust and the destruction of Jewish life in Europe. She clearly questions the purpose of this destruction and the causes behind the plan of their extermination. Yet, these sentiments beg the obvious question: So, what was the reason for this anti-Semitism that resulted in the Holocaust and how does this view square with her criticism of Jewish practices as responsible for anti-Semitism in the first place?

Arendt does offer an explanation, arguing that anti-Semitism climaxed when Jews "lost the public functions and their influence, and were left with nothing but their wealth" (1951, p. 4). Seeking to identify a cause she suggests that anti-Semitism is the hatred of the powerless since it is easy to hate those who have wealth without power (Arendt, 1951, p. 5). This explanation is odd given the experiences of anti-Semitism that even in Arendt's time was borne of anything related to wealth. One has to consider the pogroms in Russian since the late 19th and early 20th centuries to question the wealth variable as a possible cause for anti-Semitism. Even if Arendt's explanation makes sense in one particular location at a particular time, namely Western Europe, is not such an experience the proof that other causes are at hand and that wealth in the hands of Jews is nothing but an excuse for deeper resentments? Finally, when did Jews lose their public function and their influence? She has claimed all along that they never had it or that they failed to acquire it.

Unlike Lazare, anti-Semitism, argues Arendt, is racially based and as such it is a modern phenomenon. She rejects any connection to antiquity in explaining anti-Semitism. What she fails to see is that even an anti-Christian form of anti-Semitism, as the one espoused by the Nazis, had its roots in the Christian tradition (Gager, 1983, p. 267). She is convinced that "modern anti-Semitism must be seen in the more general framework of the development of the nation-state, and at the same time its source must be found in certain aspects of Jewish history and specifically Jewish functions during the last centuries" (Arendt, 1951, p. 9). In other words, a historical confluence of events related to the development of the nation-state also gave rise to anti-Semitism, whereas when she contemplates a more specific source for the rise in anti-Semitism, she finds it in Jewish functions. Arendt would go back only as far as few centuries to locate the source of anti-Semitism, and she would find it in the unfortunate relationship Jews developed with the nation-state in which they resided. Specifically, Jews were unaware of the predicaments they put themselves in by supporting the nation-state as a new form of political entity. But this explanation makes sense only if anti-Semitism did not exist before; which, clearly, is not the case.

In Arendt's view, "if, in the final stage of disintegration, anti-Semitic slogans proved the most effective means of inspiring and organizing great masses of people for imperialist expansion and destruction of the old forms of government, then the previous history of the relationship between Jews and the state must contain some elementary clues to the growing hostility between certain groups of society and the Jews" (1951, p. 9-10). Indeed, anti-Semitism has its antecedents in earlier history, but Arendt does not wish to go too far in exploring the source of this hatred. Hence, her limited view on anti-Semitism, constrained by the unique development of recent political development and devoid of deeper and more entrenched historical animosity that functioned much more than just a backdrop.

Indeed, for Arendt, modern anti-Semitism bares no relationship to earlier anti-Jewish sentiments and actions. She argues that

> The history of anti-Semitism, like the history of Jew-hatred, is part and parcel of the long and intricate story of Jewish-Gentile relations under the conditions of Jewish dispersion. Interest in this history was practically non-existent prior to the middle of the nineteenth century, when it coincided with the rise of anti-Semitism and its furious reaction to emancipated and assimilated Jewry. (1951, p. xii)

Anti-Semitism, then, is a modern phenomenon, borne out of emancipation and assimilation of Jews which was disruptive to the larger society. She is also concerned by the Jewish obsession with anti-Semitism, and thereby her argument that Jews would find more anti-Jewish hostility than history could merit. Such a measured approach in her view is important for quality historiography, but in so doing, she has minimized and even undercut Jewish history. She appears to argue against those who supposedly have claimed a longer and deeper case of historic anti-Semitism, seeking to present a more limited case of this experience. But why claim that the history of anti-Semitism is more episodic than continuous, and what does it matter if anti-Semitism was more continuous or more punctuated? Arendt is likely seeking to argue that anti-Semitism was not as bad as Jews have made it appear, at least not until the nineteenth century. Indeed, the key word in her analysis is "coincide," whereby intense anti-Semitism and interest in the history of anti-Semitism just happened at the same time. For Arendt, then, anti-Semitism, from a Jewish perspective is not so much historical as rhetorical — an obsession not borne of historical facts.

The history of anti-Semitism is indeed, a collection of many stories and episodes in various locations and communities. One is hard-pressed to point to a period or location in Christendom when anti-Semitism did not exist to one degree or another. From mild hostile attitudes, to professional restrictions to humiliation of numerous sorts, to physical attacks and murder, Jewish history of the past two thousand years and anti-Semitism cannot be set apart. And yet, there were times and places when Jews fared better than their brethren in other geographical locations. However, these relatively calmer periods cannot be used to argue that anti-Semitism was more Jewish polemic than facts, or that given numerous wars and other forms of societal strife, that by comparisons, Jews have not much to complain about when citing anti-Semitism. But this is not Arendt's overall perspective. Only beginning with the nineteenth century is she comfortable talking about increased anti-Semitism. The time frame she considers central to a discussion about anti-Semitism is dictated by the consciousness of historiography (her point about coincidence) but such a view is highly interpretive as it seeks to persuade others of a given narrative of history and rejecting competing explanatory narratives.

As discussed earlier, Arendt also rejects the scapegoat theory as foundational to explaining anti-Semitism. She argues that the scapegoat theory implies that another culprit is at fault and that the selected group for hatred implies its innocence. But since Arendt does blame Jews for causing, or for bringing upon themselves the very anti-Semitism they reject, it is not surprising that she would reject the scapegoat theory. Those using the scapegoat theory, she claims, simply attempt to find the most suitable group for convenient hatred, cautioning us to consider the fact that once someone engages in the scapegoating explanation, one leaves scapegoating altogether and enters the "more common historical research looking to explain why one group was more suited than others for the role of the scapegoat." In other words, for Arendt, scapegoating is an arbitrary form of identification, whereas Jews becoming the primary victims of the Nazis was not done arbitrarily, therefore it was not an act of scapegoating (pp. 5-7). It was the Jews fault of not realizing their culpability in bringing anti-Semitism on themselves.

She blames those seeking to explain anti-Semitism by using the scapegoat explanation as an attempt "to escape the seriousness of anti-Semitism and the significance of the fact that the Jews were driven into the storm center of events" (p. 7). Arendt's thesis remains constant as she puts the weight for bringing or causing anti-Semitism on Jews themselves. Given her thesis, the rejection of the scapegoat theory (discussed earlier) makes sense as Arendt seeks to find a cause in internal forces and thus her focus on Jewish behavior and practices is the weighty causes for anti-Semitism.

Arendt also rejects the opposite explanation "of an 'eternal antisemitism' in which Jew hatred is a normal and natural reaction to which history gives only more or less opportunity," that of killing Jews for such a long time that it has become a common and "normal" practice (1951, p. 7). Arendt rejects the notion of a long standing practice of anti-Semitism that reached a level of normalcy and she also rejects the case for a convenient group-hatred. What is left, then, in explaining anti-Semitism according to Arendt? If the arbitrary is rejected, if the convenient is rejected, then what is left is the responsibility of the self — the Jew him/herself.

Her point about the responsibility of self is part of Arendt's worldview as well as her understanding of historiography. The agent is responsible for the act and in turn the motives for the act can be found in the agent. She cites Plato's *Phaedrus* to make her point about shallow instead of serious historical analyses of anti-Semitism and its causes. For students of rhetoric, this reference is illustrative of her world view. Arendt uses Plato's *Phaedrus* to make the point that opinions are established by persuasion and not by the truth. She writes that

> The most striking difference between ancient and modern sophists is that the ancients were satisfied with a passing victory of the argument at the expense of truth, whereas the moderns want a more lasting victory at the expense of reality ... The old manipulators of logic were the concern of the philosophers, whereas the modern manipulators of facts stand in the way of the historian. For history itself is destroyed, and its comprehensibility — based upon the fact that it is enacted by men and therefore can be understood by men — is in danger, whenever facts are no longer held to be part and parcel of the past and present world, and are misused to prove this or that opinion. (Arendt, 1951, p. 9)

Arendt's insightful analysis of Plato's critical view of the art of rhetoric is the vehicle she uses to argue the accuracy of her historical explanation and against those engaged in shifty constructs of history. In her analysis of recent history, Jews failed to understand the historical forces that drove them to the center of the storm, implying that had they realized these forces, they would have been more astute in their behavior and actions. Specifically, she points to the Jewish tendency to be too close to the state (the government and the political elite), thus inadvertently causing any group that opposed the state to identify Jews as working in cooperation with the state and thus with power. Consequently, those opposing the state also opposed Jews and thus became anti-Semitic (1951, p. 25). She comprehends why the Jew sought the closeness to the state, primarily for protection but also because of their aloofness from society and that because of their close family circle, they were "suspected of working for the destruction of all social structures" (1951, p. 28). These, argues Arendt, are the facts of history and not an opinion open to an alternative explanation.

In a larger sense, Arendt takes people's prejudices and blames them on the victim and not on the victimizer. She rejects assigning the *agent-act* framing to the victimizer but readily assigns it to the victimized. Neither does she challenge the prejudice itself for being false and for carrying malicious intents. Indeed, some Jews were close to government officials, some were wealthy, and some used their wealth to support the government and many of its enterprises. Some Jews became revolutionaries who sought to change political structures, some became socialists, and some belong to the bourgeoisies. But so were many non-Jews while more Jews were poor and belonged to none of these groups. The use of reasoning by signs that lie at the foundation of anti-Semitism in general can also be detected in Arendt's analysis. Arendt falls into the same trap that anti-Semites have followed — generalize from specific signs. The rhetorical process at hand is often referred to as a rhetorical syllogism (or an enthymeme) whereby signs are acceptable representations of conclusions thereof once they fall within agreed-upon premises. The pariah is but a sign, a rhetorical device, a metaphor and a metonymy, convenient and available whenever a community "needs" an explanation for setbacks and difficulties and blaming the Jew was historically acceptable.

Arendt also suggests that "as long as defamed peoples and classes exist, parvenue -and pariah qualities will be produced anew by each generation with incompatible monotony, in Jewish history and everywhere else" (p. 66). This statement is in complete contradiction of her rejection of eternal anti-Semitism. She clearly sees the Jew as belonging to a defamed group that cannot escape the judgment of others (hence, a scapegoat). Thus, this statement, especially the phrase "produced anew," contradicts her rejection of the scapegoating explanation. The key question here is why the Jew cannot escape the judgment of others? For Arendt, the answer lies in Jewish behavior and practices that set them apart from the larger society.

The *Dreyfus Affair* which brought Lazare to realize the intensity of anti-Semitism in French society is also featured prominently in Arendt's analysis of anti-Semitism. It is with this *Affair* that she solidifies her pariah thesis, arguing that the *Dreyfus Affair* showed how dependable Jews were in society precisely because "they did not belong in it" (p. 97). Again, Arendt resorts to a simple cause-and-effect reasoning to explain anti-Semitism. The premise on which the pariah thesis rests is that Jews did not belong in France. But the *Dreyfus Affair* became so prominent precisely because of the successful integration of Jews in society; in this particular case, a French military officer serving in a respectable position at the military headquarters and at an advanced rank. After all, the accusation against Captain Dreyfus was false, intentionally so, and the entire *Affair* was based on concocted lies. Perhaps the more accurate question to be asked here is who made the claim that the Jew did not belong? The average Frenchman made this charge; not the Jew. Yet, the Jew made the effort and even succeeded in integrating in the society in which he lived, taking full pride in his community participation. The Jew acted just as Arendt advocated and yet he was rejected and hated.

The Jew in the *Affair* was but a convenient agent when the truth was not the central issue but the honor of the state: The honor of France was more important than the truth — more important than Dreyfus' acquittal. But why did the *Dreyfus Affair* shatter France? Because there were enough individuals, Jews, like Bernard Lazare and non-Jews like the writer Emile Zola, who decided to fight for the truth. This fight made the *Dreyfus Affair* a metaphor for the soul of France. That a Jew stood at the center of the *Affair* was not taken well by the French. That much is understood. But why would Arendt argue that Jews did not belong in

France? Is it because they fought for the truth and in so doing revealed to the French something about their character and ethos as well as the Big Lie they were willing to accept? Did the *Dreyfus Affair* expose French anti-Semitism for its raw scapegoat logic? After all, the entire *Affair* centered on a Jewish army officer who was well respected and promoted for his own merits. Is not this a case of belonging, integrating and functioning in a society?

The only positive result of the *Dreyfus Affair*, argues Arendt, was that "it gave birth to Zionist movement — the only political answer Jews have ever found to anti-Semitism and the only ideology in which they have ever taken seriously, a hostility that would place them in the center of world events" (1951, p. 120). But as we have already observed, Zionism for Arendt was a limited concept and when it was translated into emigration into Palestine and the creation of a Jewish state, the visionary movement turned pragmatic. Such a transformation, from a vision to reality, in Arendt's view, included state practices such as engaging in military actions that were no longer warranted in her estimation.[7]

From the *Dreyfus Affair* onward, Arendt observes the rise of racism, especially the Pan German racism which, according to her, is based on "the nature of tribalism rather than in political facts and circumstances" (1951, p. 229). In racism, the rhetoric of hierarchy had become prominent whereby the Aryan was put above the Semite. Racism, explains Arendt, is the denial of common origin and the repudiation of common purpose. It is based on the conception of divine origin of one group over others. In the context of anti-Semitism, the Jews as God's "chosen people" are replaced by the Aryan, thus making the Jew the "*un*chosen" (1951, p. 234). In other words, in racism one finds the religious grounding of anti-Semitism, the narrow perspective Christians have taken Judaism as the religion of "the chosen people," a state that must be reversed into becoming "*un*chosen." Though Arendt is on to a significant postulation here, she cannot end the analysis with a society's basic need to construct its hierarchy at the expense of another or the "other." She looks for reasons and causes for the placing of the "other" group at the bottom of the hierarchy, and this she finds in the Jews' own behavior and practices.[8]

Conclusion

The difficulty in accepting Arendt's thesis of the pariah lies in her focusing only on recent development of the nation-state as well as certain aspects of Jewish history. This explanation hardly holds relevance to anti-Semitism prior to the modern age, and it does not explain the wide-spread anti-Semitism in Eastern Europe and Russia, including during the years of *Dreyfus Affair*. Neither does it explain the surge in Islamic anti-Semitism since the 1930's. The need to find different causes for anti-Semitism in different parts of the world ought to caution us about the certainty of any assessment of anti-Semitism or that a more convincing cause is yet to be understood.

In settling her thesis on the pariah, Arendt consistently blamed the victims — the Jews for anti-Semitism and for the Holocaust. In an astute observation about Arendt's view of the trial of Adolph Eichmann in Jerusalem, Wendy Flory notes that Arendt was looking for Eichmann to display guilt for his role in sending Jews to concentration camps, and that when Eichmann did not show such an emotion, she looked for the "missing guilt" elsewhere. Flory argues that Arendt "fell into the common fallacy of 'blaming the victim'," and she did so in order to point to Jewish leaders who "cooperated in one way or another, for one reason or another, with the Nazis" (in Curtis, p. 248).[9] Instead of rationalizing the situation in which these Jewish Councils were forced to operate, a *scene-act* ratio, Arendt consistently blames victimizers and victims such that guilt must be shared by both. The obvious facts surrounding Eichmann's role in planning the mass murder of Jews were not sufficient for Arendt to draw clear conclusions about morality and guilt.

In a larger sense, what both Lazare and Arendt failed to realize is the faulty reasoning in the logic of finding temporal or local causes for anti-Semitism and that the practice of finding different causes and possibilities proves a deeper reason and a more serious cause than the transient ones to which they have clung. The case for the pariah is simply not convincing and though it explains some cases of anti-Semitism, it cannot be generalized. Rhetorically, Lazare and Arendt differ in the motive they assign to Jews and from that difference two distinct explanations for anti-Semitism are presented. While Lazare would take the situation Jews were put in to explain and rationalize their historical predicament, Arendt's view of history and the role of human action put the onus of anti-Semitism on Jews themselves. As such, Jews should have realized their predicament and acted accordingly to save themselves from anti-Semitism.

Notes

1. Even as early as 60 CE, there were no confusions between Christians and Jews. Jews were allowed to maintain their practices and rituals while Christians have abandoned numerous Jewish practices (Goodman, 2007, p. 374).
2. A ratio is a linguistic device that points to a dominant world view that is expressed rhetorically. Burke considers the ratios as "principles of determination" (Burke, 1969, p. 15). The ratios are rhetorical implications one can draw from any two elements of the Pentad — a framing of human motivation exemplified grammatically. The Pentad and its ratios can reveal motives, even those obscured from the rhetor who constructed the message. As such the Pentad and its ratios offer a rich tool in the hand of the critic who is able to gauge significance in a given rhetorical act.
3. Born in 1632 Amsterdam to a Portuguese Jewish family, Spinoza was a brilliant student destined to be a rabbi but excommunicated from the Jewish faith at age 17 for allegedly doubting the existence of God. He would later become an important philosopher whose treatise *Ethics* is considered his greatest work.
4. Lazare finds an analogous case in the hatred of the Templars as they, like Jews, have suffered because "they were hated for their pride, their orientation, their wealth in the midst of misery." And that the Templars recognized no other authority but that of God (Lazare, pp. 92-93).
5. The Warsaw Ghetto uprising took place in the spring of 1943, pitting Jews with pistols and homemade hand grenades to face the German army. It took the Germans about a month to crush the revolt which was the largest urban uprising they encountered during World War II.
6. A seventeenth century mystic who proclaimed himself the Messiah who would take Jews back to the land of Israel. Eventually, many believed him and followed him on his journey to the Holy Land but the Ottoman authorities arrested him and Shabbtai Zevi converted to Islam crushing the hopes of his followers who believed he would return the Jews to their ancient land.
7. Arendt was critical of Israel's military victories during its early days which

she considered "complicated and very dangerous." She considered military wins of a very small country against a poorly armed enemy that represented multiple nations and many millions of people to be ill-advised and that it did not bode well for the "long range reality" (Arendt, 1978, pp. 237-238).

8.   Though speculative, perhaps Arendt's thesis on St. Augustine and his "milder" anti-Semitism relative to those of other Church Fathers, conditioned her view of anti-Semitism as not necessarily a Christian construct but a Jewish one.

9.   Arendt pointed to the Judenrate, or the Jewish Councils who were forced to cooperate with their tormentors, as sharing in the guilt (Flory, p. 248).

7

The Durban Conference and the Reinvention the Past

On August 28, 2001, the United Nation's sponsored the *Durban World Conference on Racism, Racial Discrimination, Xenophobia and Related Intolerances* opened. The conference included 2,300 representatives from governments and some 3,000 representatives of non-governmental organizations (NGO's). The primary objective of this global conference was to deal with the issue of racism, including reparations, environmental racism, race and poverty, and migrants' rights, to name a few. This was the first "race conference to be convened after the UN General Assembly had revoked the infamous 'Zionism' as Racism resolution" (Schechter, 2002, p. 176). The objective of the United Nations conference was "to get governments to commit themselves to remedying and ultimately eliminating racism and related violations" (Schechter, p. 177). The preparations for the conference made it clear that Israel would be the primary focus of the conference. In light of this development, the United States sent a low-level official instead of Colin Powell, the Secretary of State. As anticipated, the conference, turned quickly into a relentless anti-Semitism in the forms of attacks on Israel as well as the displaying of offensive cartoons and statements. The blurring of anti-Semitism and anti-Israel was clearly in vogue and the pretence that the two forms of hatred were different, was now exposed. If any, attacks on Israel were replete with Nazi symbols while, at the same time, attempts were made to deny the Holocaust its historical place in public memory.[1]

During the conference, the Arab Lawyers Union distributed anti-Semitic pamphlets that depicted Jews with hooked noses, Israelis wearing Nazi emblems with Palestinian blood on their hands, and surrounded by paper currency (Bayesfsky, 2001, p. 2). Syria and Iran opposed references to anti-Semitism and the Holocaust, arguing that anti-Semitism was "complicated," "curious," and "bizarre" concept (Bayefsky, 2001, p. 2). There were even arguments about spelling the word Holocaust with an upper- or lower-case "h" (Timmerman, 2003, p. 7). A conference declaration that was prepared in Tehran, called the creation of the State of Israel a "third holocaust" (Timmerman, p. 7). The Iranian delegation also insisted that "anti-Semitism be struck from the conference's official register of bigotries because it is not a contemporary form of racism" (Timmerman, p. 8). The vehement racism inside the halls of the Durban Conference was replayed in outside demonstrations as well. One flier depicted Hitler asking: "What if I had won?" Two possible answers were supplied in the flyer: the first one stated "The good things — there would be NO Israel and No Palestinians' bloodshed," and "The bad thing — I wouldn't have allowed the making of the new Beetle" (Timmerman, p. 6). The Nazi killing machine and Israel's existence were conflated as if they belong to the same entity.

The shock of confronting anti-Semitism of the Nazi era became a warning sign to many Jews who thought that, after the Holocaust, this kind of attitude was no longer present. Instead they heard that Zionism "is based on racial superiority" ("U.S., Israeli Representatives Walk Out of Durban," p. 1). The glaring omissions in the Durban conference were equally revealing whereby those accusing Israel avoided discussing their own human rights failings such as Arab terrorism, Iraq's use of chemical weapons against the Kurds, Palestinian suicide bombers who blow themselves up on buses and in malls in Israel, human rights violations in many Arab countries, slavery, as well as the slaughter of minorities in Sudan. The main topic of deliberation was anti-Semitism; a topic that was not even on the conference agenda (Timmerman, p. 2).

The language of human rights, stated Ann F. Bayefsky, was utilized in Durban "to demonize, and then to dismember, the opponent," using the United Nation's conference as a cover for "rampant anti-Semitism" (p. 2). The real aim of many participants was to systematically remove the "vestiges of Jewish victimhood . . . by deleting the references to anti-Semitism and the Holocaust" (Bayefsky, pp. 1-2). Author Kenneth R.

Timmerman opined that the objective of the recent increase in anti-Semitism is to engage in a "semantic theft" that seeks to deny the word "Holocaust" to describe the murder of 6 million Jews and to use "holocaust" and "genocide" to describe "virtually any action by Israeli soldiers against Palestinians" (Timmerman, p. 4). The battle, then, was highly rhetorical, paying close attention to the use of words and their potential impact.

Yet, this development in Durban, South Africa, was part of a purposeful attempt to demonize Jews — a long-held intense form of anti-Semitism. The language of human rights has been transformed into the rhetoric of hate whose purpose is to hide the evil done by perpetrators and transfer it to the victim. The anti-Semitism in Durban, with its heavy focus on the Holocaust, was blatantly Nazi in orientation and its focus was on primarily on Jews and only secondarily on Israel. Here, I argue, lies an interesting admission — that it may be easier to attack Israel by focusing on its Jewish identity than dealing with specific Israeli infractions. If Durban is an exemplar for a shift in fighting Israel, it is the use of anti-Semitism as a device for unifying the Islamic world behind a common hatred. The focus on the Holocaust may reveal another significant truism — that in the Islamic world, the Holocaust is granted a primacy in understanding how Israel came about and that in countering the Holocaust as a cause for establishing the State of Israel, Israel would lose its primary justification for existence. In short, anti-Semitism is the tool of those who not only do not wish to see a negotiated end to the Arab-Israeli conflict, but who wish to negate Israel's right to exist.

The real victims of the rhetoric of hate in Durban were set aside and with them also the elimination of history and its replacement with falsehood. In short, several real victim groups are obscured in the rhetoric of hate, so that Jews and Israel could be singled out as the world's greatest menace. The consequences of the Durban rhetoric of demonization were in full force only a few days later — on September 11, 2001. Nineteen Arab individuals, mostly from Saudi Arabia, sent airplanes and their passengers to their deaths in the twin towers of the World Trade Center, at the Pentagon and one, intended to hit the White House, crashed in a field in rural Pennsylvania. Close to 3,000 individuals died that day at the hands of terrorists, making it the worst terrorist attack on the United

States. Yet, the very identification of the suicide terrorists and their country of origin were quickly rejected in the Arab world and the attack would be construed also in anti-Semitic terms.

The Arab media, educators, and religious leaders alike were quick to point the finger at "4,000 Jews who had been tipped off to stay away from work at the World Trade Center and the Jewish film crew that had advance notice to be on the scene to film the planes plowing into the towers" (Lelyvel, 2001, p. 53). An influential cleric in Pakistan stated that "Jews sold their shares in United and American Airlines before September 11" (Carlson, 2001, p. 24). The father of Mohamed Atta, leader of the suicide bombers, suggested that the "Zionists must have kidnapped him in order to steal his identity and make the mask that the agent carrying Mohamed's passport could then wear onto the plane" (Lelyvel, p. 53). The press in the Arab world was equally supportive of these claims, arguing (incorrectly) that no Jews died on September 11 as proof of their role in the events of that infamous day (McNeil, 2001, p. B1). The Syrian defense minister stated that "the destruction of the World Trade Center was part of a Jewish conspiracy" (Rosen, 2001, p. 50). None of those making the charges have bothered to suggest the motives Jews would have had in perpetrating such a terrorist attack, though a hint of a financial motive is suggested in the selling of stocks. The other motive is taken for granted — that Jews sought to implicate Arabs and point the finger at "innocent" Arabs.

Though the absurd claims of a Jewish plot have been rejected in the West, many people in the Arab world continue to believe that Jews are behind the September 11 attack.[2] Such a view fits a long-held conviction of a larger and continuous Jewish plot to control the world, a view taken directly from *The Protocols of the Wise Elders of Zion*. Arab hijackers, goes the claim, cannot be guilty of such a heinous act because Arabs do not perpetrate terrorism. Instead Arabs are victims while Jews who like to consider themselves victims, are the real perpetrators of terror. Timmerman may be correct in asserting that the anti-Semitism of the Durban conference served as the "ideological prologue" to September 11 (Timmerman, p. 1).

In the language of Kenneth Burke, the *agent-act* framing, that of admitting Arab and Muslim responsibility for terrorism as the one of September 11, 2001, is rejected and is projected instead to a counter agent in order to identify a convenient culprit — the Jews as the historical scapegoat and the agent of evil. What is also at work here is the national identity formation standing at the core of this Islamic hateful rhetoric. M. Lane Bruner (2002) writes that "the rhetorical dimensions of national identity are politically significant because different types of collective identities lead to different forms of community" and that national identity and the rhetoric that supports it can foster community characteristics — democratic, authoritative, and/or xenophobic patterns of identification (p. 2). Bruner suggests that "controversial public speeches articulating national character are taken to be useful sites for analyzing the rhetorical strategies involved in competing characterizations of the nation or the people" (p. 2).

Indeed, the projected controversial narratives are often laced with strong invectives that are familiar to Western audiences patterned on centuries of anti-Semitic rhetoric. This is clearly the case with Islamist anti-Semitism where myth and outright lies stand at the foundation of a xenophobic worldview that functions to identify and solidify its community. Put more succinctly, anti-Semitism has become a strategic political tool that functions to unify the Islamic world around an extreme and radical ideology that seeks to delegitimize Israel. Often, the Israeli-Jewish defensive stance is no match to the voluminous and vitriolic attacks on Jews and Israel. The dichotomy and incongruent identification of these two national identities is echoed by philosopher Frederick Dolan who maintains that "the most fateful characteristic" of the contemporary world order is "the replacement of experience by fiction," and that those who would seek to deal with the violence of inequality must first deal with the fabrication of collective identities. According to Dolan, "Ideology and the atomization of individuals combine . . . to form a 'fictitious world,' one that replaces the real world constituted in a genuine public sphere" (Dolan, 1994, p. 168). Indeed, the struggle against anti-Semitism is a struggle against long-held fictional beliefs that are embedded in people's psyche, their daily rhetoric, and myth-wrapping national narratives. Attempts to counter such fictions are often difficult. The case of Islamist anti-Semitism points to such fictions that are accepted as "facts."[3] But intense Islamist hatred of Jews was not always the case.

Islamist Anti-Semitism as a Political Tool

Islamic attitudes toward Judaism have for centuries been negative but also measured. In Islamic communities Jews (and Christians) were considered *dhimmis* — second-class citizens with limited but protected rights. The relationship between Islam and Judaism has guided attitudes toward Jews in a fairly systematic way for centuries. Traditional Islam did not develop nor support strong anti-Jewish sentiments. Historically, Islam has not been inherently anti-Semitic, and unlike Christianity, Islam does not consider itself as a new form of Judaism (Lewis, 1999, p. 118). The Prophet Muhammad fought the Jews of Medina and won, but that struggle was of minor consequence in Islamic history. Judaism and Islam are closer to each other than to Christianity (for example, the use of dietary laws) (Lewis, pp. 119-120), and though Islam carries some derogatory commentary toward Jews it did not promote intense polemics against them, the kind seen in Christianity (Lazarus-Yafeh in Wistrich, 1999, p. 112).

While at different periods in Islamic history Jews have fared better or worse, their treatment by Muslims was never as bad as under Christian rulers. There were no charges of "Jewish conspiracy" or "diabolic evil" such as poisoning wells and spreading the plague (Lewis, p. 122). Jews were considered a protected minority who, as the Quran states, "were afflicted with humiliation and poverty, and they felt the wrath of God. This was so because they used to disbelieve the signs of God and kill his messenger unjustly. This was because they disobeyed and transgressed" (the Quran, Chapter 2:61, cited in Lewis, p. 128). This is the prototype of the humiliated Jew that Islam has held for centuries. Yet, this historical prototype became incongruent with contemporary Judaism, and this explains much in the intense hostility toward contemporary Jews and Israel. Wistrich (2010) takes a different view whereby descriptions of tolerance between Muslims and Jews were not as idyllic as often described and that Zionism was not the cause for breakdowns in Islamic communities (p. 690). What is more probable is that Zionism became the scapegoat for many social struggles in the Islamic world at the end of the nineteenth century and the beginning of the twentieth century.

A change in the Islamic relationship with Jews takes a significant turn when Christian/Arab communities in the Middle East began to import European anti-Semitism. Islamic anti-Semitism was first precipitated by Arab Christians, a minority themselves, and primarily as a result of commercial competition that was actively supported by Christian missionaries and European emissaries in the Middle East (Lewis, p. 132). The introduction of anti-Semitism to the Arab world is also attributed to Greek and Catholic clergy, seeking to unify various nationalities during the growing ethnic strife during the final days of the Ottoman Empire.

One of the most infamous cases of anti-Semitism, the blood liable known as the *Damascus Affair* in 1840, was perpetrated by the French consul to that city. The first anti-Semitic tract, published in1869, and many thereafter, were translations from French. The *Dreyfus Affair* brought additional anti-Semitic tracts but also condemnations in the Arab world for such base racism. At times, the Ottoman authorities even prohibited the dissemination of anti-Semitic tracts considered a threat to public order (Lewis, pp. 133-137). However, during the last days of the Ottoman Empire anti-Semitism was also used by the authorities to argue that the success of the Young Turks was attributable to a Jewish plot (Lewis, p. 138). What is significant about this anti-Semitism is that the demonization of Jews, a staple of European anti-Semitism, is imported from Europe, that it set root in Islam prior to the systematic immigration of Jews to Palestine (which began in 1882), and that it commenced at about a century prior to the establishment of Israel in 1948. And though most historical accounts of anti-Semitism in Islam are explained as the result of Jewish immigration, especially during the 1920's and 1930's, and following the Balfour Declaration, the origin of anti-Semitism in the Middle East is much older and not the cause of Jews settling in Palestine. Anti-Semitism, then, is long established before the State of Israel was established, hence prior to any anti-Zionist or anti-Israeli rhetoric. A more accurate description of Islamist anti-Semitism in the Middle East is that it is initially a historical phenomenon and only later it has turned rhetorical, a persuasive means for differing objectives ends.

Even more surprising, given today's hostilities surrounding the Arab-Israeli conflict, are accounts of Arab support of the Zionist movement. Initial Arab attitudes toward the Zionist enterprise were rather supportive. Indeed, early reactions to Jewish settlements in Palestine, formalized in 1917 by the British Government under the Balfour Declaration, were quite encouraging. Ziwar Pasha who would later become Egypt's Prime Minister, participated in celebrating the Balfour Declaration. Zionist official, Frederick H. Kisch, met Egyptian officials in Cairo and reported their official support of the Zionist project and the rather conventional belief at the time in the prosperity of the region based on Jewish enterprises. In 1925, Egypt's Minister of the Interior traveled to Jerusalem to partake in the opening of the Hebrew University (Kuntzell, pp. 6-7, 16-18). Even in Palestine, reactions to Jewish settlers were not all antagonistic. While some Palestinians began to spread anti-Semitism as a means to opposing the Zionist project, others sought accommodation and even supported the Zionist movement in the form of signing petitions in support of Jewish immigration (Kuntzell, p. 37). In short, Zionism as movement to bring Jews back to their homeland was not only supported by several European states but also by governments, officials, and local leaders in the Near East. The more conventional description of unified Islamic opposition to Zionism from the outset is simply not true.

Islamism Meets Nazism

The initial positive sentiments toward the Zionist project, however, were soon replaced by vehement rejection of Zionism. A significant change took place in the 1930's, initiated by a combination of forces: the Husseinis, a powerful tribal clan in Palestine, the Muslim Brothers in Egypt, and most importantly, Nazi anti-Semitism. The Moslem Brothers, founded by Hassan al-Banna in 1928, ushered in the concept of jihad, a holy war against "Western decadence" and "Jewish amorality." In his essay "Industry of Death," Al-Banna advocated that Muslims should love death more than life. He also identified the enemy of Islam as the "Jews who were migrating to Palestine" (Kuntzell, pp. 12-15).

Al-Banna's activities were perfectly timed just as the Nazis began to infiltrate Egypt, fostering strong anti-Jewish attitudes. Though initial attempts to spread anti-Semitism failed with the Egyptian government objecting to such a policy, the threat of economic pressure, specifically the boycotting of Egypt's cotton export, brought the official change in attitude the Nazis sought (Kuntzell, pp. 18-19). By 1936, a significant change of attitude of Islam toward Jews took place. In Palestine, the Arab revolt against Jewish immigration commenced and, in Egypt, the Muslim Brothers associated their struggle with their brethren in Palestine. Yet, even at this stage the religious establishment in Egypt opposed the fermentation of Al-Banna and his movement. The rector of Al-Azhar even "forbade his Palestinian students from indulging in any anti-Jewish propaganda." As late as 1937, when the Peel Commission proposed a partition of Palestine, the Egyptian government, though officially opposed to an independent Jewish state, stated nonetheless its appreciation and respect for the Zionist ideal (Kuntzell, p. 22).

No other person, however, was as successful and tenacious in his anti-Semitism as the Grand Mufti of Jerusalem, Haj Al-Amin al-Husseini, who was the culprit for the significant change in attitudes toward Jews settling in Palestine. Al-Amin al-Husseini, whose anti-Semitism predates his cooperation with Nazi Germany, gained much from his alliance with Hitler's Germany. The Grand Mufti took control of the resistance to Zionism in 1929, and injected the secular movement with religious fervor, shifting "the emphasis to Islamic myth and to the defense of sacred Palestine and Jerusalem" (Rowland & Frank, 2002, p. 90). In so doing, he leaned heavily on the Muslim Brotherhood's brand of Islamism in developing the resistance to Jews and Zionism. Indeed, from the 1930's to today Islamist anti-Semitism, the one developed by the Grand Mufti, is a bland of twentieth-century fundamentalist interpretation of early Islam and Nazi anti-Semitism.[4]

The Peel Commission of 1937, which called for a partition of Palestine into an Arab and Jewish states, made it clear to Nazi Germany that a Jewish state was not in Germany's interest and thus the official embracing of the Grand Mufti as their person in the Middle East. Though the Grand Mufti's anti-Semitism gained much from Nazi anti-Semitism, it is founded, among others, on the teaching of Rashid Rida, a Saudi Wahhabite who also influenced Al-Banna (Kuntzell, pp. 31-34). The Nazi support and encouragement allowed the Grand Mufti to have the means to push for his view of the Zionist project against more moderate forces that were seeking accommodation and even supported the plan for a partition of Palestine. Indeed, the support for the partition plan was quite widespread among local Muslims, but the Mufti who tolerated no opposition to his power, ushered multiple attacks on Jewish as well as on Arab brethrens. All told, in the final tally, more Palestinians died at the hands of the Grand Mufti than Jews (Kuntzell, pp. 51-52).

The Nazi regime found in Middle Eastern Arabs the allies against England as well as staunch supporters in the plan to annihilate Jews. It did not take much convincing to turn Nazi propaganda also as a tool to confront Jewish immigration into Palestine. Nazi encouragement of the Muslim Brothers and the Husseinis came with financial aid and a propaganda expertise that included the use pamphlets and radio broadcasts to sway public opinion against Jews and their supposedly "atrocities" in Palestine. The radio broadcasts by Germany to the Islamic world were most extensive and effective, reaching millions of Muslims in several languages and local dialects. The broadcasts were replete with anti-Semitic statements and it is little wonder that traces of European and especially German anti-Semitism became familiar in the Arab world. The propaganda campaign succeeded in gradually shifting Arab and Islamic public opinion against the Zionist project (Kuntzell, pp. 24-25).

Following the Arab-Israeli war of 1948, Sayyid Qutb, who in his essay titled "Our Struggle with the Jews," written in 1950, constructed the shift from the Jews as *dhimmis* — a protected but also humiliated minority that lived in Islamic world — into an evil entity (Nettler, in Curtis, pp. 98-100). He did so by pointing to hostile acts Jews displayed toward the Prophet as justification for contemporary Islamist hatred toward Jews; a hostility that was not realized nor expressed centuries earlier. But what exactly has transpired during Muhammad's experience with the Jews that had now become the source for a new Islamist anti-Semitism? The tract takes its cue from the difficulties Muhammad had with the Jews and their refusal to accept his preaching, tension that have transpired in a time and a place when Islam's political and social destiny was beginning to be established but also challenged (Nettler, pp. 98-99).

Qutb's "Our Struggle with Jews" was based on both Quranic and early non-Quranic sources constructing an eternal hatred of Jews (Nettler, p. 100).[5] Qutb writes the following:

> The Jews confronted Islam with enmity from the moment the Islamic state was established in Medina. They plotted against the Muslim Community from the first day it became a community. The Quran [in fact] contained directives and suggestions concerning this [Jewish] enmity and plot. These directives were sufficient to portray this bitter war which the Jews launched against Islam, the Messenger of Allah [Muhammad], and the Muslim Community during its long history. This is a war which has not been extinguished, even for one moment, for close on fourteen centuries, and which continues until this moment, its blaze raging in all corners of the earth. (p. 102)

Qutb writes that the "struggle between Islam and the Jews continues in force and will thus continue, because the Jews will be satisfied only with the destruction of this religion [Islam]." Finally, states Qutb, "Anyone who leads this Community away from its Religion and its Quran can only be a Jewish agent — whether he does this wittingly or unwittingly, willingly or unwillingly." No doubt, the war of 1948 etched in the Arab world as *The Catastrophe* (*Nakba*) precipitated this document, yet it has become since very influential with radical and fundamentalist sections of Islam (Nettler, pp. 103-105). Qutb also opined that Jews deserve the Holocaust and Hitler's punishment because they are "the source of evil in the world." Wistrich (2010) writes that "according to Qutb, the struggle [with the Jews] had to be redefined as a war of religion waged by Judaism (representing defective and corrupted truth) against the final and absolute truth of Allah" (p. 49). As I have noted earlier, ultimate terms drive anti-Semitism and, when put in a theological setting, their influence is profound. The hierarchy Qutb outlines is similar to those observed in Christian theology in antiquity and through the Middle Ages; that of putting Judaism, the paternal/maternal religion from whence both derive, as submissive to both and thus eager to destroy Christianity and now Islam. This narrative is much more appealing than the admission of the historical timeline of all three religions.

For Qutb and his followers, writes Kuntzell insightfully, that "not only is everything Jewish evil, but everything evil is Jewish" (p. 84). A profound yet subtle rhetorical shift transforms an association between two disparate entities, Jews and evil, to a causal link whereby the association between Judaism and evil is reversed in order to present all evil as caused by Jews. Such a profound link allows for a persistent worldview and an easy explanation/convenient rationalization that often fits a reason for things gone badly. Rhetorically, then, anti-Semitism is generic, a fitting response that is so familiar and functional that its use is a preferred mode of operation as it has already secured previous adherents.

This accusation against the Jews of Muhammad's time and since is rather similar to the one made by early Christians about their expectations that Jews should accept the newly founded religion and, once they rejected the efforts, hatred settled in. Also similar to initial and long-standing Christian theology, the struggle between Islam and Judaism was constructed in the twentieth century as eternal and necessary now that Islam sought to defend itself against "aggressive" Judaism. Qutb also adds a conspiratorial caveat, whereby anyone not following the Quran must be an agent of the Jews, whether they know it or not. As Wistrich opines, political Islam requires a conspiracy (2010, p. 806). Such is the case against the Jews: tight an uncompressing, and with no alternative explanation in this all-consuming charge.

But why resort to anti-Semitism in the first place? Because, for Al-Banna, Qutb, Al-Husseini, and those supporting Islamist Jihad, the religious cause is central to Islam and, in the Palestinian struggle, they had the perfect religious grounds. It was from Jerusalem that the Prophet Muhammad is said to have been taken to the heavens and thus "only the struggle over Palestine could be inflated into a life and death issue." Jerusalem which for centuries was not featured prominently in Islamic concern has become one of Islam's holiest cities, functioning as the ideal means for a movement's cause — the unification of the Islamic world and the re-establishment of the new Caliphate. In short, "only Palestine offered the starting point from which the *umma*, the community of all the world's Muslims, could be united behind one and the same goal" (Kuntzell, p. 58). The Jew portrayed as the evil "other" became the primary means and therefore the target of this struggle. The scapegoat mechanism and the "means-to-an-end" logic that can be found throughout the history of anti-Semitism is the device that Islamists have used close to a century of Jewish-Arab tension.

What is striking in recent and contemporary Islamist references to Jews is the significant departure from the minor role the Quran subscribes to Jews and a growing obsession with the Jew as evil and the cause of all the problems in the Islamic world (Lewis, p. 193). This obsession and occupation of Arab media, the result of the radicalization of the Arab world especially since the 1950's, is aptly described as the "Islamization of Jewish imagery" (Yadlin in Wistrich, p. 316). The obsession with the Jew also functions as a way to rationalize the continuous defeat by the hands of those prototyped for centuries as weak, humiliated and cowardly.

The Islamist anti-Semitism of the past century is based on two different contexts: the first and short phase of Mecca when Muhammad's struggle with various pagan tribes was supported by Jews. Muhammad learned much from his Jewish neighbors and the Islamic reference to the Jews as the "People of the Book [the Bible]" is attributed to this peaceful period. The second experience is related to Muhammad's emigration to Medina when he and his followers began to spread Islam and the Jews resisted his efforts to accept the new religion. The antagonism toward Jews sprung from the Jewish resistance to Muhammad's efforts, and this struggle found its way into verses in the Quran. Yet, the verses cited today as the cause of much hatred were rarely used to promote serious antagonism until they became the foundation of Islamist anti-Semitism in the twentieth century. Such verses describe Jews as changed by Allah into apes and pigs (cited in Sura 5 verse 60), and that Allah describes Jews as "Be ye apes, despised and rejected" (cited in Kuntzell, p. 77).

After being beaten by the Meccans who put a siege of Medina, Muhammad slaughtered many Jews as a means to asserting his authority. The Jews of Medina, then, were but a convenient group whose slaughter was meant to project fear of Muhammad's rule and a lesson to anyone seeking to resist the Prophet. Subsequent tradition has justified the killing of Jews by claiming their challenge to the Prophet (Kuntzell, p. 65). Thus, a non-religious but a political struggle has been given a religious cover as if to justify murder. The post-hoc logic of Islam's hatred of Jews is but a likely excuse for the unjustified attack on them that included killing of the entire Jewish community. Once such sentiments were inscribed religiously, perhaps out of guilt of the unwarranted murder, the theological cover and its sanctioning power were sealed. Thus, contemporary anti-Semitism is rationalized as justified by the sanctity of Islamic scriptures, allowing for a persuasive narrative that is timeless, scared, and therefore, warranted, though the original cause for this attitude is rather suspect.

This intensified narrative that has grounded the Al-Banna, Qutb, and Husseini brand of Islamist rhetoric, is operating today in the Arab and the Islamic world whereby Israel's very existence is rejected, where most attitudes toward it are rationalized in anti-Semitic terms, and where the Holocaust is denied. Historical and political explanations in comprehending Israel and Zionism are discounted, relying instead on anti-Semitism as the sole explanation of historical forces, and a direct link between Nazi and Islamist anti-Semitism is clearly the case. What is intriguing about this connection is the Islamists' rejection of the Holocaust while at the same time wishing Hitler was more successful in murdering all Jews. Even more intriguing is the frequent accusations of of engaging in Nazi-like behavior. In choosing to accuse Israel as a Nazi-like regime, Islamists hope to deflect the very behavior and ideology they have adopted for decades. Knowing rather well what the Nazis did to the Jews, what could be more painful to Jews than to accuse them of behaving like those who tortured and exterminated them? Yet, this accusation makes the denial of the Holocaust such an incongruent argument.

Kuntzell argues that the "consequences of this historiographical gap are huge and play a decisive role in the Arab-Jewish conflict to this day. As long as it continues to deny the Shoah [Holocaust], Islamism can continue to explain international support for the establishment of Israel in 1947 in exclusively antisemitic terms." Thus for example, in a lecture at Gaza's Islamic University, a history professor could declare that the Holocaust did not happen and that concentration camps such as Dachau or Auschwitz were but disinfection facilities, while another university official asked that Arabs "show the Jews no mercy, regardless of where they are, regardless of which country. When you meet them, kill them" (cited in Kuntzell, p. 105). The denial of mass murder and the advocacy of mass murder are the twin rhetorical staples of contemporary Islamist anti-Semitism.

The attractiveness of the Nazi anti-Semitism offers Islamists a favorable rhetorical stance whereby opposition to the State of Israel is rationalized as a rejection of a state that was created out of the ashes of the Holocaust. This event, the Arab world argues, was caused by Europeans and not by Muslims, and thus Palestinians should not suffer the consequences of Jewish colonialism. This rhetorical stance is persuasive as it identifies a clear cause for the establishment of the State of Israel while also exonerating Palestinians from having any hand in this process and consequently, justifying their struggle for their own homeland. However, although this rhetorical stance is convenient, it is only partially correct. As stated earlier, anti-Semitism enters the Middle East around 1840, some hundred years before the State of Israel was created. Immigration to Palestine began some sixty years prior to the establishment of the State of Israel. The Balfour Declaration, which advocated a Jewish homeland, was issued some thirty years prior to the Holocaust, and the British Mandate, issued by the League of Nations in 1919, instructing England to assist in the formation of Jewish homeland by building the institutions of a forthcoming state, came on the heels of World War I. Whatever arguments have been brought into this history, the fact remains that a state in formation began decades prior to the Holocaust, and though the Holocaust may have expedited the formation of the State of Israel and pressured England to end its Mandate, a Jewish State was in the making since the 1920's with, for example, distinct governing institutions and labor unions.

But this complex historical account is not supportive of the Arab and Islamist narrative whereas Nazi anti-Semitism is easily transformed into God and Devil terms, hence its preferred use. Subsequently, as Yadlin has shown, the portrayal of Jews as the devil, a demon, or a Nazi in contemporary Arab-Muslim journalism is the result of selecting preferred images as well as the adoption of Christian anti-Semitism (Yadlin, p. 310). Yadlin also contends that narratives "are particularly powerful in the contemporary Arab-Muslim world, where language has for centuries exerted a special fascination" (Yadlin, p. 310). In the Arab-Muslim world, "words are aggrandized by the deep love and appreciation of language, its nuances, rhythm, and incantation," and that the power of language is especially acute in the public domain (Yadlin, p. 311). The power of language in the Arab-Muslim world is considered "the fiercest and most severe of all wars" (cited in Yadlin, p. 312). In the context of the Arab-Israeli conflict, words take on an added importance given the perception in the Arab world that "The 'Hebrew State' fully realizes that in the modern world every author is an explosive, every writer a combat commander" (Hamid Rabi cited in Yadlin, p. 312).

Not surprising, the Star of David, the metonymy for *both Judaism and the State of Israel*, when viewed in the contemporary Arab world, is symbolic of "a major abomination." Such an abomination has given light to numerous charges whose purpose is extreme hatred. A study by Dr. Muhammed Jala Idris of Tanta University in Egypt considers the Jews as not belonging to the world of sane people; that they are deranged and that, after careful studies, has concluded that the Jewish personality "is abnormal, irregular, marked by considerable deviation and derangement" (cited in Yadlin, p. 313). A book published in Egypt in 1992 repeats medieval blood libels, claiming that the Jewish Matza (the unleavened bread eaten on Passover) is made with Christian blood (cited in Yadlin, p. 314). One prominent Egyptian journalist claims that Jewish physicians in Egypt "tend to specialize in obstetrics in order to abort Muslim women and eliminate future generations of gentiles" (cited in Yadlin, p. 314). And the editor-in-chief of an Egyptian weekly writes that the Jew "has not changed for thousands of years. He is base, contemptible, scorns all moral values, gnaws on live flesh and sucks blood for a pittance . . . let us cast aside this distinction (between Jews and Israelis) and talk about the Jews" (cited in Yadlin, p. 318). Such contemporary depictions, argues Yadlin, are possible because "the negative attitudes toward Jews are taken to be self-evident maxims" (p. 313).

While in traditional Islam, Jews fought the prophet and lost and their struggle is afforded "a certain dignity and courage," contemporary attitudes toward Jews attributes to them all "that befell the Islamic world in early as in later times" (Lewis, p. 196). The gap between the traditional humility portrayal of Jews and contemporary display of Israel's military might is rationalized in contemporary Islam as a Jewish plot to avenge earlier loses to Islam and to gain strength through cunning and conspiracies. This rationalization sits better in the mind of Arabs who had to explain how the prototype of a people known as weak and meek managed to win several wars against Arab armies (Lewis, p. 197). The return of Jews to their ancient land and the creation of the State of Israel resulted in a rhetorical dilemma for the Arab world by disrupting the traditional Islamic narrative. The inconsistency between the Jew-*dhimmi* and the Jew-Israeli was solved not by changing attitudes toward Jews but by rejecting the new image of the Jew. Self-blame is never easy and rarely exercised. It is much easier to resort to a conspiratorial explanation, the kind that will keep the Arab narrative coherent. The need to extricate Jews from the Middle East narrataively and subsequently, physically is necessary then for the fidelity of the Islamic narrative.

For the Israeli delegation, as well as members of other delegations, Islamist anti-Semitism displayed at the Durban Conference brought the realization that the large reservoir of European and especially Nazi anti-Semitism is now appearing in the guise of anti-Zionism and that "an early Christian invention has now become the province of Islam" (Salpeter, 2004). Hal Lindsay dubbed the Durban Conference as "The U.N.'s Wansee Conference," after the infamous Nazi Wansee conference that planned the "Final Solution" to exterminate European Jewry (*WorldNetDaily*, Sept., 5, 2001). The context of the Durban Conference and the rhetorical text it presented in speeches, pamphlets, demonstrations, slogans and banners, reiterated familiar arguments often lashed against Israel in recent years. What was new to Israeli and Jewish experience in Durban was the intensity, depth and extent of the anti-Semitism voiced at the Conference, and that anti-Semitism and anti-Israeli sentiments took center stage, diverting attention from the original objectives of the Conference.

A recent report by the *Israeli Intelligence and Terrorism Information Center* calls Islamist anti-Semitism a strategic threat to Israel. The semi-official study center considers the intensification of Islamist anti-Semitism not a theoretical prejudice but an ideological incitement whose aim is to prevent a peaceful solution to the Arab-Israeli and Palestinian-Israeli conflicts. At the heart of contemporary Islamist anti-Semitism is an elimination ideology that is spreading in the Islamic world, calling on Israel to be destroyed. And while European anti-Semitism has grounded Islamist anti-Semitism in adopting various cabals and canards such as the forged *Protocols of the Elders of Zion*, contemporary Islamist anti-Semitism, in turn, is now being exported to Islamic communities world-wide (Rettig, 2008).

Indeed, one of the most frequent refrains used in the context of the Arab-Israeli and Israeli-Palestinian conflict is questioning "Israel's right to exist." The rhetorical implication of this seemingly naïve and commonly used phrase is clear — that perhaps Israel has no right to exist. This is the ultimate objective of many in the Arab world and its repetition is meant to hammer this notion and perpetuate the aspiration of a completely Islamic Middle East. The irony of it all is that just when attempts in various circles in Western Europe, well exemplified in 1965 by Vatican II's official rejection of the collective guilt of Jews for killing Christ, and introducing a significant step in seeking to end anti-Semitism, the Arab world turned more anti-Semitic, borrowing heavily from the same tracts that Europe began to repudiate.

After Israel won the Six Day war of 1967, Arab leaders declared that "Jews had strayed from the Law of Moses, killed Jesus, and were cursed by God through the Prophets forever" (Fakenheim, 1986, p. 33). European anti-Semitism has moved to the Near East, complete with all the prejudices from ancient times, through the Middle-Ages, and to the modern era. Its reliance on religious anti-Semitism is clearly standing at the foundation of this transformation. As Emile Fakenheim (1986) suggests, "the post-Holocaust transformation of anti-Semitism is 'anti-Zionism'," and reflecting a sobering note about this transformation he states that before the State of Israel, anti-Semites argued that Jews had no right to exist but after 1948, their argument is that Israel has no right to exist (p. 36).

Not only did the Arab world turn anti-Israeli sentiments into anti-Semitism after 1967, many outside the Middle East turned anti-Semitism into anti-Zionism, and for the same reason, that of seeing Israel win in the Six Day War as transformative whereby Israel changed from a vulnerable state to a powerful one (Fakenheim, p. 55). Indeed, the Six Day War of 1967, as the impetus for new anti-Semitism, has frequently been used in the Arab world to rationalize the change from anti-Semitism to anti-Zionism. This rather quick transformation though begs the question whether the 1967 war was a cause or just a convenient pretext. If it was a cause in the West, it was due to the changing perception of the post-Holocaust Jew; the victim being transformed into the Israeli-Jew the victimizer. Such a perception, argues Wistrich (2010) allowed some Europeans to feel absolved of the Holocaust guilt and perhaps this is the real motive. Anti-Zionism has given many European still suffering from the "hidden anxiety . . . at their belated realization of the enormity of the crime in which they were so deeply implicated," a way out (Jankelevitch in Wistrich, 2010, p. 502 and p. 631). Accordingly, "anti-Zionism was likely to provide the providential and unexpected opportunity for much-needed relief, for it offered the freedom, the right, and perhaps even the duty to be anti-Semitic in the name of democracy" (cited in Wistrich, p. 631).

If at issue is just a convenient excuse, then it is clear that old stereotypes are hard to change and that the post-Holocaust lull waited for the opportunity to resume hating Jews. In the Arab world, the transformation was a likely excuse given the reality that Zionism, at least in a spiritual form, has already been in existence for some seventy years prior to the establishment of the state of Israel. The creation of Israel has revived in the Arab world Muhammad's own difficulties with Jews of Medina whereby sentiments about Jews that were peripheral for Muslims for centuries have become central to various arguments whose ultimate objective is to challenge Israeli's existence.

Jewish refusal to accept first Christianity and later Islam has been cited as the primary "justification" for anti-Semitism in both religions. Indeed, both religions have displayed either an inherent misunderstanding of Judaism (or the relationship Jews have with their God), or worse, they have advocated a purposeful conversion whose failure was known in advance. Both religions have also advanced the argument about the superiority of their respective religion, thus presenting Judaism, at best, as inferior, and at worst, as null and void. These erroneous premises have manifested themselves in the rather naïve expectation that Jews would quickly abandon their millennia-old religion and embrace the new religion. Since both religions are based on Judaism and the Jewish Bible, adoption of the new religions, the assumption goes, should have been an easy step.

It is also baffling to ponder Islam's criticism of Jews for rejecting not only Muhammad but Christ as well. If one follows this logic, what would have happened if Jews have accepted Christ; clearly they could not have also accepted Muhammad's Islam. Yet, behind this assumption stands the serious notion that as replacement of Judaism, Jews must embrace the new religion otherwise the continued existence of Judaism is seen as posing a challenge to the new religions. This challenge could be taken as either Judaism's questioning the merit of the Christianity or Islam, or that both religions, for inherent doubt thereof are not keen on seeing Judaism exist. Therein lies the basic motive for anti-Semitism and in that motive is hateful rhetoric. As long as Judaism survives, Christianity and Islam will likely remain uncomfortable about their respective theological and foundational claims unless the theology is modified.

The motives for hateful rhetoric that stand behind such doubts and uncertainties are clearly present when one examines the invective against Jews portrayed as a needed defense of Islam against the "aggressor" Jews who seek to destroy it. Here the rhetorical process is fully displayed whereby Jews, victims of Islamic attacks, are portrayed as aggressors, and if the portrayal of the Jew as aggressor is accepted then the only solution against the aggressor is his complete annihilation. Israel, no doubt, has done enough to cement the "aggressor" accusation by building a strong military, winning wars, occupying the West Bank, and attacking Lebanon and Gaza. That its actions have been arguably defensive and often as means of survival are discounted in such an analysis, leaving the aggression charge decontextualized. The struggle against the Jew is therefore uncompromising and no matter how false its reasoning and how manipulative the history from which the invectives are drawn, the rhetoric is fundamental and it requires complete obedience. Only rhetoric can turn a victim into a victimizer and a defenseless into an aggressor, hence rhetoric's function as a powerful weapon.

Ostensibly, regardless of the gap between original historical account and contemporary interpretations thereof, what counts today, argues Nettler, is that "Islam's historical memory of these allegations has been long and strong." And so, "if for medieval Christianity the Jews were a deicide people, here for Islam they were a *potential* destroyer of creed and society." And when Israel was created centuries later, "this koranic accusation became a 'proof text' that contemporary Muslim thinkers could invoke in building their response to Islam's contemporary Jewish problem." Finally, Nettler's thesis is most significant; that the "Jews were both metaphor and literal instrument of the secularization that had wrecked contemporary Islam" (Nettler, p. 99). As a metaphor, the Jew is the prerequisite counter-agent needed for the coherency of the fidelity of the Islamic narrative whereby one's illustrious narrative requires an evil "other" as the protagonist for the narrative to be coherent and complete.

The larger implications of Islamist anti-Semitism bring us back to the tried-and-true anti-Semitism of Christendom. In a striking parallel with the Christian messianism of the end of days, culminated with the arrival of Christ, *again* (following Armageddon, which includes great war, upheaval, death, destruction and the conversion of Jews to Christianity), Muslims await the final hour that will come only if all Jews are killed. Shi'ites, in particular await the Imam-Mahdi, whose arrival would involve a terrible war and untold suffering that ultimately would usher a new Shi'ite rule in the world (Sharon, 2008). The 15th day of the Muslim month of Shaban is considered one of the holiest days in the Shi'ite calendar, the birthday of the 12th Imam, known as the *mehdi*, or the hidden savior, whose return at the end of days would herald a messianic era ("Mullahs in Space," 2008; Wistrich, 2010, pp. 884). In both Christianity and Islam, the hope for the end of days, conceived in messianic terms, is impossible without the intervention of Jews as the primary agency in, and of, the narrative. The Jew carries an important sign imprinted on his sought dead body — the ushering of the end of days, the arrival of the savior (Christ or the Mehdi), and the implementation of ultimate peace and good-will. But for such a utopia to be realized the Jew has to die.

Anti-Semitism in the Middle-Ages and now in the Middle-East has remained the mechanism of mass persuasion and the tool-box for societies seeking to manage their attitudes and belief systems, preserve power and avoid internal strife by constantly pointing the finger at a common enemy — the Jews-Israel — as the scapegoat. Anti-Semites have done so, often by constructing antagonistic entities to depict a simplistic good-versus-evil struggle. Such depictions are possible because the corresponding narratives can easily be transformed into an attractive and a salient myth or foundational tales.

Of all the charges, the opposition to Israel's existence and the hatred of Jews displayed at the Durban Conference were the most salient and indicative of a renewed anti-Semitism as a vehicle to confront Israel. The question of Israel's right to exist was taken as a serious warning, the kind that Kenneth Burke forwarded in his seminal essay "The Rhetoric of Hitler's *Battle*." To borrow from Burke's methods of analysis, Hitler's language in his autobiography *Mein Kampf* fully described his motives and since motives are indicative of planned actions, all the more the reason to heed such ominous words (Burke, 1941, pp. 744-757). Indeed, Hitler's *Mein Kampf* showed just how far he would go with his anti-Semitism and that he intended to "purify" Germany of its Jews — a short hand reference for killing them. These sentiments ground current Islamist ideology as the words used by Islamists ought to be understood as clear indications of motives.

Islamists such as Iranian president, Mahmood Ahmedinejad, who has denied that the Holocaust ever existed, employ the Nazi rhetoric used against Jews in the 1930's. Islamists' rhetoric of hate is replete with Nazi symbols, Nazi cartoons, and Nazi discourse; the source of this rhetoric could not be clearer. What is shocking about this rhetorical strategy is not just the contradiction between the denial of the Holocaust and the frequent use of Nazi symbols, but rather the fact that Islamist rhetoric denies the Holocaust while at the same time it is replete with statements about the need to destroy Israel and kill Jews — in short, a Holocaust. Equally shocking is the fact that these statements which began to be made in Islamist circles only few years after the Holocaust are widespread in contemporary Islamist world. This ideology is now owned by Islamists — be they by Iran, Hamas or Hizbullah. So, while denying that the Nazis ever executed a plan to the exterminate European Jewry, Islamists have not been hesitant to state their plan to do the same.

Yet, the question remains: Why the denial of the Holocaust and the wish to plan for it? There are several reasons for this inconsistency. First, because such a denial is sure to anger Jews and Israel, denying Jews their own narrative of a lingering trauma. Second, because the Holocaust is seen, especially in the Islamic world, as a legitimating act for the establishment of Israel, a "cause" that Islamists wish to erase from the narrative of the Middle East. Third, Islamic anti-Semitism today is not only based on Nazi anti-Semitism; it wishes to do one better – to "succeed" where Hitler failed. The denial, then, is meant to obscure a similar plan. Indeed, one repeated refrain by Islamists is the lamentation, as evidenced at Durban, that Hitler did not completely succeed in his plan to exterminate Jews. Of course, this sentiment contradicts that assertion that the Holocaust did not take place. But who pays attention to such minor inconsistencies?

If Israel's right to exist is challenged and its "behavior" is described as racist and Nazi- and apartheid-like, then the motives for its annihilation are present and can be considered "legitimate." Indeed, some of Israel's practices against the Arab residents of the occupied territories are harsh and sometimes, counter-productive, but the terrorism against Israel is muted if not ignored altogether. Israel's actions are rarely contextualized and instead are quick to be equated with behavior of autocratic or ruthless regimes. Using Burke's terminology, the recipe for killing is present once the language of killing is present and the narrative around it appears reasonable. In his passage "The Kill and the Absurd," Burke argues that if the image of killing is stressed more than the dialectic of a given conflict, "such a doctrine leads *towards* the Holocaust rather then *away from it*" (emphasis in the original) and that "the slogans of the Absurd can easily transform a truth into half-truth" (Burke, 1953, p. 254).

Conclusion

The racism accusation against Israel and Durban can be seen as an attempt to intensify the tension between the Islamic world and Israel, just when talks of compromise and accommodations were underway. Accusations of racism are value laden and thus emotional and deep, and not easily mitigated, whereas political and territorial conflicts are factual and material, can yield a stasis, and are, therefore, potentially soluble. Anti-Semitism and racism, whether consciously or not, make it impossible to reach a peaceful resolution and to find a comprise formula.

With a bit of hindsight, the Durban conference, the attacks of September 11, 2001, only few days later, the ensuing US war in Iraq, the insurgency in Iraq thereafter, and Al-Quida attacks elsewhere, have ushered in a new era of geo-political upheaval and multiple conflicts. Israel is often drawn into these conflicts even without having any direct or even an indirect link to any of them. The hallmark of putting Israel at the center of these conflicts has been consistently the same — anti-Semitism as a means to an end; that of blaming the Jewish presence in the Middle East as offensive to Islam. Hence, Islamic rejection of Israel as a legitimate state is today no longer just anti-Zionist; it is anti-Semitic, and as such it points to the primary motive at hand — that of scapegoating — seeking a convenient "evil-other" to obviate internal strife, dictatorial and theocratic regimes, poverty and many other societal ills that are difficult to solve. The Jew-Israel is the vessel for exporting domestic challenges to an external foe everyone loves to hate.

The vehement anti-Semitism in Durban was an exemplar of contemporary attitudes and thinking in the Arab and the Islamic world that featured Nazi propaganda statements combined with anti-Israeli rhetoric. The Durban conference made clear that anti-Semitism and anti-Israeli diatribes are indistinguishable and are borne of the same anti-Semitic source. Had the protestors in Durban limited their vehemence to anti-Israeli sentiments, they might have engaged in more legitimate criticism of Israel. When Islamists accepted and adopted the Nazi version of anti-Semitism during the 1930's, the Holocaust was yet to take place. Islamists invested heavily in building their propaganda machine and did so with much help from Nazi Germany, both financially and ideologically. That the Holocaust would later be factored in a sympathetic worldview about hasting the creation of the Jewish State of Israel, was clearly not the outcome for which Islamists hoped. As a matter of fact, the very Nazi anti-Semitism Islamists adopted would ill serve the Islamist world once the horror of the Holocaust became known. This simple fact explains why denying the Holocaust is one of the Islamists' most frequent refrain as are the attempts to describe Israel and Israelis as Nazi like. Rhetorically, the guilt of ill-advised policy would be purged under constant attacks of Israel and its "Nazi" acts whereby the victim of Nazi Germany has become the victimizer of Palestinians. With this balancing act, narrative coherency has been restored and its mass influence remains effective.

The convenient argument often cited in the Arab world that the creation of the State of Israel— the consequences of the Holocaust — should not have come at the expense of the Palestinians since they had nothing to do with Holocaust. But this argument goes only so far; clearly, many in the Near East listened attentively to Nazi Propaganda broadcasts whose anti-Semitic impact would last until the present day Middle-East. Finally, the key Palestinian leader in the 1930's and 1940's has been supportive of Hitler and his "final solution," was a guest of the Nazi leadership in Berlin, opposed the Nazi's plan to allow 5,000 Jewish children to leave Germany (these children were not saved), and took special interest in preventing the governments of several Balkan nations under Nazi control to allow several thousands of Jews to emigrate to Palestine. After the war, Yugoslavia would put Al-Husseini on the list of war criminals for his role as "organizer of the Muslim SS division on Bosnia-Herzegovina" (Kuntzel, 2007, p. 36, 45).

As Kuntzell writes, "Al-Qa'ida and the other Islamist groups are guided by an anti-Semitic ideology that was transferred to the Islamic world in the Nazi period" (p. xxiii). Kuntzel's thesis is that "Jihad and Jew-hated belong together," and therefore "the struggle against jihadism . . . requires zero tolerance for anti-Semitism" (p. 149). Since the premise of this volume is the exploration of the rhetoric of hate in order to bring it to an end, it is important to note Kuntzell's key argument: That if anti-Semitism of contemporary Islam is not taken seriously, no solution to the Arab-Israeli conflict is going to be possible. It is equally plausible that those espousing anti-Semitism in the context of the Arab-Israeli conflict, do not wish to see an end to the conflict. Exposing this very notion may be important to any solution to the Arab-Israeli conflict.

Notes

1. The final statement of the UN conference in Durban was so inflammatory to Israel and Jews, that organizations such as Amnesty International,

Human Rights Watch and others "dissociated themselves from the offensive language." The refusal of the Secretary General of the conference to submit the final NGO document spoke loudly of how troubled were the conference officials with its outcome (Schechter, p. 180).

2.   Given the prevalence of conspiracy theories about Israel's involvement in the September 11, 2001 attack on the World Trade Centers, the Department of State issued a report rejecting these conspiracies. See, "The 4,000 Jews Rumor," Bureau of International Information Programs, U.S. Department of State, November 16, 2007.

3.   I am using the term "Islamist" as distinct of "Islamic" in order to distinguish between those in Islam who are bent on anti-Semitism — the hatred of Jews and Judaism— and those who do not take such a view. Not all Muslims subscribe to anti-Semitism and the rhetoric of hatred. By implication, being anti-Israel is not to be equated with being anti-Semitic.

4.   For a detailed documentation of the direct connection between Islamism and Nazism, and the role Husseini played in fermenting a hatred that was not experienced previously, see, Kuntzell, 2007, pp. 6-60.

5.   Note the take on Hitler's Mein Kampf (My Struggle) in Qutb's title.

8

The Diabolic Jew and Visualization of Anti-Semitism

The process of persuasion is not limited to verbal statements, as non-verbal cues and images can be as persuasive and oftentimes offer even richer persuasive cues and suggestive context for action. Patriotism, for example, is often triggered not only by verbal appeals but can be intensified by the sight of one's national symbols such as the flag. Specific symbols, such as the swastika, can stand metonymically for an entire political entity and ideology. Likewise, the iconography or visual rhetoric in Judaism, Christianity, and Islam can cue believers into historical and foundational markings of origin, basic narrative, myth, and theology. These visual images are part of the larger religious context and ritual, meant to reinforce theological directions and commitments as well as to differentiate the "in" group from those outside, or the "us" from "them."

Images that can carry important function in reinforcing religious beliefs can also draw clear markings of separation between those of other religions. Hatred, then, is often the means for such separation, promoting hatred in order to erect a wall between believers and non-believers. In the case of anti-Semitism, diabolical images of the Jew are as old as Christianity, and to a lesser degree in Islam, and they tell much of the story of the relationship between these fratricidal religions. Indeed, one of the more worrisome aspect of anti-Semitism is the role of visual rhetoric in Christianity. Despite the formal decision to repudiate anti-Semitism by the Catholic Church in Vatican II, as well as by other Christian denominations, the implications of such images and their continued rich meaning and persuasive function, continue to perpetuate long-standing attitudes of hatred, dislike, and suspicion. While formal policies that sought to bring anti-Semitism to an end have done much to confront anti-Semitism, the visual rhetoric of Christianity has remained fundamental and, at times, incongruent with the verbal uttering of closeness and friendship. Probably not fully realized or easily amenable to change or modification, Christian iconography and images have continued to impact anti-Semitism: iconographic images of the Church in general, and the cross in particular, have done much to solidify negative attitudes toward Jews. Added to these images, those visual images depicting Jews as the devil and the ruler of Satan, and the overall picture is of a consistent pattern of hostility toward Jews.

Indeed, the visual depictions of Jews are quite often rooted in anti-Semitism. One needs only to consider visual distinctions between Judaism and Christianity to find images and visual texts that compliment and sharpen the focus on specific religious narratives and attitudes. One feature that distinguishes Judaism from Christianity is that the Jewish deity is anti-visual whereas the deity of Christianity is most visual. In Christianity and Islam, supremacy of its deity is assigned to a human being. Not so in Judaism, as no human being has risen to the level of a Christ or a Muhammad. God alone is the only central figure of the deity. Taken from the perspective of the body, the deity in Judaism is body-less while in Christianity and Islam, the deity is body rich. In Judaism no person is considered God or is associated with the authority of having any familial relationship with God.

It stands to reason, then, that in Judaism religious imagery is rather constrained, abiding by religious sanctions against the creation of images of God and iconography in general. On the other hand, Christianity in particular is rich in iconography and visual texts. Yet, for a religion that emanated from Judaism and whose primary claim for centuries has been that it has replaced it, the gap in visual rhetoric is not only revealing but indicative of the larger divide between theological claims and practices. When considering the foundations and practices of anti-Semitism, the richness of visual rhetoric in Christianity has been instrumental in its fermentation and sustainability. From the cross to diabolical images of Jews, to passion plays that reinforced foundational narratives, these visuals have provided centuries of negative images of Jews. One has to recall the controversy surrounding Mel Gibson's *The Passion of Christ* (2007) film to realize its charge of deicide in the most horrific visual depictions and the strong emotions it evokes in believers and non-believers. Such visuals have been part and parcel of the history of Christian anti-Semitism. The direct consequence of these images has been the perpetuation of the guilt Jews supposedly carry in Jesus' crucifixion. These negative images have complemented as well as reinforced written narratives about the Jews' role in killing Christ and their evil rituals and practices.

The Cross as an Instrument of Death: The cross is an instrument of death, used frequently in antiquity as the ultimate form of punishment for various crimes. It was a gruesome instrument of killing, meant to be seen and as such it stood as a warning to others not to engage in unauthorized and illegal activities that were known to bring condemnation to the individual nailed to it. However, as a crucial symbol in and of Christianity, the cross is foundational as it stands for the single act that established it. In the words of James Carroll, the cross is a "sighting device." As a foundational icon, the cross is everywhere; in churches, on peoples' neck, and hanging in peoples' homes. In some depictions, the cross has a nailed Jesus figuring on it, in others the cross is bare, yet the meaning of the cross is unmistakable. The cross stands for death and death is the principal act of Christianity; it stands for the way Jesus was put to death and since Jews have been blamed for centuries for his killing, the charge of deicide is in perpetual presence. At any time and place, Jews are guilty of the act of killing Christ on the cross, and lest anyone forget that, the cross is the reminder of what happened.

When compared with other religions, the central representative symbols such as the crescent in Islam, or the Star of David in Judaism, are not instruments of death. Christianity, on the other hand, is unique in having an instrument of death as its basic symbol and iconography. Such a foundational and principal image is replete with symbolic meaning that is specific relative to the more general symbolic meaning of principal images of other religions. The cross' impact as a visual text, then, is the construction of presence — it carries metonymically the entire narrative of Christ on the cross with all the implications vis-à-vis the supposed Jewish role in his crucifixion. The cross tells a story in vivid terms whereby Jews are narratively tied to the cross with Jesus, and there is no easy way to extricate or dissociate them from it or Him.

The cross stands for Christ's suffering and blood, clearly painful images that collectively ask believers to maintain a specific and unified memory of Christ; a memory that could not be erased given the multitude images of the cross in all things Christian. As a religion founded on the death of one person, Christianity's visual rhetoric is aligned with the verbal rhetoric of Christ as its source and foundation. Since a painful and cruel death stands at the foundation of Christianity, the visual depiction of the crucifixion carries the charge and the guilt without its verbal imperative. Therein, then, lies anti-Semitism in its row materiality and in a visually compelling form. Just as evidence in court is most profound when images such as photos are used as proof, the cross is "proof" of a sustained and eternal charge that has already been "proven." The cross will not cease to exist as the most fundamental symbol of Christianity and subsequently, Jews cannot be completely disassociated from it.

Jesus' Non-Semitic Features: Most European depictions of Christ in multiple art forms carry one consistent feature: the visual displays of Jesus portray him as European, in skin color and facial features. In some African displays, Jesus assumes African, therefore black features. What is clearly missing from numerous art forms are traces of Jesus' *Jewish features*. In fact, Jesus' Jewishness is non-existent. The erasure of Jesus' Jewish background, upbringing, and Middle Eastern features can hardly be found. One can claim that having no pictorial or image of Jesus has allowed for multiple artistic interpretations. This possibility is a reasonable explanation only if the features of other individuals, not always occupying the same artistic space, such as disciples or antagonists are depicted similarly. Take for example Bouts Dieric's (1415-75) painting titled "The Last Supper," wherein Christ is depicted as very European looking and so are his disciples, but not Judas. Judas is portrayed in black and red colors, signifying malevolence and death, he appears bitter and his nose is hooked (Becket, 1999, p. 55). Clearly, the intent of the painting is to juxtapose Jesus' benevolence and love of humanity with Judas', and by implication, Jews' malevolence.

Hatred of Jews, whether subtly or not, is clearly the intent behind images that depict Jesus in European and Nordic features while Jews who occupy the same artistic space or other related spaces (such as Middle-Ages wood carving or Nazi propaganda films) carry the most exaggerated, and ugly Semitic features. The gap between the physical characteristics of many European Jews who looked like most of their neighbors and their ugly, repulsive, and demonic depiction in films or newspaper cartoons is evidence of hateful intents. The marking of differentiation and separation could not be starker. So, whence did the demonic image of the Jew come from?

The Demonic and Monstrous Jew: The cross is one central feature of the eternal guilt of the Jew, but it is not the sole icon that carries Jewish responsibility for Christ's death. Numerous other images have been used to construct the most diabolic image of Jews. These images, flourished primarily during the Middle-Ages, were influential on Nazi propaganda, and are currently fully utilized in Islamist anti-Semitism. They all share one common theme; that of presenting the Jew in the most hateful ways, complementing and intensifying verbal diatribes against him with diabolical depictions that can ensure repulsion and, subsequently, hatred.

In his seminal study *The Devil and the Jews*, Joshua Trachtenberg (1943) accounts for the wide-spread charges of the most heinous Jewish practices and the horrific punishments. These unbelievable accusations included sorcery, magic, murder, Satanism, and diabolic acts, often depicted and intensified in annual passion plays that collectively fermented the image of the Jew as the devil. The net effect of these images was the construction of powerful persuasion whereby diabolic images succeed in causing fear and loathing. The modern Jew, argues Trachtenberg, is but an heir of the Middle-Ages Jew, and the Middle-Ages Jew was but a fiction of Christian imagination that bore no relation to the Jews living among them (p. xiv).

One is tempted to ask, as Trachtenberg has: how could reasonable people "believe of the Jews what common sense would forbid them to believe of anyone else?" (Trachtenberg, p. 1). The diabolic images of the Jew were so entrenched that they were taken for granted as true. It is also tempting to suggest, and many scholars have, that this question ought to indicate that anti-Semitism is not to be approached logically or with the usual resources of reason and common sense. Trachtenberg argues that the Jew was viewed as "the arch-degenerate of the world, infecting its literature, its art, its music, its politics and economics with the subtle poison of his insidious influence, ripping out its moral foundation stone by stone until it will collapse helpless in his hands" (p. 3). With such an explanation, suggests Trachtenberg, it is likely that the usual resources of reasoning would fail us. I argue to the contrary, that it is rather "normal" and reasonable to expect hatred of an individual or a group when fear of them is so great. Placed in the context of Middle-Ages superstition, the diabolic accusations against Jews were likely taken as reasonable by contemporaries. The compilation of negative and intense attributes may explain the overall great fear among the masses of the Jews as evil and, thus, intent on destroying Christendom. With such seemingly ample evidence, conclusions are not that difficult to draw and actions thereof are not difficult to predict, no matter how false the image constructed for mass consumption.

The consequences and responsibility of this image construction may not lie in the tendency of many to believe untrue charges, but, rather, in those who concocted them in the first place and whose design was the wide-spread hatred of Jews and Judaism. At the heart of the matter is the rhetorical process that accounts for successful persuasion that constructed these images, knowing full well the subsequent hatred these images would spew. The visual texts on which anti-Semitism is founded ought to indicate that a substantial resource of this hatred lie in a different kind of rhetoric — that of visualization, especially those images of body and blood. The net effect of these visual images has clearly intensified fear, yet its consequential hatred is not without logic. When Jew hatred includes the accusations that Jews require Christian blood for ritual purposes, that Jews are associated with Satan, that they have two horns, and that they practiced black magic, witchcraft and sorcery, such charges would naturally cause fear that subsequently would lead to defensive measures, no matter how hurtful and unjustified (Trachtenberg, p. 6). The key to repudiating the charges of the Jew-devil is not to argue that they are illogical or unreasonable, precisely because they are logical and reasonable in the context in which they are presented and consumed. The only counter argumentative stance that makes sense, albeit a most challenging form of refutation, is to argue compellingly that these images are untrue. Yet, the resources of argumentation are most frustrating when the verbal charges are complemented with even richer reservoir of diabolic images.

Trachtenberg states that the "medieval allusions to the Jew is of a hatred so vast and abysmal, so intense, that it leaves one gasping for comprehension. The unending piling up of vile epithets and accusations and curses, the consistent representation of the Jew as the epitome of everything evil," and that "the intensity of the reaction is so disproportionate to the reasons given that we are forced to pry deeper for the source of the emotional bias which made it possible for the Middle Ages to believe anything and everything reprehensible about the Jew" (p. 12). One important answer Trachtenberg forwards is that the Middle-Ages Christian could not conceive the Jew as human, and that, indeed, "the Jew was *not* human," but "the devil's creature! Not a human being but a demonic, a diabolic beast fighting the forces of truth and salvation with Satan's weapons" (p. 18). Fear, as the paramount emotion triggered in these diabolic images, ought to indicate a sinister motive of those who stood behind spreading these images and who knew well how to play on people's emotions. This purposeful strategy was not too dissimilar to Hitler's own anti-Semitic campaigns that began first with exaggerated charges of impending danger instigated by the "loathsome" capitalist and/or Bolshevik (regardless of the inconsistency between the two) Jews and consistently complemented with diabolic images in propaganda films as well as in children's textbooks and in other popular media.

Christendom constructed basic images of hatred on which others were piled through the ages. Already in antiquity, Jews were accused and depicted as associating with Satan. John states that "they [Jews] are of their 'father the devil'" and St. Chrysostom considered the synagogues a place of idolatry and devil. Similar accusations can be found in the writing of Eusebious of Alexandria (cited in Trachtenberg, pp. 20-21). On this root association with the devil, a host of tales and legends have been created, all "proving" that the Jew and Satan work together. The graphic depictions of the Jew-Satan, incorporating Semitic features that emphasized "grotesque exaggeration," were sure to intensify hatred (p. 26).

The belief that Jews have horns, argues Trachtenberg, is more than based on a mistranslation of the Hebrew word "shine" or "rays" to describe Moses beaming with sun rays on his way down from Mount Sinai. The association of Jews with the he-goat was a known superstition that found its way into art form in numerous depictions. One such portrayal can be seen in a relief on one tower of a bridge in Frankfurt, Germany, depicting a Jew with two goat's horns. And since the goat was also "the devil's favorite animal," the Jew was easily associated with a goat and Satan. Not surprising, in some illustrations, Satan, too, has goat's horns. The slippery slope of associating the Jew with evil and Satan is such that those creatures, in turn, assume Jewish characteristics. Reasoning by association and guilt by association appear to be at the foundation of the visual rhetoric of Jew hatred.

From a Devil to a Murderer: Since the Devil was taken by some as a metaphor and others as a literal evil to be resisted, and since the Jews were Devil's children, they were prone to behaving likewise. The Jews then were capable of the most heinous acts. The Devil as a central figure in Christianity meant that "he had to be permanently fought" (Laqueur, p. 55). Indeed, no other accusation, however, was as devastating to the Middle-Ages Jews then the charge of needing Christian blood and the murder of Christians. Such tales were widely chronicled and illustrated such that they became "a conspicuous part of medieval folklore" (Trachtenberg, p. 125). Among the early tales of blood libels is the case of the Jews of Norwich, England (1144), and the case of Hugh of Lincoln, England (1255). Hundreds of Jews were put the death as punishment for these alleged crimes. In 1247, a committee appointed by Pope Innocent IV to study these charges, concluded that there was no truth to the charges. Pope Gregory X stated in 1275, "that no Jew should be arrested under such silly pretexts" (Laqueur, pp. 55-56). Yet, the blood libel would continue and among the most infamous cases is the Damascus blood libel of 1840. Clearly, the edicts of early Popes did little to stop these false charges.

Jews were made to be viewed as obsessed with blood via the false accusation that they engaged in ritual murder for the blood needed in Jewish rituals, especially those associated with Passover. This so-called obsession with blood would force Jews to serve as torturers and executioners, a practice that was designed to intensify hatred and distance those behind death sentences from the ire of the community (Trachtenberg, p. 129). The overall consequence of the diabolic images of the Jews as killers and blood-thirsty was to develop a "common knowledge" of Jews that was far removed from the actual Jew that lived among them. The Jew was trapped in a perceptual world that was taken by Christians as reality and that bore no resemblance to the Jews in their midst.

The blood libels, as well as the other diabolic charges, could not be more foreign to Jews, for in Judaism individuals are prohibited from defiling themselves with blood. Also, the dietary (and hygienic) laws regarding the slaughter of animals are such that the killing of animals is not only instructed to be done humanely, but that the blood of the slaughtered animal not be mixed with the body of the animal. Yet, Christianity was bent on arguing the opposite; associating Jews with blood and all terrible implications that are associated with blood. This theme, for example, would be incorporated into popular plays such as the *Endigen Judenspiel*, a popular drama in 1476, Baden, Germany, whereby Jews are portrayed as needing "Christian blood 'to alleviate the wound of circumcision'." In another play from the sixteen century titled *Wendunmuth* ("When You Must") by Wilhelm Kirchhof, Jews require Christian blood to smear other Jews on their deathbed. The reason for this practice is "to play it safe" since Jews, as the claims goes, knew all along that Jesus was the Messiah but rejected him to spite Christians. However, on their deathbed, when in urgent need to secure their place in heaven, in using Christian blood, Jews accept Christ as the last resort. In this perverted tale, Christian blood is spilled, *again*, in order for Jews to secure their place in heaven (Trachtenberg, pp. 149-153). No tale was too improbable and no narrative too fantastic for Christians to concoct in justifying the hatred of Jews.

The primary question one must ask is, why cause fear and hatred of Jews in the Middle Ages in the first place, so small in number, so dispersed, and so poor? The answer can be found in the one consistent charge against Jews and their supposedly association with all things evil; that in rejecting Christ their aim is to destroy Christendom. Christians believed that since Jesus is the Messiah, and the Jews have rejected Him and are still waiting for theirs, and given the fact that Jews are wrong about the Messiah, then the Jews must waiting for no one else but the anti-Christ.[1] Subsequently, the allegation goes, Jews are preparing for battle with Christendom and against this feared development it is incumbent upon Christians to do everything to defend themselves against such vile Jews. In this construction, fear is placed as the primary motive for such hatred. Under these circumstances, the hatred of Jews, then, appears rather reasonable. In facing such danger and such an unholy adversary, the devil himself, or his associates, it is reasonable for any community to hate the perpetrators of evil and to defend itself against such calamity. Indeed, the economic calamity and the sense of persecution it brought to many in post-World War I Germany, was compensated and channeled by projecting the persecutory instinct on the "other" — the Jew (Swartz, 1996, p. 188). And though for the believers, it was reasonable to resort to all means against a diabolic evil, for the perpetrators of such evil, the construction of the Jew as the devil incarnate was more of a means than an end. Hatred of Jews was the means to a Christian end: that of Christianity that was not second to Judaism but independent of it.

This constellation of the Jew as the devil allowed for the ease of making anti-Semitism defensible to any reasonable challenges. As Judith Gold (1999) writes, anti-Semitism is "immune to social, political and religious restraints, equally endemic among the ignorant and the intelligent — the loathing and hatred of Jews and Jewishness — crosses all barriers of human society: Subtle, blatant, clever, crude" (p. 170). The Jews, she argues, is the "classic monster," an image in use since antiquity. As found in the Christian Bible: "You [Jews] are of your father the devil, and your will is to do your fathers' desires" (John 8:44), or speaking of Judas, John states ". . . one of you [twelve disciples] is a devil " (John 6: 70-71), ". . . the devil comes and takes away the word from their hearts, that they may not believe and be saved" (Luke 8:12). Later Church fathers perpetuated this early writings with individuals such as Irenaeus calling Jews the "sons of the devil," and St. Cyprian declaring that "the devil is the father of the Jews." The list of Church leaders espousing this view is long (see Gold, pp. 171-172).

Finally, the Jew in Christian theology was to be taken primarily as a body — a presence — whose function is a continuous reminder of his terrible act of deicide. The function of the Jew is to disappear by continuing to exist (Carroll, 2002, p. 50). The complete disappearance of the Jew, however, would negate Christianity while his normal existence would cast doubt on Christian theology. Hence, the Jew is to survive but suffer in a suspended status of a hated entity. The rhetorical constellation of such a theology cannot stand on firm grounds and is thus prone to self-doubt. Since no other explanation to Christian theology has been seriously contemplated, the Augustinian formula of the fourth century is still in vogue.

Visually, the survival of the Jew would show the degree to which the non-Jewish community, whether Christian or Muslim, needed to "know" who is a Jew. The identity of the Jew, often sanctioned by the respective governing body, would mandate specific signs for the ease of such identification. The use of the Nazi yellow star badge was a take on an earlier Islamic practice of forcing Jews to wear a sign for identification purpose. As Jews entered most professions in the nineteenth century, following their emancipation, it would become harder to find the Jew among the larger populace. The Jew was happy to shed his Jewish features and seek assimilation, but the Nazi would resort to the practice of old, of forcing a sign — the yellow badge — to secure the Jewish identification (McWilliams, 1948, pp. 90-93). This is the essence of the Nazi propaganda film, *Jud Suss* (the Jew Suss), wherein the plot of the film centers on the ability of the evil Jew, in dress and habits, to hide his true identity and appear like anyone else. The identity of the Jew was to be in the hands of non-Jews, viewing any shedding of Jews of their visual identity as conspiratorial and malevolent. The Jew had no right to construct his/her own identity.

The essence of the tension between Christianity and Judaism, then, lies in the lingering doubt Christianity holds about its foundation and theology vis-à-vis Jews and Judaism. Amidst this controversial and complicated theology of these two religions, the hateful theology was accompanied by constructed images of the Jew as evil, Satan, and the anti-Christ. These images that made the Jew-devil vivid and fearful, have allowed Christianity to reduce its complex theology into a simplistic narrative of two antagonists, identified in God-Devil terms, both symbolically and literally.

Conclusion

The theological foundation of Christianity was (and perhaps in some quarters, still remains) the pivotal reason for the hatred of Jews, and no accusation, however diabolical or twisted, was held back. The rise of anti-Semitism, in early Christianity and later during the twelve century and onward, gave rise to the use of visual images of Jews that emphasized multiple charges against them (Trachtenberg, pp. 159-151). Slandering the Jew was the way the early Church sought to establish the new religion and along the centuries the slandering "piled up so many fabulous accounts of Jewish venality and treachery that it became commonplace to attack Jews" (Trachtenberg, p. 162). Thus, Christians claimed that Jews

> mock and despise the Christian faith and profane its sacred objects; they stink; their eyes are permanently fixed earthward; they often wear a goat's beard, and at their conventiclers disguise themselves with goats' head masks; their heads are adorned with horns, and their wives trail tails behind them; they suffer from secret ailments and deformities; they are cruel and rapacious; they buy or kidnap children and slaughter them in homage to Satan; they consume human flesh and blood (Trachtenberg, p. 215).

This hostility toward Jews was mitigated initially by the Church fathers and later by the clergy. The diabolic images were a powerful tool in the hands of anti-Semites, and they used them rather successful with the masses. Though numerous popes sought to stop various attacks on Jews, their defense of Jews was usually restrained as they sought also to appease the unruly crowds demanding the blood of the Jew (Laqueur, p. 54). The diabolical images of the Middle-Ages Jew were not quickly forgotten in modern times. One need only to look at Nazi propaganda in films and newspaper cartoons to realize that they imported Middle-Ages images of the Jew with all of the grotesque depiction of repulsive figures with hooked nose and blood dripping from their hands. The Nazis even went as far as to repeat the charge that Jews emit bad smell, with a caveat that Jews now emit "'faint sweet' racial odor" (Trachtenberg, p. 49). Contemporary Islamists have borrowed heavily from Nazi depictions of

Jews. The image of the Jew today, especially in the Islamic world, continues to present a fictional creature that never existed but is, nonetheless, a powerful source of much hatred.

Note

1.   Christians believe "that the anti-Christ would be born to the tribe of Dan," therefore, the anti-Christ is taken as of a Jewish origin. See, Trachtenberg, p. 32.

9

Nostra Aetate and the End to the Charge of "Eternal Guilt"

Anti-Semitism is founded on the notion that the past cannot pass, and that it is experienced in the presence, now and forever. This sentiment about the tendency to consider the past as an endless and timeless *topos* from which human can draw relevant experiences is an apt description of anti-Semitism's longevity; a medicine that has always been available in case it was needed. Psychologist Rudolph M. Loewenstein reports that among his patients are those who "have such strong sense of the link between the past and present that they consider Jews of the present generation and of all future generations guilty of the death of Christ" (cited in Bergmann, 1988, p. 42). This is a remarkable observation given the passing of some two thousand years since Jesus' crucifixion. This observation is not an account of a mass psychology but of individuals whose idea-fix is entrenched and ostensibly operational in their daily behavior and action. How is it possible to link an event that took place some two thousand years earlier as justification for action today, tomorrow, and forever? How come anti-Semitism, rooted in Jesus' crucifixion, has remained the basis of anti-Semitism despite the passage of millennia? And, what operational practices have maintained this charge eternally?

Anti-Semitism, as described throughout this volume, is entrenched and enduring, and its practices ranging from antiquity to the present must yield a profound surprise at the longevity of such hatred. While it is possible that the root cause — that of blaming Jews for killing Christ — has morphed into an expedient reason for other motives and causes, the accusation of deicide has remained intact, sometimes verbally, and at other times, visually. Yet, the charge of eternal guilt of the Jew and centuries of anti-Semitism are grounded on one biblical verse that implicates the Jews in the death of Christ — Matt 27:24-25, wherein Jews are said to declare "let his blood be on us and our children." With this singular statement, all Jews were branded the murderers of Christ and assigning to them permanent responsibility and guilt for the death of Jesus on the cross. While anti-Semitism may appear in different forms, and at different times, to include religious hatred, social antagonism, economic blame, psychological scapegoating, racial elitism, and others, events of two thousand years ago are still, arguably, the primary reason for such persistent hatred.

The Council of Nicaea in 325 CE had Roman Emperor Constantine declare that the Jews have committed a terrible sin and should be scorned, stating that "it is unbecoming that on the holiest of festivals we should follow the customs of the Jews; henceforth let us have nothing in common with their odious people" (cited in Carroll, p. 55). Thus, has been formalized the early Christian antagonism against the Jews. The lapse of some three centuries since the "commission" of the sin was not a contested issue but an acceptable thesis. Indeed, the passage of three hundred years since Jesus' crucifixion may have offered the plausible notion that extending the accusation of deicide into the future was a possibility worth considering.

Though restrictions on Jews began earlier than Emperor Constantine's policy, his edict added a formality to an already existing practice of hatred, prejudice, discrimination, forced conversion, and worse. In 438 CE, the *Code of Theodosius II* made Christianity the only legal religion in the Roman Empire. Jews were now collectively accused of deicide, responsible for killing Jesus, and outlawed as a community of law and teaching. From now on, the "theology of collective guilt held that 'the blood of Jesus falls not only on the Jews of that time, but on all generations of Jews up to the end of the world'" (Julius et al., p. 5). Particularly effective in spreading hateful anti-Semitism were the "Passion Plays" which allowed for annual rituals of Jesus' trial and death at the hands of the Jews, thus repeatedly "renewing" the charges against Jews in such a way that they became embedded in many European traditions, some of them still performed, as in Oberammergau, Bavaria

(Wistrich, 2010, p. 90). Other inflictions include blood libels, crusaders mass massacres, severe restrictions over habitation and professions, clothing, expulsions, pogroms, and finally the Holocaust as an extreme case of anti-Semitism. All of these experiences run the gamut of some seventeen centuries, thus adding to the longevity of anti-Semitism and the many nuances developed along the way.

The key to Christian anti-Semitism, writes historian Rosemary Ruether, is "the theological dispute between Christianity and Judaism over the messiahship of Jesus" (1974, p. 28), and that "as long as 'the Jews,' that is, the Jewish religious tradition itself, continues to reject this [Christian] interpretation, the validity of the Christian view is in question. The 'wrath upon the Jews', poured out by Christianity, represents this ever unsatisfied need of the Church to prove that it has the true content of the Jewish scripture" (Ruether, pp. 94-95). The theological statements about Christ are inherently anti-Judaic. For Ruether, to use an oft-quoted phrase of hers, "Christian scriptural teaching and preaching per se is based on a method in which anti-Judaic polemic exists as the left hand of its christological hermeneutic" (p. 121). Ruether laments the notion that Christianity devoid of anti-Semitism is taken as impossibility — a realization that lies at the roots of Christian anti-Semitism. Subsequently, "the word Jews took on the role of a hostile symbol for all those men and women who dared to resist and reject the gospel teaching." Ultimately then, "for Christianity, anti-Judaism was not merely a defense against attack, but an intrinsic need of self-affirmation," (Reuther, p.181) and that "possibly anti-Judaism is too deeply embedded in the foundations of Christianity to be rooted out entirely without destroying the whole structure" (Ruether, p. 228). In being accused of killing Christ, the Church conceived the Jews as carrying a collective guilt that would last until the Day of Judgment (Bergmann, p. v).

The notion of eternal anti-Semitism lies in this theology and, since the Day of Judgment is yet to arrive, despite the passage of two thousand years since "committing" the charge, the guilt, likewise, is eternal and collective. This has been the theology of the Catholic Church, officially, until the Vatican II statement of 1965. One can rationalize that, from a Christian perspective, the longevity of anti-Semitism was the result of a continuous attempt to prove Jews wrong about their rejection of Jesus as the Messiah. This rationalization assumes that at any time and age, Jews must be reminded of their "mistake" in not accepting Jesus as the Messiah prophesized in the Old Testament. Yet, even if one attempts to sympathize with this advocacy, it hardly explains the depth of religious hatred and its physical consequences in the form of massacres, deportations, torture, and annihilation. Even more puzzling is the contradiction between Christ's prediction of his death as a necessary act of redemption and blaming Jews for his killing. If the death of Jesus was foretold as a heavenly act, then how does one square this foretelling with the guilt of his killing? Or, how can anyone be guilty of an act that was already foretold and prophesied, especially as a divine act? Christianity which often argues that the Old Testament foretold Jesus' arrival has abandoned its principal reliance on such prophesying when it comes to his death, and selected instead to hate, justifying the hatred by claiming that the Christian God does not like the Jews.

At the heart of the rhetoric of anti-Semitism is a temporal variable, consistently argued as eternal, and the proof of the heavy hand of the temporal is inherent to Christian anti-Semitism has been furnished by no other than the Catholic Church itself. In the 1965 Synod, known as Vatican II, under the initial guidance of Pope John XXIII and implemented later by Pope Paul VI, the Church has focused precisely on the temporal issue, claiming that though "True, the Jewish authorities and those who followed their lead pressed for the death of Christ; still, what happened in His passion cannot be charged against all the Jews, without distinction, then alive, nor against the Jews of today." The statement known as *Nostra Aetate* ("in our time") went as far as to ask that the

> Jews should not be presented as rejected or accursed by God …
> Furthermore, in her rejection of every persecution against any man, the Church, mindful of the patrimony she shares with the Jews and moved not by political reasons but the Gospel's spiritual love, decries hatred, persecutions, displays of anti-Semitism, directed against Jews at any time and by anyone. (Pope Paul VI, 1968, p. 176)

The statement by Vatican II, though likely not sufficient from the Jewish perspective as it did not exonerate Jews of the charge of deicide (Forster and Epstein, 1974, p. 2), is nonetheless profound and significant. Most importantly, the cause of anti-Semitism is identified as accusation of Jews for the killing of Christ and the nature of anti-Semitism is identified as eternal blame thereof and its persecutory manifestations through the ages. For the first time the Catholic Church has rejected the eternal guilt of Jews for the death of Christ. The Pope went as far s to insist specifically on removing the "cruel words *perfidies judaeis* ('perfidious Jews')" (Carroll, p. 39). In arguing and explaining this point prior to finalizing the official Vatican II statement, Cardinal Bea, who advocated a new approach to Christian-Jewish relationship, stated the following:

> The Jews of our time can hardly be accused of the crimes committed against Christ, so far removed are they from those deeds. Actually, even in the time of Christ, the majority of the Chosen People did not cooperate with the leaders of the people in condemning Christ … If therefore not even all the Jews in Palestine or in Jerusalem could be accused, how much less the Jews dispersed throughout the Roman Empire? And how much less again those who today, after nineteen centuries, live scattered in the whole world? (p. 128)

As argued earlier, the transformation of religious hatred into racial, ethnic, and national hatred, are rooted in Christianity's foundational act — the events surrounding Jesus' crucifixion. In Islam, anti-Semitism as a relatively recent development is now said to be rooted in events surrounding Muhammad's struggles to establish a new religion and his struggle with the Jewish rejection of the Prophet's conversion attempts. Out of these so-called "root causes," hatred of Jews developed to include a host of related and unrelated manifestations, often accompanied by manufactured narratives; yet, no other accusation has been more devastating and consequential than the argument for the eternity of anti-Semitism and, hence, the foundation of its longevity.

It is noteworthy that though anti-Semitism has undergone many changes, not the least of them was the shedding of the religious aspects and its replacement with other potent descriptors such as racial theorizing, the Vatican took upon itself the formal and painful task of admitting its role in the history of anti-Semitism. With so many non-religious entities being responsible for anti-Semitism, especially since the emancipation of Jews in the eighteenth century, the Catholic Church could have claimed lack of complete or sole responsibility for this hatred. The Catholic Church could have even pointed the finger at other Christian churches, especially Protestant ones, as hotbeds of anti-Semitism. It could have pointed to non-religious entities such as Tsarist Russia, Nazism, or Italian Fascism, as sources of anti-Semitism. Yet, it chose the formal and thus dramatic venue of a Church Council with all of its importance and significance. It is possible to read this development as admission that the roots of anti-Semitism lie in the religious context, specifically in early Church theology that formalized hatred of Jews, as this much is specifically stated in Vatican II statements.

There are several possibilities why the Vatican took the formal repudiation of anti-Semitism: The Catholic Church may have felt guilty, either directly or indirectly, for its complicity in the Holocaust and the centuries of anti-Semitism that led to it; it may have opted to stand as an example for all Christians, thus guiding the larger Christian world to follow suit; Or it may have even seen a direct line from Christian antiquity to the present, thus putting the onus on the Vatican to correct earlier dogmatic teachings of hatred against Jews. To one degree or another, the papacy has attempted some protection of the Jews throughout the Middle-Ages and it is thus possible to view Vatican II as continuing this practice. However, the papacy protection of Jews was qualified, nuanced, and quite ineffective in carrying any authority over the clergy, often considered the primary culprit of anti-Semitism and violence at the local level.

Not to be overlooked is a significant precursor to Vatican II Council to be found in the writing of Cardinal John Henry Newman (1801-1890) whose *Essay on the Development of Christian Doctrine* (1845) formulated the notion of "development as a norm in Church history," whereby the "truth does not develop, but the categories and formulas we use to describe dogma do and must as we move from one language to another and as our understanding increases" (*Roman Catholicism Historical Perspectives, Patheos*, ¶7). The interfaith website *Patheos* asserts that while a segment of Catholics considered the Church as unchanging and fixed in time —indeed, this was quite appealing and comforting to some eyes — others followed the logic articulated by John Henry Newman in the late 19th century, that the Church had been undergoing development and change throughout her history. The label 'Tridentine church', referring to the Council of Trent that had concluded in 1563, was used to label and sometimes slander a Church set in stone and backward in thinking, but in reality it had only been during the last two centuries or so that the Catholic Church had closed herself off from modern developments stemming from the Scientific Revolution and Enlightenment of early modernity. (*Pathoes*, ¶3)

Though a theological paradigm shift had been underway for about a century, the Holocaust, I argue, must be seen as the immediate cause for the urgent need to repair the Church's relations with Judaism. It is also significant that Pope Paul VI paid a visit to the Holy Land in 1963, the year of becoming a Pope, and the year of deciding to go ahead with his predecessor plans for a Vatican Council.

Nostra Aetete removed "the taint of guilt from the Jewish people then and now," but it did not completely remove the charge of deicide. Its positive impact lies in viewing "Judaism not as a decadent and defunct precursor of Christianity which the latter had replaced and superseded, but as a lively parent and brother faith that had survived against all the odds and would, no doubt, continue to survive" (Foster and Epstein, 1974, p. 2). Yet, despite the remarkable development, the sting of anti-Semitism has remained in come circles of the Church, and so has its temporality of old. Recent developments in 2009, under Pope Benedict XVI, have cast doubt on the accomplishments of Vatican II, and pointing to the inevitability of Jews' eternal guilt charge as central to Catholic theology. Appearing to embrace those who opposed Vatican II's accommodation with the Jews, Pope Benedict has sought to accept the credentials of Bishop Richard Williamson who has denied the Holocaust as well as opposed Vatican II's accommodation with Judaism.[1] Christopher Hitchens writes in *Newsweek* that "what makes the present case so alarming is that concessions are being made to Holocaust-deniers and anti-Semites, and that this is not a departure from 'original intent' Catholicism but rather part of a *return* to traditional and old-established preachments" (2009, pp. 58-60).

At the heart of the problem is a growing opposition within the Catholic Church to the doctrine of Vatican II and its rejection of Jews' eternal guilt. Hitchens points to the absurdity of the charge of eternal guilt which is mentioned in only one verse of one Gospel (Matthew 27:24-25) and that the calamities that befell Jews since are all the result of this verse (p. 60). Indeed, when contemplating the nature of anti-Semitism, one must ask some basic questions not only about the nature of anti-Semitism and its length but also its justification. The longevity of this hatred must have a life and reasoning of its own but what about the nature of the charge itself? What has allowed this longevity in the first place and what variables made anti-Semitism survive despite the many historical, political, geographical and social changes? In seeking to explore the longevity of anti-Semitism, I turn briefly to discussing the notion of temporality in narrativity as a necessary step in contemplating the rhetorical aspects of anti-Semitism.

Temporality in Narrativity

The longevity of Christian and Islamic anti-Semitism and its reliance on eternal guilt is rooted in "original causes" that both faiths selected to consider as continuous and timeless. Time was intentionally frozen for centuries once an inherent cause has identified Jews as guilty of a major religious offence. In Christianity, the offense is that of deicide — the killing of Jesus as God, and in Islam the charge is that of rejecting Muhammad's teaching, quarreling with him, and supposedly, seeking to kill him. The notion of freezing time or extending time to eternity is a unique argumentative stand since any logical assessment of the inherent argument therein would lead one to quickly dismiss as absurd the extension of guilt from one person to another, not to speak of extending guilt from one generation to another or extending guilt from one century or from one millennia to another. Yet, anti-Semitism's presence over seventeen centuries for Christianity and thirteen centuries for Islam proves that such argumentative stands are possible.

Philosopher Paul Ricoeur (1985) theorizes that "the time of narrating is separate from narrated time" and that narrated time allows for "temporal compression," making it possible for "anticipations and flashbacks, the inter-linkings that enable the memory of vast stretches of time to be included in brief narrative sequences, creating the effect of perspectival depth, while breaking up chronology" (pp. 79-80). A narrative, states Ricoeur, is but a semantic innovation where a "work of synthesis — a plot" is "brought together within the temporal unity of a whole and complete action" (1983, p. ix). He also stipulates that "time becomes human to the extent that it is articulated through a narrative mode, and narrative attains its full meaning when it becomes a condition of temporal existence" (1983, p. 52). Time, Ricoeur says, "becomes human time to the extent that it is organized after the manner of a narrative; narrative, in turn, is meaningful to the extent that it portrays the features of temporal experience" (1983, p. 3).

Ricoeur calls our attention to the "games with time" we play, that this game "has as its stakes in the temporal experience intended by the narrative," and that "these temporal qualities are brought to light only by the play of derivations and insertions" (1985, p. 80). In paraphrasing Ricoeur, Severson argues that the games we play with time allow us to bring death and eternity together "as the twin limiting horizons within a 'narrative consciousness' that has historical and fictional components" (1995, p. 15). For Ricoeur, the "time of history" bares no relationship to "the time of action," and this is so because "history cannot . . . sever every connection with narrative without losing its historical character" (1983, p. 177). History, then, is neither an ontological nor purely a chronological account of events because time is punctuated by narrated events (1985, p. 218).

In other words, human discourse or narrative allows us to extend time beyond its physical or measurable qualities. The consequence of reconfiguring time is that historical truth and fiction become a major issue of contention (1983, p. 92). In the case of anti-Semitism, as discussed earlier, the objective of extending Jewish guilt of Jesus' crucifixion beyond his immediate generation was the result of continuous doubt and uncertainties regarding theological statements foundational to

Christianity, hence, continued guilt. With timeless and eternal guilt, a rather difficult and uncomfortable situation was "solved" by developing a narrative that followed a story of origin in simplistic yet profound ways. The narrative of origin centered on describing the act of Jesus' crucifixion such that the major culprit of his death would quickly result in hatred and sought retribution. The "punishment" of the Jew, then, became the end result of this child-like narrative, carrying the instruction of guilt projected for eternity.

It is in eternity (timelessness) that one finds the device that has kept anti-Semitism for centuries. The device that has allowed anti-Semitism to be extended to eternity, to connect different temporal points, is the *metaphor*. By metaphor I mean the ability to condense meaning of a given entity in one representation. Time, argues Jens Brockmeier (1995), has no "ontological entity to which the term time might refer." Rather, time is a metaphor, and that "it is in narrative that we construct the *most complex* constructions of temporality." And the most complex constructions are time-syntheses whereby individuals can create autobiographics, memories and identities (pp. 107-110).

It should come as no surprise, then, that Time has taken on religious metaphors and functions interpretively as in a theological construct whereby "God is more than just the source of a 'physical' time: God is the *agency* of time" (Severson, pp. 149-150). Perhaps here lies the logic of timeless guilt that, once it is said to be sanctioned by God, is carried with the ultimate credibility and therefore cannot be questioned. Indeed, anti-Semitism would continuously be addressed as "sanctioned" by God or by divine inspiration (recall Hitler's statement that in killing Jews he was doing God's work), much on display these days in Islamist rhetoric.

This theoretical point about how time can be manipulated is undertaken here in order to focus on the crucial variable of anti-Semitism I highlight here — the argument that it is not only eternal, but that it *should* be eternal. This is the stance that the early Church undertook and kept intact for centuries. Strands in contemporary Islam are bent on following the same logic. The theoretical stance that has grounded the longevity of anti-Semitism is that time or temporality is a rhetorical construct, a metaphor punctuated and molded to fit coherent argumentative and mythic narratives.

Such mythic narratives have allowed the construction of anti-Semitism as justified by divine intervention, without which such hatred would be deemed illogical and unethical. Yet, those seeking to extend Jewish guilt centuries after the charges were first leveled have succeeded in doing so by developing mythic narratives that incorporated simplistic plot lines that identified a culprit who would carry the guilt for eternity. In seeking to have the guilt eternal, the victimizers are always assured of having a way out of their action by continuously having a handy culprit to identify, absolving them of their own guilt. In the anti-Semitism of both Christianity and Islam, one finds a creative temporal tales that merge biographical sketches of their respective founders, their initial struggle with Jews, the Jew as their primary foe, the Jew who sought to scuttle the founder from forming a new religion, and, therefore, the Jew as the *ultimate* enemy who must be done with. Such a narrative of origin is foundational and, as such, its sanctioning by God made it easy to turn the Jew into the evil entity par-excellence, and on whose shoulders others' sins are to be carried.

A Theological End to Anti-Semitism

Jews have committed two acts that made Christianity possible: they gave literal birth to Jesus the person as well as to the religious conception (the Messianic idea on which Christianity is based), and in "killing" Jesus they have also established the foundation of what would later become Christianity. A certain understanding of this tautological reasoning seems to have been accepted by the Church in Vatican II. Though vaguely expressed, Vatican II's *Nostra Aetate* sought to amend its relationship with Judaism, by absolving them of the eternal guilt (but not the guilt) associated with Christ's death. And by embracing Jesus' Jewish upbringing, the Church recognized and appreciated the Jewish foundation on which Christianity was borne. Most profoundly, Vatican II centered on the key variable in anti-Semitism — the temporality of eternal and collective guilt. With this variable taken out of anti-Semitism's rhetorical formula, the scapegoating mechanism has been exposed as well. As such, *Nostra Aetate* is a remarkable document and an important attempt in some two thousand years to end anti-Semitism. Yet, so simple, logical and straightforward a statement, it took two thousand years to correct an obvious injustice. It took the Holocaust and its horrendous mass murders for the Catholic Church to assume some guilt in conceiving and perpetuating anti-Semitism.

If the Church read historical events more objectively, it would find out that Jesus was part of a large progressive movement in Judaism and that there is strong evidence that the Romans and not Jews were responsible for Jesus' crucifixion. As Pawlikowski writes "Until we reassociate Jesus with the wider Jewish struggle of the period against spiritual and political oppression, the crucifixion narrative will continue to carry the seeds of anti-Semitism despite the official condemnations of the deicide charge" (p. 109). In similar fashion, Islam found in its origin the timeless formula for eternal anti-Semitism. The fact that this retrospective viewpoint is also a product of Nazi propaganda does not change the effect of this rhetoric. On the contrary, Islamist anti-Semitism has taken over where European anti-Semitism, at least in vicious form, ended with the collapse of the Nazi regime.

Temporality in the case of anti-Semitism has had a devastating impact on the Jewish people as it sustained the hatred beyond all logical extensions. From one generation to another, Jews were made to suffer anew an act committed centuries and millennia earlier. But temporality by itself does not explain anti-Semitism beyond its ability to extend a given argument beyond its contemporary setting and timeframe. Temporality implies something else that is simple yet sinister — it allows individuals to accept the notion that people inherit guilt and that this "inheritance," a notion that is possible only rhetorically — is an act of persuasion, conviction, and belief. This is precisely how anti-Semitism has remained eternal and rationalized as such. The ability to accuse Jews as accursed and guilty of crimes committed against the founders of Christianity and Islam is possible, logically, if one accepts the premise that guilt is transferable from one generation to another. No such logic is associated with another group or community, yet this reasoning process has been sustained for centuries in the case of Jews.

The rhetorical process of establishing a successful campaign of anti-Semitism in the Islamic world is quite similar to the process undertaken by the Church centuries earlier whereby an original religious quarrel became foundational for future sentiments. Just as killing Christ was constructed as a sin carried by all Jews forever, Muslims, reacting to Zionism, have re-discovered Quranic verses to "prove" an eternal and religiously sanctioned hatred. With such verses against the Jews, uttered by Muhammad himself, all contemporaries have the right to repeat them and to follow their sentiments. Thus, a foundational story functions to legitimate the cause of hatred, absolving Muslims from contemplating a more complex assessment of historical as well as contemporary situations. Clearly, it is easier to fall back on foundational archetypes of hatred than to deal with the more complex realities of the contemporary Middle East, the strife within the Arab and Islamic world, the ties Judaism has with its historical land, as well as the differing approaches within the Arab world and its relation to Israel and the Arab-Israeli conflict. The foundational story of Muhammad and his struggle with Jews as the perspective from which the Arab-Israeli conflict is, or should be, assessed leaves no room for compromise or accommodation between the warring parties. Yet, this foundational narrative works only if time is frozen whereby events of the seventh century CE are accepted as a justification for attitudes and actions some fourteen centuries later.

Despite the clear distinction between the accusation of killing the founder of Christianity and the struggle with the founder of Islam, contemporary Islamist anti-Semitism is so vicious, so crude, and so outmoded, that the only explanation for its intensity must be put in the context of anti-Zionist hatred. Indeed, just as the Catholic Church have come around after some seventeen centuries of anti-Semitism, the anti-Semitic slogans of medieval Europe began to pervade the Islamic world in the twentieth century. Islamist anti-Semitism has adopted long-standing European anti-Semitism, including tracts such as the *Protocols of the Wise Elders of Zion* and slogans that have long been considered passé, and interjecting them into verses from the Quran to prove a much greater animosity than is warranted between the Prophet Muhammad and Jewish inhabitants of the Arab peninsula during the early seventh century.

Christian antiquity constructed the rhetoric of hating Jews as the means to creat a new religion that was to be distinctly different and separate from Judaism. Islam has found the same rhetoric of hatred as useful and effective weapon to fight Israel. Anti-Semitism, then, has, and continues to be a convenient means-to-end rhetoric because it can inflame feelings and yield hatred precisely because those behind it do not wish to pursue more moderate and accommodating policies. Vatican II exemplified the possibility of correcting grievance and errors by removing eternal guilt and collective punishment. It also recognized the role Judaism has played in the foundation of Christianity. If the temporality of eternal guilt is to be taken out of the relationship between Muslims and Jews, including the recognition of Jewish history and theology, a more realistic dimension of the Arab-Israeli conflict, I believe, is a likely possibility.

Conclusion

Nostra Aetate as the single and most profound statement on the origin and longevity of Christian-Catholic anti-Semitism was a watershed in the Christian-Jewish relationship. The document took out one of the most hurtful cause of anti-Semitism — the charge that all Jews are to be considered Christ-killer at any place and time. The dramatic reversal after almost two millennia was an admission that a single rhetorical device — temporality — made the longevity of anti-Semitism possible. That this single linguistic device could have done so much to establish anti-Semitism speaks volume to the role of rhetoric in anti-Semitism and hateful discourse in general. Yet, taking out the eternity of the deicide charge on whose principal Christianity sought its foundation did not go unnoticed by those currently seeking to re-introduce it. And though one hopes that no such reversal will take place, the suspicion that Christianity and anti-Semitism are too closely related is a continued cause for concern.

Similarly, the Islamist eagerness to charge Jews with a similar "crime," that of seeking to kill its founder, seeks to construct an unyielding and eternal hatred of Jews. Such a perspective is meant to prevent any possible accommodation between Muslims and Jews, and subsequently, any reduction of tension between Arabs and Israelis. The latter might be the real aim of this theology. Hatred, and its opposite, accommodation and peace are possible then only when the rhetorical intensity therein is greatly reduced, and for this to happen, a temporality of eternal charges cannot and should not be accepted. In short, individuals and groups cannot be charged with act allegedly committed millennia earlier by their co-religions.

Note

1. Richard Williamson, the rector of the Seminary of Our Lady Co-Redemptrix in La Reja, Argentina, a member of the ultraconservative Society of St. Pius X, has opposed Vatican II for the overall liberal stand the Church Council took, specifically its repudiation of the eternal guilt of Jews in Christ's crucifixion. On January 21, 2009, Pope Benedict XVI lifted his ban on Williamson and several other bishops for an earlier infraction related to an unauthorized appointment in 1988. Just as the Pope lifted his ban, Williamson gave an interview to a Swedish television station denying the Holocaust. The firestorm this interview generated brought Pope Benedict XVI to issue a statement of solidarity with the Jewish people and claiming that the Vatican was unaware of Williamson's earlier views on the Holocaust. German Chancellor Angela Markel as well as prominent German Bishops issued a stern condemnation of Williamson and his anti-Jewish sentiments. With such criticism, the Vatican now demanded that Williamson issue a clear and unambiguous retraction. Though several vague apologies were issued, Williamson did not fully retract his. He was finally removed from his seminary post and the government of Argentina revoked his visa and forced him to leave the country (New York Times, February 4 and April 19, 2009).

10

The Founding of Christianity and the Rejection of Judaism

The case studies and instances of anti-Semitism in different times and places point to several consistent and predictable patterns. Crucially, the origin of anti-Semitism lies in Christianity's early struggles to establish itself as a separate religion from Judaism. The formative first three centuries are replete with tensions between Christianity and Judaism such that any discussion about the eradication of anti-Semitism cannot proceed without first engaging the thorny origin of anti-Semitism in antiquity. Recent scholarship into this period has shown the degree to which early Christianity found it necessary, as the mechanism for its own survival, to reject Judaism. This thesis by itself is not surprising or new; what is revealing is that the struggle for an independent religion was set in the context of Judaism's rather successful inroads into the Greco-Roman world. And since less extreme means of separating the two religions proved unsuccessful, a hateful rhetoric was developed, purposefully designed to advance the cause of Christianity at the expense of Judaism.

Rhetorically, the need to have an enemy to be demonized can be explained by the need of early Christians for a clear *identification*:

[T]his rhetorical identification of personalized enemies enhances establishment of self-hood in several ways. By identifying against an other, one may delineate his own position — locate himself by contrast. By painting the enemy in dark hued imagery of vice, corruption, evil, and weakness, one may more easily convince himself of his own superior virtue and thereby gain a symbolic victory of ego-enhancement. The rhetoric of attack becomes at the same time a rhetoric of ego-building, and the very act of assuming such a rhetorical stance becomes self-persuasive and confirmatory (Gregg, 1971, p. 82).

This passage, written by rhetorical critic and scholar Richard B. Gregg in reference to protest movements of the 1970's in the United States, is applicable to describing the transition from tension between early Christianity and Judaism to a full-pledged anti-Semitism. This explanation allows for comprehending the roots of anti-Semitism as a rhetorical, purposeful, and self-fulfilling discourse of hate. Hatred, in this context, is strategic, calculable and a means to an end.

Against the more dominant notion that once Christ appeared on the scene Judaism would decline and perhaps even disappear, the opposite has happened. Judaism thrived and flourished during the first three centuries CE, influencing many pagans to adopt Jewish practices as well as encouraging early Christians to continue their Jewish practices. It is against this background that a hateful rhetoric was developed, designed to attack Judaism as a means of succeeding against a rival religion, and that in this context anti-Semitism set roots.

The tension in the early days of Christianity was not so much between Christians and Jews as between those that wanted to be outside Judaism (such as Hellenistic groups) and those who wished to stay within. For those wishing to stay within Judaism, Jesus' crucifixion was not seen as the transforming act that necessitated the rejection of Judaism, especially given the higher importance attributed to Jewish symbols such as the Sabbath, circumcision, the centrality of the Temple, and dietary laws. Indeed, there is sufficient evidence to show that some "pre-gospel traditions placed little or no emphasis on the cross as the key to understanding Jesus and his mission" (Gager, pp. 25-28).

If any, the evidence is strong that Jews were not only well integrated in the Roman society but that Judaism was seen by many Romans as a philosophy that was much admired and emulated. A century or so after Jesus' crucifixion, Judaism was acceptable and, in some Roman circles, it was considered influential and respected despite the Jewish revolts of the first and second centuries CE. Romans were fascinated by the Jewish religion and philosophy, and though future revolts in Judea, especially the revolt of 135 CE would sour the relationship between Rome and Jews in general, a renewed respectability of Judaism was apparent even as late as the early third century. For example, the respect and influence of Judah haNasi, "Judah the Patriarch," the spiritual leader of the Jewish community in the Holy Land in the third century CE, appears to have reached all the way to Rome. Evidence of Judaism's renewed respectability can be observed in Origen (ca. 185-254 CE), the Church father who appeared disturbed by Rome's interest in things Jewish (Goodman, pp. 482-484).

Following the Bar Cochba revolt of 132-135 CE, and the destruction of the Jewish community in Judea, the Roman Empire, in control, changed the name of the province from Judea to Syria Palestina, seeking to eliminate symbolically the Jewish State as well as humiliate the remaining Jews by naming the territory after the Philistines, Greek invaders who settled on the shore line of ancient Israel centuries earlier (Goodman, p. 494).[1] In the wake of this development "Christianity offered itself . . . as true Israel in a very specific sense, that is, as Israel without those elements most offensive to Romans — the strong sense of identity as a nation and the attendant commitment to the autonomy of the land and its central institution, the temple" (Gager, p. 66).

Yet, this popularity of Judaism in Rome must have been disturbing to those wishing to see Judaism lose to the new religion. That such positive receptiveness prevailed even after Emperor Constantine officially embraced Christianity in 325 CE was a source of great irritation. The anti-Christian and pro-Jewish attitudes of Emperor Julian (360 CE) in particular must have caused great concern to Christians (Gager, p. 94). It is this context that brought attacks on Judaism that subsequently manifested itself in anti-Semitism as the vehicle for separateness. Disturbed by the popularity of Judaism, Church leaders were bent on countering those features that were attractive to Romans such as Judaism's sense of morality, monotheism, customs, and the nature of God (Gager, p. 83).

Gager argues that in St. Chrysostom we see the standard practice of "rhetorical invectives" lashed out against Jews, a stylized approach to addressing a perceived opponent. Similar invectives were uttered by

Ephrem (second half of the 4th century) who uses the term "crucifier" as synonymous with Jews (Gager, pp. 120-123). Yet, Church leaders, including St. Chrysostom and others were the exception while "popular Christianity was not nearly as convinced as were its leaders that the beliefs and practices of Judaism had been rendered powerless by the appearance of Christianity" (Gager, p. 133).

This point ought to be sharpened: *the anti-Semitism of the early Church does not originate within Judaism or by Judaizing Christians but prompted purposefully by those Church leaders who would have nothing to do with Judaism and who were disturbed by the popularity of Judaism.* Rosemary Ruether (1974) sees anti-Semitism as inseparable from early Christianity, and that at the heart of the dispute between the two religions is "the messiahship of Jesus" (p. 28). Ruether contends that for "Christianity, anti-Judaism was not merely a defense against attack, but an intrinsic need of Christian self-affirmation" (p. 181). Judaism had to be rejected completely for Christianity to survive. It is equally important to consider the possibility that Christianity is much more Hellenic than Judaic, and that "among some Christian scholars the contrast between Judaism and Hellenism masked a crude anti-Semitism," and that "the Church had captured the hearts of the Roman Empire only because Pauline Christianity was Hellenized and not a Jewish phenomenon" (Goodman, p. 107).

The anti-Semitism of Christian antiquity came about for several reasons, chiefly among them was the realization that Judaism did not end as some wished. Only after the revolt of 133-135, when Rome suffered severe losses in Judea, did the Christian Church take advantage of the anger and hostility toward Jews by co-opting Judaic practices many favored while at the same time denigrating Judaism. Yet, even these measures were insufficient for a while to drive a wedge between Judaism and Christianity as well as between Judaism and Rome.

A point of caution is also merited regarding scholarship on Christian antiquity and its struggle with Judaism. Citing G. F. Moore, Gager argues that "Christian interest in Jewish literature has always been apologetic or polemic rather than historical" (p. 31). Christian theology and scholarship continued earlier polemics and did not pursue a more honest account of the historical record; in so doing, such theology/scholarship has allowed anti-Semitism to continue, by passivity if not by design. One example of such biased attitudes toward the historicity of Judaism during the Roman period is the assessment of Longinus, a teacher of rhetoric and the sublime, whose praise of Judaism was initially dismissed as erroneous interpretation. Once refuted it was revised such that a new assessment declared that he must have been Jewish which he was not. The accurate assessment would take Longinus' attitude toward Judaism as the "broad and deep penetration of Judaism in the Greco-Roman world of the first century," an assessment clearly not to the liking of many scholars of Christianity (Gager, p. 83).

The larger mischaracterization of the history of the early Church's attitudes toward Judaism lies in the fact that, until recently, the voice of the many Judaizing Christians, those who saw no need to abandon their Jewish origin, was not heard. Instead, a corrected assessment of wide-spread Jewish philosophy or monotheism in the Greco-Roman world makes the role of anti-Semitism as means-to-an-end that much clearer. Though recent scholarship into Christian antiquity is laudable for its corrective stance, centuries of accepting Christian polemics and the longevity of suspect scholarship bares much responsibility for promoting and perpetuating anti-Semitism. For example, recent scholarship has sought to temper Paul's supposed hostility toward Judaism (Gager, pp. 7, 21-31, 198). Specifically, Paul's teaching, and especially his view that the "Torah and Christ are mutually exclusive categories," though now taken with greater caution, has stood for centuries as the justification for the denigration of Judaism (p. 247).

At the core of the tension between Christianity and Judaism is the Hebrew Bible as the source of documentary evidence for claims made by both religions regarding the Messiah. Both religions seek legitimacy to be confirmed by biblical proof. From the Jewish perspective, rejection of Jesus as the Messiah is consistent with the Hebrew Scripture since the acceptance of Jesus as the Messiah would have amounted to a rejection of biblical precepts about God. Christianity had to answer this challenge since its foundation and identity rests on biblical proof, but it has selected to do so by rejecting Judaism and claiming to be its replacement. "Replacement theology" became the principle argument Christianity presented, claiming to have taken over Judaism, replacing it, nullifying Judaism, and holding those still pursuing it in contempt. St. Augustine advocated this theology by claiming that the House of Israel has been cast off by God, formulating replacement theology as an official Church doctrine (Laqueur, p. 53). Though replacement theology has been rejected by several Christian denominations, especially in the United States, for centuries, claims Brog, "Replacement theology led inexorably to anti-Semitic opinion, legislation and action. Rejected by God, the Jews found little mercy from man" (pp, 3-5, 14, 22).

St. Augustine added a vicious twist to the Christian "need" of Judaism, advocating the continued existence of Jewish communities as necessary to overcome Christianity's credibility difficulties. Accordingly, St. Augustine feared that given the Old Testament's many references to the coming of the Messiah, those doubting such prophecies would dismiss Christian claims as forgery. As Laqueur puts it, for St. Augustine, "the survival of Jews was necessary — as proof of the essential rightness of Christianity; their misery was to help to let the glory of Christ shine all the more" (p. 53). The principal rhetorical move here based on the notion that if the credibility of a source is in the hands of the enemy or a hostile entity, its authenticity cannot be doubted. Put differently, if the Jews as "enemies of Christ" have the best proof of his coming, who could doubt Him? Jews, Christians hold, then, have an important mission — their continued existence as "proof" of Christ's rightness. Of course, no one bothered to ask Jews if they were willing to take on this mission. Ostensibly, Jews were to be protected but humiliated and punished repeatedly. Thus perhaps developed the tradition of some popes who sought to protect Jews when put under attack. This twisted logic has made anti-Semitism not only possible but it encouraged its perpetuation. But there is a more profound implication to this theological point — that of Christianity needing to prove its theology correct. But if Christianity is morally and ethically "right," it needs no such proof in the first place. Here, I contend, lies the rhetorical origin of anti-Semitism: *self doubt of religious acts and its guilt thereof resulted in projecting the charge of eternal guilt onto a perceived antagonist — the Jew — from whom religious origin and foundation is derived.*

Indeed, the foundation of Christianity on Judaism was difficult for Christianity to accept and any attempt at theological maneuvering thereof would be judged against the norm, context, and practice as established in Judaism. Though the decision to repudiate Judaism was not without controversy among the leaders of the early Church, as some wished for a complete repudiation of the Old Testament, in the end, the Jewish foundation of Christianity was accepted but with it also came an anti-Judaic stance and a hateful rhetoric (Gager, pp. 134-159). This decision illustrates that anti-Semitism was not a spontaneous reflection of contemporary sentiments but a conscious decision made with specific intent and objectives.

Thus developed a theology, and a rhetorical stance, that argued that not only is Christianity superior to Judaism, but it also argued that God had rejected the Jewish people. Even this stance was not enough as the early Church also selected to demonize Judaism. As Gager aptly states, "when neither textual criticism nor exegetical discussion proved capable of settling any of the major issues, Christians resorted to the simple assertion that the Jews, as God's rejected people, were blind to the meaning of their own scriptures. At this point debate ended and diatribe began" (p. 159). The diatribes that came were most malicious, mocking the "biblical god as envious, ignorant, malicious, blind and jealous," or dismissing "as a laughingstock every hero ([e.g.,]Adam, Abraham, Isaac, Jacob, David, Solomon, the twelve prophets, and Moses) of the Jewish Bible" (p. 171). Accusing Jews of deicide was not enough, as Carroll argues, Christians went further to argue that Jews were not only their enemy but God's enemy as well, and that "when later, mainly Gentile Christians misread the story, is what made it lethal" (2002, p. 92).

Absent the ability to confront logically the theological challenge Judaism provided, especially those related to the Messianic idea, and given the attractiveness of the Jewish faith in the Roman Empire, attacking and denigrating Judaism became the rhetorical weapon of choice. Anti-Semitism became the tool for Christianity's survival, demonizing Jews and Judaism as the preferred *modus operandi*. Though initially the strategy was unsuccessful and questionable, Christian dogma gradually gained strength and credence and was institutionalized. The promise of redemption over one's sins made all the difference; it offered a solution, or absolution, to most, if not all who chose to believe it. The hope for the end of days and its promised salvation was attractive. The Jewish messianic conception was key to Christendom's success as it founded faith on hope; an appealing formula for dealing with life's sins and guilt.

The rhetoric of charging Jews with carrying an eternal guilt was transformed into a rhetoric of invented causes whereby Jews were also charged with causing malevolent occurrences. This rhetoric of cause would display itself most clearly in the strategy of reversing arguments. For example, while Jews were well integrated and respected and whose practices were often emulated, they were accused of espousing separateness; the dietary laws that in essence preserved hygiene and cleanliness also brought charges of poisoning wells and causing disease in others; or, the miniscule number of Jews would not stand in the way of charging Jews with seeking to control the world. This rhetorical device of reversing accusations and lacing them with negative attributes, of blaming Jews for acts others committed, would be found time and again all the way into modern and contemporary anti-Semitism. Finally, in its anti-Jewish invectives, Christian antiquity sought to cover its own doubts, questions, and uncertainty that stood at the foundation of its theology.

Carroll argues that the charge of deicide dates back to the pronouncement of Bishop Melito of Sardis during the second century CE (p. 7). Killing Christ would be the ultimate rhetorical weapon as evidenced in the homilies of Church Fathers primarily in the 4th century. While Jesus' crucifixion was not an important feature in the theology of early Christians, not as long as the Romans used it as a tool of capital punishment, it would gain much credence later and become the primary accusation against Jews. The accusation of decide would intensify the rhetorical war individual Church leaders undertook in the hope of finding a stronger argument and a more lasting case against Judaism.

The deicide charge, as Carroll shows, also ignores the role of Pilate, the Roman governor, whose savagery was quite known, and his later slaughter of worshipping Samaritans would result in his recall back to Rome (Carroll, pp. 84-85). Ostensibly, the Jews would carry the brunt of the crucifixion and not the Romans. The charge of killing the founder of Christianity would prove devastating to Jews throughout history and become a justification for retribution of all kinds, including genocide. Killing those who killed a founding figure would become the ultimate rhetorical formula and the most succinct and justifiable argument, no matter how remote in time or how erroneous the facts of the case. Thus, "the hatred of Jews has been no incidental anomaly but a central action of Christian history, reaching to the core of Christian character. Jew hatred's perversion of the Gospel message launched a history . . . that achieved its climax in the Holocaust" (Carroll, p. 22).

Conclusion

Anti-Semitism was not an afterthought but a conscious decision of the early Church, disturbed by the continued success of Judaism in Rome despite several revolts against the Roman occupier of Judea. Ostensibly, the early Church settled on the strategy of repressing Judaism. It took until the fourth century for the Church to separate itself from Judaism. Recalling events that took place several centuries earlier, the Church intensified the attack on Judaism by the use of invectives until the new strategy yielded the sought results. The most crucial and devastating development for Jews would be the charge of deicide with the specific instruction by Church leaders to construct the charge of Christ-killer as eternal. With the additional instruction to keep Jews humiliated and scorned, anti-Semitism was set in motion as a lethal weapon that would last for centuries. Subsequently, Jews would pay a heavy price for events that they did not witness nor were part of.

Rhetorically, it is significant that reasonable arguments did not yield the separation from Judaism Christianity sought. Only by intensifying the charge and constructing it around the act of death and killing, and accompanied with a heavy dose of visualization and the body rhetoric thereof, the kind that secure continued emotional involvement, did the early Church succeeded in pinning the charge of Jesus' death on the cross on the Jews.

Note

1. The Bar Cochba (or Kokhba) revolt of 132-5CE, is named after its leader Shimon bar Kosiba, was perhaps the most violent of the Jewish resistance to Roman rule. The revolt was not easily crushed as exemplified in the official statement to the Roman Senate that did not include the customary reference to the health of the legions (Goodman, pp. 468-469).

11

Guilt as Foundational to Anti-Semitism

As discussed earlier in Chapter 1, rhetoric scholar Kenneth Burke has argued that guilt is inherent to human beings and that it can manifest itself in various feelings and sentiments such as doubt, uncertainty, or inadequacy. Any imperfection can yield guilt that subsequently promotes a rhetorical process Burke calls *dramatism* — a process by which people overcome guilt through the projection devices of scapegoating, victimage and sacrifice, meant to achieve redemption and ultimately, purification (Burke, 1973, pp. 39-40). Burke would find the terms for his perspective in the religious context where the dramatistic process would be exercised both literally and metaphorically. The application of this perspective however can cover all contexts, not just religious ones. As he explains:

> a dramatistic analysis shows how the negativistic principle of guilt implicit in the nature of order combines with the principles of thoroughness (or "perfection") and substitution that are characteristic of symbol systems in such a way that the sacrificial principle of victimage (the "scapegoat") is intrinsic to human congregation. The intricate line of exposition might be summed up this: If order, then guilt; if guilt, then need for redemption; but any such "payment" is victimage (Burke, 1968, pp. 445-452).

In a poetic, yet instructive manner, Burke outlines the human rhetorical process:

Here are the steps

In the Iron Law of History
That welds Order and Sacrifice:
Order leads to Guilt
(for who can keep commandments!)
Guilt needs Redemption
(for who would not be cleansed!)
Redemption needs Redeemer
(which is to say, a Victim!)
Order
Through Guilt
To Victimage
(hence: Cult of the Kill). (Burke, 1961, pp. 4-5)

In lay terms, Burke argues that imperfection motivates perfection, and one is motivated to achieve perfection. Such a process, however, is accomplished through sacrifice — either of self (mortification) or of others (victimage) — or, one succeeds when another is crushed (sometimes metaphorically and at other times, literally). These are the discursive and persuasive games humans play; however their consequences could be quite devastating and deadly.

Christianity has been developed around the concept of "redemption by the sacrifice of a crucified Christ," and given this foundational act Burke asks "just what happens in an era of post-Christian science, when the ways of socialization have been secularized? Does the need for the vicarage of this Sacrificial King merely dwindle away? Or must some other person or persons, individual or corporate, real or fictive, take over the redemption role?" For Burke, the answer lies in human need for "a Vessel to which will be ritualistically delegated a purgative function, in being symbolically laden with the burdens of individual and collective guilt." Burke points to the fact that in Hitler's anti-Semitism the Jews became the Vessel that "provided the secularized replica of the Divine Scapegoat (1953, pp. 31-32). Hitler did not invent the mechanism of blaming Jews for all that befell Germany; he simply took a tried-and-true line of reasoning whereby the Jew has been the primary vessel for Christian redemption centuries earlier and spanned it into racial redemption necessitated by the Jewish contamination of the Aryan blood.

Christian self doubt about its religious foundation and doctrine, and the initial rejection by Judaism, became an important source of concern and guilt, and thus the impetus for anti-Semitism. Attacking Jews and Judaism became the weapon of choice in overcoming such doubt, and thus developed a persistent anti-Semitism as the *modus operandi* of the Christian doctrine. Christianity claims to be an extension of Judaism and stands for the fulfillment of the messianic idea initially developed in Judaism.[1] However, despite the many efforts to convince Jews of this premise, Jews rejected this replacement theory in their religion. In rejecting Christ, Jews were taken as casting doubt about claims that are central to Christianity. That Judaism's existence was taken as a challenge to Christendom has ultimately brought upon an inherent guilt about theological claims.

While Jews have countered Christianity in its early days, when it was still a Jewish sect, and sporadically during the Middle-Ages (often by the Church's instigation), for the past several centuries, Jews have rarely challenged Christianity and its claims. When Christianity felt a bit more comfortable debating Jews, especially during the Reformation era, these debates, instigated by the Church and set in such a way as to ensure "the Jews lost even when they presented superior arguments" (Lazare, 1967, p. 75). This way of thinking has pervaded most centuries and, only in the post World War II era have relationships between Judaism and Christianity improved in recognition of earlier harsh treatment. Given the passage of time since the outset of Christianity, that after two thousand years, Christianity is likely no longer insecure and its future is no longer in jeopardy. Yet, the improved relationship between the Church and Judaism is largely the result of responsibility felt by Christians over anti-Semitism and the role it has played in the murder of millions of Jews during the Holocaust.

But why is Christianity in doubt? Why the constant need to prove Christianity's foundational claims? The case studies and episodes of anti-Semitism covered here, and many others not included in this volume, point to several explanations. The reliance on Judaism and the continuous need to prove Christianity's foretelling in the Old Testament is indicative of the uncomfortable, if not suspect, relationship between the two religions. Christianity is completely reliant on the persona of one individual — Christ, while Judaism is not dependent on the existence of one individual, nor is its survival contingent on one and only one iconic figure. This transformation of Judaism from an invisible God (non-human)-based religion to Christianity which is God/human/visible being-based religion had to be accompanied with proof and justification for such a radical transformation from the Jewish conception. The contention raised here is not about the theology at hand but about the rhetorical stance taken, whereby a theological transformation was accompanied by a hatred that was seen as necessary to carry such a significant change. This very selection of hatred as strategy/theology in itself represents the weakness of the theological arguments Christianity offered instead of a well-reasoned argument for its theological position.

When the tension is caused not by two agents who are far removed from each other, but by agents who are actually rather close, and one of them claims to complete the other, the result is more, rather than less, antagonism. Indeed, the proximity of the two religions, especially during the first three centuries, is a significant reason for the tension Christianity developed with Judaism. The obsession with Judaism would continue into the Middle-Ages. Such tensions, at least in dramatic and rhetorical plot lines, usually require that one agent be slain for the other to succeed.

In Martin Luther's diatribe *Against the Jews and Their Lies*, one finds the ultimate dramatistic process. In proposing how to deal with Jews, Martin Luther suggested the following:

> First, their synagogues should be set on fire, and whatever does not burn up should be covered or spread with dirt so that no one may ever be able to see a cinder of stone of it. And this ought to be done for the honour of God and of Christianity in order that God may see that we are Christians, and that we have not wittingly tolerated or approved of such public lying, cursing and blaspheming of his son and his Christians . . . Secondly, their homes should likewise be broken down and destroyed. For they perpetuate the same things there that they do in their synagogues . . . Thirdly, they should be deprived of their prayer books and Talmuds in which such idolatry, lies, cursing and blasphemy are taught. Fourthly, their rabbis must be forbidden under threat of death to teach anymore (cited in Cohn-Sherbok, 2006, p. 32).

Martin Luther's destructive plan of Jewish homes, houses of worship and forbidding Jewish practices, as if taken directly from the sermons of St. Chrysostom, is presented as acts in honor of God. The very action of destruction would not only please God but would be considered a sign of one's Christian duty to God. The implied hierarchy in this act of destruction is Christianity's supremacy over Judaism, but what justifies this ultimate act of destruction?

The harsh treatment Luther calls for is partially the result of his anger over his earlier attempt to argue against the anti-Semitism of the Catholic Church and his rather sympathetic view of Judaism as the mother religion. But Luther also assumed that given his favorable view of Judaism that Jews would be grateful enough for his generous views and convert to his brand of Christianity. Though many Jews were quite happy with the new wind of progress of the early sixteen century, conversion was not the subsequent act they contemplated. Hence, Luther's anger and his claim that Christianity needs to assert its supremacy was premised on Paul's assertion that "the Jewish nation had been rejected by God and that the old covenant had been superseded" (Cohn-Sherbok, p. 33). The assumption that conversion for Jews was an easy if not an act of gratefulness shows, at best, a naive and shallow Christian conception and understanding of Judaism, and at worse, a vengefulness in retaliation to Jews refusal to convert.

The Wedding in Cana

A unique and perhaps even a radical if not controversial perspective on the notion of guilt as foundational to anti-Semitism is the study of the wedding in Cana by Judith Gold (1999). She finds the wedding in Cana (a village outside Nazareth in the Galilee region of ancient, as well as modern Israel) to be a fertility cult event and that its central feature — the turning of water into wine — is representative of a Dionysian festival known as *Bacchanal*. The theme of this ritual is the reenactment of "the life cycle of the young god of the wine" (Gold, p. 154). Both Mary and Jesus are present at the wedding and according to specific statements and instructions between Mary, Jesus, and the attendants present, Gold argues that the wedding in Cana is between Jesus and his mother.

The central theme of a Dionysian ritual is the turning of water into wine which is also Jesus' first sign. Thus, the act that establishes the epiphany of Dionysus also marks the Christian Epiphany. The wedding in Cana, writes Gold, "indelibly stamps Cana with the 'imprint of Dionysus'" (p. 155). What I glean from Gold's discussion on the wedding at Cana suggests that the roots of anti-Semitism are inherently rhetorical and motivated by guilt.[2] At the heart of this event stands an incestuous relationship between Mary and Jesus, a story that appears only in John 2:1-11, an act that Gold opines is similar to other "incestuous unions between deities."[3] Incest, writes Gold, is "a religious expression [that] was often made obligatory in the rites of fertility religions" (p. 151). The material evidence for this perspective lies in several features of the story such as the turning of water into wine and the celebration of the Dionysus rite on January 6 which is the same day of the reading of the Cana liturgy (Gold, p. 155). Gold's thesis is that the Dionysian wedding at Cana is disguised, presented instead as a Jewish ritual which it was not. Gold's thesis is that "the Christ story is an incest tale. A fertility cult drama with Judaistic façade" (pp. 157-158, 163).

What Gold draws from the wedding in Cana is that "anti-Semitism is incest fear" and that the principal fear of incest has been used to construct an image of the Jew as a monster "materialized into flesh and blood." The roots of the monster and devil images lie in the view of the wedding in Cana whereby "as God, Jesus is 'absolved' of earthly transgression . . . But as man, Jesus is bound by the incest taboo. He is subject to retribution." Thus, more profoundly, "as God, Jesus is 'Christian': the emerging Deity of Cana, the offspring of Father and Virgin, the Firstborn to be sacrificed, the suffering, dying God of Calvary. As man, Jesus is a Jew." As God, Jesus is innocent of incest, but as man, Jesus, a Jew, committed incest, an abomination as far Judaism is concerned (pp. 183-184). Jesus the Jew becomes the generic Jew while Jesus the God is absolved of any sacrilegious act. If anti-Semitism is incest fear, as Gold puts it, then the anti-Semite is the one who hates the Jew as a rhetorical process of cleansing oneself of the incest guilt. The Jew, then, is the vehicle for transferring one's sins.

What is intriguing about this early Christian story is the attempt to saddle a Dionysian ritual of an incestuous relationship between mother and son with Jewish practices. Such ritual is foreign to Judaism and is clearly Greek in origin. But why accuse Jews and Judaism of promoting this practice? Because the story is disturbing, and if true, would shed different light on Jesus and Christianity. One way to fend off any potential lessening of Jesus' stature regarding the wedding in Cana is to accuse Judaism of promoting this ritual. Jews, then, are guilty of promoting incest and Jesus is the innocent victim of evil Jews. If the wedding in Cana carries the significance related here, then the fear of incest would explain, at least in part, why, throughout the ages, anti-Semites have often been intrigued by Jews' sexuality. The Dionysus ritual of mother and son cohabitating, clearly considered a sin in Judaism, ushered in the long tradition of accusing Jews of sins they have not committed. The false charge takes us back to the motives played out in this drama, accusing the "convenient" culprit, the Jew, as the agent of evil instead of dealing with the guilt inherent in the plot. The rhetoric of projection, then, appears time and again as the formula for promoting Christianity at the expense of Judaism.

A Foundational Narrative

A closely related source of tension between Christianity and Judaism with implications for anti-Semitism is the possibility that the Jews are envied for possessing an attractive story and a foundational narrative that has grounded its origin, history, conception of the deity and related moral and ethical guidelines. Both Christianity and Islam have claimed the Judaic narrative, or portions of it, as theirs, either by copying the story, chipping away at its authenticity, co-opting it, or arguing that its parts or its whole do not belong the Judaism. An appealing or a "good story" is attractive when it encapsulates the totality of a people's historical and mythic narrative. Rhetoric scholar Walter Fisher considers humans as "essentially storytellers" whose communication and decision-making follows the mode of "good reasons," and that the "production and practice of good reasons is ruled by matters of history, biography, culture, and character" (1984, p.7). Operationally, rationality is a matter of assigning *narrative probability* — an assessment of coherency of the narrative, or *narrative fidelity* — and assessment of truthfulness assigned to the narrative (pp. 7-8). Narratives as "good stories" that stand for human experience, explains much how in anti-Semitism a foundational story was co-opted and its authorship denied.[4]

In rather simplistic terms, the Jewish story is a foundational story about the origin of human development; about historical origin and about the relationship of humans and their God; about the lineage of founding patriarchs and matriarchs; and, about the progression of generations. It is a story whose primary metaphor is about continuity and purpose; about a cherished land and its centrality to a people's identity with many climatic events that carry moral imperatives, such as Noah and the flood, Abraham's journey from Ur to Canaan, Abraham and Isaac, Jacob and Joseph, the story of Moses and the Ten Commandments and their moral and universal implications, the Exodus from Egypt, of King David and the building of the Temple, its destruction and its re-building, among others. And above all else, it is a story about a people and their rather unique approach to the deity — a supreme but invisible God.

As a historical narrative of one people, the Hebrew Bible is indeed such a foundational storybook, replete with good and bad characters, the rise and fall of individuals and nations, of climatic anticipation and utter despair. The Bible is an attractive storybook because it incorporates many morality tales that are instructive and climatic, and whose lessons are rather universal. The Bible, as a collection of mini stories, develops a tale of a people with a distinct progression from a beginning through multiple accomplishments and failures that has become a foundational narrative, not only to Jews but to Christians and Muslims as well. Ultimately, the Bible is attractive because it is about the power of hope. No wonder others sought to co-opt the Bible; and co-opting they did and with dire consequences. Although this narrative cannot be ascertained to be accurate (though Archeology has, for the most past, confirmed many of its stories), it is *also* foundational to a belief system of two religions, Christianity and Islam, as their respective narrative sprung out of this Hebraic foundational narrative.

The "good story" was founded on a special relationship established between God and the Jewish people via their Patriarch Abraham. The

Jewish historical narrative begins with this contractual selection known as the Abrahamic covenant whereby God has chosen a people who would carry a specific purpose for humanity (Gen. 12: 1-3). Yet, the "good story" of Judaism, which covers some three thousand years of history, includes many unpleasant and even horrid chapters, and though the return of Jews to their land of antiquity completes a historical cycle, it is an experience accompanied with so much pain that many would have preferred not to have been "chosen" in the first place. Indeed, the co-option of the Jewish narrative is often limited to primarily accounting for its two poles: the beginning — God's covenant with Abraham, and the end — the return to the land of the covenant, ignoring the lengthy and troubled middle exemplified in centuries of persecution, hardship, and slavery. In short, those who approach the Jewish narrative from the outside, do so selectively.

Since the temporal variable is instrumental in constructing anti-Semitism as eternal, one is tempted to wonder whether the temporal is but a rationale for other reasons for hatred. In other words, in rationalizing eternal hatred by expanding and extending an original cause into a timeless guilt, are other reasons for anti-Semitism kept obscure? The cooption of Judaism is not without complications and one of them is the very guilt that exists in the act of "borrowing" from Judaism some of its tenets, symbols, holy places, and biblical stories. This guilt, emanating from such cooption, has been, and likely remains, a source of concern over issues of authenticity, originality, and numerous implications. Is it possible, then, that charging Jews with killing Christ was the preferred strategy in order to counter the Jewish charge of co-opting Judaism? By one pole stands the visual clarity of a crucified Jesus and by the other pole stands the Jewish Bible — a complex collection of tales and their moral implications. In its reductionist form we have the tension between Christianity and Judaism represented by the dead body of God on the one hand, and the narrative of His people who crucified him in the other; the visually simple vs. the complex and evolving. As an argumentative stance, Christianity's ostensibly powerful charge trumps Judaism's defense, but it does not relieve Christianity of its guilt.

Hatred of Judaism for being the mother religion from whom much was taken but rarely acknowledged is the rhetorical consequence of the "borrowers," allowing for a way out of the uncomfortable situation and a "necessary" step in order to feel secure and pure precisely because the act of cooption without acknowledgement is anything but an honorable act. The ultimate wish of the "borrowers" is to have the one borrowed from cease to exist; hence for Judaism to cease to exist so that Christianity (and later Islam) could feel secure in their claim of perfection.

St. Chrysostom came close to advocating this thought and, with his vicious attacks on Judaism, anti-Semitism was firmly established as a Church doctrine. Since Judaism's mere existence is seen as a continuous affront to those who claimed to have replaced it, anti-Semitism has persisted as well. The frustration over the Jews' rejection of Jesus has been very difficult for Christianity to accept. The decision to punish Jews for killing Christ and to keep them in that state of punishment until the Day of Judgment (which means forever) is but the activation of guilt.

If Christianity were to account for the complete story surrounding Jesus, it should have begun with the appreciation of Judaism for bringing Jesus to life, thus making Christianity possible, and then move to second part of the story — the accusation of killing him. However, the birth of Jesus as a Jew has rarely been part of the Christian narrative; only his killing is featured prominently. (Only beginning in late 19th Century have several Christian denominations, primarily Protestant ones, opposed the replacement theology, emphasizing instead Jesus' Jewish heritage and upbringing.) Subsequently, "the Jew is held responsible for the crime from which the Christian reaps moral and psychological benefit in redemption from sin" (Loewenstein, in Bergmann, pp. 44-45). One important manifestation of anti-Semitism as a strategic and purposeful hatred of Jews was to demonize them and equate them with Satan as the ultimate devil. The devil in Christianity is a rather prevalent concept, and, accordingly, Christians are to engage in a permanent fight with the devil, and since the Jews are the "devil's children," they must be fought permanently as well (Laqueur, p. 55). The temporality of anti-Semitism expressed as an eternal fight may have originated in this simplistic enthymeme.

This rhetorical process of hating the original religion has been complicated by the establishment of the State of Israel primarily because of its material and symbolic act. The return of Jews to the holy land, beginning in the late nineteenth century, closed the circle of two thousand years in Jewish history and Jewish narrative, not only by persisting despite all odds, but, for the first time, sharing their holy places with Christians and Muslims. This is not the way the plot was supposed to have developed; not from the Christian or the Islamic perspective, because Jews were not to inhabit Jerusalem or the Holy Land *again*. The temporality of the return of Jews to their ancestral land worked this time against the temporality of the Jews' eternal guilt and their banishment from their ancient land. Unable to integrate with local communities due to multiple restrictions regarding habitat and profession, and unwilling to forgo their religion despite harsh treatment over the ages, the return of Jews to their ancestral land after the passing of many centuries was taken as the symbolic victory for Judaism, thus an affront to those wishing for ages to have Judaism long disappear. What would Christianity say now of Jewish iniquities and the loss of the Holy Land? That the formula of punishment was wrong? Or that God had a plan that differed from what Christianity conceived? Probably not! Since religious dogma is rarely fallible, its rhetoric has to be consistent through the ages.

Given the establishment of holy places of the Christian and Islamic faiths on the ruins of Jewish sites such as the ancient Temple, the return of Jews to the Holy Land and their reclaiming of the same sites, was quite an unexpected and undesirable development. What is a Christian or a Muslim to do with their narratives, when the Jewish narrative had come full cycle? Yet, the Catholic Church did indeed correct itself in 1965, and though scholars would point to the Holocaust as the reason for the change, it is equally possible that the establishment of the State of Israel was an added and compelling development that the Church could not ignore, forcing itself to reconsider the theology of the Jewish people's estrangement from the Holy Land. In recent decades, this issue has been of a much greater concern for Islam than for Christianity, whereby the Islamic approach has simply been to deny Judaism its holy places while numerous Christian denominations have actually embraced Zionism and consider the return of Jews to the Holy Land a significant sign for Christianity in the form of the return of Christ.[5]

Take for example the competing Jewish claim that the holy places in

Jerusalem were built on the ruins of its ancient Temple originally built on the rock on which the patriarch Abraham planed to sacrifice his son Isaac, a claim that is also central to Islam. A simple chronology dictates that the Islamic holy place was originally the Jewish Temple built by Kings David and Solomon. Here is the heart of the tension; Judaism is the scorned religion precisely because it has original claims not only to the Biblical story but to the holy places, thus tying together a community, time and place. Thus, with Israel's establishment, anti-Semitism rhetoric shifted from hatred of Jewish people to hatred of the Jewish state, challenging the foundation of the State and its right to exist. This attitude is well illustrated in a recent statement by an Islamic cleric, Sheikh Raed Salah, who claimed that "The Al-Aqsa mosque was never the site of a Jewish temple," meaning, the holy site has no connection to any ancient significance. The cleric also challenged Israel's historical claims to the city of Jerusalem and denied "that there ever existed a Jewish temple on the Temple Mount" ("Arab Leader Denies Temple Ever Existed," *The Jerusalem Post*, 2008, March 10). Such is the rhetoric of denial when faced with historical evidence. Yet, this attempt at dissociating Judaism from Biblical sites is indicative of how important is the holy sites as foundational to each religion and its narrative.

Subsequently, the enactment of ancient roots in a modern state, meant to allow Jews to escape the difficulties of living among others, brought a new level of anti-Semitism and a new twist on an old hatred. Following World War II, anti-Semitism abated in Europe, primarily out of guilt of the horrendous killing of Jews in the Holocaust. In the Near East, however, anti-Semitism, primarily of the European kind, set roots in the Islamic world. The ancient city of Jerusalem, the city of David and Zion, became the capital of Israel, resuming the link to a distant past. The objection of most nations to recognizing Jerusalem as Israel's capital is indicative of how volatile the city is in others' perception and just how difficult it is to accept Israel operating from its ancient site. Here the religious and the national sites have merged to combine a site of peoplehood — a nation's capitol and Judaism's eternal city.

At issue, then, are differing perspectives on how different people view a national perspective. Most Israelis, and to an extent, many Jews throughout history, have followed a theological and spiritual perspective (hence, the Zionist ideal) that ties their theology to its ancient history, and thus to its ancient land. Muslims follow a similar, though not an identical perspective, whereby its theology and spirituality are tied to the same historic-religious site — Jerusalem and, by extension, the Holy Land. Outside the Middle East, other considerations such as international law and human rights often trump religious considerations and, hence, the source of tension and misunderstanding. But the most difficult tension is not between dissimilar perspectives on the role of Jerusalem or Israel as the materiality of ancestral land, religion and community, but the similar perspective taken, primarily by Jews and Muslims with the same connection to land, religion and community thereof, cherishing the same sites in the old city of Jerusalem and deriving important features of their respective narratives from this and other holy sites.

Claims that Israel has no right to exist and seeking to have Jews reside where they do not choose — very much the activation of anti-Semitism, is to deny Jews their right to develop their own perspective on their nationalistic expression. Yet, the very denial of Jews of their historical land on the ground that such reasoning is no longer acceptable is fine, theoretically, but it should apply, then, to all people who seek the same; not just Jews.

These competing narratives cannot be dismissed as not warranted or as not foundational to the notion of Jewish or Arab peoplehood. However, these competing narratives need also be acknowledged for their historical and expressive qualities. The Christian and Islamic religious narratives are developed out of the Jewish/Hebraic narrative. This very acknowledgement can do much to resolve both anti-Semitism and even the Arab-Israeli conflict. Put more simply, a clear and straightforward recognition of the Jewish people's heritage and connection to the ancestral land, as well as Israel's right to exist could be the formula for ending anti-Semitism and its goal of delegitimizing Israel. From this point onward, the chances of solving the Arab-Israeli conflict are much greater.

Conclusion

Both Christianity and Islam have roots in Judaism, have borrowed heavily from its biblical narratives, rely heavily on its primary symbols, sites, and agents, and seek converts to their faiths reasoned as a perfected form of the latter. With such proximity to Judaism, it is no wonder that hatred developed shortly after the establishment of both Christianity and Islam. After all, how can one borrow heavily from another and claim to be original? It is this proximity of Christianity and Islam to Judaism that stands at the root of anti-Semitism and the root cause for its longevity. This is the essence of guilt — Judaism's presence as a constant reminder that Christianity and Islam would not have come to life without Judaism as the prior and earlier religion, and that Judaism's prior existence does contradict the "order" of things as Christianity and Islam would have preferred. Only the elimination of Judaism can allow Christianity and Islam to claim theology and geography with no recrimination. But as long as Judaism stands, a constant doubt creeps into the other two religions, casting suspicion about various claims.

Throughout history, Christianity, and later Islam, have been willing to accept or adopt the most bizarre accusations against Jews — sorcery, devil-worshiping, blood libels, and the like. It begs the question though as to why have such outrageous accusations been so easily accepted? The answer I submit lies in the constant need to demonize Judaism as a way of keeping Jews submissive and humiliated for fear that they would otherwise challenge a borrowed theology. The possibility of Judaism reclaiming its ancient land was not contemplated in Christianity and Islam for centuries, yet when Zionism was introduced to world politics, Christianity and Islam would differ in their approach, primarily due to geo-political reasons.

Though European colonial powers were entrusted in administering the Near East, this temporary arrangement did result in competing claims to ancient sites. Christianity, for the most part, would keep its anti-Semitism European, with Philo-Semites supporting Zionism, while anti-Semites would settle for the racial grounding. Islam, in control of vast territories of the region for centuries, would not take lightly the resurgence of Judaism in their midst, hence the greater intensity and a change in attitude from the *dhimmi* to a hostile entity. Cooption of religious sites would thus be more acute in the relationship between Islam and Judaism than between Christianity and Judaism. For Christianity, the passage of time from antiquity and, especially, the Holocaust, would bring about a more accommodating relationship with Judaism. Islam would intensify its relationship with Judaism once it was realized that the Zionist movement and, subsequently, the creation of the State of Israel, became a reality. The resultant effect of the growing conflict was the conflation of religious with political rhetoric and with the aid of Nazi Germany, the grounding of Islamist anti-Semitism in religious texts and vile images.

Notes

1.　Similarly, Freud contemplated the possibility that hating Jews was the result of jealousy of those who brought monotheism and considered themselves chosen by God. See, Laqueur, 2006, p. 37.
2.　For Gold the wedding in Cana is a "festival for Mother and Son, in which the mother goddess asks her son to show forth, to engage with her in the archetypal sexual rite of the sacred marriage ceremony. The inaugural event of a fertility drama in which the son — hesitant, reluctant, reticent — ultimately accedes to his mother's wish." Gold claims that "Jesus' incestuous relationship with his mother is underscored by the episode of the cleansing of the Temple" which comes immediately after in John 2:13-22. Gold, pp. 158-159.
3.　Gold cites several examples for such unions: Kronus and Rhea (father and daughter), Ishtar and Tammuz (mother and son), and Isis and Osiris (sister and brother). See Gold, 1999, p. 151.
4.　By narration, Fisher refers "to a theory of symbolic action — words and/or deeds — that have sequence and meaning for those who live, create, or interpret them." The narrative as a perspective combines argumentative and persuasive themes with literary and aesthetic theme. The force of the narrative lies in the narrative's ability to hide its persuasive intent and often appearing as an attractive story (1984, p. 2).
5.　The evangelical turn in the form of "Christian Zionism" is not without its complexity. One the one hand, it advocates a pro-Israeli stance. On the other hand, however, this support is grounded in the belief in the "end of days" when Jews would convert to Christianity. The ultimate plan for the conversion of Jews to Christianity remains a sore point for Jews who otherwise have welcomed this movement's political stance. Another problem is that Christian Zionism is, at times, grounded in anti-Muslim racism.

12

The "Jew" as an Identity of Name and Place

"Anti-Semitism," it has been pointed out by numerous scholars, is a misnomer and that a more accurate term is "anti-Judaism" or "Judeo-phobia." Regardless of the terminology used, at the core of this phenomenon is the word "Jew," standing in for a name and identity. This name and identity merit examination and the consideration such that it can shed additional light on the scourge of anti-Semitism. The word "Jew" is a shorthand European extraction of the name Judah (one of the Patriarch Jacob's twelve sons) from which the region of Judea was coined. Judea was the southern kingdom of ancient Israel and, after the reign of King Solomon, two kingdoms would be formed: Israel to the north and Judea to the south. This historically-based coinage of the term has evolved over time into two competing identities: that of Jews' self identification and those of non-Jews' identification of the Jew. These two identities would often clash in anti-Semitic discourse.

The word "Jew," then, carries a rich meaning and is a reference to more than just a personal identity; it is also a reference to a land, and later, a kingdom founded by King David. There is much symbolism attached to this particular king and his future lineage to Jews and subsequently, to Christians as well. The location of Jerusalem in the region of Judea, and its central focus as the capitol of the ancient kingdom, is of utmost and holy importance. It was in the capitol of Judea that the temple was built and from whence all political, religious and symbolic powers emanated. Though the northern kingdom, Israel, was lost prior to the demise of Judea in 772 BCE, its name has been resurrected two millennia later to name the modern State of Israel. Like the origin of Judea in Judah, son of the patriarch Jacob, "Israel," too, is a person's given name. In this case, it is Jacob himself who, after wrestling with God's angel, acquired the honorary name "Israel," which literally means to wrestle with God, and metaphorically means "to know God."

Both individuals, father and son, Jacob-Israel and Judah-Judaism, then, would lend their name to a land and a people. Hence, the centrality of the land, of its history and of its religious and historical foundation as significant to the identity of those affiliated with it. For many Jews, their identity has been a matter of a cherished land long lost and recovered, and a past that unifies Judaism as a unique entity not easily comprehended. The centuries old ritual and liturgical refrain "next year in Jerusalem," illustrates the symbolic importance of this city in connecting the ancient kingdom with contemporary life. Hence, Israel's current capitol, the same as in the ancient kingdom, is an important aspect into Jewish identity. This identity would not be missed by those espousing anti-Semitism. Whether by coincidence or by design, the same name "Judah" from whence Jew and Judaism is coined, is also the name of the individual who supposedly betrayed Jesus. One cannot escape the suspicion that perhaps anti-Semitism was reinforced by the naming Judah Iscariot as the betrayer of Christ, thus casting a cloud over Judeans and on Jews ever since.[1]

In a statement submitted to the *United Nations World Conference Against Racism*, the Jacob Blaustein Institute, a human rights organization under the auspicious of the American Jewish Committee, states that though dispersed world-wide for centuries, Jews have in common the perception that

> they are descendants (actual or adoptive) of nomadic tribes that settled between the Mediterranean and the Jordan River more than 30 centuries ago, and whose early history, culture, and religious experience are reflected in the Hebrew Bible ... And indeed, the power of the biblical insistence on monotheism, the majesty of the Hebrew Bible's poetry, the authority of its ethical precepts, and the drama of its narrative of the exodus from slavery to freedom have not only commanded the devoted attention of Jews, but also the reverence of both Christians and Moslems. (Julius et al, p. 2)

The statement also describes "the community's distinctive memory of their national existence in ancient Israel, and their aspiration to return to Zion remained powerful centripetal forces in the life of the Jewish people throughout many centuries, sustaining a sense of communal identity both among the devoutly religious and, in modern times, among relatively secularized Jews as well" (Julius et. al., p. 2).

This identity of the Jew, by and for Jews, points to time and place — a reminder of a foundational religion and with it the implied claim to an historical order not accorded the same value in Christianity and Islam. Recall that for Kenneth Burke, order leads to guilt, and guilt prompts all kinds of unsavory acts on the road to redemption. Since Christianity or Islam's primacy (or supremacy) runs suspect when put in a historical sequence (chronological order), the resultant guilt over circumventing the historical order leads to antagonism against the older religion.

As a unique form of foundational memories, Jews have continuously lamented their expulsion from their historic land. This lamentation has been part of the religious ritual for ages. The public display of memory has been entrenched in the Jewish psyche and its religious institutionalization ensured the continuation of memory as the essence of hope. In hope is the aspiration for better days and the unity of the group organized around shared symbols and narratives. Judaism, then, found a rhetorical process for its continuity amidst hostility and persecution. The essence of this continuity was to constitute the identity of Jews with their historicity, hence memory, of a past and a land.

Originally, Judaism (or the Hebraic faith) was a unique if not a revolutionary religion in the sense that it was based on an idea, a conception that the deity could not and should not be proven visually, nor be translated into a physical entity. Subsequently, in Judaism, no physical human being can stand for God, and God remains an eternal idea, a metaphor, and an invisible deity. The Jewish edict against any material depiction of God is clearly the principle operative statement about the conception of the deity. This biblical reference to the relationship between God and the Hebraic people had turned into a cause for envy and subsequently, hatred, often expressed in the "chosen people" reference. A people's belief that their God has selected them to teach and instruct others has been turned by non-Jews into a charge of

Judaism's superiority. Not only is this phrase taken for an elitist statement, in the struggle over hierarchy and chronology, the phrase "chosen people" implies that others were *un*chosen. Such a supposed selection by God is sure to turn those not chosen to hate the chosen. In short, here we find another block in the wall that anti-Semites has sought to build between Judaism and those who borrowed from it. However, the nuanced perspective allows the "antagonism toward the claim of choseness" to be considered justified (Wistrich, 2010, p. 99).

What eludes many anti-Semites is the notion that believers of other faiths often hold on to the notion that God has selected them and that their religion is superior to others.[2] Yet, despite the tendency of religions as well as nations in general to claim their unique superiority over others, it is the Jewish identify that gets criticized and is used as pretext for hatred. Rhetorically, the statement that God has chosen the Jewish people as His people must be understood in reverse, whereby the Jewish people have selected their God, a monotheistic and abstract conception. This conception, unique for its time and place, has positioned Judaism of antiquity and since as different from its surrounding peoples and their deities. The deity in Judaism is value-based and not an entity to be proven visually and/or factually. This unique conception is operative today as it has been for millennia. Neither Christianity nor Islam would emulate this conception, and this ideational deity may be the source of the "chosen people" charge, whereby Jews are accused of being elitist instead of being respected for their unique conception of the deity. The rhetoric of hate is easier than the rhetoric of respect because in hate, the hater stands at the top of the hierarchy whereas with respect, the respecting and the respected stand on an equal plane.

Equally important, Judaism in its spirituality and liturgy is also a place-based religion, perhaps a compensatory value for the lack of iconic and material essence, in short — its historical rootlessness. This is not a perspective construed narrowly as a political argument supporting the State of Israel; rather, this is a perspective that kept Judaism alive for centuries. This perspective is not the product of Zionism. If any, Zionism recognized, albeit through bitter debates, that "Zionism Without Zion" was not acceptable to most Jews. Judaism is historically tied to its location of birth and foundation, and this spiritual connection to its ancient sites is judged by some as essential for its existence, whether one resides in its proximity or not. The connection to the land was flexible enough though that when the land was lost, memories could replace it without causing much disruption to the religious foundations. Thus, despite removal from its ancient lands by various powers such as the Babylonians, the Assyrians, and the Romans, and dispersion of Jews, the connection to the Holy Land has remained constant in prayers, aspirations, and liturgy. Without the connection to the land, however remote, Judaism could not have survived, or at least not to the extent that it has. Such, for example was the case when early Zionists who contemplated different "homelands" such as Uganda, quickly discovered that only the Holy Land was meaningful and mythic to Jews. This myth, write Rowland and Frank, "was not a strategy that could be put aside when writing a message to the United Nations; it was a fundamental truth" (Rowland and Frank, p. 58).

That the land of Israel carries a "mythic importance" to Jews is often rejected on the grounds that it represents only a historical argument but that it does not necessarily carry saliency when considering other groundings such as a geo-political or legal ones. Yet, Islam carries mythic and religious connection to the same holy sites. Indeed, the complication of the connection between Judaism and its location of heritage lies in the competing claims of location and narrative ownership by Christianity and Islam. The Dome of the Rock is built on the site of the Jewish ancient temple which was built on the rock on which God initially commanded Abraham to sacrifice his son Isaac. For Islam, the Al-Aqusa Mosque is one of the holiest shrines, but for Jews, the ancient Temple lying just beneath it, is as holy, but the existing Islamic holy place above has forced Jews for centuries to limit their worship to the remaining western wall of the old Temple while being fully aware of the fact that the entire site is holy to Jews. Even though Israel has been in control of a united Jerusalem since 1967, out of respect for Islam, Jewish worship at its old Temple site is limited to the western wall.

Competing religions often build their holy places on the ruins of an older religion, purposefully designating such a symbolic act as standing for superiority, conquest and humiliation. Such an act must be seen for its message of superiority versus submission (such as building a grand mosque on the foundation of the Christian Church, Hagia Sofia, in Istanbul, Turkey). The act of destroying or burying an older religion holy site and erecting a competing one in its place is tantamount to a declaration of victory. Anti-Semitism in this context is the resultant fight over the identity of Judaism as it is tied to its location of origin. Though the tensions over the location of origin are not as acute between Judaism and Christianity today as they are with Islam, Jewish existence is a reminder that its holy places precede those claimed by Christianity and Islam. Since religious identity for all three religions — Judaism, Christianity and Islam — is closely tied with location of origin or religious narratives, anti-Semitism is ostensibly the unwillingness to admit that Judaism is an earlier religion and the first builder of the holy sites now claimed and in part controlled by other religions. The fact that Jews are the inhabitants of the holy land *again*, and of Jerusalem in particular, is seen as disruptive primarily to centuries of Islamic narrative, and to a lesser degree Christian narrative.

The identity of Jews as forever connected with their ancestral land was well recognized by Jewish thinkers in the 19th century who were quick to realize that in the nationalistic movements springing all around them was perhaps the solution for centuries of anti-Semitism. Theodore Herzl's predecessors, people such as Leon Pinsker and Moses Hess, concluded that Jews would always be considered strangers in their communities of residence. Pinsker argued that "Jews are unassimilable and therefore inevitably aliens," and Herzl considered the prejudices against the Jews so ingrained that only a Jewish state would solve anti-Semitism (Cohn-Sherbok, p. xiii). Yet, from the early days of the Zionist movement its leaders took practical steps to ensure that the return to Palestine would not only be a fulfillment of historical aspirations, but that it would be welcomed by the Arab inhabitants of the Middle East.

The Zionist movement was born during the declining years of the Ottoman Empire, in control of vast territories including the Middle East.[3] The movement was a direct response "to the twin problems of anti-Semitism and the threat of loss of identity through assimilation" and that "Zionism provided Jews with a new way of thinking that rejected assimilation and recast Judaism as a national movement with Palestine as its natural site because of the mythic energy associated with the place and its history" (Rowland and Frank, p. 36). Early Jewish settlements in Palestine were thus made under the Ottoman authorities, and when the Ottoman rule ended with the entry of Great Britain into the Middle East in 1916, Jewish immigration was not blind to Arab inhabitants. As a matter of fact, and against the more prevailing notions, Jewish immigration was mindful of the Arab residents of the region. Indeed, as discussed earlier, during the last years of the Ottoman Empire and the early years of the British Mandate in Palestine, the relationship between Jews and Arabs were quite positive.

Arab residents in the Near East actually encouraged Jewish immigration into Palestine. German scholar Matthias Kuntzel suggests that the period of 1860 to 1930 was rather flourishing between Jews and Arabs. Jews became members of the Egyptian Parliament and held various government positions. The editor of the Egyptian newspaper Al-Ahram argued that the "Zionists are necessary for this region. The money they will bring in, their intelligence and the diligence which is one of their characteristics will, without doubt, bring new life to the country" (cited in Kuntzel, p. xxx). A former Egyptian Prime-Minister, Ahmed Zaki opined in 1922 that the "victory of the Zionist idea is the turning point for the fulfillment of an ideal which is so dear to me, the revival of the Orient" (in Kuntzel, p. xxx). Kuntzel also cites a 1926 invitation by the Egyptian government of the Jewish Teachers Association delegation from Palestine to visit Egypt and a visit of Egyptian students to Tel-Aviv to partake in a sports competition. Even after tension between Arabs and Jews in Palestine broke out in 1929, the Egyptian press did not allow anti-Zionist and anti-Jewish articles to be published in the press (Kuntzell, pp. 5-6).

The sentiments of those Arabs who welcomed Jews into the must have encouraged other Jews to think of Palestine as a future homeland. Indeed, many Arabs did not display antagonism to the Zionist idea nor did they show any resentment to the connection Jews had to their ancestry land. If anything, the identity of the Jew with his ancestral land was initially not an issue. As discussed earlier, only when the number of Jews entering Palestine increased so did the hostility toward them as well as the opposition to the Zionist idea. Subsequently, the opposition to Zionism and a Jewish homeland quickly turned anti-Semitic.

Yet, the connection of Jews to their ancient land has always been known to anti-Semites and it has been used against them throughout history. One slogan anti-Semites have repeatedly uttered in Europe, especially during riots, even as late as 1819, was "Hep! Hep!" which stands for the acronym *Hierosolyma est perdita*: "Jerusalem is Destroyed," or "Jerusalem is lost" (Elon, p.101). In seeking to humiliate Jews, those shouting the slogan were rejoicing that Jews lost their ancient land, sensing rather well that the connection of Jews to their holy land was paramount in their religious and national conception, even eighteen centuries later.[4] This call also posits an interesting dilemma and admission of an important truism. In the slogan HEP is the recognition that Jews lost their land and that their "punishment" for being Jews is their estrangement from it. This joyous argument, however, is inconsistent with the claim that some anti-Semites make today, namely, that Jews have no right to the land from which they were expelled. At least, some Christian anti-Semites recognize the fact that Jews were expelled from their land but only to support the narrow theology of eternal rootlessness while Islamists anti-Semitism rejects any connection Jews have had with the ancestral land.

While for centuries, anti-Semites would use this argument to humiliate Jews for losing their ancestral land, and Jews would dream forever of returning to it, modern anti-Semitism, of both Christian and Islamic origins, would argue the opposite, that Jews had no right to return to their ancestral home. One interpretation of both ancient and modern stands regarding the land of Israel (and the State of Israel) is that just as Jews were kept to survive but humiliated as a sign for the glory of Christianity, depriving Jews of their ancestry land was designed to humiliate them.

For the anti-Semite, the identity of the Jew is that of a forever wanderer, just as Church fathers claimed some seventeen centuries earlier. True, that when the slogan HEP! HEP! was uttered, Jews were only spiritually aspiring to return to their ancient land and Zionism was yet to be borne. Yet, the reciting by anti-Semites of the connection Jews had, and continued to have, to their ancestral land, some eighteen centuries after the expulsion by the Romans, shows how entrenched the connection has been, not just for Jews but importantly, for non-Jews as well. Since the establishment of the State of Israel, a repeated claim has been made that Jews had no right to create a state on the land inhabited by others, and that they should go back to whence they came. This claim is not only inconsistent with earlier claims but it is also hateful given the long history of mistreating Jews for being strangers in other lands. The inconsistencies of these arguments are but another instance of anti-Semitism as the rhetoric of hate whereby the grounds of claims often shift to convenience the argument at hand. Yet, the central argument has not changed — that Jews, anti-Semites claim, are to reside where they can be hated and definitely not in their ancestral land.

But some Jews *did* return to their ancestral land and in so doing they, inadvertently, laid the ground for a shift from anti-Semitism to anti-Zionism. Since Zionism could have deprived anti-Semites the grounds for their perpetual hatred and the convenient scapegoat, it replaced the Jew as the focal point of anti-Semitism and kept constant the old formula of hatred. Subsequently, Israel became the metonymy for Jews so that anti-Semitism could continue unabated. Others oppose Zionism on the grounds that it is an "ideologically founded political system" (Segre in Curtis, p. 147) which privledges Jews over everyone else. But Zionism, at least in its idealistic form, is "a progressive, democratic, liberal, secular, liberation movement of the Jewish people, a successful reaction to oppression and colonialism, a nation-building effort inspired by the lofty ideals of prophetic messianism, and a precise political and historical phenomenon concerning only the revival of the Jewish people after a long period of dispersion and unmatched suffering" (Segre, p. 145). Segre suggests that Zionism is neither a national movement like Arabism nor a secular movement like Communism. Zionism, for non-Zionists, is thus an odd entity and therefore unacceptable to some, primarily for basing it on a religious kinship (Segre, p. 149). This sentiment may explain how anti-Zionism and anti-Semitism are often conflated.

Admittedly, it is not easy to define Judaism. As a religion it moulds "soul and spirit." It is "simultaneously ethics and metaphysics . . . it was law." God is not only the sole prerequisite in Judaism but the Torah, too, is of a paramount source of strength and identity, compiling history, education, morality, ethics and rituals. Devoid of its original land, the authority of the Torah increased and, thus, the Jewish law became supreme no matter where Jews settled and what language they adopted, the foundation of the religion remained intact (Lazare, p. 131). As Marrus suggests, and I suggest that this is true for some but not all Jews, Israel represents a "common denominator for Jewish self consciousness in the world" (in Curtis, p. 173). Yet such a focus is often devoid of proportionality. Just as the miniscule number of Jews world-wide cannot justify the enormous focus and attention given to them, the size of the State of Israel cannot justify the enormous attention given to it. If one takes, for example, the accusation that Israel occupies Arab land, how many more countries occupy land supposedly of others? Yet, Israel is the recipient of much scorn and disproportional focus.

In seeking to define Jewish identity, it might be productive to consider Judaism, or the Jewish entity, a peoplehood; that is, a community of people that shares a combination of religion, national aspiration, kinship, history and memory, as well as a very strong attachment to the ancient land that formed the Jewish people in the first place. Beginning with the destruction of a Jewish homeland by the Romans in 135 CE, Jews were forced to develop an entity of survival that would ensure their continuity as a people without their land and without their cultural and symbolic structures at hand. Through the development of tradition, post-Biblical writings such as the Talmud and Gemara, the development of the Synagogue, liturgy and rituals, a framework of Jewish communities living in foreign lands grew over centuries into a well-functioning modal. Despite differing locations, languages, and cultures, Jews held on to a core of Jewish feeling that ensured continuity and survival, albeit with much hatred and suffering.

Fundamental to these practices was the construction of a ritualized public memory and, under this framework, the Jewish identity has functioned, continued, and survived for centuries, integrating tradition, vision, dreams and a strong sense of attachment to an ancient land. The public memory of this identity would be transcended into liturgy with daily as well as annual rituals, festivals and otherwise, symbolic enactments of remembrance. The strength of Jewish public memory is one of its most enduring features and it explains the ability of a relatively small community, dispersed and separated by distance, language and culture, to hold on to cherished memories that bind and ground an identity despite difficult odds, threats and attacks. Admittedly, this form of public memory is a double edged sword and that would also be used as pretext for hatred.

Integration of Jews with their respective local community of residence was often complex, usually practiced by maintaining specific norms of Jewishness meant to ensure continuity of core beliefs and values. The larger community, already prejudicial against Jews for religious reasons, did not understand the complexity of Jewish survival and, thus, the conventional perception of Jews by non-Jews was a limited one, often reducing the peoplehood entity into its sub-components of religion, history, language, and customs, and assessing them separately against local norms and traditions. In short, a semiotic assessment of the Jew, often based on visual features, dominated non-Jewish perception. Any assessment thereof usually ended up portraying the Jew suspiciously and conspiratorially as different and as strangers wearing different cloths, smelling differently, or practicing a different diet. From the outcast to the hated, the distance is rather short, primarily since suspicion often breeds conspiracies. Thus, the link of Jews to each other regardless of language or location would in turn be used against Jews in various conspiratorial theories that would flourish especially in the late nineteen centuries and well into the twentieth century.

The hatred of Jews as Jews, or for their Jewishness, is but a cover for opposing an entity that is seen as threatening the community's social cohesion. The real causes of a community's difficulties are not examined, and in its place, faulty effects are associated with "causes" assigned to Jews. In short, effects are replaced with causes whose net result is fanning the flames of hatred. The Jew, then, is identified as the culprit and the cause of all things negative. Indeed, the conspiratorial accusation often functions as a unifying device when a community gathers against a hated entity blamed for engaging in some mysterious and sinful behavior. The Jew often "fits the bill," allowing communities throughout history to blame the Jews for the most diabolical behavior. Thus, the ingredients of Jewish identity are also the grounds for anti-Semitism whereby the decision to keep Jewish core beliefs and values from disappearing, and the survival mechanism developed, also became the source of estrangement, suspicion, conspiracies, and subsequently, the pretext for hatred.

Anti-Semitism, then, has always been symptomatic of guilt! Guilt of usurpation, guilt of frustration, guilt of unresolved tension within a community, guilt over centuries of persecution, and guilt of causing or aiding the Holocaust. The latter is of particular volatility as the enormity of the crime cannot fully be overcome by a call for forgiveness, reconciliation, or reparation. There is no act of contrition that can "balance" the crime (guilt) of the Holocaust, hence the motive to find in the victim the same behavioral tendencies. Since Israel's creation is often described from a narrow historical view as the result of the Holocaust, the implication is clear – Israel should not have been established because these grounds – the Holocaust – are not justifiable for such a nation-building. Indeed, Arab nations of the Middle East and the Islamic world beyond often resort to the "Holocaust-established-Israel" formula. This is the reason why Israel is constantly under the magnifying glass of the world — seeking to find in Israel the "Nazi" characteristics that would balance and perhaps absolved the guilt over the Holocaust. Such rhetoric, anti-Semites hope, could weaken the Holocaust cause in the creation of Israel, and subsequently, delegitimize Israel's founding narrative. The rhetoric of identity formation is the battleground and its ammunition can be found in dissolving one narrative and exchanging it with another.

Conclusion

The identity of the Jew by Jews, from its early history onwards, point to the strong connection Judaism has to its place of origin. This connection would develop in later years into forms of public memory, allowing a community deprived of its ancestral land to continue to function despite the loss. The identity of the Jew by Jews would also put high premium on cultural, historical, and social entities to form a community that is larger than its religious precepts. As such, Judaism, I argue, is much more than just a religion; I define it as a *peoplehood* — a community that despite different practices, socialization, locals, and languages, share a common heritage and a spiritual and symbolic memory to an ancient land. Like other minorities, the way Jews identify themselves differs from the way non-Jews define Jews and whose definition is often much narrower, usually focused on the religious aspect and a misunderstanding or ignorance of the richer variables involved. Ostensibly, anti-Semitism is often the result of a purposeful gap between the identity of Jews by Jews and those of non-Jews, and the refusal of non-Jews to allow those objectified to define themselves. This gap has been acknowledged by Vatican II, asking specifically that Christians should allow Jews to define themselves. The implications of such a dramatic change are significant, if only heeded, for Jews and for all people.

Notes

1. Recent research into the Gospel of Judah suggests the possibility of a different tale not to be found in other Gospels; that of Judah Iscariot being Jesus' closest disciple and thus much envied by others. Is it possible that the tale of betrayal is but a preferred version of Church leaders once other versions were to be excluded from the New Testament and that this version would reinforce the hatred of Jews?
2. The United States of America has been often considered the "new Israel" and a chosen nation (Hart, 1997, p. 251).
3. For the greater part of the Nineteenth Century, the Ottoman Empire (1566-1918) would be in decline, bringing European nations to repeatedly deal with the "eastern Question." The Ottoman Empire would see parts of its provinces being chipped away by Egyptians, Syrians, Albanians, Greeks, and others. During the late 19th Century, Jewish immigration to Palestine would increase and, with it, the call for a Jewish national homeland in parts of the Ottoman Empire. The Ottoman Empire would come to an end at the conclusion of World War I, and it would bring the United Kingdom to take control of the Near East (alongside a treaty with France over the areas of influence) and issue the Balfour Declaration of 1917, announcing the recognition of Great Britain of a Jewish Homeland in Palestine.
4. In the 1930's a similar call was heard: "Jews-Move on to Jerusalem," while today the call is in the opposite direction — to get out of Jerusalem (See, Laqueur, 2006, p. 15).

13

Concluding Thoughts about the Prospects for an End to Anti-Semitism

What, then, are the future prospects of anti-Semitism? Is anti-Semitism here to stay for another millennium or two? Or for eternity? This question must have been asked time and again, in antiquity, during the Middle-Ages, when the Enlightenment was in full force, and after Holocaust. The fact that this question has already been repeatedly asked means that anti-Semitism did not dissipate and will likely continue. Such an assessment is not surprising and is quite depressing. Yet, the exploration of the rhetorical causes of anti-Semitism, if understood correctly, may lead to a way out of this millennia-old scrooge — that of understanding the role of guilt and its transference to a substitute in order to construct the "perfect" enemy. If the recognition of this tendency is realized, if guilt is not to be transferred to an innocent and remote agent, perhaps Christian theological precepts would be understood for their rhetorical practices and their consequences would be assessed accordingly.

The perspective developed in several case studies reveals a consistent pattern that has been enshrined theologically but is essentially a rhetorical one — a persuasive process of arguing the superiority of Christianity and Islam on the back of Judaism (pursued either as a matter of principle or as a means to another end). That anti-Semitism is experienced *exclusively* in these two religions must be understood as borne of a unique relationship of an earlier religion and the difficulty of Christianity and Islam have had in according Judaism its historical place and influence.

The view taken in this study is that anti-Semitism is a *rhetorical* entity and that it functions as a discursive process encompassing a collection of arguments that seek to persuade others of specific positions as justification for attitudes and actions. Foundational to anti-Semitism as a rhetoric of hate is an inherent guilt that is embedded in historical and religious circumstances. As a rhetorical entity, the material essence of anti-Semitism has encompassed variables such as ideologies, beliefs, opinions, attitudes, values, and convictions, used negatively as "necessary" to justify a course of action. The means for securing attitudes and actions can be found in prejudices, stereotypes, and scapegoating, used with malicious intent. All of these rhetorical manifestations are borne out of "guilt" or "imperfection" over religious borrowing and usurpation, as well as the need to overcome them without imputing self doubt.

The unstated, or hidden, objectives of anti-Semitism include, among others, reinforcement, conformity, and unity of the community, objectives that are seen as possible when victimizing an "other." The principal operative mechanism of anti-Semitism is the reversal of terms whereby the objective of unity is achieved via division, and the objectives of strength or self worth are managed through the projection of denigration and humility into the "other." The reversal of terms is most clearly apparent with the reversal of causes and effects and their analogous extensions as in disease — Jew and its affective symptoms — non-Jew (cited in McWilliams, p. 107).

Since anti-Semitism is often reduced to generic arguments against Jews, it is a productive to consider anti-Semitism as recourse to argumentation or as a generic source of argumentation (or *topoi*, to use the terminology of classical rhetoric). The perspective that guilt is the inherent motive within anti-Semitism has manifested itself in the practice of *scapegoating* — an invented vessel on whose shoulders the sins of others are to be carried. Anti-Semitism, then, is based on immoral and unjustified arguments whereby the wrong cause and the wrong culprit are charged. As Sartre has noted, the Jew "is a pretext," and "anti-Semitism, in a word, is fear of man's fate," and "fear of one's self."

As an ideology, anti-Semitism, explains Sartre,
[i]s a scurrilous yellow myth, whereby the anti-Semite projects his criminal intention on an innocent victim by charging the victim with having organized a conspiracy which is, in fact, his own. Then, while the circumstantial evidence mounts against the

victim, the real criminal commits his crime in full view of a public whose attention is so riveted upon the scapegoat that it does not even see what a dagger is being driven in its neck (cited in McWilliams, 1948, pp. 267-269).

The transference of guilt and culpability is the objective of the anti-Semite, seeking to commit a crime and blame another for it. Such a formula works if it has been practiced repeatedly and goes unnoticed for what it is.

It is noteworthy that throughout the history of anti-Semitism, the formula of actions-following-speech is quite prevalent — of rhetoric prompting a mass psychology. Had anti-Semitism functioned at the level of attitudes alone, it would have ceased to exist a long time ago. But such is not the case as anti-Semitism has often been prompted at the level of inciting speech that turned into hostile action. A simple survey of the history of anti-Semitism, as well as the case studies covered here, reveal that whenever or wherever it has erupted, non-Jews, prompted by polemic of religious or social tensions, have often resorted, rather quickly, to violence. In short, a rhetorical act always preceded action. This tendency to resort to violence is one of the distinct hallmarks of anti-Semitism and it begs the question, why? I have tried to answer this principal question in this volume, arguing that when two competing entities are rather close (or similar) to each other, the hostility is that much greater than if they were more apart, distant, or dissimilar. And if one of these entities emanate from an earlier one, hostility is compounded. Finally, if the entity that emanates from an earlier one seeks to usurp the older entity, we have the recipe for a disastrous relationship. Hence, the need to get rid of the older entity whose origin and primacy continues to overshadow the newer one. Thus, Judaism and Christianity would develop alongside these rhetorical paths, leading the latter to hateful discourse and actions.

The phenomenon known as anti-Semitism has lasted some two thousand years and, despite the passage of time, its practices have remained rather constant. At different junctions throughout the history, in divergent localities and among different groups and communities, anti-Semitism looks rather similar, is accompanied by familiar discourse, and is replete by tried-and-true false accusations. The struggle to counter anti-

Semitism is as old as anti-Semitism itself, and the prospect of overcoming prejudices against Jews has seen few successes and many failures. Anti-Semitism has persisted because of societies' need to hate an "other" as a strategy of obviation, as means to justify different ends.

The birth of anti-Semitism, I contend, was of a rhetorical act needed to separate early Christianity from Judaism. Christianity's survival was seen as possible only by denigrating and humiliating Judaism. As a rhetorical construct, anti-Semitism was designed as a weapon to spew hatred against Jew and Judaism to limit the influence of Judaism in the Roman Empire. A century or so after Christ, Judaism flourished while Christianity was unable to construct a separate identity and attract the masses needed for its success. When the opportunity came, as a result of Judean politics and failed revolts against Rome, Church leaders began a rhetorical campaign of hateful speech. But the issue at hand is larger than that. The entire foundation of Christianity rests on its anti-Judaic stance. As Rosemary Reuther opined, "anti-Judaism is too deeply embedded in the foundation of Christianity to be rooted out entirely without destroying the whole structure" (1974, p. 228). The Danish philosopher Soren Kierkegaard said it most succinctly: "no other but Judaism could establish, by means of negation, so definitely, so decisively, what Christianity is" (cited in Carroll, p. 59).

It is, therefore, not difficult to understand why Christian theology cannot completely shed its polemic in exchange for accurate historicity. As Lloyd Gaston succinctly puts it: "A Christian Church with an anti-Semitic New Testament is abominable, but a Christian Church without a New Testament is inconceivable" (Gager, p. 11). French historian Jules Isaac who was influential in convincing Pope John XXXII to reverse centuries of Christian anti-Semitism (later implemented by Pope Paul VI in the form of Vatican II's *Nostra Aetate*), identifies the Christian Church as the real culprit for the Holocaust and all preceding acts of anti-Semitism. All forms of anti-Semitism, Isaac argues, are derived from the root cause of Christian anti-Semitism and its "teaching of contempt" toward Judaism which included the eternal guilt of the Jew for crucifying Jesus, the claim that Jesus rejected the Jewish people, and the Church's rejection of Jesus' Jewish identity (Brog, pp. 1-2). From a Jewish perspective, one wishes for a corrective, even after two millennia. The statement of a Jewish critic from antiquity is apt even today: "why do you take your origin from our religion, and then, as if you are progressing in knowledge, despise these things, although you cannot name any other origin for you[r] doctrine than our law?" (cited in Gager, p. 113).

Ultimately, the essence of anti-Semitism is the level of confidence and comfort Christianity (or Islam) have about their theological grounding and teaching and their ability and willingness to look at their respective theological resources and assess them against the prompting of hatred toward Jews. As long as Judaism is denigrated and anti-Jewish sentiments abound, the implication has to be that each religion continues to harbor some doubt about its theological precepts; that its debt to Judaism is a source of discomfort. Such a partial admission has been made, but the motives of the rhetoric of hate are present, even when hidden, as when one religion calls Judaism "old" and theirs "new," or when the struggle to re-charge Jews of eternal guilt in post Vatican II continues, or when Judaism's holy places are nullified and its history is erased.

It is written in II Corinthians 5:21 that "For our sake he made him to be sin who knew no sin." In his death, we are told that Christ sacrificed himself in order to redeem all from guilt! But if Christ's action was done for the sake of humanity, why blame Jews for his death on the cross; why accuse Jews if all humanity is redeemed from guilt? Fundamentally, why distinguish between humanity and Jews? Since sin and its resultant guilt have guided this inquiry, the end to anti-Semitism may lie in both. The charge against Jews, of killing Christ, is still central to Christian theology and mindset. Relying on the writing of R. Reik, Kenneth Burke cites the following: "The unconscious feeling of guilt, originating in the primeval crime, has never left the Jews and was only partially soothed by the destruction of the temple and other national calamities. Yet not only that unconscious guilt-feeling, but also the hidden rebelliousness against God, the mortal defied successor of the primal father, was passed on from generation to generation" (Burke, 1961, p. 259).

Eternal guilt is described as an unconscious feeling of guilt that has not left the Christian believer, seeing in every Jew a successor of a primal father. That this guilt is contradictory to the statement Jesus made about his taking everyone's guilt upon him and, in so doing, redeeming all others, is clear but why, then, charge the Jew with eternal guilt? Here is the key to the accusation of the Jew's eternal guilt — the projection device whereby one's guilt is redeemed by projecting it onto another. Yet, it is this particular point that can solve anti-Semitism. This is so because the theology at hand is essentially rhetorical — the need to act out of our motives directed by an acceptable Order. Though the charge of eternal guilt was taken out by the Catholic Church in 1965's Vatican II Council, the recent advocacy of few Church advocates to insert again the charge of the Jews' eternal guilt must be taken as a theological principle some in the Church cannot do without.

In its simplistic form, Christianity's great "moments" are "original sin" and "redemption," and they both function as the foundation of Christianity's superstructure (Burke, 1954, p. 283). Yet, these two "great moments" are impossible without the intervention of guilt and the need for its cancellation. As Burke opines, an "absolute guilt must be matched with an absolute cancellation of the guilt, and that such cancellation can be contrived by *victimage*." In contriving victimage, a victim must be held accountable regardless of the truthfulness or validity of the charge. The victim is a mere convenient agency for the sins of others. Thus, an *original sin* with its categorical motive was turned into a *personal sin*, the kind that allows the charge of the Jew-eternal guilt to become a charge of every Jew, every time, and every place. The reason for this reductionist move lies in the possibility that tribal guilt of the Jews was insufficient for Christendom in inflicting a "deserving" punishment, and an actual sin was added such that the "crime" could be taken as real and its retribution justified (Burke, 1954, pp. 283-284, 290). In essence, anti-Semitism is punishment that has been inflicted on individual Jews through the ages precisely because the tribal (collective) and temporal guilt (Jews of Christ's time) and its "punishment" were not sufficient for the alleged "crime."

Putting the entire matter in a most succinct way, the question a Christian (and a Muslim) should ask is this: Is the guilt of the Jew necessary for the survival of Christianity (or Islam)? If the answer is in the affirmative, then the realization that one's religion is based solely on the destructive charge of another ought to raise great concern. If the answer is negative, then anti-Semitism ought to end. This foundational question ought to be asked of all believers and not be left in the hands of few who set the agenda for all.

Rhetorically, modern anti-Semitism, especially the racial kind, well in use by the Nazis and more recently in the Islamic and Arab world, is but a variation on the anti-Semitism of antiquity and the Middle-Ages, focusing on evil motives and exclusiveness. The height of anti-Semitism in the form of Nazi ideology of "superior vs. inferior" races incorporated many of earlier forms of medieval anti-Semitism of demonic and diabolic charges. This racial anti-Semitism found fertile ground in the Arab world and ushered in an Islamist anti-Semitism which is largely recycled Nazi anti-Semitism, and whose purpose was to confront Jews returning to their ancestral land.

Jews as the historical victim of much cruelty have been portrayed as the victimizer of Christ, as murderers of Christian children whose blood they needed for the Passover ritual, as the poisoners of wells, as a plotters and seekers of world domination, of espousing radical thoughts, of being Bolsheviks, Communists, capitalists, and lately as the attackers of Muhammad. At every age and historical juncture there appears to be a cause and thus a "reason" to hate Jews, which means that there has *not* been a reason at all. Indeed, one primary feature of anti-Semitism is the sheer inconsistency of charges against Jews. From humiliating Jews for being driven off their ancestral land, for negating the power of Judaism without their own land, this litany of charges and hateful statements are but rhetorical devices that hide true motives of hatred. This hatred is but a means for making it easier to argue that Jews deserve all the punishments inflicted upon them throughout history. When sorting out this maze of contradictory and ridiculous charges, there stands the truth, raw and bare — the Jew as the convenient victim for others' frustrations, uncertainties, and iniquities.

The rhetorical objective of anti-Semitism has consistently been to remove the victimhood from Jews and assigning it to the victimizers. Christians have practiced this device for ages and lately it has been much in use in the Arab world. The Durban conference of 2001 was such an exemplar and so is the rhetoric coming from Israel's enemies such as Iran, Hezbollah, and Hamas. Their anti-Semitism is but classical rhetorical devices whereby key terms are switched such that an opposite construct of events and reality are presented as truthful and a reason for hatred. This rhetorical device, (also in use by Holocaust deniers), has had a devastating effect on Jews throughout history as it allowed a rather simple reversal of the victim-victimizer ratio to allow lies to be accepted as self-evidenced truth in whose name, endless atrocities and various crimes have been committed.

Contemporary anti-Semitism is also the result of a competition among a variety of groups over public sphere about whose victimage narrative is more profound and more deserving of world sympathies. Hence the hatred of Jews in contemporary world affairs is also about usurping the Jewish victimage narrative. A sinister motive lurks in the background of the victimage competition — that of seeking to rank victimage according to some nationalistic or political objectives — a competition that is not very productive as it is often more fictional than factual. This motive is clearly visible in the appropriation of the term Holocaust, a term uniquely designated to describe the deliberate killing of six million Jews by the Nazi regime in Germany. The use of the Holocaust to describe other calamities (not associated with the death of millions in World War II) than those that befell the Jewish people is an attempt to usurp the experience and thus deny its severity and significance. Arguing about the use of an upper- or lower-case "h" in Holocaust is, indeed, symbolic of this public sphere competition.

The reality is that massacres and genocide have not subsided after the Holocaust. If anything, they have continued as if the experience of the Holocaust has meant little to those bent on decimating their opponents and on mass scales. That the Holocaust is also the cause of competition about the victimage narratives and not an experience to be judged on its merit vis-à-vis a specific group of victims, be it Jews or Armenians, is but another form of hateful rhetoric. Here hatred is not directed only at the Jew for actions he did not commit but also seeks to rank this hatred as less significant than it is, accusing Jews for perpetuating their narrative for self gain while the suffering of others is abound. Subsequently, Jews are charged again and their eternal guilt designation continued. Ostensibly, anti-Semitism, the argument goes, is not as serious as Jews make it to be and it must be put relative to other forms of hatred in order to contemplate its true dimensions. Depriving

Jews of their historical victimhood, while at the same time justifying their victimage, is the persistent threads of anti-Semitism from antiquity to the modern age. Ultimately, this denial of the victim's victimhood is but a rejection of one's guilt.

As this study has shown, anti-Semitism has not changed much throughout history, and its varied manifestations should not obscure the consistent patterns that can be found in examining specific cases of anti-Semitism. I, therefore, do not distinguish between anti-Semitism of antiquity and racial anti-Semitism of the modern era — or any other kind, type, or variation of anti-Semitism. At its core, anti-Semitism is rather uniform in its rhetorical function; seeking to persuade and influence that which is false and manipulative. Indeed, the suasive objective of anti-Semitism has always been to elevate one over the other, to establish a hierarchy, to defend that which is not defensible, to "protect" a community against phony charges of the evil Jew, and to justify actions that are not warranted.

When contemplating the multiple and contradictory charges leveled against Jews, one wishes that anti-Semites would make up their mind and decide which Jewish features or habits they hate and which they accept. Let Jews have some clarity about what is it that anti-Semites hate. It is simply inconceivable that anti-Semites hate Jews for their wealth, for their capitalist nature, for their revolutionary tendencies, for their Communist attitudes, for being close to their governments, for their militaristic aspiration, for their cowardice, for their intellectual inclination, for their exclusiveness, or for their involvement in the cultural and intellectual life of their society. Put differently, if anti-Semitism is grounded by multiple and contradictory argument, then something else is going on here.

Clearly, anti-Semitism was borne out rhetorical needs and has remained a rhetorical weapon of choice. Anti-Semitism has survived the ages because it subscribes to a simple code-of-hatred whose ingredients include the "different," the "outcast," the "other", the "dirty" and the "devil." This code-of-hatred is simplistic because that is the only way such a rhetoric gets traction and is able to adapt to different circumstances, times, and locations. The code-of-hatred is persuasive because it functions by referencing verbal and visual signs that are already in use and easily observed, and thus believed. Such a code-of-hatred is not taxing on the human psyche as it offers a quick way of obviating one's attitudes toward an unwarranted development, hence the preference for projecting guilt onto others.

Final Thoughts

As we come to the conclusion of this book, I note the existence of an interesting tension between those, such as St. Augustine, who wished to keep Jews alive but humiliated as proof of Christianity's claims of being the "true" religion, and those, such as Eugen Dühring, who wished to eliminate Jews altogether and to de-Judaize Judaism such that Jesus would be declared an Aryan and not a Jew (Laqueur, p. 93). In both cases, a segment of Christianity was searching for its legitimation, a notion considered possible, literally, only at the expense of Jews; one preferring them alive and another preferring them dead. As Judaism stood in the way of this religious actualization, a rhetorical process of persuading believers of such dogma and theology had to be developed. The strategy was executed primarily by demonizing Judaism, hence a purposeful anti-Semitism as the rhetoric of hate, designed to convince believers of the merit of one religion by denigrating another.

The scapegoat theory clearly functions in the case of anti-Semitism. Ample cases identified in this study point to the selection of the Jew as the vessel, or the vehicle, on whose shoulders other problems are carried. But the Jew as a scapegoat, or anti-Semitism as an escapist perspective, point to a special case of scapegoating. The Jew was not selected for being taken as an innocent bystander, or being weak and, thus, an easy target for such a label. The Jew was selected for strategic reason: because his origin in antiquity represents the foundation of both Christianity and Islam, and as long as he remains, he is taken as instilling doubt and uncertainty about their theological claims. The Jew, then, is a well-identified agent who was made into an antagonist, a counter-agent, and worse, the enemy of God. As such, his lot was cast: he should cease to exist or be tolerated but humiliated. Both strategies have been pursued.

Along the lengthy road of hatred, the Jew was made into a scapegoat, and perhaps *the* historical scapegoat *par excellence*. Religious narratives of hatred piled plenty of accusations against the Jew such that their cumulative effect began to "function" as a scapegoat, used for any societal ill or setback. This transformation of a strategic counter-agent into a historical scapegoat and a pariah is the strategy Islamists of the twentieth century have adopted, seeking to unify the Islamic world around one cohesive narrative that is supposedly founded at the birth of Islam. The Jew who was taken as seeking to nip Christianity in the bud by being accused of killing its founder, Christ, is now blamed for seeking to do the same to the founder of Islam, planning to kill its prophet Muhammad. When the *ur*-text of two major religions, Christianity and Islam, has the Jew identified as the ultimate enemy, any narrative thereof is vested with so much power of suasion, symbolism, and perceived legitimacy that the possibility of separating truth from myth and fiction is nearly impossible. One needs only to realize that it took Christianity almost two thousand years to begin to see its foundation more accurately and in that process it came to terms with its responsibility for anti-Semitism. One can only hope that the same reflection in Islam would yield a more accurate account of its origin and its relationship with Jews and Judaism. More specifically, Islam needs a more expensive view of Judaism that is not constrained by its view of Israel and the Arab-Israeli conflict. The Arab-Israeli conflict is only a century old while Islam's relationship with Judaism covers some thirteen *other* centuries. With such a corrective Islamist's anti-Semitism can subside, and perhaps with a more objective view of Judaism, the Arab-Israeli conflict will subside as well.

Over the centuries, the religious-based anti-Semitism, motivated by guilt and insecurity over initial theology, has been pushed aside while more contemporary "causes" were featured, but by then, the Jew was cast the symbolic "other," an outcast to be feared and despised; with this formula, charges of all kinds were easy to be "assigned" to him. That from time to time, the religious cause would rear its ugly head is but an indication of the primacy given to the religious cause of anti-Semitism. The operative rhetorical formula of the Jews' eternal guilt was the principal notion Christianity has adopted in seeking to redeem itself of its own guilt. After all, what better way to alleviate one's guilt than by projecting it onto an antagonist? Hence, the scapegoat mechanism that was activated operated for centuries. This rhetorical formula was in clear evidence when Vatican II's *Nostra Aetate* statement of 1965 sought a significant corrective as well as an admission of the religious cause for anti-Semitism. The religious motive reached a full cycle, from initiation to its end.

Perhaps at the level of meta-theory, the hidden motive for anti-Semitism is a struggle and a competition over memory, especially public memory. For Judaism has based its continued existence on the memories of the past: memories of space and memories of founding myths and rituals. The anti-Semite, then, wishes the world to forget Judaism's origin and heritage and, ultimately, hopes for its erasure — for as long as Judaism persists, the anti-Semites rationalizes, the public memory of Christianity and Islam are associated with Judaism. However, the process that allowed communities to divert attention for various contemporary difficulties and challenges, also kept the scapegoated group united and cohesive despite its dispersion, or perhaps because of it; focusing on its need to defend itself and keep the flame of origin and survival relatively intact. It is tempting to suggest, however tenuously, that perhaps Jews and Judaism have survived millennia of persecutions not only because of its survival mechanism and instincts, but perhaps more significantly, because anti-Semites were intent on keeping Jews a hated group so that they could blame Jews for causing the condition that they were put under by others.

But it did not have to be that way; meaning, anti-Semitism did not have to be the mode of operation for Christianity and Islam. These two religions did not have to resort to the rhetoric of hate as a means to an end. They have done so because it is easier, convenient, and even economic as it "saves" them from having to invest efforts in more honest justification of theology as well as politics. Well into the fourth century, Judaism and Christianity have co-exited to one degree or another and without spilling into extreme prejudice and violence. Only when a purposeful rhetoric of hate was instilled into Christian theology has anti-Semitism become a Church doctrine, with devastating consequences. In short, for some three centuries a *modus vivendi* between Judaism and Christianity was the primary experience and not anti-Semitism.

For the past century, those rejecting replacement theology have shown that acknowledging Judaism's foundation of Christianity, as well as appreciating the historical context of the two religions, does not weaken nor contradict Christianity. The immediate consequence of this development has been a significant reduction in anti-Semitism, at least among certain Christian denominations. There also exists an equally significant implication for Christianity; that of shedding off the hateful theology that was invented for other than religious reasons. Christianity without anti-Semitism is a possibility and a reality.

The parallel argument is also applicable in the case of Islam where hateful rhetoric is a significant development only since the 1920's and whose objective was the unity of the Islamic world. Jewish immigration into Palestine provided the ideal launching pad for a new ideology that did not exist in Islam until a century ago. Inventive anti-Semitic theology sowed extreme hatred that was not previously part of the Islamic experience. Political and geo-political reasons stand, then, at the base of supposedly theological conflict, now intensified. It, too, did not have to be that way. The end to anti-Semitism lies in reaching back to the truth — the truth of the foundation of Christianity and Islam. This discovered or re-discovered truth, however, is in the hands of Christians and Muslims.

Jews have sought to end anti-Semitism through the ages and for the most part they have failed. I am not certain whether Jews can ever end anti-Semitism and countering it has yielded little success. Those espousing anti-Semitic attitudes are responsible for ending it, but for this to happen, in both Christianity and Islam, a theological change must take place, and as Vatican II has shown such a significant change is possible. As for Jews, to follow Arendt's advice, they have a choice and that is to confront and challenge anti-Semites whenever such attitudes are expressed. In the context of the Arab-Israeli conflict, they must point to those charges that attack Jews and Judaism and not Israel or Israelis. It is in this context that, despite the difficulties of confronting anti-Semitism, I took this challenge by seeking a different approach to the study of anti-Semitism — the rhetorical perspective — because the historical study of anti-Semitism has revealed an inherent reliance on persuasive processes. It is my hope that in exploring the various rhetorical processes at hand that their sheer contemplation and understanding would bring some to take a more critical approach to anti-Semitism and hence begin to eradicate it.

References

Organization for Security and Cooperation in Europe (April 2004). *After the promise: Keeping commitments to combat antisemitism.* The Jacob Blaustein Institute for the Advancement of Human Rights.

Arab leader denies temple ever existed. (2008, March 10). *The Jerusalem Post. www.jpost.com.*

Arendt, H. (1978). *The Jew as pariah: Jewish identity and politics in the modern age.* Edited and with an Introduction by Ron H. Feldman. New York: Grove Press, Inc.

Arendt, H. (1973). *The origin of totalitarianism.* Second Edition. New York: Houghton Mifflin Harcourt.

Arendt, H. (1951). *The Origin of totalitarianism.* New York: Harcourt, Brace and Company.

Bayefsky, A. F. (2001, December 16). Terrorism and racism: The aftermath of Durban. *Jerusalem center for Public Affairs.* No. 468. *http://www.jcpa.org/jl/vp468.htm.*

Becker, J. (1977). *Messianic expectation in the Old Testament.* Translated by D. E. Green. Philadelphia: Fortress Press.

Beckett, W. Sister. (1999). *Sister Wendy's 1000 masterpieces.* New York: DK Publishing.

Ben-Itto, H. (2005). *The Lie that wouldn't die: The protocols of the elders of Zion.* London: Vallentine Michell.

Bergmann, W. (ed.). (1988). *Error without trial: Psychological research on antisemitism.* Volume 2. Berlin: Walter de Gruyter.

Brockmeier. J. (1995). The language of human temporality: Narrative schemes and cultural meanings of time. *Mind, Culture, and Activity.* Vol. 2, No. 2, 102-118.

Brog, D. (2006). *Standing with Israel: Why Christians support the Jewish state.* Lake Mary, Florida: Front Line.

Bruner, M. L. (2002). *Strategies of remembrance: The rhetorical dimensions of national identity construction.* Columbia, S.C.: University of South Carolina Press.

Burke, K. (1972). *Dramatism and development.* Worcester, MA: Clark University Press.

____. (1969). *A grammar of motives*. Berkeley: University of California Press.

____. (1968). Dramatism. In D. L. Sills (ed.), *International encyclopedia of the social sciences*. New York: Macmillan.

____. (1961, 1970). *The rhetoric of religion: Studies in logology*. Berkeley: California University Press.

____. (1954). *Permanence and change: An anatomy of purpose*. Third edition. Berkeley: University of California Press.

____. (1953). *A rhetoric of motives*. New York: Prentice Hall.

____. (1941). The rhetoric of Hitler's *battle*. In *philosophy of literary from: Studies in symbolic action*. Baton Rouge: Louisiana State University Press.

____. (1941). *Philosophy of literary form: Studies in symbolic action*. Baton Rouge, Louisiana State University Press.

Carlson, T. (2001, October 22). Our man in Islamabad. *The New York times*, 24.

Carroll, J. (2002). *Constantine's sword: The Church and the Jews*. Boston: A Mariner Book.

Chernick, M. (1980). Some Talmudic responses to Christianity, third and fourth centuries. *Journal of Ecumenical Studies* 17, 396-406.

Cohen, R. (2001, September 6). Zionism: refuge, not racism. *http://www.washingtonpost.com.*, A23.

Cohn-Sherbok, D. (2006). *The paradox of anti-semitism*. London: Continuum.

Cott, J. (1979). The problem of Christian messianism. *Journal of Ecumenical Studies*, 16, 496-514.

Curtis, M. (Ed.). (1986). *Antisemitism in the contemporary world*. Boulder and London: Westview Press.

Dolan, F. M. (1994). *Allegories of America*. Ithaca, NY: Cornell University Press.

Ellul, J. (1965). *Propaganda: The formation of men's attitudes*. New York: Alfred A. Knopf.

Elon, A. (2002). *The pity of it all: A portrait of the German-Jewish epoch, 1743-1933*. New York: Picador.

Encyclopedia Judaica.(1972). Jerusalem. [New York], Macmillan.

Fakenheim, E. L (1986). Philosophical reflections on antisemitism. In M. Curtis (ed.), *Antisemitism in the contemporary world* (pp. 21-38). Boulder, Co: Westview Press.

Fisher, W. (1984). Narration as a human communication paradigm: The case of public moral argument. *Communication Monograph*, 51, 1-22.

Flory, W. S. (1986). The Psychology of antisemitism: Conscience-proof rationalization and the deferring of moral choice. In M. Curtis (ed.,), *Antisemitism in the contemporary world* (pp. 238-250). Boulder, Co: Westview Press.

Forster, A. and Epstein B. R. (1974). *The new anti-semitism*. New York: McGraw-Hill.

Gager, J. G. (1983). *The origins of anti-Semitism: Attitudes toward Judaism in pagan and Christian antiquity.* New York: Oxford University Press.

Gilbert, M. (2007). *Churchill and the Jews: A lifelong friendship.* New York: Henry Holt and Co.

Gold, J. T. (1999). *Monsters & madonnas: The roots of Christian anti-semitism.* Revised Edition. Syracuse: Syracuse University Press.

Goodman, M. (2007). *Rome and Jerusalem: The clash of ancient civilizations.* New York: Alfred Knopf.

Greenstone, J. H. (1972). *The messiah idea in Jewish history.* Westport, Conn.: Greenwood Press Publishers.

Gregg, R. B. (1971). The ego-function of the rhetoric of protest. *Philosophy and Rhetoric, 4,* 71-91.

Hart, R. P. (1997). *Modern rhetorical criticism.* Second Edition. Needham Heights, Mass.: Allyn & Bacon.

Hariman, R. (1986). Status, marginality, and rhetorical theory. *Quarterly Journal of Speech, 72,* 38-54.

Hartman, D. (1976). Sinai and exodus: The grounds for hope in the Jewish tradition. *Journal of Religious Studies, 14,* 373-387.

Hilberg, R. (2003). *The destruction of the European Jews.* Volume II. Third Edition. New Haven: Yale University Press.

Hitchens, C. (2009, February 9). The Pope's denial problem. *Newsweek,* 58-60.

Hitler, A. (1971). *Mein kampf.* Translated by Ralph Manheim. Boston: Houghton Mifflin Company.

Hobbes, T. (1962). *Leviathan.* New York: Macmillan.

Iran's president Mahmoud Ahmadinejad in his own words. (2006, December 12). *Anti-defamation league* (on line). *www.adl.org/main_Anti_Semitisim_Internat ional/ahmadinejad_wors.htm*

Julius, A., Rifkind. R. S., Weill, J., and Gaer, F. D. (2001). *Antisemitism: An assault on human rights.* New York: The Jacob Blaustein Institute.

Klausner, J. (1955). *The messianic idea in Israel.* New York: The Macmillan Company.

Kuntzel, M. (2007). Hitler's legacy: Islamic anti-semitism in the Middle East. Unpublished essay.

Kuntzell, M. (2007). *Jihad and Jew-hatred: Islamism, Nazism and the roots of 9/11.* Translated from German by Colin Meade. : Telos Press Publishing.

Laqueur, W. (2006). *The changing face of anti-semitism: From ancient times to the present day.* Oxford University Press.

Lazare, B. (1967). *Antisemitism: Its history and its causes.* Translated from French. London: Britons Publishing Company.

Lelyvel, J. (2001, October 28). All suicide bombers are not alike. *The New York Times Magazine,* 53.

Lewis, B. (1999). *Semites and anti-semites: An inquiry into conflict and prejudice*. New York: W. W. Norton & Company.

Lindsay, H. (2001, September 5). The U.N.'s Wansee conference. *WorldNetDaily.com*.

Maccoby, H. (1973). *Revolution in Judea*. London: Orbach and Chambers.

Marrus, M. R. (1986). Is there a new antisemitism? In M. Curtis (ed.), *Antisemitism in the contemporary world* (pp. 172-184). Boulder, Co: Westview Press.

McAteer, M. (1989, April 3). Liberalism destroying church, bishop says. *The Toronto Star*.

McNeil, D., Jr. (2001, November 4). More and more, other countries see the war as solely America's. *The New York Times*, B1.

McWilliams, C. (1948). *A mask for privilege: Anti-semitism in America*. Boston: Little, Brown and Co.

Mullahs in space. (2008, August 18). *The Jerusalem Post* (on line). *www.jpost.com*.

Nettler, R. L. Past trials and present tribulations: A Muslim fundamentalist speaks on the Jews. In M. Curtis (ed.,), *Antisemitism in the contemporary world* (pp. 97-106). Boulder, Co: Westview Press..

Newman, J. H. (1845). Essay on the development of Christian doctrine. *http://www.patheos.com/Library/Roman-Catholicism/Origins/Historical-Perspectives.html*

Nilus, S. A. (1905). *The Protocols of the wise elders of Zion*. Translated by Victor E. Marsden. *www.flholocaustmuseum.org/history_wing/antisemitism/primary_sources/The_Protocols*

Pawlikowski, J. T. (1986). New Testament antisemitism: Fact or fable? In M. Curtis (ed.), *Antisemitism in the contemporary world* (pp. 107-127). Boulder, Co: Westview Press.

Parkes, J. W. (1974). *The conflict of the church and the synagogues*. New York: Hermon Press.

"Peace" object, says Ford, in an attempt to justify his anti-Semitic attitude (1921, February 17). *The New York World*, 1, 5.

Phillips, K. (Ed.). (2004). *Framing public memory*. Tuscaloosa, AL: The University of Alabama Press.

Pope Paul, VI, (1965, October 28). Declaration on the relation of the Church to non-Christian religions, *Nostra Aetate*. In *http://www.vatican.va/archive/hist_ council/ii_vatican_council/documents/vat-ii_decl_ 1965*.

Pope Paul VI. (1968). Declaration on the relation of the Church to non-Christian religions, Nostra Aetate. In the *Catechism of modern man: All in the words of Vatican II and related documents*. Boston: The Daughters of St. Paul.

U.S., Israeli representatives walk out of Durban conference. (2001, September 4).

United Nations Wire. http://www.unwire.org/unwire/20010904/17592_story.asp.

Report on global anti-semitism. (2005, January 5). *Department of state to the committee on foreign relations and the committee on international relations.* The bureau of democracy, human rights, and labor. *http://www.state.gov/g/drl.rls/40258.htm*

Rettig, H. (2008, April 21). Report: Muslim anti-semitism "strategic threat" to Israel. *The Jerusalem Post* (on line). *www.jpost.com.*

Ricoeur, P. (1983). *Time and narrative.* Volume 1. Chicago: University of Chicago Press.

Ricoeur, P. (1985). *Time and narrative.* Volume 2. Chicago: University of Chicago Press.

Rosen, J. (2001, November 4). The uncomfortable question of anti-semitism, *The New York Times Magazine,* 50.

Rowland R. C., and Frank, D. A. (2002). *Shared land/conflicting identity: Trajectories of Israeli and Palestinian symbol use.* East Lansing: Michigan State University Press.

Ruether, R. R. (1974). *Faith and fratricide: The theological roots of anti-semitism.* New York: Seabury.

Saint John Chrysostom (1984). *On the incomprehensible nature of God.* Translated by Harkins, P. W. Washington: The Catholic University Press of America. Saint John Chrysostom (1985). *Apologist.* Translated by Schatkin, M. A. and Harkins, P. W. Washington: The Catholic University Press of American.

Saint John Chrysostom. *Homilies Adversus Judeaus. http://www.fordham.edu/halsall/source/chrysostom-jews6.html.* (All references to the homilies are cited in the text.)

Salpeter, E. (2004, July 1). Islam co-opts the Jewish satan. *Haaretz.com.*

Schechter, M. G. (2005). *United Nations global conferences.* New York: Routledge.

Scholem, G. (1971). *The messianic idea in Judaism.* New York: Schocken Books.

Segre, D. (1986). Is anti-Zionism a new form of antisemitism? In M. Curtis (ed.), *Antisemitism in the contemporary world* (pp. 145-154). Boulder, Co: Westview Press.

Sivan, E. (1986). Radical Islam and the Arab-Israeli conflict. In M. Curtis (ed.),*Antisemitism in the contemporary world* (pp. 61-69). Boulder, Co: Westview Press.

Sowell, T. (2006). *Black rednecks and white liberals.* New York: Encounter books.

Severson, R. J. (1995). *Time, death, and eternity: Reflecting on Augustine's confessions in light of Heidegger's being and time.* Lanham, Maryland: The Scarecrow Press, Inc.

Sharon, M. (2008, July 16). We only get one strike, *The Jerusalem Post* (online) *www.jpost.com.*

Swartz, O. (1996). Symbols and perspectives in Burkean rhetorical theory:

Implications for understanding anti-semitism. *World Communication, 25(4)*, 183-190.

Swartz, O. (1998). *The rise of rhetoric and its intersections with contemporary critical thoughts*. Boulder, Co: Westview Press.

The 4,000 Jews rumor. (2007, November 16). *Bureau of international information programs, U.S. Department of State*.

Timmerman, K. (2003, November 12). Preachers of hate: Breathtaking wrath at U.N. *WorldNetDaily. http://www.worldnetdaily.com/news/article/asp.*

Trachtenberg, J. (1943). *The devil and the Jews: The medieval conception of the Jew and its relation to modern anti-semitism*. Philadelphia: The Jewish Publication Society of America.

Warnick, B. (1992). Leff in context: What is the critic's role? *Quarterly Journal of Speech, 78*, 232-237.

White, H. (1987). *The content of the form: Narrative discourse and historical representation*. Baltimore: The Johns Hopkins University Press.

Williamson, R. Bishop. (2009, February 4 and April 19). *The New York Times archives*.

Wilken, R. S. (1983). *John Chrysostom and the Jews: Rhetoric and reality in the Late fourth century*. Berkeley, University of California Press.

Wistrich, R. S. (2010). *A lethal obsession: Anti-semitism from antiquity to the global Jihad*. New York: Random House.

_____. (Ed.). (1999). *Demonizing the other: Antisemitism, racism, and xenophobia*. Jerusalem: Vidal Sassoon International Center for the Study of Antisemitism.

Yadlin, R. (1986). Arab antisemitism in peacetime: The Egyptian case. In M. Curtis (ed.), *Antisemitism in the contemporary world* (pp. 86-96). Boulder, Co: Westview Press.

Historical Timeline

c. 1200 – 450 BCE: Biblical period.

c. 1037 BCE – c. 970 BCE: Reign of King David.

c. 960 BCE: Solomon's Temple in Jerusalem in completed.

c. 930 BCE: The Israelite Kingdom is divided between Israel, the northern kingdom, and Judea, the southern kingdom with Jerusalem as its capitol.

c. 772 BCE: The Kingdom of Israel falls to the Assyrians.

c. 586 BCE: Jerusalem falls to the Babylonians and Jews are expelled.

c. 539 BCE: Cyrus, King of Persia, allows the return of Jews to Jerusalem.

516 BCE: The second temple is built

c. 300 BCE – c. 150 BCE: Post-Biblical period.

200 BCE - 100 CE: The Hebrew Bible is codified.

167-161 BCE: The revolt of the Maccabees (Hasmoneans) against the Seleucides, of which the story of Hanukah is based.

63 BCE: The Roman Empire turns Judea into a Roman province.

40 BCE – 4 BCE: Herod the Great rules as King of the Jews.

c. 3 BCE: Jesus' birth.

c. 30 CE: Jesus' death.

66-70 CE: The Great Jewish revolt against Rome.

131-136 CE: The Bar Kokhba revolt is crushed and Judea is destroyed.

313: Roman emperor Constantine establishes Christianity as a legal religion.

1095-1291: The crusades in the Holy Land.

1290: Jews are expelled from England.

1492: Jews are expelled from Spain.

1516: The first Jewish Ghetto (restricted enclave) is established in Venice.

1517: Martin Luther begins the Protestant reformation of the Church.

1626-1676: Shabtai Zvi declares himself the Messiah and seeks to return Jews to the Holy Land.

1655: Oliver Cromwell allows Jews to return to England.

1740: New messianic fervors bring the Ottoman Empire to ask Rabbi Haim Abulafia (1660-1744) to travel to the Holy Land and rebuild the city of Tiberia. Thousands of Jews flock to Palestine.

1791: The Pale of Settlement is established by Czarist Russia and includes a vast Jewish population of some 750,000.

1840: The Damascus blood libel.

1858: Jews are officially emancipated in England.

1860-1875: Sir Moses Montefiore builds housing for Jews outside the wall of the Old City of Jerusalem.

1882-1903: Russian Zionist Jews build a settlement in Palestine that attracts others Jews to emigrate out of Russia following a series of pogroms.

1894-1906: The Dreyfus Affair.

1897: The first Zionist Congress is held in Basel, Switzerland.

1903: The Protocols of the Elders of Zion is first published.

1917: The British government issues the Balfour Declaration.

1920: The League of Nations grants Great Britain a mandate over Palestine.

1933: Hitler is elected Chancellor and the start of a wave of anti-Semitism that forces many Jews to leave Germany.

1939: The British government issues a White Paper, limiting the number of Jews allowed entry into Palestine.

1939-1945: The Holocaust in which some six million Jews (and six million others) are murdered by Nazi Germany and their allies.

1945-1948: Pressure mounts on Britain to allow surviving Jews to enter Palestine. The struggle for a Jewish state turns violent.

1947: The United Nations votes to establish a Jewish State and an Arab State in Palestine.

1948: Israel declares its independence and the first Arab-Israeli war erupts.

1956: The second Arab-Israeli war with Great Britain and France fighting alongside Israel.

1962-65: Second Vatican Council which sought to repair Catholic-Jewish relationship.

1967: The third Arab-Israeli war known also as the Six Day War. Israel takes over the Sinai Desert, the Golan Heights and the West Bank of the Jordan River.

1973: The fourth Arab-Israeli war known as the Yom Kippur war.

1978: Camp David Accords whereby Israel and Egypt sign a peace treaty.

1993: Israel and the PLO sign the Oslo Accords.

1994: Jordan and Israel sign a peace treaty.

2005: Israel withdraws from Gaza.

2006: Israel and Hezbollah of Lebanon engage in a military conflict.

2009: Israel invades Gaza.

Index

Lightning Source UK Ltd.
Milton Keynes UK
UKOW021830310112

186415UK00001B/107/P